"Readers who find themselves wrestling for control over what needs to be left in God's hands will see themselves in Claire."
ROMANTIC TIMES

"As a consummate crafter of words and c¹   Sam Hall weaves an engaging story of one wom⸍   ʰerself and her God."
BILL MYERS,
Author of Eli

"Bravo to author Sam Hall on ⸍   ⸍, *Daughter of the Cimarron*! His heroine is a chₐ   ⱼou'll never forget. Troubled, but always determined, shₑ ₐnd the love of her life struggle through the Depression and the Dust Bowl in a twister of a story. Sam doesn't shy away from the tough issues, both in life and love, and his hard work has paid off in a memorable tale of what really matters."
LESLIE GOULD,
#1 Best-Selling and Christy Award-Winning Author

"Sam Hall writes the kind of narrative I love most, the search for self amidst the search for faith."
GINA OCHSNER,
Author of *The Necessary Grace to Fall*
(Winner of the Flannery O'Connor Award)
and *People I Wanted to Be*
(Winner of the Oregon Book Award)

"*Daughter of the Cimarron* grips the reader's heart while at the same time illuminating the historical period in which the story is set. Author Samuel Hall hits all the right notes in this compelling debut novel. Recommended!"
ANN SHOREY,
Author of the *At Home in Beldon Grove* and *Sisters at Heart* Series

"Sam Hall's debut novel, *Daughter of the Cimarron*, kept me reading when I should have been doing other things. A historical novel based on real life, its readers are plunged into Claire's struggle to live down a divorce and find a way to earn a living in 1928, at the beginning of the Great Depression. How do we find faith after we've been disillusioned? Crawl under the covers if you plan to read this book before bedtime, because you won't want to put it down."

MARION DUCKWORTH,

Author of 16 Books, including *Naked on God's Doorstep* and *The Greening of Mrs. Duckworth*

Daughter

OF THE

Cimarron

A Novel

by

Samuel Hall

Ashberry Lane

© 2015 Samuel Hall
Published by Ashberry Lane
P.O. Box 665, Gaston, OR 97119
www.ashberrylane.com
Printed in the USA

All rights reserved. No part of this publication may be reproduced, stored in a retrieval system, or transmitted in any form or by any means without the prior written permission of the publisher. The only exception is brief quotations in printed reviews.

This story is based on actual events, though it is purely a work of fiction. In some cases incidents, characters, and timelines have been changed for dramatic purposes. Certain characters may be composites, or entirely fictitious.

ISBN 978-1-941720-08-0

Library of Congress Control Number: 2015936415

Cover design by Miller Media Solutions
Photos from www.bigstock.com, www.dollarphotoclub.com, and Samuel Hall.

Scripture quotations from The Authorized (King James) Version. Rights in the Authorized Version in the United Kingdom are vested in the Crown. Reproduced by permission of the Crown's patentee, Cambridge University Press.

FICTION / Christian / Women's Fiction

Dedicated to the real
Claire and Elmer, my parents ...

And to Allison, Loren, and Ethan, my children.

CENTRAL ARKANSAS LIBRARY SYSTEM
MAUMELLE BRANCH LIBRARY
MAUMELLE, ARKANSAS

Chapter One

CLAIRE

Mama always said, "People put out stories to make themselves feel superior. Ignore the tales and the people who tell them."

But I couldn't ignore the envelope in my purse.

"Sunday driver!" My husband shook his fist at the car in front of us. Turning the steering wheel to the left, he pulled the throttle lever down. The engine revved faster as we moved beside the other car's back bumper. A moment later, the car jolted.

Our '26 Ford coupe jerked to the right and skidded into a shallow ditch beside Illinois Highway 3. No sound but the creaking of metal.

The car we'd been trying to pass kept on going.

Harold sat rigid as a post, knuckles ivory white over the steering wheel. My husband's thick brown hair looked as if he'd combed it with an eggbeater. With a stream of curses, he swept his hair off his forehead.

"Are you all right?" Why had he taken such a risk? Did he *want* to die?

Harold shoved his door open and, without another look at me, stepped down.

I pushed against my door, but a barbed wire fence gleamed on the other side of the ditch so I scooted across the seat and followed him out.

He ducked to catch his reflection in the side window and commenced finger-combing his hair back in place. "Lookit that," he muttered. "Clear in the ditch and stuck besides. How am I going to get this flivver back on the road?"

A battered red truck rolled to a stop beside us. The driver, a rangy farm hand with a gap-toothed grin, vaulted out. "Hey-ee. Close call. Everybody in one piece?"

I pulled myself upright. "I ... I guess so. It was so quick, I—"

1

"Things can happen mighty fast. People driving thirty, forty miles an hour. Like maniacs. You coulda been killed." He shook his head.

"What?" Harold puffed out his chest. "You didn't see nothing. Who you think you are?"

The tall man's smile faded. He seemed to be deciding whether to fling Harold over the fence or simply to leave.

I stumbled forward. "No. No, he didn't mean it that way." My voice caught. "Yes ... you're right. We should've been careful ..."

"Claire, I *did* mean it that way!" Harold's right eyelid twitched, a sign things could get out of control—quickly.

I wheeled between the two and grasped Harold's arm. "Elmer expects us in St. Louis *today*. We need this man's help. He didn't intend disrespect." I turned back to the farmer. "He's ... we're just upset. That was very frightening. We're so glad you stopped."

The man stared at Harold, as if daring him to pop off again. Finally he got into the truck and backed up to our car. Within minutes, he'd hitched on to our coupe and pulled it up beside the pavement. He unhooked from the Ford and dropped down to look underneath. "That right tie rod's bent. I'd get it fixed as soon as possible if I was you." He directed the words at me, not Harold.

I reached into the car for my purse.

The farmer shook his head. "You don't owe me nothin'. I'm glad to help *you*." Without further ceremony, he climbed in his truck and chugged off.

⌘ ⌘ ⌘

My heart still beating double-time, I choked back tears. I wanted Harold to pull over and comfort me, but I knew better than to expect it. At least, he should've apologized for scaring me and nearly getting us both killed. No reason for him to drive that fast; he was always taking risks—as if he were more important than anyone else.

The crew at Deluxe Art Studio, where we worked selling enlargements and frames, knew what he was like. What they didn't know, they made up. Rumors followed Harold like flies after a manure spreader.

He said they were all lies.

I didn't know. I didn't want to know.

Suddenly, the steering wheel vibrated with a thudding racket.

2

I grabbed the door handle. "Harold, that man said the tie rod's bent. You should take this car straight to a shop."

"That sounds like something your old man would do."

"Don't call him that."

"He's an old fossil. If he was the saint you make him out to be, he'd run his own house instead of telling other people what to do."

"And what's that supposed to mean?"

"Don't play dumb. You know your mama wears the pants in that house."

I swallowed hard and blinked back tears. "We're driving down the road in a wrecked car ... and all you can do is insult my parents?"

"Buzz off, Claire. You're giving me a headache. *If* we stop for a mechanic—*if* we could find one—we'd be lucky to make St. Louis by Monday." He cocked his head to one side. "Hey, feel that?"

"What?"

"Exactly. You don't feel nothing 'cause the shimmy is gone. Let me take care of the car. You keep still for a change."

"That's so ... disrespectful." Still fighting tears, I turned to the side window. After two years of marriage, I still didn't know Harold Devoe. Not on the inside anyway. His response to the farmer who'd helped us was typical. Aside from the things that annoyed me—playing the big shot, trying to run other people's lives like he ran mine, his brass, and his idea that a dimpled chin made him a lady-killer—he was a swindler. A self-centered cheat.

He wants trouble? I'll give it to him. I reached into my purse and fingered the envelope the desk clerk had given me that morning.

"You know, Claire, you'd be a lost child if you didn't have me around to look after things. Better to keep quiet so you don't expose your ignorance. But here you are, telling me—a man—how to take care of a car."

"You nearly got us killed."

"That idiot wouldn't give way. He could see I was trying to pass."

"You had no business passing there."

"You're suddenly the authority on operating a motor car?"

"You won't admit you made a mistake. I've done nothing—"

"Yeah, nothing but run your yap since we left Paducah."

I gasped. "I have the right to speak. While we're at it, why is it

3

that Ferva seemed to be the only one who knew where you were last night?"

The car jerked slightly.

Caught him off guard. I touched the envelope again. "Well?"

He looked straight ahead. "You don't let things go, do you? Always seeing things or making up stuff that never happened. I told you I was playing cards with Wiley and Spessord. Ferva came in with Wiley, but she left when we started a card game." He slid the window open and held his arm out in the stream of air.

I raised my voice against the rush of wind. "Harold, you agreed not to gamble. We barely have money to cover expenses. And everyone knows Ferva's reputation. Besides, she's a grass widow."

"So, she's separated from that drunk. Is that so bad?"

"Not separated—divorced. She's a divorced woman."

"That really bothers you, doesn't it?"

Yes, it does. "What bothers me is you being around her. I—"

"I was not *around* her." Harold held his mouth half-open, his upper lip curled.

I hated that look. "That's not what I heard."

"Well, you've been listening to the wrong people on the crew."

Harold always had a smart answer no matter what I said. My chest tightened like it had when I got lost out in the pasture, only five years old, sure the coyotes would get me. I was never so glad to see Pop.

I couldn't imagine Harold ever coming to rescue me. More like he was only waiting for an opportunity to leave, to end it. I couldn't let that happen.

Harold glowered at the road. "No matter what I say, you won't believe me."

Without looking down, I grasped the envelope and pulled out the newspaper clipping. My hand shook, but finally I had proof of something. I held the clipping up. "Can you explain this?"

Harold pulled his eyes from the highway and squinted. "What's that? Give it here."

I jerked back. "It's Ness County Court Notices—from the paper."

"*The Ness County News*? They make up most of their stuff. You're awfully naïve if you believe anything in that rag."

"They don't make up court notices."

4

"What do you know about the legal system? Who sent that drivel anyway?"

It so happened, I'd learned too much about the legal system since I'd married him. "The letter didn't have a return address."

"Oh, yeah. I'll bet you know who sent it. And what's it supposed to be about?"

"It's about you, Harold."

His mouth drew into a hard line and the color drained from his face.

I'd rehearsed my little speech at least twenty times. Once I began, my words came out like marbles pouring from a can. "It's a paternity suit, Harold. Claims you're the father of a little girl born last month. A child that was conceived when ..." I gripped my purse. "When we were in Ness City last year. It's true, isn't it?" Amazed at my outward calm, I leaned back.

His eyelid twitched—three or four times.

I couldn't let this die on the vine. Something had to come from it, as clear-cut as Mama's world that divided truth into neat little patchwork blocks of black and white.

The steering wheel shuddered again in Harold's hands. More swearing.

"Aren't you going to answer me? What do you have to say about this paper?"

"I don't have nothing to say about it because it's a pack of lies." He sounded like a little dog barking. "If you believe that claptrap, you better go soak your head. Just because some gold digger files a lawsuit doesn't mean a hill of beans. And you treat it like gospel. From someone you don't even know."

Gold digger? I hadn't thought of that. But I'd play this out. Anyhow, there was no gold to be dug from Harold. "I didn't say I don't know who sent it. I only said it didn't have a return address. It's Gar's handwriting."

He snickered. "Gar? Your cockeyed brother? He just wanted to get a dig at you by spreading gossip about me. And you fell for it."

"Don't change the subject." *Yeah, that would be like Gar.* I took a deep breath. "I deserve an explanation. This didn't appear out of thin air, or it wouldn't be in the newspaper."

5

He turned serious, expression as flat as the Illinois horizon. "I'm telling you, Claire, there's nothing to that article. If I'd known about that suit, it would already be dismissed."

"Oh, really?" Such a liar.

Harold didn't move his gaze from the road ahead. Smooth as cream, he said, "No one with an ounce of sense would believe those out-and-out lies. That's some desperate dame trying to get ahold of your dad's money—through me. Why don't you throw that piece of paper in the garbage? I'd never betray you. You mean too much to me, sugar. This hurts, that you'd think I'm that kind of man. I got my faults, honey, but I'd never cheat on you. You believe me, don't you?"

Harold had done bad things, but he called them "misunderstandings."

Yet if I could *not* believe him, that would mean the end of the marriage. I'd never be a mother.

He stroked my arm with his free hand, fingers sliding to the tips of my own.

My arm trembled. I looked away and stared at the roadside. Green fields, baking in the hot sun, flowed past as far as I could see. So much like back home, in western Kansas. I pinched the clipping between my fingers. Some way, I had to find out which spoke the truth—the newspaper or Harold.

Chapter Two

The rattle of a key sounded through the transom. I turned from the closet, hanger in hand, and edged past the double bed. *About time Harold got here.* I unlocked the door and peered out just in time to see a woman go in an adjoining room. I spun back into the room and flung the hanger.

It clanged off the cast iron headboard and skittered across the floor.

Another look out the window to the Union Station tower clock. St. Louis was a big town, but it shouldn't take him three hours to drop off the car and catch a streetcar back here.

Elmer Hall was getting tired of Harold's excuses. Made me look undependable too.

Suspicion fogged my mind.

Only traffic noises outside and the thud of my heart competed with silence in the room.

No. Can't let the negatives get me down. I grabbed Harold's suitcase and heaved it onto the bed. After undoing the straps, I flipped back the lid. Striped pajamas lay entwined with the white shirts and trousers I'd carefully pressed. I could only stare at the wrinkled mess.

He'd expect me to re-iron all of it. Where was the justice in that?

I flung it over a chair.

A paper fluttered out like a disturbed moth and settled on the floor. With a sweep of my hand, I snatched it up.

A racing form dated exactly a week previous, Saturday, July 7, 1928. On the back, Harold's careless scribble—two words, "St. Lou," and what looked to be a phone number.

His ironing could wait.

I fluffed my hair. A few dabs from the powder-puff took care of my face, as well as the white splotches on my neck and left elbow. Doc Lane had called that vitiligo. Said it was inherited but harmless.

Yeah, but he didn't have to put up with the stares I got.

7

I slid my feet into the Mary Janes I'd bought in Memphis. A walk along the promenade would clear my mind and there'd be plenty of time to get back before dark.

Not that it would make any difference to Harold.

As I swept through the lobby, I gave it a quick scan. Would've been fun to have my friend Geneva join me. But there was no one but Spessord and Frank Wiley.

Frank rose when he saw me.

Uh-oh, I don't want to talk about Harold. I waved and hurried out the door. Soon I was simply another tourist strolling along the river. I'd enjoy my walk, even if it was just by my lonesome. Pop always said one may have to wait till evening to know how splendid the day has been.

Several blocks east, there it was, the biggest river in America. People swarmed the space. Vendors hawked sweets, hot dogs, and souvenirs. A dance marathon was underway, complete with a three-piece band. The last four couples leaned against their partners like broken fence posts. Beyond, acrobats and a skinny juggler performed.

A magician lit up when I slowed to watch his show. "Hey, beautiful, I need an assistant for my next trick. How would you like to be a star?"

Not interested in having a strange man pawing me, I backed away and attached myself to a group of tourists.

A red-haired boy thrust a handbill in my face.

Immediately, I thought of the racing form in Harold's suitcase.

Gambling every chance he gets. I'd like to know what that phone number is about. Harold's no planner, but he's a schemer.

Afternoon shadows slanted across the promenade. The tourists paused to watch small boys toss bread crumbs at a mallard hen and ducklings.

Time for me to go find my supper too. I turned back toward the hotel and detoured through a neighborhood showing its age.

Strains of "Who's Sorry Now?" floated from a doorway. Two colored men sat on the front fenders of a sedan, giving women the eye.

I quickened my pace and cut across the street toward the opposite sidewalk. As I maneuvered between cars angle-parked at the curb, dampness touched my foot. First time I'd worn my new shoes and I'd stepped right into a pool of water that darkened the pavement.

I stepped back, pulled off my shoe, and wiped my foot against my other calf.

The puddle of liquid ran toward a black coupe on my left. Its front fender looked like an accordion and the headlight sat askew on its mount.

My breath caught.

A crocheted green and white shawl lay behind the passenger seat—exactly like the one Mama had given me. I didn't have to check the license plate. It was our car. I looked around, my breath held like a cracked egg.

To the left, a high porch and turret dominated a three-story Victorian house. Red velvet curtains covered the windows. The place reeked of evil, of Baal-worship and lewd secrets. Other houses like it stood down the way. Seedy shops and vacant lots with knee-high weeds had overtaken the area. A locust rasped overhead.

I jumped. In all my twenty-two years ... *Relax, Claire, you'll be all right.* My blouse felt like a wet mop on my back. I took a deep breath and finally stopped trembling. I checked the angle of the sun again. Still time to get back before dark. An alcove offered a place to watch the Ford and the house with the velvet curtains.

What would I say if Harold showed up that minute?

Around the corner, a blatting saxophone vied with a honky-tonk piano for attention. The sidewalk filled with tourists but no sign of my husband.

A door opened on the alley side of the big house, and a heavyset man stepped out. He glanced both ways, pulled his hat brim down, and rounded the far corner. Minutes later, a small man slipped out the same door and disappeared down the alley like a leaf in the wind.

More men left the house as I waited, one every few minutes.

Bunch of saps. I couldn't tell where they entered the place, as only one man, maybe a tourist, took the front steps and rapped on the paneled door.

He probably had a wife waiting too.

After several minutes, the door opened a crack, then widened, and a woman wearing satiny blue waved him in.

9

Street lights flickered on. Shadows overlapped the sidewalk and filled the recessed openings of the shops. Two men walked by and gave me a look.

I felt like a cornered rat, but they kept on going. They'd likely be back. I almost bolted.

Maybe this is crazy. It was at least twenty minutes back to the hotel. I'd wait five more minutes. Maybe ten. No reason for our car to be parked on this street. Not a repair garage in sight. *But these houses—I know what they are ...*

A hoarse giggle brought my attention across the street.

A man and woman, arms draped around one another in a disgusting way, weaved toward the Ford. The man stumbled a couple times and his shirt tail flapped below his coat. His boater concealed his face. But there was no mistaking who it was.

Harold.

With a hussy I'd never seen before.

Instinctively, I covered my eyes. Electrical impulses of pain arched across my forehead to my temples. I gasped and tears streamed down my face. I couldn't stop it, and my nose began to run.

Somehow, I had to get myself together to confront him. Otherwise, he'd brush it off as mistaken identity; say I was all wrought up again, imagining things.

I slipped out of the shadows and stopped in front of the coupe.

Harold escorted that "lady" to my place.

As he sidled around the car, smirking, I caught a whiff of booze.

He stopped about four feet away and started running his mouth. "Why doncha move, lady?" Then he looked me full in the face. He backed away and flailed one arm as if to keep from tipping over. His lips puckered and he looked like a dying goldfish, its face at the surface of the water, eyes round with panic.

Where I got the strength, I don't know, but I yelled, "Get her out of that car!"

Ten people or so circled around us as if they knew something was about to happen.

Harold stuck out his hands like he expected me to lay a slice of forgiveness in each palm. "You don't understand, Claire. It's not what you think—"

"Get her out!" I stuck my finger in his face. "Now!"

Harold jumped like a puppet on a rubber band. He tripped to the passenger door and pulled that hussy out of the front seat like she was on fire.

The woman's rouged cheeks flamed even redder. She jerked loose and backed against the fender, glaring at him. "Dahling, do you have to leave now? Don't forget our agreement." She stuck out her hand, voice now hard as a hammer. "Two dollars, mister. Right here."

I'd never seen Harold in such a pinch. Like that time Gar pinned a garden snake to the ground with his boot. Its tail had squirmed awful, like it knew it was a goner.

Harold thrust a bill at the woman.

She snatched it out of his hand and hissed, "Where's the rest, buster?"

Someone snickered.

A woman called out, "Pay her what you owe her, big shot."

I felt faint.

Harold wilted, hands shaking, but he pulled out another bill and tossed it at the floozy. He whipped around and elbowed through the crowd. Then he staggered back toward the curb, shuffled between parked cars, and ran across the street.

The tears came again. I didn't try to stop them.

Women's voices came from somewhere. What they said, I couldn't hear over my sobs, but I knew they cared. I wiped my tears away. Once my vision cleared, two bleached blondes, smiling like rescue angels, came into focus.

They drove me back to the hotel and seemed as upset as I was. The one with the orange lipstick said, "I could tell he was a rat. He's not even smart. That tramp looked like a cow, honey. You wanna make him pay—really pay—before you let him back."

The other was indignant. "I wouldn't have him back! He doesn't deserve someone as nice as you. He ain't got no class."

They brought me through the hotel lobby as if I were the Queen of Sheba.

The night clerk raised up from his chair behind the lobby desk, but they gave him a look that would stop a clock, and he handed over the room key without a whimper. They escorted me to my room.

11

"Thank you. I'll be all right."

After hugs, they left.

And returned minutes later with the extra room key.

Miss Lipstick said, "We want to make sure Prince Charming doesn't disturb your sleep."

We hugged again and then they were gone.

After the door clicked shut, I leaned against the wall for a long time. Not crying, though. I'd shed enough tears over my marriage and its long, rutted road. Instead of confronting Harold, I'd smiled my way past the warning signs and potholes of his deceit. Half the time, we were off on one of his impulsive detours. He went; I followed. I'd lost track of who I was. Could I ever find myself again?

That court notice from Gar had taken off my blinders. Gar meant to hurt me, but he'd done me a favor. No way could I pretend everything was okay now. Even if it meant giving up my dream—a home, a husband who cared for me, and, most of all, children of my own.

That had never been Harold's dream.

But I wasn't yet done with that sneak. He'd come back, give me a big line about mistakes and misunderstandings and how it would never happen again. I would be expected to pretend our marriage was back on track … and I wouldn't have to explain a divorce to Mama.

Mama said God forgave sins. She also said he hated divorce. Maybe it was too extreme for God's mercy. Again and again, I'd asked the Almighty to adjust Harold's attitude. As far as I could tell, God had more important things to fix than my marriage.

A chill shook my shoulders. What was done was done. I'd have to learn to sell on my own. The marriage was over. I pictured Mama telling me she understood. The thought stuck, a fish bone in the throat, and I knew.

Mama would not understand.

Divorce could ruin an entire family. People talked. And how could Pop stand before the church as Sunday school superintendent, proclaiming God's holiness? Everyone would know his sweet daughter lost her marriage.

No way would they let me back in the house after that.

Chapter Three

The hotel window framed a dimming sky. Given a thousand tomorrows, maybe my pain would go away. Until then, I'd have to deal with—*What will people think?* Mama's message, but I'd taken it as my own.

Now I was damaged goods. Dropped like dirt for a streetwalker.

Had I let it happen? I'd sensed an invisible connection between Harold and certain kinds of women. Women who would've caused Mama to narrow her eyes and pull at Pop's sleeve. I recalled the hard-looking woman hanging around our hotel room in Kokomo, Indiana. Suspicion had coated my mind like rust on an old skillet. Harold had done nothing to remove it, and I'd been too spineless to confront him.

I scooped up his clothes strewn on the bedspread. By the time I'd flung them into his green suitcase and strapped it shut, I was panting. I checked the hallway.

Empty.

I tugged the bag to the far wall, next to a soiled room service tray outside Room 848. Back in the room, my gaze fell on his clothes I'd separated out to iron. I heaped them on his bag in the hallway. Inside again, I slid the latch and sat to write a letter to Mama and Pop.

After I finished and addressed the envelope, the clock on Union Station showed 10:20. *Should've called Ben.* Too late now. If I stayed on the crew, I'd need a roommate.

A different roommate.

My mind so muddled I couldn't think, I fell into fitful sleep, barely aware of sounds outside my door.

My name repeated, steady as a headache. "Claire … Claire …"

I turned over and pulled the sheet over my head.

The voice, more insistent now. "Claire."

I sat up and held my breath. This was no dream. Someone was at the door. Still scarcely breathing, I slid out of bed, slipped on my robe, and crept toward the dim light from the transom.

13

Three raps vibrated the door.

Then a hoarse voice said, "Claire, open up. We need to talk. Let me in …" Harold's little dog bark.

My forehead pounded. "No. There's nothing to talk about. Take your clothes and—"

"Look, we had a misunderstanding, okay? I admit it. I'll make it up to you. We need to talk, though, but not out here."

My face felt hot even as my toes curled against the chill of the wood floor. "Maybe you need to talk, but I don't. Go away. I don't want to see you. There's nothing to say. You did—what you did. You shamed me."

He responded with the familiar promises and excuses—plus some new ones.

I let him go on for a while and leaned over to check the time.

6:05. He probably waited to sleep off what he'd had to drink. "Claire!"

I jumped.

"You there? Listen … give me five minutes. Before somebody on the crew comes out here. I don't want a scene. I know you don't, either …"

No, I didn't. "Five minutes?"

"That's all. Just five minutes. I promise."

What if he wouldn't leave once I let him in? But I didn't want questions as to why he was standing out in the hallway, locked out of his own room. I flipped on the light and slid the latch.

He slouched in and sat, pulling on his nose.

Looks like he slept in the street. My robe hugged about me with arms crossed, I waited.

"Look, Claire, what you saw wasn't … anything. That woman wasn't what you think."

The nonsense he tried to pass off was so pathetic. Something about a friend he'd run into, Harry Crosswhite, whose sister had joined them over a couple drinks and he was going to take her home before dropping the car off at the shop.

"You really think I don't have any brains, don't you, Harold?"

He stopped, mouth open. "Well, no, Claire, I didn't say that."

"Is that the best you've got? Just come in here and see if I'd

14

believe another pack of lies?"

"Look, you got it all wrong. She was Harry Crosswhite's sister. His sister."

"His sister, my foot. Why'd you give her two dollars?" My stomach churned. "I was wrong, Harold. I *do* have something to say. We're done—you and me. I put up with your schemes, your excuses, and the lies. I wanted children, a real family. You wouldn't hear of it. Told me the first week of our marriage, 'There'd be no *brats*.' Remember? That about killed me. Never to be a mother! And now, this street tramp—"

"You never believe me."

Oh, now I'm supposed to feel sorry for him? The gall! I grabbed the bedstead to steady myself. "Why should I believe you? I've lived with you, Harold. You took things that weren't yours. You—"

"You're nuts. I never took anything except what I earned fair and square."

"Really? What about the money from that blind man in Milwaukee? And that heirloom ring from the nice widow in Buffalo? You're a thief, Harold. Not just a philanderer, you stole—"

"Lies, lies, lies. Claire, look at me." He gave me that sideways smile, the kind I never trusted.

Oh, boy, here it comes. I stared at the wall. I'd seen levelheaded people practically fall over themselves to do anything he asked. "You're not going to get me to disbelieve what I already know."

"I can explain every one of those … things. That ring, she—"

"If I remember correctly, you almost wet your pants when that Tennessee deputy came looking for you about a stack of hot checks."

He stiffened and his face clouded up. Strangely, he suddenly seemed unable to interrupt me.

"But that's dishonesty. Cheating and lying. This other—those two women in Chicago, that hussy in Kokomo … You called it 'innocent flirting.' Then Ferva, *always* around. And that *thing* you were with last night. You've no right to expect anything. I've given and given. You've just been a taker." Tears came but I brushed them away. Two deep breaths. "I want you out of my life. Leave. You've had your five minutes anyway."

He worked his jaw like a terrier chewing wire. "So that's the way you want it? You can't make it on the crew without me. I've carried you. I'm the salesman; you're the helper. You better get your train ticket back to Kansas 'cause you'll never be able to keep up on this crew."

Such brass. "That's not true. I can sell and you know it. Hateful—that's you. This shows what kind of worm you really are." I flung the door open.

⌘ ⌘ ⌘

No tears after he left. If I didn't get busy, he might hustle me out of my job. I threw on some clothes and slipped to the end of the hall where I'd seen a house phone. After a call to the front desk, I took the stairs down a flight and knocked on the door of Room 712.

No answer.

A church bell bonged eight times.

I rapped again on the door.

Stirring came from inside, followed by the sound of colliding objects and a curse. "Who is it?" The voice sounded irritated.

"It's me, Claire." I couldn't bring myself to say my last name.

Silence, then the snick of the latch. The hallway light followed the door edge to reveal a heart-shaped face haloed by a frizz of hair. "What on earth? Claire, what are you doing this time of morning?"

"Geneva, can I come in? I really need to talk."

"Sure. I've gotta get ready for confession, but come in." Geneva's lips seemed in a perpetual pout, with a blush converging on her mouth. She pointed me to a chair as she grabbed clothes from the closet and tossed them on the bed. "Siddown, honey." She groaned. "My head hurts."

I sat. "I have a very important—uh, a very personal request to make."

Geneva turned from the mirror, right eyebrow lost behind mouse-colored hair. "Personal? Go ahead."

"Something has come up, and I need a place to stay. That is … can I room with you?"

"Why would you need a place to stay? Has Harold left you?" Her voice ascended half an octave.

She leaned so close that I remembered I hadn't brushed my teeth. "Harold stepped out on me with a streetwalker."

16

"That rat. I knew he was a lowlife." She smacked the brush on her makeup kit, puffing a pink cloud into the air. She extended her hand as if dispensing a cup of mercy.

Her touch spread calm throughout my body. "All the rumors I've been hearing about Harold … I ignored them. But they were true."

"I know, Claire. Hard to accept, but I've been there. Two years ago …" She leaned back and shook her head. "I'm sorry to say I understand."

The church bell pealed again.

"Men are all alike. Yes, you can room with me. Bring your things here anytime."

"Oh, thank you."

She dressed in a frenzy of movement, ending with a final adjustment of the coral pin on her blouse and a smile for me. "If I looked like you, toots, I could throw my clothes on with a pitchfork and still look good. After I get back, I'll take you to lunch."

"Lunch would be nice. I saw a cafe yesterday within walking distance." My burden lifted. "Geneva, I really appreciate this."

"We single girls gotta look out for each other. I've needed a roommate since Lucille left the crew. Never thought *we'd* room together." She glanced at her watch. "Gotta move. I'll get you a key after Mass. Now relax and make yourself at home."

As Geneva's heels clicked down the hallway, I whispered a prayer of thanks. The phrase *single girls* had caught my breath. I was used to being married, to being a missus.

Bright sky drew me to the window. A train chuffed from Union Station, headed west. West, to Mama and Pop, to Myrrl and Ethel and all the others.

I couldn't even go back to visit—at least, not the same way. I'd have to start everything over, all on my own. I'd squandered the choice of a lifetime, marrying a man I thought I knew. I'd always believed optimism would carry me through. Now my confidence had clumped like cold oatmeal into self-blame.

I wasn't a bad person. After all, I was Sam and Lillian's youngest, the one they doted on. I shut my eyes and visions appeared—me and Myrrl playing in the yard, looking for crawdads beside the farm pond, even that awful time with the lawn mower when I was three. Myrrl

17

pushed the blade, and the razor-sharp reel spun and nipped the ends of two of my fingers. In the pain and spurting red, I'd been alone for endless minutes while Myrrl flew to get Mama. The hurt seemed like it would never stop but, somehow, Mama doctored me through it all.

This pain was deeper than that and even more hopeless. I opened my eyes and looked down at the two middle fingers on my left hand. The nails curved down over the blunted ends like little seashells. A great sadness swept over me.

ELMER

Door-to-door sales was high-pressure business. Manipulators and crybabies, blaming instead of sharpening their own skills, weren't needed. When necessary, I'd straightened them out. Some called it bullying, but that came from jealousy. After all, my crew usually led Deluxe's monthly sales figures. From farm boy to head of regional sales, my skills were self-taught.

I drew a deep breath and rang the telephone.

Finally the front desk connected me with Ben Dial, the managing partner of Deluxe Art Studio. The third ring was interrupted by a click on the other end of the line. "Yeah, it's Ben."

"Morning. Elmer here. Got a minute?"

"Sure, glad you called. I'd like your take on sales territories anyway. What's up?"

"Harold. Got me outta bed this morning. Didn't talk sense—wants us to make changes. Said Claire's making trouble."

A snort echoed from the receiver. "So? That's his problem, not yours."

"He wants me to let her go."

"Let her go? We can't find enough good salespeople now, and that swell wants us to drop a producer? Claire *is* doing all right, isn't she?"

I sighed. "She's learning. But Harold's the better salesman and he's using that against her. Guess their marriage is on the rocks. He wants her gone. Says it's him or her."

"Listen, Elmer. Harold may be good, but he's not running this outfit."

"But that's it—he's good. Shall we talk over breakfast?"

"Sure. Make it seven thirty. Best to meet away from the hotel. How about Morry's? That's north, on Sixth. We can walk over together."

"Yeah, Morry's." I set the handset down. *Can't find good salesmen as it is. Harold's not winning this one, though.*

CLAIRE

A siren cried in the distance. The muffled hum of an awakening city erased my dream, and I reveled in thinking only about myself. A woman has the right to rid herself of a man like Harold. Pop would say, "Let's look in God's Word." But he did that for everything. Maybe God had put a loophole about marriage in the Good Book.

I groped in the dresser for a Bible. There, in the bottom drawer. I hefted it, flipped it open. Now what? Where to read? I stared at the book for a few more moments, then slipped it back into the drawer. I stepped into the hallway and stopped, hand on the doorknob.

I didn't have a key to Geneva's room, and St. Louis was a big city.

A door opened down the hall.

I squinted at the figures in the dim light.

Martha and Lowell Dial—nice couple. Like teenagers in love, the way they held hands and smiled at one another. And Lowell was Ben's younger brother.

"Why, hello, Claire. Are you on this floor?" Martha's cheeks dimpled as she smiled.

"No, uh … that is, not yet." I groped for an explanation. "I guess Geneva is, uh, I thought maybe she'd be here. Yeah, so I—"

Lowell cut in, eager as always. "Martha and I are going out for breakfast. Would you and Harold like to join us?"

"No! I mean … no. I've got to move some things … Harold's somewhere …" Leaving the door open a crack, I forced a smile and walked toward the stairs like a lost lamb, ducking my head as I went past them.

Their footsteps receded toward the elevator. They probably wondered what had come over me. Well, they'd find out soon enough, like everyone else.

I had completed three trips from my room, down the stairs, and across to Geneva's room without running into anyone else from Deluxe. In case Harold returned, I wanted to be out of there. My arms felt as if they were going to drop off. Perspiration soaked the back of my dress, and I probably smelled like an ox.

I flung a mishmash of yarn, my sewing kit, scraps of cloth, and various other items into a tattered paper bag, then threw my bathrobe and two dresses over my other arm and spun into the hallway. As I turned to shut the door, the sack ripped.

Scissors and balls of yarn bounced across the floor.

"Oh, good night!" I dropped to my knees.

A familiar voice with a touch of mirth in it rang out above me. "What's the commotion out here?"

I glanced sideways.

A black wingtip oxford appeared on the floor next to my hand.

I looked up. *For crying out loud.*

Elmer, my crew leader, stood outside Room 848. "You nearly bowled me over. What's the toot?"

I lurched up so quickly the blood rushed from my head, and I almost toppled over. "I'm moving. Right now." No point in beating around the bush. "Harold is not … here. I'm moving in with Geneva. But I'll be ready for canvassing tomorrow morning." *Of all people to catch me like this.* "I've got one more load, so if you'll excuse me."

He seemed to weigh what to say. "I meant to call you anyway. Need to talk with you and Harold before I hand out territory assignments. Maybe we can resolve some things. Why don't you meet us downstairs in the morning, say, eight thirty?"

Meet with Harold? Nothing could be resolved involving him. I tried to invent a question, a word to bring understanding.

Nothing came.

"Tomorrow, then?"

I gave a half nod to Elmer and headed back to Room 712.

Chapter Four

Geneva and I followed the waitress to an outside table under a giant sycamore. The aroma of spring flowers made me think immediately of the lilac bushes that Mama pruned religiously out at the farm. Of course, Mama did everything religiously. I snorted with laughter.

Geneva gave me a surprised look.

I mumbled something about wishing I could enjoy the season back in western Kansas.

Pop would've told me to pray, but I hadn't seen any results in that department. I needed down-to-earth advice from a real live person.

Geneva asked, "Do you know what you want to do?"

"What *I* want?" I stared at her.

"Yes, you. What is it you really want to do, now that you're on your own?"

I swallowed. "Well, it's, uh, not so much what I want to do as what I have to do."

Geneva dropped her menu and lit a cigarette. "You don't *have* to do anything."

That wasn't right. Mama had always taught me there were certain things a girl had to do. Be nice—always be nice. Be careful of the company you keep. Guard your reputation ...

"But I have to get things right," I stammered. "All of it ... the divorce, making a way for myself, telling my family. I'll have to ... Geneva, I need to re-make my whole life, and I don't know where to start." I teared up. "My family—Mama, really—she said I was headed for disaster when we left Ness City to work with Deluxe."

Geneva shook her head. "Sounds like your mama wanted to keep you tied to her apron strings. Look, Claire, we all make mistakes and Harold was yours. But that doesn't mean life is over." She tapped the ashes off her cigarette onto the ground beside her. "You're right; you have to re-make your life, start over, whatever you call it. Is that all bad?"

I gave a half laugh. "Well, I can't go home. Not after what's happened. So staying with Deluxe is my only choice."

"Don't be a goose. You've always got choices. Besides, it's your home, your family. What would they do if you show up, shoot you?"

"You don't know Mama. Divorce just isn't done."

She rolled her eyes. "So, you're here. Stay with Deluxe. Things might get tense if you have to work with Harold, but you could—"

"Don't say that." I waved my arm and nearly knocked my glass of water off the table. "I won't work with him. I'll join another sales team."

"Okay, calm down. But remember, Elmer would have to okay any changes. And Ben will have an opinion too."

I caught my breath. "Maybe that's why Elmer wants me to meet with him and Harold tomorrow morning."

The waitress came and took our order.

When she left, I told Geneva what Elmer had said.

"Can you trust Elmer?"

"What kind of question is that?" I took a gulp of water, suddenly aware of my thirst. "You think I shouldn't?"

"He's been your boss since you came on with our crew, right? That's been more than a year. You tell me."

"Well, I guess so. Why wouldn't I?"

"Because men run things to keep themselves in charge. Not many men will make the effort to stick up for a woman. You might be out on a limb. Depends if Elmer's fair."

"I won't work with Harold. I'll make that real clear to Elmer." Right then, I would have taken them both on.

"Good for you. But Elmer isn't a man who likes to have a woman tell him what to do."

"Where else could I work, Geneva?"

The couple at the next table turned and stared our direction.

I lowered my voice. "I don't know anybody here in St. Louis."

"I didn't mean *here*. Go home, someplace where you know people."

"Those people ... my family has probably disowned me by now."

Geneva exhaled smoke out the side of her mouth. "You're telling me you're afraid of what might happen here and you're afraid to go

22

home. You can't do nothing."

"I'm not afraid, but I'm not very sure of myself anymore." How had I even considered climbing Elmer's frame to demand *anything*?

The waitress came to take our orders.

We both ordered salads. I wasn't very hungry and Geneva was likely short of cash.

She leaned forward. "Claire, you suspected Harold was a no-good, but you didn't confront him till last night. Why?"

"I didn't know *how*. You can't believe his excuses. I could never get a straight answer."

"Claire, everyone—except you, I guess—everyone knew Harold's reputation. He's a wolf." Geneva pulled out her hand mirror to check her makeup. "See what happened when you finally stood up for yourself? You exposed him for what he was."

"I knew he was a grifter. Always asking Pop for money. Said he needed several hundred to set up a barbershop in Ransom. Three months later, that was gone and he said he never wanted to barber anyway. Then he jumped into a string of get-rich-quick schemes that fell apart. Finally Pop started asking questions. Questions he should've asked Harold at the beginning."

"Once a skunk, always a skunk." Geneva shook her head. "You saw enough of him to know he wouldn't change. And you never held him accountable."

"I kept hoping he'd do the right thing." And I'd been gullible.

"Does no good if there's no penalty. He does what he wants. A man needs a woman to keep him in line. What's done is done, but you've been way too passive. Sometimes you have to take charge so you don't get run over. Understand what I'm saying?"

"I hear you." I looked down. The thin silver band on my finger glinted in the sunlight like a flaring match. I twisted the ring off and into my hand. "I wonder what would've happened if I'd stayed back in Kansas."

"But you didn't. You wanted more, like we all do. What was your dream?"

"I don't know. I guess I wanted to find out what I was meant to be."

Geneva's eyebrows shot up.

Doesn't she realize God has plans for everybody? Maybe not. "Does that not make sense to you?"

"What you were meant to be? What do you mean? You're free to be what you can be. We're right back to where we were five minutes ago. Nobody's telling you what you have to do."

While the waitress set our salads down, I held my tongue. As soon as she moved on to check with the next table, I said, "I don't mean following a set of rules for my life. I mean, if there was a plan for me—like maybe from God."

"From God?" Geneva snuffed her cigarette out. "Well, uh, maybe some real religious people believe that. Mostly, though, you make your own plans. You're the one … Unless, yeah, unless your preacher-man tells you what God says. But why would he let a tomato like you marry someone like Harold?"

"That's just it. What if Harold wasn't part of God's plan? Harold talked about himself, what he was going to do. He was very sure of himself. He came from a good family. That was very important to me, to Mama."

"Did you love him? Really love him?"

That question. "I thought I did, at first. After months of disrespect, whatever I had felt for him died. At the end, I couldn't stand to be around him."

"You ever date anyone else? Harold's not bad-looking, but he's no Valentino."

"Harold came along after Walter Davis stopped courting me. Walter was a fine man, and nice-looking too, in a rugged sort of way. He would've married me. But my oldest brother, Gar—he told some stories that Pop believed. They weren't true, but by the time I got it straightened out with Pop, Walter never called again." I dropped the ring into my purse and drew my knuckles to my mouth.

Geneva thrust me a hankie. "Sounds like there's more to your story."

I dabbed my face and managed to speak. "Yeah, I guess there is." I pictured the rose arbor at the farm place, Myrrl leaning over the garden fence, white pickets spiking his overalls. "My brother and I looked after our sisters' children, pushing them in our front yard swing and telling them stories. They loved going out in the pasture to

24

scout for prairie dogs and rabbits."

Geneva leaned across the table. "You wanted a family since you were a kid, didn't you? You assumed that any decent man would want the same thing."

"But Harold wasn't ... he thinks only about himself."

"I keep telling you; you're done with Harold. But you're not done with *you*."

I slumped back in my chair. "I might as well be. There's nothing I can do now. I went against Mama's wishes. She was right, and I was wrong."

"Claire!" Geneva's voice rose to a falsetto.

Several people around us turned to stare.

"Forget your mama for a minute. It's your life, not hers."

"Well, she showed me in the Bible—God hates divorce." I stabbed a tomato.

"Claire. Claire." She spoke quietly now.

I looked up and stilled my fork.

"You have to forgive yourself for your part. But remember, Harold's the rat in the chicken coop, not you. I ended my marriage when it had to be done—"

"But divorce is a sin. You're Catholic. How did—?"

"Annulment. No divorce. That's where we have it over you Protestants." She held her cup with both hands and peered over the rim.

"But is that legal? Were you ... excommunicated?" I hesitated to discuss my own beliefs, much less those of someone else.

"Yes. And no. Yes, it's legal. In fact, even getting a divorce isn't a sin. No, I wasn't excommunicated. Actually, I took Communion this morning. But why're you asking about all this? You're not considering becoming Catholic, are you?" She flashed a cheesy grin.

"No, I only want to do right. But Mama said the Bible—"

"I don't know about the Bible, and I don't have any idea what your mama believes, but divorce in itself isn't always wrong, according to what my priest told me."

I stared at her. She didn't have to worry about pleasing God or her family as long as she pleased her priest. But it couldn't be that simple, the way people back home whispered about marriages breaking up.

25

Geneva plowed ahead. "Father Rooney said it depends on what you do *after* you're divorced. If you remarry after divorce, well, that may not be good."

I coughed on a piece of lettuce. "Don't say that. I want to have a family."

She frowned. "You better talk to your preacher-man—make sure what you can and can't do. That's why you're tied in knots. You want to have kids, but you think you can't remarry. Is that it?"

Tears again. I blew my nose. "Yes. So, I'll talk to my 'preacher-man.' Should have done that before I married Harold. Money was everything to him, and he was always in trouble. When things got too hot for him, he signed us up with Deluxe. So we picked up and left Ness County. I found out later that the law was after him."

"I'm sorry, honey." Geneva's voice softened. "Do you have anything else you can fall back on?"

"I got my cosmetology license when I was eighteen. Mama didn't think much of beauty operators."

Geneva rolled her eyes again. "Your mama."

"After my correspondence course, I worked in a beauty shop in town. First time I had a steady income. People noticed me. I was a woman, not just a farm girl. Those society ladies trusted me. They told me ..." I lowered my voice. "They shared some very private information while I did their perms and facials. A lot of women simply want someone to talk to, about their boyfriends, husbands, secrets. You wouldn't believe the secrets some women are carrying around. A trip to Wichita is an adventure when all you've known is western Kansas. But even they'd be amazed at the places we've seen with the crew."

"Yeah, it's a big world out there once you get out of Joliet. Lotsa women are doing things, almost anything they put their minds to."

"Amelia Earhart. Osa Johnson—she's from Chanute. Aren't they something? And I'd like to think I could do something special ... *be* special."

"You've got what it takes. Why shouldn't you?"

"'Cause my mistakes are hard to live with. I was crushed when Walter went back to the Otis girl. Then Harold came along." I pulled the tortoise shell clasp from my hair and caressed it. "I should've given myself more time."

"Both of us have lots of 'should haves.' You do the best you can. It'll take time to get over the divorce, but face it, Harold's a crumb. You deserve better."

"Didn't you hear what I said, Geneva? I can't marry again before God since he hates divorce."

Chapter Five

A fried egg stared back from my plate, its golden eye quivering each time the hefty waitress thudded past.

7:30. One hour before my meeting with Harold and Elmer.

I must've checked the clock in the hotel coffee shop five times before I finished my toast. Enough. I left a nickel tip and headed up to my new room.

I entered and eased over to the mirror to re-check my makeup.

Geneva stirred, sat up, and then half stood and leaned against the wall.

"Good morning."

She gave a snuffled response before she felt her way to the lavatory.

Time for me go.

I scanned the lobby when I stepped off the elevator.

A man in a gray suit and straw boater leaned across the counter from the desk clerk.

I shrank against the wall.

The figure in the gray suit straightened; he was at least four inches taller than Harold.

Exhaling, I chastised myself and started across the lobby.

Two men rose from the overstuffed chairs near the east windows. Against the morning light, I saw only silhouettes but identified them at once. Spessord's six-foot, seven-inch frame loomed over any crowd, and Frank Wiley, who walked like he had a pebble in his shoe.

I forced a smile as they approached.

"Claire, where's your husband gone to?" Wiley asked with a grin. "He's not still in bed, sleeping off that moonshine, is he?"

Spessord frowned. "Frank, be respectful!" He turned to me. "We expected to see Harold when you got to St. Louis, so—"

"So he could pay us the dough he owes us."

No surprise—Harold gambling again.

28

"Frank." Spessord directed his gaze back to me, his mournful voice more agonized than usual. "Harold shouldn't never play poker—or play the ponies, either." He looked at his shoes. "He lost a wad. We thought we'd better outline a plan for getting our money."

I rubbed the back of my neck. "You mean he still owes you?"

"A hundred thirty-six smackeroos is what I got coming," Wiley said. "And Spessord—a hundred fifty-five, ain't it? That's two ninety-one, grand total."

Over two months' worth of commissions?

"Claire, we're being straight. I wouldn't try to fool you." Spessord's deep-set eyes flickered beneath the thatch of continuous eyebrow.

At least Harold's troubles no longer had to be mine. "Of course, Jim."

Wiley rattled on, like a milk wagon on a cobblestone street. "We had a few drinks. Played cards until two or so. Harold went to get his stash, so he said. We waited over half an hour, but he never showed. I get peeved, Claire, when somebody lies to me like that."

"I understand. Harold should take care of his own affairs." Had they caught my drift?

Spessord waved a huge hand. "We need to settle these obligations before he, uh, forgets. You wouldn't happen to know where he is?"

"I haven't seen Harold. Not lately, that is." I pasted on a bright smile. "You might catch him outside the meeting room, down the hallway." My neck prickled with heat.

The two men exchanged glances.

I turned down the hallway. What might Spessord and Wiley do? And what would Elmer say if the situation turned ugly? When it came to business, he tolerated few distractions.

Harold habitually arrived a few minutes late, but he might be early for this meeting. What if he already had Elmer cornered, running his mouth?

I peered inside the meeting room.

Elmer sat alone at a small, round table, pencil in hand, gazing at scattered papers and a wrinkled map. He looked up. "Have a seat."

Spessord and Wiley popped their heads in from the hallway behind me.

"Jim, what's up?"

Spessord dropped his eyes. "Sorry, Elmer. Understood that Harold might be coming down here, but we'll catch him afterward."

"Jim, there's Harold." Wiley pointed and the two men hurried away.

The sound of scuffling feet and agitated voices jerked Elmer upright and out of the room.

A babble of disagreement rose and fell in the hallway.

I moved toward the open door. *Wait, stop right here.* More times than I could count, angry men had confronted Harold. He had an uncanny ability to slide out of tight spots. I edged forward and peeked into the hallway.

Thirty feet away, Spessord and Wiley had Harold backed against the wall.

Elmer, a solid six-footer, stepped in front of Harold, forearm raised, facing the other two. "Back off, Jim. You too, Frank. Now, what's this all about?"

Spessord waggled his index finger in Harold's face. "What it's about, Elmer, is that we have a tinhorn on the crew. He thought he could weasel out of what he owes us. He's a liar, besides, and—"

"It's a simple misunderstanding, Elmer." Harold smoothed the front of his coat and avoided eye contact. "Jim has his facts mixed up, that's all. He—"

"Shut your mouth, you little snot, or I'll mop the floor with you." Spessord turned to Elmer. "Frank and I'd like a word with you. Privately."

Elmer laid a hand on Harold's arm. "You, stay right here." Then, to the others, "All right, Jim, let's hear it, over there. Then I'll get his side of the story."

I edged back into the meeting room and sat at Elmer's table. Abruptly, I arose and hurried to the window, gazing outward as if transfixed by activity on the street. I maintained this pose until movement came from behind me.

Thankfully, it was Elmer, alone, shaking his head. He took a deep breath. "Claire, why don't you come back in half an hour? I'll have the sales meeting then. It looks like I've got a row to settle."

I stayed where I was. What if Harold was waiting for me?

As if he knew my thoughts, Elmer gestured to the door. "Don't you worry. The hall is clear now."

⌘ ⌘ ⌘

My heart felt as if it were going to jump out of my chest as I approached the meeting room. The buzz inside ceased the instant I came through the door.

All eyes turned to me.

Only two open seats, in the front row.

Where was Elmer?

Whispers stirred but quickly shushed when voices in the hallway approached the open door.

Elmer strode to the front of the room. Behind him, Ben settled against the side wall, one hand thrust into a coat pocket, the aroma of his expensive cigar wafting after him.

Elmer didn't mince words. "Some changes—so I'll get down to brass tacks. Ben and I met with Harold. He's taking a break from the crew, effective today." He flicked a glance at me. "There are no other adjustments."

I had a sudden urge to bolt from the room but instead raised my eyes to the street map taped to the wall. Elmer's baritone continued, peppered with a finger-jabbing assignment of territories and schedules. Finally he said, "Claire will partner with Ruby. Lowell, I'd like you and Martha to take them to their territory. They'll be next to you. Ben says we'll be in the St. Louis area for three weeks. Maybe four, if Paducah sales are any indication. I'll spend most of my time with the new people. The rest of you know how to reach me. Any questions?"

Sweeney raised a hand, but his wife hissed and pushed it down.

Elmer collected his lists and maps.

As the room emptied, Martha Dial approached and put her arm around my waist and smiled right at me. "We'll take care of you, kiddo."

I wanted to collapse into her arms.

⌘ ⌘ ⌘

Not having a car meant occasional long treks to rendezvous with Lowell and Martha. Through every neighborhood, I lugged my frame and photo samples, plus all my invoices and records. Once, Elmer

31

ferried me and Ruby around our territory for half a day, but he had two other teams working without a car so we were afoot more often than not. When we returned to the hotel each evening, I checked the mail, ate a quick meal, bathed, and collapsed into bed.

I had lunch several times with Lowell and Martha in the following two weeks, but they never mentioned Harold. Surely Lowell had heard about the drama from his own brother. No way would I ask if he had.

Maybe Spessord and Wiley would be enough to keep Harold away. I saw a lawyer, only once, to file divorce papers. Whenever I caught a few minutes with Geneva, which wasn't often, I poured out my anxieties.

She told me not to fret.

Sunday afternoon of our third weekend in St. Louis, Geneva breezed into our room. "Hey, toots, where you been? You're taking work too seriously. I never see you awake."

"I never see you, awake or asleep. You got time for me?"

"Oh, Claire, I do. Sorry I haven't been around. I've been seeing an old boyfriend—before Johnnie. He lives here, so I called him. We've gone dancing a few times. He's a real sheik."

"Is he friendly? Because, uh, you might want to re-touch your lipstick." I snickered, then broke into laughter.

She raced to the mirror, eyes wide. "Oh, I'll never hear the end of this." She grabbed a towel and rubbed her face vigorously. "Sweeney saw me in the lobby. Of all people, I had to run into that lout …" Her words trailed off behind the flailing towel. She peeked around it and we both lost control, Geneva snorting as she did when carried away.

That threw me in a tizzy. "So, Sweeney saw you? Now everyone will hear about it."

We must've giggled for five minutes. It had been months since I'd felt like laughing about anything.

Both of us gradually wound down.

I got up off the bed, swiped a comb through my disheveled hair, and gave her outfit a once-over. "Is that new? Did your beau get all that for you? I haven't seen that floral blouse before."

Geneva flashed a Clara Bow pose. "Stunning, isn't it? Mama sent it for my birthday."

32

I moved over to get a better look. "That silk scarf didn't come from Mama. He's got good taste. I'll bet he didn't find that cameo pin in Duckwall's, either." I gave her a long look. "He must think you're pretty special, Geneva. Harold never bought anything like that for me." In fact, all I ever remembered getting from him was a handkerchief—a handkerchief!—and some stationery. Not that I expected fancy gifts, but one would think that in two years of marriage, a man would've gotten more for his wife, considering birthdays, anniversaries, and Christmases. I had papered over a lot of demeaning, hurtful things from him.

"Maybe, but we'll leave St. Louis in a week, and then what? He goes back to whoever he's been seeing. I don't dwell on it." Geneva sighed. "But I need to look after you. You all right?"

"I took your words to heart. This isn't the end of the world." I clutched the comb tighter. "But I thought I'd hear from home by now."

"From their viewpoint, being in St. Louis is probably like being on the moon. The best thing—Harold's gone. I know you don't walk out of a marriage like getting off a bus but you *do* get to start over." Geneva mounted a search, probably for her cigarettes. "You ready for when Harold comes back?"

"I don't let the thought enter my mind. I can't tell you how many times I saw him play the big shot, with his boater tipped up like a rooster's comb, eying the women and flipping a four-bit piece like he owned the joint."

"Yeah, no one likes an overbearing swell but we don't want to dirty our hands with them. So they get their own way. Finally, it gets so bad we have to do something. Takes courage."

"Don't remind me what a wimp I was."

"Sorry, toots. Better luck next time." Geneva collected her purse. "Let's go downstairs for lunch. I found a dime on the sidewalk."

⌘ ⌘ ⌘

The following week, a letter came from home, written in Pop's hand.

Missed you every time I called. Can't tell you the grief I feel. You said you had no marriage to save. Such an ungodly man. Wish I'd been there to deal

33

*with that selfish lout. He had plenty of chances to
show he was worth his salt. Failed every time, far as
I can see. But divorce is a serious matter in the eyes
of the Lord. Even though you're not to blame.*

*You didn't give many details. I take it Harold
violated the marriage covenant. A monstrous sin. My
soul weeps for you, babe. I can help if you need a
lawyer. Do you plan to come back to Ness?*

*Regardless, we want you to know we are praying
for you.*

I stared at the sheet for a long time, imagining the scratch of Pop's
Sheaffer pen as it bled his emotions in a race across the page.

And him wanting to know if I planned to come back to Ness. Not
really an invitation.

I flipped the page over.

Not a word from Mama.

I didn't try to stop the tears.

⌘ ⌘ ⌘

After a quiet meal and a walk, I went back to the room and wrote a
short note back.

*Don't worry, Pop. The big boss got me a lawyer.
My responsibility anyway. If it's okay, I'll come home
in two weeks. We're going to Peoria after we leave
here. I'll check with my boss to be sure I can get
away. Let me know if a different date would be better.*

So much Pop hadn't said. Did they want to see me? Would we all
sit around the big oak table and discuss how I'd start all over again?
Pop would have his Bible …

I had my Bible already, there, under my letters.

Where to begin?

Too bad Pop's not here. I cut the book like a deck of cards.

Psalms again. "Save me, O God … thou dost know my folly …
Dishonor has covered my face. I have become estranged from my
brothers and an alien to my mother's sons …" Whoever wrote that

felt like me. "But God is the strength of my heart and my portion forever." I grabbed a pencil stub and underlined the words.

Probably wrong to mark sacred Scripture, but I was glad I'd done it anyway.

I hurried downstairs to catch Elmer in the hotel restaurant. How would I talk to the man? Harold had always represented the two of us. I spotted him in a booth with Wiley.

Elmer wore a black three-piece suit set off by a gold chain and watch fob across his vest.

I withdrew a mirror from my purse and confirmed the white splotches on my neck were covered.

Elmer laughed at something Frank said.

I studied his profile. Prominent cheekbones, wavy black hair, strong chin. Nice-looking. He never seemed to notice the way women watched him when he entered a room.

He turned before I could look away.

Seized by a coughing fit, I walked toward him, eyes watering. I tried to smile. "Good morning, Elmer. I was, just—hello, Frank ..." I swallowed and plunged ahead. "Elmer, if I could discuss something with you. Won't take but a minute."

Wiley stood. "Elmer, that's all I had. Let me know." He squinted at me. "Claire, you heard from Harold? Me and Spessord need to finish our business with him."

"No, I don't hear from him at all, Frank." I gave him a sharp look until he left.

Elmer pushed Wiley's cup and saucer aside and waved for me to sit. "Well, are you and Ruby becoming a team?"

"Not a team. I'm more like a helper. Ruby doesn't take no for an answer."

"That's why I put you two together. Now, what can I help you with?" He beckoned the waitress. "You had breakfast?"

"Coffee will be fine, thanks. What I want to talk about—to ask you—would it work for me to take a few days off so I can go back and see my family, maybe in a few weeks?"

"What's up? You looking for another job?" His face creased in a faint smile.

Was he serious? Or mocking me? "No, of course not." My reply had an edge I hadn't intended.

His eyebrows went up.

He must have been teasing. It annoyed me all the same.

Elmer pulled out a folded calendar, marked like a battle map. "Probably a week in Peoria. The weekend of the twenty-fifth to get to Davenport. Two weeks there. Those hay-shakers all want pictures of their family trees. It's been a good area for us." He looked at me, serious. "How long do you need to be gone? You and Ruby are just getting acquainted with one another's quirks, so I can't stumble around very long with someone else filling in for you."

"Five days, counting a weekend. The train takes a day each way."

He stared at me. "You understand personal matters shouldn't take precedence over work as a matter of practice, yes? But I'll treat this as an exception. Let me know exact dates after you get your train ticket."

Though his brusqueness put me off, I forced a smile. "Thanks. Of course, I'll tell you right away. I won't wait for that coffee. I need to get ready to join Ruby." I stood and nearly collided with the waitress, who had arrived with a pot of coffee. Whirling around her, I muttered an apology and swept out to the hotel lobby. I'd get my tickets when I returned that evening.

Not that it would do a lot of good if I wasn't even welcome back in my own house.

Chapter Six

Eighteen months previous, Harold had spirited us out of town. Now I'd be crossing Mama's threshold again. My throat constricted, and my palms slicked with sweat. Then I thought of Pop, arms outstretched, and breathed easier. And Myrrl, easier still. Five years older, my brother was always there when I needed him. He was driving down in Pop's Studebaker to pick me up at Dodge. Maybe Grace too, if they left their baby with Mama. I loved my sister-in-law, so naïve she made me laugh. I could tell them anything they asked about. Almost anything, really, and they wouldn't tell Mama.

I gazed out the train window. Furrowed fields flowed past, opened moist and rich to the hot blue sky. A red-tailed hawk settled on a far post. I couldn't help but smile. Deluxe Art Studio—even Peoria, which I'd left the day before—seemed like a dream compared to the reality of a Kansas prairie.

The frizzy-haired woman in the window seat next to me finally lapsed into twitching slumber. In the morning light, her pouty lips and dangly earrings reminded me of Geneva.

When Geneva had taken me to the Peoria train station, I'd told her going home would be trouble. "Mama already has her mind made up. Thinks this divorce proves I'm unstable."

Geneva's jaw dropped. "This is your mother. Mothers don't say stuff like that." Then she started rattling on about the women in her home parish, sacrificing for kids and husbands.

"Geneva, listen to me. You don't know Mama. She *does* say that. She gets her mind made up and there's no changing it. Pop doesn't want to ruffle her feathers, either."

Geneva frowned. "Sounds like a controlling family if they gloss over disagreements like that. Some folks think *looking* good is the same as *being* good. They trip over themselves to paint a pretty picture when all they need is to face reality."

"I remember Mama's first words when I told her I wanted to go to beauty school—'What will people think?' She's surely asking that same question now. Am I suddenly a bad person?" Tears seeped from the corners of my eyes.

Geneva proffered a hanky. "You need to go home. Face them all. Settle it. And no, you're not bad. Get off that, honey."

I took the handkerchief and dabbed my eyes. "I can count on one hand the number of divorced women in Ness City. Guarantee the women at the beauty shop can name each."

⌘ ⌘ ⌘

As the train glided to a stop at the Dodge City station, I spotted Myrrl. Goody—Grace was with him, clutching her hat. Tumbleweeds bounced down Front Street.

After sidestepping down the aisle to the door, I gratefully took the conductor's hand.

Grace's voice came through the wind like the chirp of a lost bird. "Claire! Claire!"

Flying sand lashed my face and I blinked.

Irrepressible Grace waved a white hankie.

Then they were beside me, and I fell into the lattice of their arms.

As Myrrl collected my luggage, Grace took me to the Studebaker.

I slid into the front seat with a gasp. "Oh, this weather. How could I forget the wind?"

"Welcome back to Kansas, little sister." Grace got in the backseat and reached up to hug me again. "You look so pretty."

I dearly loved this unassuming woman. Her functional dress and hair pulled back in a bun would be dismissed back east as old-fashioned, but Myrrl said he loved her inner beauty—her pure heart and loving spirit. It didn't hurt that she was a great cook too.

He yanked his door open and started the car.

As we headed north out of town, I turned sideways to study him.

"What you looking at, sis?" He gave me that impish grin.

"Oh, I'm memorizing what you look like. Lucky I didn't get in the wrong car."

"Who you kidding? You'll never forget this mug."

"I shouldn't tell you this, but Helen Schweitzer said you were handsomer than any of her beaus. I told her she'd change her tune if she had to live in the same house." I reached across to squeeze his

38

shoulder.

Myrrl pressed my hand against his face.

The stubble of his cheek against my skin brought to mind Walter Davis. My face felt hot.

Myrrl shot a glance my way. "Whillikers, sis, you *have* missed us. A weekend isn't going to be long enough to catch up on everything."

Grace caressed my hair. "I can imagine what it's been like, away from family with no one to really talk to. I've missed walking out by the pond with you, sharing secrets."

"Now it's your pond, and the farm too. I'm glad Pop and Mama moved into town and let you do the farming. Do you like being out there?"

Myrrl grinned. "Since Pop already built a house for Gar on the east quarter, it worked out swell for me. He couldn't very well ask for Pop's farm."

Grace launched a flurry of questions: would I ever come back to Ness to live, and if I'd seen the soup kitchens and marchers in the streets back east, and so on. Before I could answer, she said her brother would like to meet me. Then she asked if I ever had time to go to church.

So like my sister-in-law. "Well, I have a wonderful roommate, Geneva, who's so, so real. I loved the bluegrass country of Kentucky—white fences winding over green hills. Don't tell Mama, but I went to a jazz club in Cleveland."

Grace's eyes widened. "You didn't! Tell us."

"They had a Negro band, if you can imagine. Could they ever play. Have you heard of Jelly Roll Morton? He strutted around that stage in a fancy tuxedo, white shoes, and spats. A tap dancer brought everybody to their feet. You would've been floored by that show."

Grace closed her window and leaned forward. "Did they serve beer ... or whiskey?"

"Oh, yes. The bar was as long as Pop's house. Whiskey bottles across the entire back wall."

"But that's illegal!" Grace gasped.

"Bootleggers," Myrrl said. "They're in Ness too. People just ignore the law."

Grace shook her head slowly. "Wasn't it scary, with all the drunks around?"

I suppressed a smile. "Some people drank, but most came for the music and dancing. Besides, the management had three big fellows watching to make sure no one got too rowdy. One man got on a chair, waving a bottle, and those big men had him out of there in a jiffy. His wife nearly cried. She wanted to see the show, but she finally took his coat and left too."

"Goodness!" Grace sank back into her seat.

I told about the time we got lost in New York City and almost went the wrong way into the Holland Tunnel. Grace gagged when I described Geneva eating oysters on the half shell at Chesapeake Bay. Myrrl asked if men in suits actually peddled apples on the street. I said I wept when forty hungry women and children came into our hotel in Pittsburgh; and no, I hardly ever got to go to church and that was what I missed the most.

Myrrl looked back at Grace in the rear-view mirror.

I quickly changed the subject to their family.

Grace thrust a picture forward. "Here's our little boy, Lynn Dean."

"Oh, so precious. Your baby." I touched the image. "And Pearl—she's got a new baby?"

"That's her fourth," Grace said. "Ethel and Ed are expecting again, and ..." She faltered.

Myrrl mumbled something about Gar farming the south quarter.

Helen Schweitzer would know more about the latest around town. I'd talk to her later.

Twice, Grace seemed ready to ask about Harold but didn't.

I'd tell them if they asked, but I wasn't going to bring it up. Weariness and the drone of the car eventually overtook me. I cushioned my head against the door and dropped like a pebble into a pond of blissful sleep.

I awoke as we came into town. Behind coverlets of trees, the houses—in turn dignified, plain, friendly, fair, or faltering—huddled along the sleepy streets I knew by heart. Windows stared back at me like blind men. I could name the families in most of the houses. Would they care that a lost daughter had returned home? I felt a twinge of regret that no one was out to greet me, ridiculous as that was to hope for.

Myrrl teased me about being bored with their company. We broke into laughter like twittering birds, and just as quickly cut to nervous silence. Myrrl stopped in front of the white stucco house at Park and Chestnut.

With butterflies in my stomach again, I thought of the prodigal son. That father had welcomed his wayward child with open arms.

Pop appeared on the porch as I opened my door.

I hesitated … then flew up the steps into his arms. "Oh, I'm so glad to see you. To be here."

Mama's alto voice. "Claire, come in out of the weather."

Was that a hint of sharpness? Had she shut me out of her soul … or was it my imagination?

Grace and Myrrl brought my luggage, and Pop and I followed them inside.

Mama set out five plates of her Rosenthal china and cut an equal number of pieces of black currant pie. We sat around the big round oak table and drank blissful hot tea. I went through my travelogue but didn't tell about the night club or the whiskey bottles along the wall. Exhausted, I realized I was the only one talking. I closed my performance, even though I wanted to peel back my skin and open up my heart.

Look, Mama! I'm bleeding, all inside of me. I need you to touch me where it hurts and help me heal.

⌘ ⌘ ⌘

Ethel and Pearl came over later that evening. I'd hoped they, especially Ethel, would ask what I'd gone through. They both said they missed me and asked about my travels. Everybody stopped talking each time Mama entered the front room to restock refreshments.

What were they afraid of? Were they waiting for Mama's permission to ask about the divorce?

Pop sat next to me, listening without speaking.

As the evening wore on, I felt an urge to shout. *Somebody—ask about me. Tell me you care what happened to me. Ask me if I'm hurting. Tell me I'm okay, that you accept me.*

Pop finally excused himself for bed, Mama collected the cups and dishes, and the visitors went home.

I went upstairs and cried myself to sleep.

Helen Schweitzer, dear Helen, came over as I finished breakfast.

I got two blankets, and we cocooned ourselves out on the front porch in the cool of the morning. I told her about my ruined years with Harold.

She understood, like always. That afternoon we took a picnic out to the pond on the home place. We walked into the quiet countryside, into a private corner of heaven.

⌘ ⌘ ⌘

How many times had I wished to be with family on Sunday? I stared out the living room window.

Mama came out of the kitchen. "Not everyone knows you're back. But they'll be surprised—glad—to see you."

"Church? Not today. People will ask questions. And last night, Ethel couldn't even ask how I was." Tears came in a rush, wetting the front of my sensible, cream-colored blouse.

Pop whipped out his bandanna and handed it to me. "No, Mother. Our girl doesn't need to go to church. She came to see us. It's too much to expect. She'll be fine right here, while we go." His hand on my arm, he bent toward me. "Babe, we'll be back, right after services. I'll tell Reverend Lewis you wanted to see him, but next time. He'll understand."

"Thanks, Pop." I mopped my face and honked into his kerchief. "I'll be all right."

Mama turned and collected the breakfast dishes.

⌘ ⌘ ⌘

Packed and ready for the drive down to Dodge, I sat with Mama and Pop around the dining table that afternoon for a last cup of tea. Pop's attempts at small talk fizzled, and I fidgeted. If they weren't going to ask me, I'd tell them. "I'm not sure when I'll be home again. Deluxe has a year-end banquet that everyone is expected to attend. I don't want to jeopardize my job, so I may come home for Christmas, then go back east for the banquet."

"So, you'll continue traveling?" Mama's words came like rocks thrown against a concrete wall. *Smack ... smack ... smack.*

I wanted to jump up and smash the teapot against the stone fireplace. Instead, I simply looked at her before speaking. "I have my job, Mama. I can't give that up, at least not right now."

Pop leaned forward. "You can stay here, babe, you know that."

"That means so much—to hear those words. But I need to make my own life."

Mama folded her arms in front of her. "You didn't have to leave Ness in the first place."

"That was Harold's decision, not mine."

"Didn't you have any say?"

"Mama, it was go or be left behind. I was doing everything I could to save the marriage, even then. You probably don't understand how it was with Harold 'cause you've got Pop."

"Oh, I think I understand. But it seemed you kept going from one crisis to another. Why didn't you ever come and talk to me about it? I would've listened to you, maybe even given you some helpful advice."

My stomach clenched. Did she feel as shut out as I did? "I wish … I'd done that. With Harold, nothing was easy. I wanted to talk with you, many times. He didn't like me being independent. Said I was selfish. I tried to build trust between us, but he didn't care. By the time I really needed to talk with you and Pop, we were gone. Cleveland, Kansas City, Chicago—always on the move."

For a few moments, no one spoke. My emotions tugged like an insect struggling in a spider's web.

Mama broke the silence. "After you left, to join the photography people, I didn't know when you'd come back. Harold's troubles seemed to never stop. Sam, you knew more than you let on. I can imagine what other people thought—"

He raised his hand. "I didn't want to bother you with all that, Lilly, and I thought Harold would get ahold of himself. I talked to him once, man to man, and he promised he'd never betray my trust again. He could seem so sincere. I wanted to believe him, for Claire's sake."

"I'm glad to hear you say that, Pop." I gulped in a breath. "I wondered if you thought I was so gullible, marrying him in the first place. Harold could be very convincing."

Mama leaned forward. "A woman can tell certain things about a man. You know that. It comes down to what she wants to admit she knows. She can be ruled by her heart or by her head. I never thought for a minute that Harold was the man for you—"

The words scalded my ears. "Mother! Why didn't you say something?"

"You had your mind set on marrying him, that's why. Frankly, I would've been happy if you'd continued seeing Walter Davis. Perhaps he was a bit unpolished, but he seemed stable."

I looked from Mama to Pop, then back again, "Oh, Mama! That was so hurtful, what happened. Gar was responsible for Walter never calling again. Remember, Pop?" I looked at him, helplessly.

He dropped his head again, as if to etch the pattern of the throw rug onto his memory.

Mama seemed about to burst. Finally she expelled a single word. "Well!"

Pop raised his head and his right hand at the same time. "Lilly, I'll explain, but later."

She frowned and turned to me. "You surely felt some hesitation about Harold—"

"Mama, who can ever know for sure?" I swiped away a tear and met her gaze. "Nobody can."

"But didn't you pray about it?" Her voice was soft, yet with a hard insistency. "God shows the way. He always shows the way if we ask him."

"Yes, I prayed, Mama." The words came out flat. Had I really?

Her voice crystallized, almost celestially. "In God's eyes, divorce is a sin."

"Oh, Mama! What could I do?"

"Yes, Mother, what could she do?" Pop sat beside me and pulled my head over on his shoulder.

I almost broke down.

"It's all right, babe. You put up with that sorry excuse for a man longer than he deserved, and it cost you. The last time you came home was almost more than I could bear." He stroked my hair, his arm like Moses's staff. "I'm glad it's over. And I don't believe God would judge you for ending this."

A tattoo of footsteps turned all heads toward the front porch as a battered straw hat passed the window.

Gar. I'd wondered if my oldest brother would spare the time to see me.

44

After a token greeting, Gar withdrew a sheaf of papers from a linen folder. "Take a look at this." He thrust the papers between Mama and Pop, with a glance at me.

Something was up. I leaned forward.

Pop fumbled for his glasses. "What is this? What are you trying to do?" He had an uncharacteristic edge to his voice.

"Look at it. Just take a look. This shows what I've been saying. It's costing the family a pile to support that man." He darted another sharp glance at me.

I scanned the papers, eyes burning as I comprehended what Gar had presented. He'd listed Harold's offenses down the left side of each page and beside each were notations and a dollar amount. I had an urge to slap him. I started to speak, but my brother wasn't finished.

"This has got to stop." His voice was nearly a shout. He seemed emboldened by our silence. "Why is our family money being used to support this—this wastrel? Why, it's criminal, what he's doing with our money."

"Our money?" I'd had enough. "How can you say that? This is Pop's money. He gave you a house! If he chooses to help someone else in the family, what is that to you?"

Pop pushed his chair back from the table and stood, all in one motion, a fearsome expression on his face, a look almost of horror, certainly of blazing anger. Facing Gar, he spoke, voice grating. "This is disrespectful. It's hurtful to Claire, to your mother, to me." With that, he stacked the papers and ripped them in half, glaring at Gar.

Gar's arm jerked up, as if to save his precious accounting. He caught himself and backed out of the room. Then he turned and left the house in a storm of mumbling and stomping.

The house now silent, Mama got up without a word and stored the washed dishes.

I stared at the china cabinet and waited for Pop to speak.

By the measured sounds from the crockery, Mama expected a statement too.

He slumped in his chair and then drew a hand to his temple, as if to erase the scene from his mind. Was his distress more about his eldest son's attitude than it was about his youngest daughter's pain?

My marriage had been a destructive seed planted in the garden of

45

the family, and its weeds and briars had poisoned relationships and isolated me from those I loved. Obviously, Gar had been told nothing about the breakup with Harold.

I stared at my father. "Pop?"

He still sat with downcast eyes, then looked up and stared out the window, eyes rimmed with tears. "How can Gar be so unfeeling?"

"You haven't told him about the divorce. Why?"

Pop exhaled. "There never seemed to be a good time, knowing the tension between you and Gar over the years. It was none of his business anyway."

Mama rejoined us. Hands on her hips, she said, "You told the others. Several at church already know." She snatched a doily off the end table and worked it between her fingers. "I never knew you had given Harold—Claire—so much, just to pay for his forgeries and thefts."

I looked from one to the other.

Mama flung her hand up. "That much money! How could he go through all that money?"

Pop's voice rose like a sudden wind. "I don't know. I don't understand people like Harold. And I guess I don't understand my own son, either. Gar would not have acted differently, regardless if I'd told him. He can be so bent on himself. But I should've told …"

"Now he'll be upset that you kept it from him," Mama said.

"He'd be mad either way." Pop huffed. "Even though he overdid it, he'll fume and grump at being misunderstood. But he was way out of line. First time I've confronted him in a long time. It just took the right situation to bring it out. Gar and I will have other talks." He stood and gazed about the room, looking as if he'd been aroused from a nap. "We'd better get to cracking, babe, or you won't be ready when Myrrl arrives. Don't want to miss that train. Lilly, did you get that spice cake wrapped up for our girl? And make sure you save a piece for the gardener." He grinned and wrapped me in a hug.

⌘ ⌘ ⌘

I told Myrrl about Gar's visit.

Tight-lipped, he said, "Gar always comes first. Pulls that stuff on me sometimes. Never thought he'd let Pop see his true colors."

"Gar did it to hurt me. Afterwards, Pop was the one hurt." A dust devil whirled across the road, flinging debris in its wake as we passed. "He doesn't care who he hurts."

"Pop had to confront him, Claire," Myrrl said. "He couldn't let Gar get away with that."

Grace leaned up from the backseat. "Your father can take care of himself."

"Are you sure? He's always so careful around Mama. And he hadn't told Gar about the divorce. Maybe he thinks that would only stir up more of an uproar."

We each seemed to retreat into individual caves of silence. Only when the northern fringe of Dodge City appeared on the approaching ridge line did we stir. I checked my makeup while Grace reviewed a list of things she needed to get in the big town.

Good-bye approached with each sweep of the second hand on the station clock. As the black locomotive pulled in, we had one last tear-stained hug.

Finally on the train, I looked out the window at those two sad-eyed people waving. They knew as well as I did that no one in the family could voice the necessary questions, much less come up with the answers to go with them.

Everybody on the crew liked me—why not my own mother and brother?

Chapter Seven

"You won't believe what happened." I dropped my bags inside our hotel room in Peoria and hugged Geneva. "Mama didn't care about me or why I left Harold. She simply didn't want to face the scandal of my divorce."

She hugged me, then stepped back, hands still on my shoulders. "Claire, this boils down to respect. You need to let people know you got feelings and an opinion or two, and they'd better listen."

I could only shake my head. "Don't get me started, or I'll only cry. For now, Deluxe has to come first. I need to make some sales or Elmer will send me down the road. Harold was a no-good, but he knew how to sell. Now, it's just me, and I've got Ruby to deal with too."

"Glad it's you and not me."

"I try to do what she says, but she's so impatient. If Elmer had more time, I could learn from him. I've never seen anyone size up a prospect the way he does. No matter what questions they have, it's like he's already rehearsed the discussion."

"He's very smooth." Geneva settled into a chair. "So smooth, in fact, that you might miss his technique. But he can be awfully impatient sometimes. You weren't here when he bawled out Sweeney, but Elmer practically had him in tears."

"He can be abrupt with the men, but I've never seen him speak to the women that way."

"He doesn't have to. I get the feeling he expects women to know their place."

My forehead pounded. I'd grown up with that attitude back in Ness County. "You think he'd run over me?"

"Maybe. If he thought he needed to. I'll say this—he's not uncivil, like Ruby."

"As long as he treats me with respect, I can handle anything he dishes out. Besides, he's considerate. Have you noticed how he always speaks to the little guys—the shoeshine boy, the bellhop? He's got a basic respect for people in general. And he doesn't let a flashy pedigree intimidate him, either. I wish I could be that way."

"Why can't you?"

"Geneva, I told you I only went through ninth grade."

"You never act like it bothers you."

"I put on a good face. Mama always told me a big smile goes a long way."

"Well, you don't have to please her now. Only Elmer and Ruby, and me." She winked. "A foot rub would go a long way."

⌘ ⌘ ⌘

I learned to respond to Ruby's outbursts with a smile and a nod. Over the next six months, my sales figures climbed. But door-to-door canvassing was still hard. This particular day had been tedious; I'd never seen so many indifferent people. A warm bath would feel good.

Room key in hand, I headed for the elevator.

Elmer hailed me from across the lobby. "Claire, would you have time for dinner this evening?" He seemed to be looking past me.

I turned around but saw only Cosmo Grenada joking with the bellhop. I looked up at Elmer. A manager-employee meeting? "Why, yes. Shall I meet you in the hotel restaurant?"

"Why don't we go out? Ben said Tilly's has good seafood and steaks. It's about twenty minutes away. I can meet you here in the lobby. Six thirty okay?"

I hated to forgo a relaxing soak in the tub, but the idea of eating someplace besides the sandwich shop or hotel restaurant seemed very appealing. "I'll need to freshen up, but that will be fine."

The maître d' treated Elmer like an old friend and seated us at a quiet table with fresh carnations. "Clair de Lune"—my song—came from a piano nearby.

Why hadn't I worn a nicer outfit? Tilly's had good food, but I enjoyed most the easy pleasantness of Elmer's company.

Conversation flowed like an unhurried stream. Elmer said I might be ready to work with a new work partner. "Your sales are picking up. I think you've got what it takes to make good money at this. You still like what you're doing?"

"Well, I enjoy people. They're nice—most of them. I didn't think it would be like that, here in the East."

"People are people. They talk faster here than out on the prairie. If you treat them with respect, they'll think you're a great judge of character." He grinned, shooting wrinkles toward his cheekbones.

"They talk so fast. Sometimes I have to guess at what they're saying."

"Don't guess, ask." Elmer opened his valise. "You have to find out what they want. A customer trusts you when he believes you really want to understand him." He spread a printed page on the table. "Read this. My ideas on typical customer objections. I tell how to handle each one. That should help you refine your close. We'll work out the hiccups so you can approach every customer with confidence. You want to be successful, don't you?"

I instinctively touched my left hand to my neck. "Well, yes. I might need some help." Elmer had a dominant personality. I liked that in a man, but it made me wary too.

"I'll help you. You've been with Deluxe for well over a year now. I want you to feel this kind of work is for you."

"Traveling sales is different from what I'm used to. I counted up the other day and I've already been in twenty states. I never imagined I'd see so much of the country. Before this, I hadn't traveled much. Just a vacation trip to Yellowstone with my family."

"You'll see more if you stay with us. Ben has definite ideas of where he wants to take the company." He raised his eyebrows. "Of course, you might be planning to go back to … western Kansas, is it? You have roots there?"

I looked down. "Yes, Ness County. All my family lives there. I'm the youngest so my folks expected me to stay under their protection. You know how parents are. It was hard leaving Mama and Pop. It seemed best for me to honor them."

"'Honor them'? Why do you say that?"

"It's Biblical. 'Honor thy father and thy mother that—'"

"Yeah, I get it. You stayed home because you were the youngest."

Goodness, didn't everyone know the Ten Commandments? "Yes, to honor them. Pop retired from farming, but he's always busy. He taught me how to do things by myself. Old Litchfield, our neighbor, nearly fell over when I hitched up a team of horses without any help.

Mama and Ethel and I cooked and canned together, crocheted and baked too. My brother, Myrrl, is five years older. He's my best friend, next to Helen Schweitzer. His wife, Grace, is a dear friend too." I grinned at him. "I don't expect you to remember all those names."

"It's all right; I'm a little slow, but I think I have it. You make friends easily. It's …" He seemed to search for words. "It's good, that you refer to your family as friends."

I had blabbed the whole time like a giddy schoolgirl. "Elmer, I talked all about myself, but what about you? Tell me about your family."

He grinned. "There will be lots of time to tell you about the great and wonderful things I've done. After we work on your sales close, I want you to see the new line of frames Ben's getting for us."

⌘ ⌘ ⌘

The following morning, Geneva motioned me over to her breakfast table in the hotel restaurant. "Sit down, Claire. Tell me about your date last night with Elmer."

"That was no date; we just had dinner and—talked. Technically, I'm still married, and I don't date married men, that's for sure."

"Elmer's not married. Where'd you get that idea?"

"Haven't you noticed the child who's sometimes with him?"

"That's the boss's son. Elmer likes the boy. Wouldn't surprise me if there's a kid back in his past, though." Geneva tapped her cigarette on the saucer under her coffee cup. "So, you did have a date, whether you knew it or not." She cocked her head sideways and smirked.

Hot-faced, I gave her a tight-lipped smile and quickly ordered eggs and toast.

⌘ ⌘ ⌘

Elmer asked me to dinner again a few days later. Maybe it had been a date. Well, I *had* filed the divorce papers. No sense in waiting for the formality of signing the final approval.

We went out several weeks running. Workdays, I always wore colors he liked in case I'd see him. I felt giddy when his eyes sought me out, even in a roomful of people. After a while, we stopped pretending. Others on the crew knew we were an item.

He made casual excuses to have me ride with him each day of canvassing. His Oakland sedan was equal to anything the banker back

51

home had. Elmer seemed pleased at my success. He helped me with the toughest prospects—a Catholic bishop, a family-run manufacturing company, owners of a big horse farm.

My sales surged. We became a real team. Ben commented that Elmer should've had me as his partner six months earlier. I did everything but carry Elmer's black valise. He kept his personal items in it—the *New York Herald Tribune* or *Kansas City Star*, a dog-eared address book that he never let out of his sight, the latest issue of *Argosy*, and perhaps a week-old racing form.

One day I mentioned how much my church back home meant to me. He said "yeah" and changed the subject.

He had an endless mine of fun things to do on weekends rather than go to church. He took me canoeing on the Ohio River—the most romantic afternoon ever, except for my sunburn. Another time we explored fish markets around Chesapeake Bay and ended that day with a grand seafood dinner. We discovered a new attraction in Chicago—a miniature golf course—and I nearly beat him. One treasured afternoon, Amelia Earhart appeared at an airport outside Pittsburgh two weeks after the first women's cross-country air race. So many people came, cheering and waving, that Elmer helped me up on a flatbed truck so I could see.

I called down to him, "You should see her, Elmer! She's so elegant." My gaze followed the caravan until it disappeared into a distant hangar.

He extended a hand to help me down.

I crouched on the truck bed, then dropped into his arms.

He didn't release me right away. "Hey, not bad. Let's do that again."

I must have blushed several shades of pink before I could speak. "I think we better go."

He laughed. "All right, we'll go dancing tomorrow night. How about that?"

Butterflies fluttered in my stomach. "Oh, I've never danced. I don't know how." I ducked my head, stuck for words again.

"Never danced? Don't tell me those plowboys never took you dancing." Elmer twirled me before we got into the car.

Breathless, I spoke as if nothing had happened. "Myrrl took me to barn dances, but I never danced. Mama didn't think it was proper for a Christian girl."

"Not proper? You didn't say your mama was a foot-washing Baptist."

"Because of the fights and the drinking—almost every time, it seemed."

"Your mama tried to keep you from having fun." He wiggled his eyebrows. "Well, hang on, we're going dancing, and your mama's not here, so you're going to have a good time."

I stared at him, wide-eyed. Everything I'd done with Elmer had been fun.

Afterward, we ate at a restaurant that overlooked the Allegheny River. I got carried away talking about my family—the gatherings, Mama's cooking, Myrrl's pranks, and snowy drives to church.

He laughed, which made me feel warm inside.

I told him about dreamy fall afternoons when I'd sit in the hay barn all by myself, spellbound by the patter of rain on the roof while the cattle stirred quietly in the stalls.

Elmer seemed fascinated by everything I talked about every time we were together. Thoughts of him filled my every spare moment.

⌘ ⌘ ⌘

I lingered in the lobby of our downtown hotel in Reading, Pennsylvania. Elmer usually contacted me by Thursday if he was taking me out that weekend, but I hadn't seen him for two days. Was this one of those mysterious weekends when he disappeared? He didn't account for those absences, and I couldn't find the words to ask.

Bitter memories of Harold's disappearances swept over me. I couldn't shake the haunting memory of belonging to someone yet having nothing.

I went back to the room. A quick bath—wouldn't hurt to be ready in case Elmer called.

Sounds of street traffic below floated past the window. A siren cried, then another, converging across the street. My mind refused to think of anything but Elmer.

The door closed behind me and I jumped.

Geneva. She gave me a funny look. "Kind of quiet without Elmer here, isn't it?"

I stood. Talking to her was better than being alone, but how could she see right through me?

"You miss him, don't you?"

"Miss him?"

"Don't give me that. You know what I mean. You're like a lost puppy dog when Elmer's not around, aren't you?"

"I wouldn't say that. I've got lots of things to do."

"Sit down, honey. Let's talk." Geneva motioned toward the armchair. Her eyes slanted up, foxlike, adding an exotic look to her otherwise plain features. "Look, Elmer is a fine man. Everyone respects him. But you don't know much about him, do you?"

I plopped down, my lips in a pucker. "He'll be thirty-eight in January. His folks live in Kansas City or Tulsa, I'm not sure which. He has four brothers and a sister. They all live back that way, in Kansas and Oklahoma. And yes, I think he's a fine man. What more should I know about him?"

"Elmer jokes around a lot, but he doesn't say much about himself." Geneva took a deep breath. "Has he ever mentioned Ada?"

"What are you talking about? Who's Ada?" I felt weak and my head swam.

"I should have kept my mouth shut—"

"No. Tell me. Who's this Ada?" I dug my fingernails into my palm.

Geneva leaped up. "She's some dame he goes to see sometimes. Lives in Colorado. I saw a letter when we were in Wichita last summer. Elmer wasn't there to pick up his mail. Ben waved it at me and said, 'Elmer's flapper.' I debated if I should tell you. You're such a prize I was sure Elmer would forget her."

"I guess Elmer doesn't hold to that same opinion." I scowled but my heart ached. "So—what else did Ben say about him?"

"Not much. I guess Elmer drives out to see this Ada every so often. Once, I heard Ben grumble about his Colorado trips. Said he didn't want Elmer leaving him flat for another job. Elmer's a very impressive man, but I didn't think it was right for him to—"

"Geneva, how could you not tell me about this woman before now? Makes me look like a fool." Nausea threatened. "I don't expect anything from Elmer. He's got other women chasing him. Reba's always flouncing around him, like some floozy."

"I wouldn't worry about Reba, if I were you."

"I don't worry about anybody, Geneva. And I don't want to talk about ... about Elmer anymore!" My voice climbed in pitch and I struggled for control. I could shut off my affections anytime I wanted, couldn't I? I waved Geneva away and stumbled downstairs and outside.

The cloudless day chilled me. I should have grabbed a sweater. At least the cold air cleared my head. I shut off all thoughts of that man. The rumble of streetcars and traffic used to excite me, but now I yearned for the peacefulness of western Kansas. How could I have been such a fool? *He doesn't care for me. I'm just another one of his harem.* I was tired of this gypsy-like life, never having anything, never staying anywhere—

The squeal of tires and blast of a truck horn sounded behind me, and the dark machine swept past in a commotion of sound and wind.

I wobbled to the curb and retched. Cold beads of sweat coursed down my forehead. Was I coming down with the flu, or was my emotional state causing this? Either way, I headed back to the hotel.

I felt dry and used up, brittle as a charred wick. No fun being a woman alone, trying to compete in a man's world. For the first time, I wondered how Geneva managed ... If only I had someone to baby me.

Ben kept the crew four more days in Pennsylvania. At least that gave me time to recover before we moved again.

The following Tuesday, I pounced on Geneva the second she walked in the door. "You have time for a talk?"

"Sure, toots, what's on your mind?"

"I've been doing a lot of thinking the last few days." I took a deep breath. "It doesn't make sense for me to stay with the crew."

Geneva dropped onto her bed. "Why?"

"I'm not making a fortune. I can work back home. Frankly, always being on the move is getting me down. Why should I stay here?"

"Don't you want to keep your job? Shouldn't you ...? Well, you and Elmer might ... he likes you. You spend a lot of time together. He's a swell guy."

"He's been seeing that ... Colorado woman while I sit and wait, like I don't count. I need to figure out where I'm going with my life. I'm surely not staying with Deluxe Art Studio." I paced to the window and back. "In fact, why do *you* stay here? This gypsy life—doesn't it bother you? I feel like a … a twig floating along after a heavy rain. No purpose, but drifting along with the flow. I don't want to be like that! Someone who simply drifts along, alone."

"Well, toots, that's a pretty strong judgment. I kind of like the adventure. You shouldn't leave unless you have a plan."

"I don't know what I'm going to do. I wish I could talk with my parents, have them listen to me." I took a deep breath. "When I lived at home and went to that country church, life seemed so simple. I miss Sunday school, the hymns. But here? Nobody except you believes anything. You pray with your rosary beads every night, and you go to church—Mass—every chance you get. But Sundays don't mean anything to the rest. Sundays are for sleeping off Saturday night's party or for travel to someplace down the road."

Geneva stood, her mouth open. "I've never heard you with so much fire."

"My father believes. He believes in God—like God is really real. I don't do that. I want to. Instead, I'm a drifter, never having even a room of my own. Makes it hard to know who you are and where you should be going. I'm just using up space."

"What are you going to say to Elmer?"

My voice dropped to a monotone. "He saw me in the lobby, asked how I was … wants to take me to dinner Friday. I'll talk to him then. Depends on how he responds to what I say—after that I'll decide what to do."

Geneva grasped both my hands and squeezed. "Claire, you don't need me to tell you what to do. You've got it already figured out."

I could almost see the swallows gathering for the night at the home place, twittering in the single-minded knowledge of where they belonged. The week before, Pop had written, reminding me "… we still love you. We always love you. And we are here for you."

Geneva squeezed my hand again. "I hope I haven't said the wrong things. You're really a special gal. You know that, don't you?"

"You are too, Geneva."

⌘ ⌘ ⌘

Friday evening, Elmer took me to a small place tucked in a hickory grove that served home cooking. The maître d' greeted him by name. How many other women had Elmer taken to this restaurant?

We sat near a large window in a secluded corner, and I tried to look upbeat while he talked. "We'll go on to Scranton from here. That's one of the top vaudeville stops in the country. You've been to Scranton, haven't you?"

"Of course, the last time we made this swing through—after Harold left." I waited to see if he'd pursue that subject. He never had before. "I wasn't sure if my folks would let me back in the house when you approved my trip to visit them. They were death on divorce, but I was the only one trying to make that marriage work. Harold stepped out on me." Tears gathered and I fought for self-control.

Elmer raised his eyebrows. "I guess I never knew why he left—why you split."

"Harold was dishonest—pure and simple. Hot checks, 'misappropriation' of other people's money, 'forgetting' to pay his debts. I was a fool to put up with it." I looked out the window.

Snow swirled lazily through the yellow halo under the street lamp. I wanted to tell Elmer everything on my heart. But the moment wouldn't last forever, even though I wished it would. I looked into his eyes and willed him to ask more.

He didn't speak.

"I need to take a break from the travel, Elmer. Christmas is less than three weeks away. I'm twenty-three—it's been two years since I've been home for Christmas. I know that's where I want to be for the holidays, home with my family."

I didn't tell him I wasn't coming back.

Chapter Eight

ELMER

After I dropped Claire at the train station, the rain turned to sleet and the wind sliced into the car. I swerved around a stalled jitney as thoughts of Claire filled my mind. I liked her spunk, even if she had practically pushed me out of the station.

A man stood behind a black coupe stopped on the shoulder. Nobody deserved to be stranded in awful weather.

I pulled over, crammed my hat down around my ears, and turned up my coat collar. As I stepped out, the wind almost ripped the door out of my grip and sleet flew sideways into my face.

The poor devil didn't have a hat, but sported a pair of swanky shoes. He waved toward the front of his car.

The left tire was totally flat.

For crying out loud, are you helpless? Jack it up and put the spare on. "What do you want me to do for you, mister?" I yelled above the howl of the wind.

He stepped beside me, close enough for his voice to carry though he held a coat over his head. "Need a ride downtown. You know where Hotel Brunswick is?"

Brunswick? That's where the Deluxe crew ... That reedy voice—I jerked my head to the side and looked him full in the face.

Harold, Claire's ex.

His eyes met mine and an obscenity erupted from his mouth.

Typical. The man hadn't changed since Ben Dial tied the can to him after his run-in with Spessord and Wiley. I jerked a thumb toward my car. "Get your stuff and get in. I'll take you where you need to go."

Aside from small talk about how cold he was, he remained remarkably quiet as we drove.

I wasn't inclined to volunteer any information either. Why did he just so happen to be in Lancaster at the same time as the Deluxe

crew? Harold was a grifter, to use Claire's term for him. *Claire ...
wonder if he knows I've been spending time with the woman he
discarded for a tramp.*

"Elmer, you still with Deluxe, I reckon?"

I nodded. "Still with Deluxe. What about you? What have you
been up to?"

"Oh, I been lots of places since I parted with the old crew."

Yeah, I'll bet you have.

"Worked awhile with Chambers down in Carolina, but I could see
they had no future." He prattled on about how he'd tried to get them
to do this and try that, but no one would listen to his voice of
experience. "Uh, is Ben Dial traveling with the crew this week?"

"You need something from Ben?" Answer a question with a
question—Ben's training, ironically.

Harold was silent for a minute. "Well, maybe. I'd gotten the, uh,
idea that Ben might be looking for a top salesman."

"Where'd you hear that?" I glanced over.

He worked his jaw. Then, like sour milk slopped into a pig's
trough, his words splattered all directions. "Ferva. She heard—at least
she thought Ben said he'd give anything—pay high dollar—he'd pay,
like, he wants another qualified, you know—highly experienced—
salesman. Not that he'd replace current salesmen, but—hey, I tried six
times to catch him. I been wanting to get back to Deluxe. Good
company. You suppose Spessord still holds a grudge? Ferva said
Deluxe would be in Lancaster. So I came. Here." He looked at me as
if he deserved a medal for driving cross-country on a hunch.

I slowed to let a horse-drawn buggy turn in front of us, then
wheeled into a parking space near the hotel.

Harold's gaze followed the black-clad Amish couple in the buggy
as they passed. "That's taking religion too far. Like Claire—she was
always sticking the Bible in my face, telling me what her dad—"

"That so? I hadn't pegged her for being very religious." I caught
my breath, throat dry. *Have I missed that about Claire?* If Ferva had
told Harold about my relationship with Claire, he could have been
toying with me the whole time.

Harold gave me a strange look as I cut the engine. "Thanks,
Elmer." He grabbed his bag and headed into the hotel.

I stood beside my car for long minutes despite the sleet and wind. Finally I trudged inside. Maybe I wasn't as smart as I thought I was.

CLAIRE

Wheel against joint, like the measured strike of a blacksmith's hammer, each dull click took me farther away from the man I'd chosen to leave. From the charming, attentive man I thought I loved. When Elmer had driven me to the station the previous evening, I'd deflected his questions regarding my return to the crew and boarded the train almost feeling jaunty. Now, the memory of his voice caressed my emotions like a velvet glove.

My breath caught in little choking sobs, and the woman beside me turned to stare. I found a hanky and dropped my head until the locomotive whistle signaled a crossing east of Dodge City. I stood and pulled my valise and sack of Christmas gifts down from the overhead bin.

Stockyard pens and an auction barn swept past like a military encampment, followed by bleak houses and scattered false-front businesses. The station platform reached out to the oncoming train and flagged it to a stop beside a dozen people huddled outside the entry.

I scanned for Pop's face.

The chill wind snaked through the train car as the doors opened.

There he was, hand held aloft.

I flung the blue scarf around my neck before I stepped onto the platform.

Meticulous and energetic, Pop loaded my bags into the Studebaker, impressive for a man of sixty-seven. He waved me in and then seated himself. He grasped my hand and held it against his cheek. "I'm glad my small-town girl has finally come home from the big city."

"I'm glad to be home too, Pop."

On Front Street, he spoke again. "Your mother missed you. Sometimes she forgets you're gone and calls out your name when she's working in the kitchen."

"She does?" I smiled. "She was so disappointed in me last time I came home. I wasn't sure if I should look for a rooming house elsewhere—maybe Bazine or Dighton."

"Claire, don't talk that way. Yes, Mama was let down, but not by you. She was disappointed by the way things turned out. After your visit, she and I had a long talk. She wants the best for you."

I stared at him. "Did she say that?"

"Didn't need to. You're our daughter, our people. We won't abandon you. I was kicked out of my mother's house when I was fifteen because old Ruff said there was no room for me. But we'll always have a place for you."

"Pop, you may feel that way, but I want to make sure Mama … agrees."

"I understand. Given time, you'll see that your mother feels the same. So let's have no more talk about our daughter living among strangers when she has family."

I squeezed his arm. "Pop, that means so much to me. But even though I'm your youngest—I'm also grown-up."

He seemed to consider this. In a voice so soft I had to lean over to hear above the noise of the car, he said, "You don't want me to call you 'babe'?"

"It's not about what you call me. It's how the family treats me. I'm a woman, not a child." I patted his leg. "Call me whichever—babe, Claire. But I want people to realize I'm not a giddy young girl to be looked after. Pop, if you only want me under your roof only to keep an eye on me, I won't have it. I'll live by myself."

"You'll be free to make your own decisions."

"Mama thinks my divorce is more than a mistake. She's always condemned failed marriages. But if she understood Harold's dishonest nature, how he thought only of himself … she surely wouldn't expect me to live with a man I can't trust."

"You did what you had to do, babe. It was right to leave him."

"That long talk you had with Mama. Did she change her mind?"

"Your mother has … opinions." Pop worked his jaw.

"I doubt she'll want to paper over this." I cleared my throat. "Pop, I haven't been in church for, uh, for a while. My friend, Geneva, suggested I talk about the divorce with my pastor. She had her first marriage annulled."

"Catholic, is she? Talking with Pastor Lewis would be good. He'll be coming over to see me this Saturday. Wants me to go with him to visit a new family." Pop's blue eyes bore into mine. "Or you could see him at church if you come with us to Sunday services."

"I'd—yes, I'd like that. But I probably won't go to Sunday school. No need to get the third degree from Matilda." The woman was a Nosy Nellie to the extreme.

"Matilda will be there. Loud as ever. Getting a bit forgetful, but if she recognizes you, the whole church would listen in while she 'makes over you,' as she calls it."

"Also, I need to get three more Christmas presents. Plus, I might go see Helen Schweitzer this weekend."

"You don't have to get presents for me or your mother. Having you home is enough." He stared straight ahead.

I took a deep breath. "Just before I left Deluxe, the lawyer called to say the divorce is final. I had him mail a copy of the decree to your address. Harold can't do anything to me now, can he?" I searched his profile. "I mean, he won't come to our house sometime, will he? I want to move on with my life and be done with that cad."

"Harold's gutless. He won't come around because he'll never get another nickel out of me." He pointed out the window. "See that wheat? Mine's even better. Good enough for me to pasture it a few weeks. Won't hurt the crop, and I'll save on feed. Gar sniffed at the idea, but they're my cows, not his."

⌘ ⌘ ⌘

Pastor Lewis pushed his Bible under my nose. "No getting around it. You look at Malachi—see here."

I followed his ridged fingernails as they traced the lines of text.

"And he—that's God—God hates 'the putting away.' Some people might not see it but that's what it means. God hates divorce. You've done a hateful thing in the eyes of God."

This was the Lord's word for me? "It wasn't my fault! I couldn't put up with—"

"*He* defiled the marriage, Hiram." Pop's voice came like the growl of a mastiff. "Claire wouldn't have left that marriage if Harold hadn't broken the marriage vows. He was seen with a streetwalker. What was she supposed to do?"

"Oh, Sam. Nothing is ever as clear as we'd like for it to be, is it?" The reverend flipped toward the back of his Bible. "The Apostle Paul says she's to remain unmarried if she divorces."

A cloud of despair descended on the kitchen table, strangling me. *Never to have children?* I vaguely heard Pop asking about exceptions, betrayal, infidelity ...

Pastor Lewis grunted and glanced at me. "Yes. There is an exception. I'll study it more." His huge paw reached across the table and brushed my hand. "I'll get back to you and your folks. Sounds like you were the victim in this case. Though that's ignoring the fact that you may have been a bit hasty in marrying this man, little lady." He stood and pushed his chair back.

Mama, who'd said nothing the entire time, avoided my eyes as she got up and escorted the reverend to the door.

⌘ ⌘ ⌘

The distance between Ness City and the East Coast was measured in days, but soon mail from Elmer began to arrive. I stared at the letter in my hands, similar in sentiment to the one I'd received the day before—and to those which would surely follow.

> *It's impossible to tell you how disappointed I was when I realized something had delayed you. Please tell me you'll be back. You don't know how much I miss you.*
>
> *The New Year's banquet is set for Columbus. I'm wiring money for you to come back. No point in my going if you're not with me.*

I shook my head. How annoying. I didn't care what he said. He'd had his chances. Now he expected me to chase after him. *Well, he's got another think coming.* I sent a telegram with a message not to expect me.

Elmer responded with a succession of telegrams—all with the same offer of getting me to the banquet.

I ignored every one. I'd already made up my mind to forget that man from Deluxe, even if he didn't get the hint. I received a special delivery letter five days later. I stared at handwriting I knew as well

63

as my own.

So this was what it was like to feel like a princess—and the prince had written a personal letter, delivered by a king's messenger right to my door.

Other letters soon followed, and the contents were tender, even devoted, compared with anything I'd ever gotten before. Anticipation replaced doubt. I began to let myself believe what he'd written. As far as I knew, he'd never lied to me. But he had disappointed me. He'd let me think I was very important to him—while still seeing that Ada woman. Not exactly lying, but not being forthright either. Why should I have expected this charming man to commit himself to me?

Finally I located my pink rose stationery. I would write back, telling him it was nice to hear from him. That I appreciated him as a friend.

But that was a lie. Stars flashed across my vision when I thought of Elmer. I knew men well enough to know that no man who cared about a woman wanted to be called "a friend."

Elmer had given me his photo, taken at a resort in New Hampshire. I found the Whitman's chocolate box where I'd put it. I'd intended to throw it away, but now I held it before me and examined the handsome face. I caressed the flat image and leaned it against the dresser mirror.

It took all afternoon but I composed a carefully worded message. Before sealing it, I dabbed a touch of his favorite perfume on each page.

So began a thrilling little game, but one I could quit anytime.

⌘ ⌘ ⌘

Right after Christmas, Ed Jackson asked me if I'd set up a beauty shop in the back of his drug store. The business took off almost immediately. The society ladies in Ness City talked up my facials, but they were most intrigued because I'd been back east. I spiced accounts of my travels with references to famous people I'd seen, and they ate it up.

Myrrl and Grace invited me out to the farm one mid-week evening for supper. Russell, Grace's brother, just "happened" to stop by. Right away I knew it was a setup, but he was charming, had a keen sense of humor, and hung on my every word.

The next day, I told Mama about the evening with Myrrl and Grace. "I've been working such long hours at the shop, I almost forgot my own family. I met lots of interesting people on the crew, but there's nobody like my brother."

She chuckled. "Who could forget how he used to hide under the table and grab my leg? That boy almost gave me a heart attack."

"Or when he'd tie your apron strings to a kitchen chair. Mama, you were in another world, singing away to yourself. Then you'd whirl around to grab something off the stove—dragging that chair right with you!"

The telephone interrupted our laugh. "That's probably Helen. She promised she'd call this afternoon." I lifted the handset to my ear. "Hello, this is Claire."

A man's voice, but whose?

A smattering of words penetrated my confusion.

"Russell ... happened to be in town ... walk in the park."

My breath caught.

"Hello? Hello, are you there, Claire?"

"Yes, I'm here." I looked out the front room window, where the elms bent before the wind and ragged clouds scudded across a leaden sky. "A walk in the park? It's starting to snow!"

"Let it snow. I've got a coat. I'll bring an extra if you don't have one." He laughed.

I laughed with him. "All right, if you're game, I am too. But I'll bring my own coat." I rang off. *What would my pastor think of this?* No matter. He'd never gotten back to me anyway.

Mama called, "Who was that?"

"Russell. Grace's brother." I stood stock-still, trying to understand how I had just committed myself to a mid-day walk in a high wind with a man I scarcely knew.

"Didn't you say he stopped by Myrrl's last night?" Mama ceased kneading and dusted her hands. She leaned forward, hands resting on the bread board.

"Yes. He's, uh, quite the conversationalist. What do you know about him, Mama?"

She went into the pantry and returned shortly. "His first marriage only lasted a year. By then, his wife had a baby—"

"He was married before?" I vaguely remembered the Johnson girl and now felt flustered about going out with Russell, even if he was my brother's brother-in-law.

"You knew that, Claire. Myrrl told us when the wife left him. Went back to Sterling—"

The sound of a vehicle in the driveway ended the discussion. "He's here already? He just called, and I haven't even combed my hair!" I flew upstairs to my bedroom.

"Let him in!" Mama hollered. "He'll catch his death of cold, standing in that wind!"

Better head off Mama's interrogation. I quickly retrieved my long woolen coat and a brush to swipe at my hair. Struggling into the bulky garment, I flew through the parlor and almost knocked a lamp over.

Mama stood next to the door. "Here's your scarf, you silly girl."

A succession of knocks rattled the adjoining window.

"Coming!" I snatched the blue-green scarf from Mama's outstretched hand. Catching my breath, I composed myself before I turned the doorknob.

The storm did bring snow, which jabbed our faces and coated the streets and paths with sparkling slate as we walked. I had to hang on to Russell's arm to keep from falling, but he didn't seem to mind. Neither did I. We finally sought refuge inside the drug store for hot cocoa before heading back to our house.

Over the next month, I spent many weekend evenings with Russell. He planned excursions and adventures strictly for me, a practice I found mostly delightful but sometimes presumptuous. I also went out with Milt Shaw or Harry Minor whenever either was able to catch me free.

However, Elmer's letters still came with dependable regularity.

⌘ ⌘ ⌘

The March wind abated for the first time in three weeks. Pop went out to work in his garden.

I prepared a pot of hot tea, collected two cups, placed it all on Mama's wicker tray, and went outside. I waited while he finished planting his early peas.

"If it weren't for that chill breeze, I'd be too warm for tea," he said as he pulled his wooden chair out to face the afternoon sun. "Sit." He motioned me to a straw bale. "Your work and social life have kept you so busy, we don't talk much anymore."

"I thought the same thing, Pop. In the same house but we hardly see each other." I poured tea and framed my question. "You think jobs will be hard to find for a while?"

He squinted. "You looking for work someplace else?"

I shifted my position on the bale and shaded my eyes against the sun. "No. It's Russell. He hasn't had steady work in seven months. Doc Hinkle hires him occasionally. Then he takes me to the ten-cent matinees. Not something to build anything on."

Pop stopped his cup halfway to his mouth. "He asked you to marry him?"

"No, but I think he wants to." I peered at him over the edge of my cup. "I'm determined not to get myself into another hand-to-mouth existence like I had with Harold."

"You better make that clear with the man." He wiped his mouth. "Looks like my girl is highly popular—all that mail and the young men calling. You can afford to be particular."

I smiled. "Tell me again what happened between you and Mama. How you knew ..."

His eyebrows went up.

I quickly added, "That's one of my favorite stories, and you tell me something new each time."

He took out his red bandanna and wiped the sweat from his forehead. "It's one of my favorite stories too. Your mother could've had her choice of several young men."

"So, how did she know that you were right for each other?"

"Well, a few months after I homesteaded on the place, I heard about this neighbor, Stedke, with a flock of beautiful daughters. Five of them! They lived a ways over the hill behind my farm. Later, I saw them at community gatherings at Rosedale School. Several of us young bucks stood outside the first time old man Stedke drove up with those lovely girls in their buggy. Us boys got quiet as midnight. Everyone pretended there was nothing out of ordinary—but as soon as they went inside, we stampeded for the door."

I giggled. "I wish I could've seen it. But you saw Mama—she was there too?"

"I saw her. I saw *all* of them! I'd never seen that many lovely girls in one group. We boys nearly knocked one another down 'casually' getting in that schoolhouse door." Pop chortled.

"But you didn't talk to her that first night?"

"There were too many others crowded around. I watched old Stedke. He didn't cotton to all the commotion, so I stood back. I didn't say a thing, but I caught her eye. She smiled, and I almost melted into my shoes. Lydia gave me the once over. But Lilly was the one I wanted."

"Did you pursue her right away?"

"Well, this was on a Saturday, and I was bound and determined to see Lilly before someone else horned in. So, on Sunday afternoon, I accidentally on purpose ran out of sugar and went over the hill to borrow some."

"To the Stedke's. And the girls were there."

"They were all there. It was a bit awkward, as Lydia had set her cap for me, and she waltzed over and grabbed my arm. Then I thought to tell her I wanted to borrow some sugar. While she went after the sugar, I mustered up the courage to speak to Lilly. I must have stood there a minute or two, looking at her like a wall-eyed calf."

"And then she knew you liked her?"

"It was written all over my face." He laughed again.

⌘ ⌘ ⌘

The August afternoon settled quietly over western Kansas. In all my twenty-three years, I hadn't yet tired of it. I straightened up my beauty shop—scissors, combs, lotions, and paraphernalia in their places—then turned the skeleton key and latched the side door. I rounded the corner for the short walk home and nearly fainted.

A black sedan sat in the driveway.

I'd ridden in that black sedan many times. The last time had been the previous December when Elmer had taken me to the train station.

A host of memories descended, like little stars falling from the sky. For a moment, I savored them, not moving. Finally I stepped forward, heart pounding, and wended past the polished automobile.

The ten steps up to the porch seemed tilted and steep.

Maybe I should run away. No. I smoothed my hair. My lips seemed stuck together. How would I speak? With a deep breath, I opened the door to Pop and Mama's house.

Elmer sat opposite the entry. The evening sun blazed over my shoulders, spreading amber light on the throw rug at his feet.

My eyes took a few seconds to adjust to the cool contrast of the dark area outside the splash of sunlight. Surely the handsome man with the penetrating hazel eyes could hear the thunder beating inside my chest.

Chapter Nine

Mere feet separated me and the man from my recent past. The clink of crockery located Mama, busy in the kitchen. Pop sat on Elmer's right in dignified silence, waiting for me to explain this unexpected visit.

Then my parents faded from consciousness, and it was just me and Elmer. The slight crease at the corners of his eyes, a faint smile— almost a smirk, the glimmer of knowing me like waves of summer heat. I wanted to touch Elmer's curly, black hair, slide my fingers down the side of his face and touch his mouth. This handsome man had traveled hundreds of miles to see me. The thought made my head swim.

"Hello, Claire." That voice, resonant, almost silky. He rose, hat casual in his hand. "I just arrived. Was telling your dad that the crew was in Kansas City for two weeks and I thought, why not come and see you? Figured I'd surprise you."

Moisture fogged my vision. I blinked to focus.

He reached out and grasped my elbow.

The scent of his shaving soap, the warmth of his masculinity, swam around me. A quick glance toward Pop, and I pushed away.

Elmer guided me to the nearest chair.

I sat, back stiff, as he returned to the couch. *Oh, my. What does Pop think of this?* I sought his face.

Pop stared back in apparent wonderment, eyes warm and sad. That look, proclaiming the depth of his love for me.

I arose to get the ever-present pitcher of iced tea from the kitchen and nearly bowled Mama over. After an exchange of apologies between us and a "Hello, Mama," from me, I swept the pitcher from the icebox and re-filled Elmer's and Pop's glasses. In the next few minutes I offered Elmer a refill on his iced tea not twice but three times.

Mama made a brief appearance, which only heightened the tension until she returned to the kitchen. During that interlude, I grasped two truths: Mama knew why this traveling salesman had come to see her daughter, and she had no intention of allowing him to stay overnight in her house.

What to do? I stuttered, "Oh. Yes. You'll need a place to stay. Let me call Myrrl and Grace. They'll be glad to have you with them tonight, Elmer." Without waiting for an answer, I tripped into Pop's office and cranked the wall phone. After the operator put the call through, I was struck by my stupidity—*Grace is Russell's sister!*—and started to hang up.

Myrrl answered.

I whispered the situation.

"Sure, he can stay with us. Why don't you two come out for supper?" His voice moved away from the receiver. "Grace, Elmer's staying the night. Claire's Elmer, the fellow from the picture company. The one she said she was never going to see again ... Yes, I told them to come out ... The old rooster? Yeah!" Without lowering volume, Myrrl's voice was back at the phone. "Claire, we—"

I jumped, ears ringing. "Myrrl, you nearly broke my eardrum! I'm right here."

"Oh, sorry, sis. We'd like to have the two of you out for supper— fresh corn on the cob, homemade bread, Grace's rhubarb pie, chicken and noodles. And I've needed an excuse to send that old rooster to glory. He's a flogger. It'll be fun to have you out. Wanted to meet that Elmer guy, anyhow."

"Oh, thank you."

"Shall I invite Russell over too?" He chuckled.

"Myrrl. Stop that." I covered the mouthpiece. Had Elmer heard? No, he and Pop were talking wheat prices.

"Myrrl, behave, you hear. Wait a minute, let me talk to Grace."

"Now?"

"Yes, *now*, if you please."

Her cheery voice came on the telephone, "Claire, I understand you have a visitor."

"Yes." I sighed loudly. "Grace, I need your help."

"Of course, Claire. What is it?"

I swung around again to check on Elmer before returning to the phone. "You know I've been seeing your ... seeing Russell. But Elmer's here for a day. A couple days, maybe, and I want to spend time with him. What I'm asking is—can you make that wonderful brother of mine behave when we're out at your place tonight? Not a word about Russell?"

"Don't give it a thought. In fact, I'll tweak his beak if he so much as opens his yap about—about anything. Myrrl kids around, but he knows he'll be in hot water with me if he doesn't act the gentleman. Never mind about Russell. I already told him he's on his own as far as you're concerned. We'll just have a good time."

⌘ ⌘ ⌘

A breeze wafted through the screen door, carrying a mockingbird's medley into the great room of the old house. Evening light cast animated shadows of Grace on the far wall as she bustled between the stove and the table.

Every time I looked up, it seemed Elmer was looking at me. Surely Myrrl and Grace saw it too.

Elmer was always a good conversationalist and seemed especially clever that evening. After dessert, he turned to me casual-like and said, "It's a nice evening. Why don't you show me around the farm?"

We went outside, my heart pounding. The descending sun shot gems of light through the elms I'd played among as a child, and I felt reckless and dreamy. I let my shoulder converge along his arm as we walked through the pasture toward the pond. The path muddied as we reached the cattails at the edge.

Elmer stopped and pulled me to him, voice soft. "Claire, I forgot Kansas was so far away. Evenings after work, I'd look to the west. I thought of you someplace under that setting sun and it about broke me to pieces. I could hardly stand it." His hand touched my face, left traces of warm emotion and tenderness. In a whisper, he said, "I'd imagine what you might be doing that instant and wish I were with you."

The firmness of his chest and his muscled arms made me feel secure. There seemed a consent between us, as if the glimmering reflection from the pond blended with the distant call of the mourning dove, serene and insistent.

Elmer whispered again, "I want you to be my sweetheart. More than anything."

No one had ever called me that before. "Sweethearts can only be that if there's no one else."

"There's no one else. Hasn't been, not since you left. Won't be anyone else ever again."

I searched his eyes. Not a blink. He was as earnest as a child.

"You've been out of my sight, but I've thought of you—every day. There wasn't a morning I didn't come downstairs to the hotel coffee shop, no matter what city we were in, and right away look for you. Expect to see you. I'd listen for your voice, mistake someone else's laughter for yours. I could see your dark eyes shining and think that smile was only for me. Claire, I love you." He lifted my chin with his left hand. His voice dropped lower, grew more intense. "Say you'll marry me."

There were so many reasons to say no. That Ada woman, my pastor's strong condemnation of remarriage, Mama ... I touched his lips with my index finger and looked into his eyes. "Yes, Elmer. I've never forgotten you. You should know that, simply by looking at me. Yes, I'll marry you."

We kissed, how many times, I couldn't remember. When he stopped, I was breathless. He lifted me by the waist, took a step, then he glanced down and dropped his arms, a look of disgust on his face.

I stumbled back and followed his gaze.

His black dress oxford had left a neat imprint in a fresh cow pie. He scuffed his shoe against a clump of buffalo grass and gave me a silly grin.

I stepped forward, wove my arms under his vest, and buried my head against his chest.

Barn swallows flitted toward the farm buildings, as if drawing the curtain of night over the prairie. We walked across the meadow to get in his car and drove away with a wave to Myrrl, seated on the front step.

We roamed the back roads between Myrrl's farm and Ness through the night, stopping here or there to enjoy the solitude and quiet when the world belonged to us and no other. The expectant hush that divides the darkness from yellow-robed dawn had almost dissolved by the time Elmer headed for my home. I wanted the moment to go on forever. With the awakening of the community would come the call of work and necessity. Elmer would be gone.

Halfway into town, he pulled the car off the road. He opened his door, slid out, and pulled me after him. We stood there and watched the glory of first light. The morning chill finally drove us back to the car.

"Can you stay another day?"

"Sweetheart, I don't want to leave, but I have to be back and ready for work tomorrow morning. I have to keep this job so I've got something to take you back to. I'll be back before you—"

"When? When will you come back, Elmer?"

"After the next eastern swing. When I get within a day's drive. I'll call you as soon as I know I can break free. I'll even let your daddy's preacher do the honors—"

"If he'll do it. I am divorced, you know. But anyway, we'll get married here, in Ness?"

"Wherever you want it to be." He kissed me again. "Better get you home, before I fall over. I need to catch three or four hours of sleep at Myrrl's before I hit the road for Kansas City."

"So this is good-bye."

He shook his head. "Not good-bye. Just so long … for a while. I'll be back before you know it." He started the engine and took me home.

The front door sighed as I pushed it open. My eyes probed the interior gloom.

Sure enough, Mama sat, facing me, in the upholstered chair—thankfully, asleep.

I tiptoed upstairs.

A meadowlark trilled from a fence post on the far side of Pop's garden. In the brightening sky, the crescent moon rested on a locust branch like a basin of promise.

The rest of my life would be with that man. Handsome as Douglas Fairbanks—and I was the one he wanted. I couldn't have wrought this on my own if I'd tried. I wished his eastern tour had already started. The sooner it was done, the sooner he'd return.

⌘ ⌘ ⌘

I awoke with a start at ten o'clock that morning. Russell! Russell had said he'd pick me up that very evening. My heart pounded as I tried to gather my thoughts. Should I call him to say I was engaged? I stood before the mirror, fluffing my hair.

Russell—such a tenderhearted man. It didn't seem right to blurt out bad news over the phone. I'd tell him the right way, in person.

Mama met me as I came downstairs. "Claire, we didn't get much chance to talk to your visitor." Her eyebrows arched with expectancy.

My words burbled like a spring freshet. "Mama, we're getting married. Elmer asked me—last night. I knew, as soon as I saw him sitting in that chair, I knew why he came. And I knew I still loved him. I haven't told you much about Elmer, but he's very special to me."

"Getting married? You've been seeing Russell. For months. Doesn't seem like Elmer or Russell's very special to you with all the other fellows you're running round with."

"Mama! I wasn't committed to Elmer. Not until he asked me to marry him."

"He asked you and, just like that, you said yes?" She stared at me, as if I'd sprouted wings. "Are you sure you know your feelings? After all, he's a *salesman*."

"Mama, I'm a saleswoman. I know what he does." I wanted to shout at her.

"But he's not a man of God, my daughter. He smokes—a pipe. I saw him."

So, he's too worldly for your divorced daughter? "He's a good man, Mama, and he cares for me. Not only that, he'll provide for me. He's highly respected in the company."

"How's our girl this morning?" Pop ambled out of his study. "Good to meet Elmer yesterday. He seems keen on you, babe. Quite a surprise, having him arrive out of the blue."

"Yes, Pop. I'm glad you got to meet him. As I told Mama, we're promised."

Pop's expression clouded over, his blue eyes uncomprehending. He finally spoke. "He did seem ... bent on a purpose. That's why he came?"

Mama snapped a dishtowel over her shoulder. "He's older—considerably."

"Yes, he is older, but he treats me as an equal, if that's your concern." *Should have known it might come to this.*

Mama had that bright look in her eyes.

"If we can talk about this later, I have an appointment at eleven." I gathered my things and hurried to the door.

Mama would keel over when Russell showed up.

All day, I fretted about what Mama's reaction would be when Russell came by. I didn't know how *I'd* react, for that matter. Perhaps I should have had Russell meet me at the shop, or simply told him not to come at all.

No. I'd see him, explain, and everything would work out.

After work, I told Mama I wasn't hungry and for them to have supper without me. I hurried upstairs before she could respond. My bedroom, which had always seemed like a refuge, now felt like a prison. Almost panting, I tried to focus my thoughts. For long moments, I sat on the bed, clenching my hands. I suddenly stood up and went downstairs.

This won't be easy. I entered the dining room, words already forming. "I wanted you to know that Russell will be … is coming over to see me. I need to talk with him."

Pop looked gray, like he was about to throw up. Mama just chewed her lower lip.

Before either spoke, a car pulled up outside. Russell!

I hurried to the door before he could knock and threw a good-bye over my shoulder. "Mama, Pop. Have a good evening."

Russell jumped when I burst outside. "Claire! What's—" He recovered and greeted me with a smile. "Boy, I'm glad to see you. You look stunning. Come on, let's go for a walk."

Anything—just so I can get out of here. "Why, yes, that would be nice."

"That's swell. I knew you'd like that. Afterward, we'll get a chocolate at the drug store."

The heat of the evening had drawn people outside to their porches, to fan themselves, gossip, and watch children play stickball in the streets.

Russell seemed to watch me closely, as if he expected some declaration.

Had Grace or Myrrl told him about Elmer? I stopped and faced him. "Why do you keep looking at me that way?"

"I'm merely admiring my companion." He smiled and pointed toward an unoccupied bench in front of the courthouse. "Why don't we sit?"

This was it. My stomach churning, I halfheartedly listened as Russell described a job opening at Dighton, thirty miles west.

Finally his voice ran down.

The shouts of children cut through the dusk.

He pursed his lips. "I heard you had a visitor. I gather he didn't stay long. Did your mama run him off?"

"No, he had to get back to the crew in Kansas City. So he's gone."

"That's nice—for now." Russell stared into the distance. "Is there more I need to know?"

"I suppose there is." I had to be truthful, not only for him, but for myself. I gave a sad little smile, my voice barely a squeak. "He asked me ... he asked me to marry him."

Russell's smile disappeared and he swallowed hard. "And what did you tell him?"

A dog set up a racket.

I waited for quiet. "I told him yes."

For moments neither of us spoke.

Another dog answered the first.

Then all was silent.

Russell took my hand. "I don't see an engagement ring on your finger. Claire, you know you mean the world to me. Unless you tell me you don't want to see me again, I want to keep calling on you."

My mouth seemed filled with paste. Sitting there with Russell—a man not my fiancé—I couldn't understand my emotions. As crazy as it was, I was still fond of him. Finally words came. "If you'd like ..."

"Yes, I'd like—so much." Russell leaned toward me but quickly stood and pulled me to my feet. "I'm not giving up that easily. Not when it comes to you."

⌘ ⌘ ⌘

I'd finished getting dressed for the day when a soft knock fell on the bedroom door.

"Babe, could you check in with us before you leave for work?

Your mother and I would like to talk."

My left hand flew to my neck. "Sure, if it won't take long. I have a facial appointment in forty minutes." I straightened Elmer's picture, which was propped against the dresser mirror, then hurried down to the dining room, my heart pounding with every step.

Pop motioned to a chair. "Claire, we're … confused about what you're doing."

"Yes. What I'm doing." I dropped my gaze as Mama emerged from the kitchen, then forced myself to lift my head.

Her mouth held in a thin line, and her eyes flashed. "How can you say you're promised to marry this … Elmer, while you've pranced around town every weekend with another man or two?"

"I don't suppose you understand how hard this is. I'm trying not to cause greater hurt. This is something I have to work out, and I hope you'll let me handle it."

Mama moved beside Pop. She placed both hands on the table and leaned forward. "But you're *not* handling this. You're merely giving the whole town gossip material."

"Lilly, please!" Pop spoke very sharply to her. "Other people can gossip all they want. Claire, what we want to know is, what are your plans? You seem to have forgotten this man Elmer already. What about him?"

I swallowed. "My plans are to marry Elmer. But I can't dump Russell as if he has no feelings. Elmer's coming back when he can, and we'll be married. I told Russell all this."

My mother pressed her nubbed fists into her blue, floral dress. "If you keep up this willful hypocrisy, don't expect me to stand with you."

Her disappointment, her anger, broke the skin of calm that overlay my pain. "Mama!" I kicked a straight back chair against the wall.

It cracked and a splintered leg skidded across the floor.

"You're awful! You and your … your self-righteous attitude! How about a word of love? You don't know what I've been through. Never asked. You only want to blame." Face burning, I grabbed my scarf and sack lunch and fled out the front door. For lonely moments, I leaned against the stuccoed wall of the porch and wept.

Pop's baritone rumbled inside. "You satisfied with what you got?"

Over the next two weeks, I proved Mama correct. Engaged to Elmer, I still took weekend walks with Russell. It was deceit if not disloyalty. Beset by guilt, I avoided conversations that might get Mama going on a new line of questions. Every night, I asked God for insight, for answers, but expected—and got—nothing in return for the mumbled prayers I cast to heaven.

A dozen roses arrived from Elmer the following week. They were the deepest red I'd ever seen. But then, I'd never gotten roses before. I put them in Mama's ceramic swan vase and then placed the arrangement on the dining room table. I pirouetted away from the table, then caught myself against the living room archway and looked back over my shoulder at the bouquet. Slowly, I advanced toward the table, mimicking the elegant promenade of Delores del Rio in *The Red Dance,* which Elmer had taken me to see in Cincinnati. I swept over to the pressed back chair, swung it around, and posed, resting my chin on the back and gazing at the glimmering roses. Their fragrance anointed the room, and I sat entranced, remembering that night.

Mama's footsteps on the walk interrupted my reverie.

I rushed to the front door and opened it. "Mama, look."

She stared past me, working her jaw as if fighting off a frown. "Yes, they're nice. I wonder how much they cost." She dropped her shawl on the end table. "Can you help me with supper?"

"No, I can't. I've got plans." *Why play games?* I faced her. "Russell is coming. We're going to have a picnic out at the farm this evening."

She stood with hands on her hips for half a minute and then turned toward the kitchen.

Russell arrived ten minutes early, and Mama called up to my bedroom. "Clair-ee! You've got a guest at the door, and I'm up to my elbows in dough!"

I dashed downstairs, patting my hair into place. I ushered him in with a smile and a wave at the picnic basket.

He grinned. Then his eyes widened as his gaze swept past me.

I gasped. I'd forgotten to relocate my precious roses. Unable to bridge the silence, I waited for him to speak.

He took the basket in one hand and my arm in the other, as if he hadn't seen a thing, and strode to his dad's Packard.

After the picnic, we watched a covey of quail that chirped out from a fencerow. We'd never had trouble communicating before, but now talk came brittle and stiff.

Twice, Russell started to speak and then stopped.

I waited, knowing he could never talk about *us* until he had settled the issue of *him*. A man had to have a job if he planned to support a wife.

⌘ ⌘ ⌘

In September, Russell left for Kansas City—a long day's drive from Ness City. He vowed to come back for me when he had the right job.

I said I'd miss him. The next day, I helped clean Mama's house, and then went to my room, solitude a surprising relief.

Helen Schweitzer invited me over for Sunday dinner. Afterward, we had tea on her back porch. I remarked that sending romantic letters to two men at the same time reminded me of a Hindu firewalker I saw in a Chicago park.

Helen frowned. "If you're not careful, somebody is going to get burned."

I swallowed. "Helen, I can't bear to hurt either one. I'd stop it if I only knew how."

"You mean, you'd stop if you wanted to. I don't know how you kept up this charade as long as you have. Are you serious about your engagement?"

I blinked. Was she against me too? "Well, yes, I am. But Elmer left me sitting out here on the prairie until it suits his fancy to come back. Don't you think that's a little presumptuous?"

"Or trusting. A promise is a promise. Does he know you've been seeing Russell?"

I choked but managed to speak. "Oh, how could he?"

"You tell me, Claire. Seems like you're being a bit presumptuous yourself."

"Helen! I don't have a ring. And I'm supposed to wait until he decides to show up—"

"You agreed to that. To love and be loved in return requires trust, not evasions or fear."

The words stung. I bit my lip so hard I tasted blood. "But I'm afraid, Helen. Afraid I'll be hurt again. I don't want to be hurt again."

Helen gazed over the edge of her teacup. "Life doesn't give you that kind of guarantee."

⌘ ⌘ ⌘

A letter from Elmer in early November hit even harder, like a mallet at a strongman's test. Covered in unusual scratch-outs and re-writes, it said:

> *Should've told you a long time ago, but I've been married before too. We've been separated—haven't seen her in nine years. The divorce will be final in two weeks. It's your privilege to change your mind. I sincerely hope you don't. I don't know what I'd do if you called it off ...*

In a reply that I delayed three days, I hinted about another man, but I appreciated his honesty and wasn't calling anything off. How could I say anything else? I surely hadn't been straightforward with him.

An envelope with Elmer's bold cursive lay propped on the buffet when I came home from work a week later. I snatched it and swept to my room.

> *Yes, I've known about this other guy. I wondered if you'd let me know. You mind telling me what you're going to do about it?*

I gasped and a chill flashed up my back. So he knew about Russell. How? And what else did he know? I slumped into a chair, my mind a whirl of imaginings.

Helen. Helen would know what to do.

The clock downstairs bonged the half hour.

I practically ran down the stairs to the phone. *Please, please be home.* I rang her and waited until she picked up. "Oh, Helen, it's me. Do you ... Could we talk—right away? Can you come over?"

A few minutes later, I paced between the door and window of my bedroom, watching for her familiar Ford to appear out of the dusk. I thought of Russell's last words—that I meant the world to him. With his employment status and the wife and child that he'd never mentioned, I wondered what else I didn't know. Or even if what he said was true.

Yesterday, I had two suitors.

Today, it appeared I might have none.

Shame at my pathetic lack of character made me want to run screaming into the night.

Chapter Ten

"Two men and one decision." Helen sighed as if shocked at the trouble I'd gotten myself into.

A tiny spider swung on an invisible thread from the ceiling above her head. It moved constantly, all purpose and direction. It knew what to do.

Unlike me.

I *knew* what I was doing. Or rather, what I was *not* doing. Because *to do* would be to tell one of two men I preferred the other. That seemed impossible. I closed my eyes and tried to envision spending the rest of my life with one of them, going where he went, sleeping where he slept, bearing his children, sustaining us both under his weaknesses and his will …

"Claire? Claire, I don't think you heard anything I said. Where is your head?"

I dropped my gaze to Helen. Then back to the corner.

The spider had disappeared.

I shuddered. "He's gone."

"Russell? Yes, I know. He's still in Kansas City. Has he written you?"

I gestured toward the corner, my hand a rag at the end of my arm.

"Claire, you're not making sense. I'm going home. We're both tired. You'll do better after you get some rest."

"No, wait, Helen. Thank you for putting up with me, for being here. But don't go."

"Do you even want me here? I'm sure it's confusing, having two men fighting over you, but since I don't know anything about that …"

I gave a wan smile to this dependable friend. Helen hadn't blamed me, hadn't whipped me with I-told-you-so's.

She looked at me straight-on. "You can't do nothing. You need to make a decision. You know the right thing to do. Do it!"

"The right thing." Impossible. I could think only of my mistakes.

All made while trying to make everyone else happy. But if I didn't make my own decisions, who would? Maybe the best decision was no decision.

Pop would say, "Follow the Book. If you don't know what to do, see what God's Word says. Look—right here." And he'd flip to a passage I'd heard dozens of times but could never find for myself. "Here it is in Proverbs—'Trust in the Lord ... he shall direct thy paths.'" A slide of his thumb across his tongue and he'd flip the pages again. "A pure treasure, the Sermon on the Mount."

Words which I'd heard from Pop and pulpit were like an endless flow washing over my mind without soaking in. Complete. True. As if the words should apply to everybody's life, any hour.

Yet it felt the words never applied to mine.

Pop had said something about "Lilies in the field ... the Heavenly Father knows your need ..."

Of course I had need! But I needed more than words. I needed a God I could touch, see, talk to, and listen to. Bible stories were too simple to answer my questions.

When Pop read Scripture, the words bolstered me, made me feel secure, uplifted, and sometimes even bold. But an hour later, the words had escaped my mind and I had no idea where to find them.

In the past, I flipped through the pages—hundreds and hundreds of pages! How could anyone find anything there? I usually placed the volume back on my closed trunk where it stayed for a while, daunting and dense.

Once, when I was eight, I'd looked up from a blind search of my Bible, trying to be like Pop and hear God speak to me, and caught Gar staring at my fumblings, a sneer on his face. I'd turned away, my face hot with embarrassment, as I did now in front of Helen.

⌘ ⌘ ⌘

Five days before Christmas, Elmer telephoned that he was en route from Kansas City and would arrive that very evening. I raked a comb through my hair as he talked. I glanced into the wall mirror. The look on my face set me to trembling. The comb fell from my fingers and clattered on the floor.

At least the decision was out of my hands.

He'd taken six days off—time enough to get married and drive to

Baltimore for the annual Deluxe holiday banquet.

Had Pop, foot resting on a chair because of a recent injury, heard what Elmer said?

"Elmer." I gripped the telephone tight against my chin. "That's not enough time. I can't ... I have to get ready."

"That's the way we left it in August. We haven't changed anything." His words echoed from the receiver like water rushing down a rain pipe, all playfulness and excitement. "I'll help you pack. Shouldn't take long. Your preacher all set to go?"

"I haven't asked. I didn't know when you were coming, so I—"

"You haven't asked him?" A pause on Elmer's end of the line. "Okay, okay. We'll get your justice of the peace. Mind giving him a call?"

"Yes. I will, Elmer." His words gave me needed direction.

"I can hardly wait to see you."

That's what Russell always said ... Russell!

I had to call him, tell him I was marrying another man because he, the now-employed Russell, hadn't shown up when the marriage train came by and ... I again drew near the mirror.

My image, wide-eyed and slack mouthed, stared back. Was that me?

The months of pondering, the telegrams and my perfumed notes, the long walks with Russell and the intense letters from Elmer, my inventions to excuse a lack of decision—everything had come down to this rush toward commitment.

I struggled to breathe and dropped into a chair. I'd treated a basic part of who I was—the power of choice—as an aggravation. I barely heard Elmer's closing words. My temples pounded.

Elmer would arrive in a few hours. I had to put Russell aside.

Mama came in the door, stamping the cold off after helping all day with my sister Pearl's baby. She shrugged out of her coat.

"Mama, Elmer's coming."

Fatigue wrote its name all over her face.

I should leave her be. But I blurted, "Mama, can you help me? The wedding ... Elmer only has a few days off, and—"

Her shoulders fell another inch. "I'm tired, Claire, very tired. This is not a good time to discuss your plans."

"Mama, all the details for my wedding. I need you to help me—"

"Do you know how much sleep I've gotten this week? That child may have whooping cough. Pearl has the rest of the family to look after too." Mama shook her head, as if disbelieving I had the nerve to want assistance with a problem I'd hatched all by myself.

After dinner, she retired to her bedroom.

I was on my own.

Pop, still with his leg up, gave me a rueful look. "Babe, you understand—your mother is worn out. Even if I hadn't taken that fall on the ice, I wouldn't be much help to you."

"I don't think it was too much to ask for help, to make sure I've covered everything. It's not like I ask Mama for favors every day." *There's a million things to do and I don't have the foggiest idea where to start.* "I'll try Helen." Two deep breaths. I rang the telephone like a swimmer frantic for air. "Helen, it's me. Can you come over?"

"Now?"

"Yes, now! I don't know how long you'll be, though. We have a wedding to plan."

"Oh, Claire, really? A wedding? I'll be over as soon as I can."

My mind clouded with how to tell Russell. All evening I tried to focus on starting my life with Elmer. *Call the JP first.* I needed to think about the wedding ceremony, Christmas for my family, packing everything I needed, all the good-byes.

⌘ ⌘ ⌘

Elmer arrived late that night, tired but upbeat. Mama had already gone back to bed, but she'd be scandalized if he stayed in the same house where I slept.

After settling Elmer in the front room with a cup of hot cocoa, I pulled Pop into the kitchen. "Pop, Elmer can't stay here." I gripped his arm, bunching up his sleeve between my fingers. "Oh, sorry." I dropped my hand and smoothed his shirtsleeve.

"Babe, I'll call Ethel," he whispered. "You go entertain your guest." He limped out of the kitchen.

I grabbed a plate out of the cupboard and threw two of Mama's sugar cookies onto it while Pop made his call. I barely had time to bring the plate out to Elmer before Pop came over to announce my sister and Ed would be happy to put Elmer up for a few nights. He gave Elmer directions to their farm while I made a quick ham sandwich and put it into a bag, handing it to him as Pop hustled him out the door.

Mama appeared from the bedroom hallway. "What are you doing up so late?"

"I'm waiting for Helen, Mama. I need her help with the wedding, with details."

"I'm sure you do." She gave me a brief look and turned to her bedroom, her blue- and white-striped nightgown melting into the gloom of the hallway.

I raised my hand and then sank into the overstuffed chair with the rosette doilies on the arms.

Twenty minutes later—time enough for my tears to dry—Helen arrived and I waved her upstairs to my room.

"Helen, I don't have anybody else to talk to about ..." I swallowed. "I need advice about what I need to do."

"What you need to do about what?"

"About ... Russell."

"You haven't told him yet? Claire, for crying out loud!"

"I know, I know. You said something like this would happen."

"You'll have to tell him, unless you plan to keep dating him when you're married."

I threw my pillow at her.

She settled into my rocker with a grin. "So, tell him."

"That's just it. I don't know what to say." How could I hurt his feelings when he'd been nothing but wonderful to me?

"He needs to hear it from you, Claire, not from someone else." Helen waved her index finger in the air. "Unless ... do you plan to call this wedding off?"

"No! Elmer's here. We're getting married. But I don't know how to tell Russell."

"You can't keep going down that road! That's why you've got the problem now. You *can* do this. Remember when you and I handled Leonard Leikem? It was your idea, but we pounded him good." She laughed. "Make up your mind to do it, and it's as good as done. You're as stubborn as your mama, only in a different way."

"I'm not like my mother."

"Well, what does she have to say about all this?"

"Mama has been helping Pearl with her little one. But she's against the marriage; never has liked Elmer." I snatched up the pillow I'd thrown at Helen and clutched it against my chest. "That hurts—really hurts—not to have my own mother on my side."

"I've known your mother since we were little. She's a controller, but I didn't think she'd go this far." Helen shook her head. "Probably shouldn't say this, but that attitude is what got you in this whole mess."

"Attitude? What do you mean?"

"Your mother—she's resisted you all along 'cause you wouldn't let her control you. Going to beauty school, marrying Harold, now Russell and Elmer—you've set your agenda."

"Why shouldn't I? It's my life." I stopped for a moment. "And how did Mama's trying to control me get me into all this … this mess?"

Helen stood and laid her hands on my shoulders. "Because, my dear, fragile friend, you like to be the boss. You're exactly like your mother in that respect."

I gaped at her. How preposterous!

"But I'm here to help you, so why don't I spend the night so we can talk this over?"

I stared at her. "I thought you were my friend."

"I am. Didn't I offer to spend the night with you?"

"Yeah, but you're also calling me names. I'm not bossy."

Helen held up one hand. "Okay, you're not bossy—you just like to run things." She tweaked my nose. "Some people call it manipulation. We can talk in the morning. You're not working tomorrow, are you?"

"The beauty shop!" Heart pounding, I clutched my neck. "How could I forget? I'm booked solid to New Year's Eve! I can't just up and leave."

Helen stood and pulled me up with her. "For the love of Pete! You are in a mess, aren't you? It's too late to get in a tizzy about something else tonight. We'll have to handle the elephants one at a time. Why don't you take a hot bath? Wake me up if you need to talk. And don't drown yourself. You've got a big day tomorrow."

My bath didn't yield any magical solutions. Finally I went to bed.

Helen slept soundly on the side of my bed closest to the wall, breathing evenly.

The sight of her still there calmed me.

Controller, indeed.

⌘ ⌘ ⌘

I paused to catch my breath outside Ed Jackson's half-open office door. *Focus on what to say—not on how he might take the news.* Helen had drilled that into me during her little pep talk over breakfast. I licked my lips. If my heart beat any harder, it might thud right out of my chest. I tapped on the door and stepped into view.

With a broad smile, Ed looked up from behind the pile of paperwork that always decorated his desk. "Claire, come in. Have a seat."

For a big man, Ed had one of the squeakiest voices I'd ever heard. I nearly choked to keep from giggling every time I talked with him. "Oh, Ed, thank you. I, uh, I wanted to tell you something. I need to, uh ..." My face felt on fire.

"Well, go ahead. It's okay. Are you all right?" Ed half pulled his bulk from the battered green chair and extended his hand.

"Yes, yes, I'm fine. Better than fine, in fact. It's that you've been so nice to me." My words turned from trickle to torrent. "Ed, I have to cancel my appointments after today. I'm getting married the day after tomorrow." I dropped my eyes.

"Claire, you—you're getting married, you say?"

I glanced back up.

"Of course, nearly everybody gets married sometime, I guess." Ed stared at his hands. A bead of sweat slid beside his pug nose and hovered above his upper lip. He whipped out a red bandanna and massaged his face, which had turned mournful. "Claire, you're not, uh, in trouble? That is, you're not expecting?"

"Heavens, no, Ed. That's not why I'm in a rush."

He looked relieved. "Thank goodness. I mean, how wonderful! Congratulations!" He struggled to his feet, a smile wreathing his jovial face. "I'm glad for you. Glad that you're not in a family way— not yet anyway. But yes ..." He swabbed his face again with the kerchief. "Yes, what will I do? It does leave me in a fix. Though congratulations to both you and that young man who walks you home from work on Fridays. What's his name?"

Could my cheeks get any hotter? "No, that's Russell. I'm marrying Elmer—someone else. A man I don't think you've met. You see, I met him when I was gone."

"None of my business." He peered at me from beneath bushy eyebrows. "This is rather short notice. Can you postpone it till after the first?"

I gulped. "I wish I could, Ed, but Elmer arrived a bit ago, and now he has to get back to Baltimore. We've, uh, been planning to get married as soon as he could get free from work."

"I see." He fiddled with a pencil. "You'll notify all your clients?"

"Oh, yes, Ed." My mind raced. "I'll tell them what I told you."

"They'll understand—at least, I hope so. And congratulations again!" He held my hand in his huge paw and patted it with his other hand. "We'll surely miss you, Claire. Make sure you tell your daddy to come by and tell me how you're doing."

Despite his graciousness, I knew I'd left him in a pickle.

And I had to call all thirty women on my client list and tell them I was closing up shop. I was letting everybody down just to get married on a minute's notice.

My temples pulsated.

⌘ ⌘ ⌘

The following morning, I'd begun packing when a familiar voice came from below.

Gar's insistent tone wafted upstairs, demanding that Pop let him run twelve new cattle on Pop's wheat pasture.

Pop's voice. "Gar, can't this wait? Besides Christmas guests, you surely know that with Claire getting married—"

"Isn't she the dependable one? Sets up her little shop, then chases after other rainbows. I'd wager the ladies of the town wish Jenny Fitzgerald still had her beauty shop. Claire's ill-timed plans have put everybody in a bind, particularly Ed Jackson. And the way she's treated Russell Hinkle is a disgrace. Not to mention the family." Gar's piping rant slowed. "She's always gotten what she wanted—why not now? I hear it's a Chicago salesman. From Harold the Crook to Big-City Big Shot! Probably not worked a day in his life."

A chair scuffed across the floor and Pop's sharp voice followed. "You can leave right now if you're going to talk like that. This is Claire's moment to start over, and I won't have you going on like this. Not here, not now, not anytime."

"You held the truth of her divorce from me because no one wanted my opinion. But mark my words, Father, your spoiled daughter will take every advantage for as long as you baby her. I've said my piece. If you please, let me know about that wheat pasture within the week."

The entry door slammed.

Jenny Fitzgerald! I'd forgotten about Jenny, the undertaker's wife. Gar would fall over if he knew what a help he'd been to me. I called Jenny right away.

Yes, she'd fill in at Ed's shop for the week after Christmas—more if needed.

Maybe God did answer prayer.

⌘ ⌘ ⌘

Elmer and I were married in the home of the justice of the peace on the twenty-third of December, 1930. Helen and Pop attended the wedding, but Mama didn't show. I watched the front door, sure she'd come through it any minute. The ceremony was over before it began, it seemed. A quick kiss with Elmer and then Pop's arms encircled us.

"You'll take care of my girl. I know you will, Elmer." He seemed to grope for words. "We—Claire's mother and I—wish the blessings of God on you both. I'll pray for you every day."

Elmer gazed back at Pop, his smile unreadable, and squeezed me to him. "I'll always take care of your girl."

My questions bubbled up. "Pop, where's Mama? Is she sick? Why didn't she come?"

Pop shook his head, sad-like.

As we ran down the steps of the house, Myrrl and Grace pulled up.

Grace jumped out and hugged me. "You didn't tell us what time the ceremony was, and now it seems we've missed it." Another failure to add to my list. I pressed a kiss to her cheek. "I'm so sorry. It's all happened so quickly."

During the hasty minutes before we left Pop's house for Baltimore, I insisted Elmer stay by my side. He carried my bags down from my room and set them by the door.

Mama emerged from the kitchen. Without explanation or apology, she hugged me and shook Elmer's hand.

Pop wept as he followed us to the car. "I want you to write. Tell me where you are, like before." He hugged us again and waved until we turned the far corner.

I swallowed back my tears and smiled at my new husband. "Now it's just us."

After a first night in Wichita, we made a stopover in Kansas City to meet Elmer's folks, "if we can find them," Elmer said.

"What do you mean?"

"They might be staying at Uncle Jim's."

We went to Uncle Jim's, and I met Cousin Effie, and Cousin Smiley and his wife, Henrietta. Elmer's younger brother, Earl, and his wife, Mae, popped in before we departed.

In the hubbub, nobody ever explained where Elmer's parents were. Exhausted, I totally forgot to ask Elmer once we got back in the car.

Elmer drove through Indianapolis so I could buy a dress for the banquet. Before he lay down in the car seat to take a nap, he gave me twenty dollars for my shopping.

I returned with a long, black chiffon, sleeveless creation with a scoop neck, an ivory lace top, and $3.50 in change.

Elmer still slept, so I returned to the dress shop and penned the most difficult letter of my life, telling Russell I was married. I wrote how I'd tried not to hurt him but that everything happened so fast.

I didn't spell out that I'd been a coward, afraid to do what I needed to do.

Deep down, I hadn't changed that much since I'd been married to Harold.

And I'd be facing the same problems all over again unless I figured out how to take control of my life.

Chapter Eleven

We hurried from the frosty night into the warm lobby of the Lord Baltimore Hotel. Laughter and chatter rippled toward us from an Art Deco archway, through which uniformed staff hurried in and out. I reached up and adjusted Elmer's tie.

He leaned down and kissed me.

I giggled, pushed him away, and redid my lipstick. Through the open doors, I saw familiar faces seated around a large horseshoe arrangement of tables.

Elmer squeezed my hand. "Sweetheart, are you ready to be a celebrity?"

I grabbed his arm. "As long as I'm with you, handsome."

We dodged a line of waiters bearing platters of food and swept into the great hall. The smells of warm delicious food, flowers, booze, and perfume overwhelmed my senses.

Cosmo Granada saw us first. He put two fingers to his lips and whistled.

Applause echoed back like a wave.

We'd barely gotten seated before Chet Orr and Cosmo pulled Elmer over to the bar. I watched out of the corner of my eye as Cosmo raised a whiskey bottle. If Prohibition couldn't keep the boys from their booze, I couldn't either, though this was not my idea for how my marriage would begin.

A cluster of women approached. Reba Stone blocked my view of Elmer—on purpose, probably. That female reminded me of a cobra, hypnotizing its prey with an unblinking stare. She masked her vulgarity with a fixed smile that tightened its grip if the victim's attention wavered. Always with an agenda.

And as long as I could remember, Reba's agenda had been Elmer.

Hair the color of Scotch whiskey, dressed fit to kill, she leaned in. Her earrings clanked against her bare shoulders. "Claire! So-o-o nice to see Elmer, and you too, of course. I heard he wasn't coming back—that your daddy might have him behind a pair of mules. Gossip, I suppose." She blew smoke past my left ear, her pig eyes daring me to respond.

Her beery aroma choked me.

Was that a forked tongue flicking between her painted lips?

I backed out of striking range. Then I caught myself. I didn't have to tussle with that awful woman. "I don't listen to gossip. Maybe you shouldn't either."

Geneva and Ferva interrupted us, Gladys and Rose and a gaggle of others soon after. Familiar faces pushed forward. It reminded me of the time I went with Pop to Petersilie's farm auction when I was twelve.

The chatter stepped up.

"Claire! How did you get that man?"

"Are you really and truly married?"

"Let's see your ring."

"What did you do? I invited Elmer to try some of my home cooking, and he always had an excuse not to come."

"How'd you snag that handsome devil?"

"No offense, but what do you have that I don't?"

Geneva quieted the babble. "Can it! We're here to wish this little lady luck, and you start a catfight. Claire, the rest of us want to congratulate you on getting *that* man. You're something, you doll." She gave me a big, welcoming grin. "Now tell us all, how *did* you get Elmer to pop the question?"

I put my arm around Geneva's waist and leaned forward.

The perfumed crowd quieted.

Had the boys gotten Elmer sloshed yet?

I glanced again toward the bar.

The men around him had started a drinking song.

"I did what nobody else did. I made him come to me."

"You're kidding. No woman can make a man—"

"Quiet. Let her go on. What *did* you do, Claire?"

I settled back, drank in the attention. "Elmer sent me telegrams, flowers, special delivery letters—trying to get me to come back on the crew. I told him I was staying in Kansas, and he didn't like it a bit."

"Oh, good for you, toots. He toed the line." Geneva threw her head back and laughed.

A chorus of cheers came from the girls.

A pang of disloyalty stabbed at me. "Well, I didn't exactly make him toe the line. But he became *very* interested. He made me feel like I was something special."

More sighs and giggles rippled through the huddle, quickly shushed by those who seemed eager to hear the rest of my story.

"Well, he didn't like what I had to say, but I'd already decided to do things on my terms. I was seeing another man—"

That revelation brought a wave of laughter and giggles.

"Though I didn't handle that so good."

Geneva patted my arm. "So what, toots? Without competition, who knows?"

"Elmer tried to get me to come back to Columbus, even wired money for the train. I told him, 'Nothing doing. You want to see me, you come to Kansas.' And you know what? He did."

"That's all? You just sat tight?" Rose sounded like a bleating sheep.

Reba snickered.

Poor Rose, so desperate to get a man.

"When I was here on the crew, he figured I was always available. Took me for granted. He was used to having women chase him. I merely played my cards differently."

A gang of men elbowed through the women. "Okay, girls. Step aside now! We gotta kiss the bride."

Glaring, Elmer popped off the barstool and headed toward us. Had he remembered the shenanigans the crew did to newlyweds?

Four tuxedoed huskies—all smiles and graciousness—blocked his path.

"Hey now, my wife isn't to be passed around like dessert."

Several men reminded him that he'd often been on the other side.

A shrill voice rang out. "If the men can kiss the bride, there's no reason a woman can't kiss the groom."

Reba!

I jerked around to see that hussy, arms like an octopus, pull Elmer's head down and smother him with a kiss.

Two weeks later, the crew moved to Philadelphia. Elmer's close friends, G.K. and Elsie Swank, took us to see The Great Blackstone. The magician surprised us by identifying me as a new bride. He called me forward to assist with several tricks. In the few minutes I was on the stage, he pulled an egg, a dollar bill and a yellow bird from my hair and my jacket. I even got to keep the money. Blackstone then escorted me back to our table, audience cheering. I started to sit, but the illusionist grabbed my hand and pulled me away. There were four eggs on my chair! As he gathered them up, that yellow bird appeared on my shoulder. I don't think I had blushed so much in my life, but I managed to wave at the crowd.

Elsie grabbed my arm. "Claire, you were fabulous. Elmer didn't tell us you were such a personality. I could never be so poised."

"It happened so fast, I didn't have time to get nervous. Now, I am."

G.K. echoed his approval, and Elmer watched me with a sly smile.

"Elmer, did you have anything to do with that?" I gave him a poke, but he only laughed.

After the show, Elmer treated us to a late dinner and dancing at a fancy nightclub.

G.K. drove us back to the hotel about midnight.

As Elmer and I got out of the car, a crowd appeared. Right away, Elmer grabbed my arm. "Let's get into the lobby—quick. Something's up."

Members of the crew filled the entry. It was a shivaree, and Elmer and I were the stars. The women kidnapped me. Elmer later told me he was given the choice of singing or dancing a jig to get his bride back. He said he was no singer, so he danced. After more pranks, they had him push me around the block in a wheelbarrow. There must have been fifty people, tooting horns and singing until the cops called a halt to the noise.

Elmer told me later that G.K. and Elsie had put the plot together. "They don't do this for just anybody, Claire. I guess they figure you're pretty special."

"I like being special—to you, lover boy."

⌘ ⌘ ⌘

Elsie took me shopping the next afternoon and we stopped for a soda afterward. She told me how she and G.K. had met Elmer. "We joined the crew about the time you left, though I don't think you and I ever met. G.K. and Elmer hit it off right away." She laughed. "Of course, they had to include me. Elmer used to talk about you when we'd go out. He was like a lost puppy."

"Really?" I hadn't thought of how my departure might have affected him. "Tell me more."

"Elmer's not one to talk about his feelings, but your personality impressed him. Said you always seemed cheerful. Reminded him of his sister Maggie."

"From what I've heard, she's a Christian woman, making the best of a bad marriage."

"Did he say that?"

"No, his aunt told me—the one in Kansas City."

"Well, I'd be surprised if Elmer said anything about his sister being a Christian woman. From the way he talks about that religious fanatic he married first time around, it doesn't sound like he puts much stock in that."

"Is that the way he put it?" Why hadn't Elmer ever told me any of this?

"Pretty much. He said he joined Deluxe after they split the sheet. He doesn't talk about his first marriage. One thing I know—drinking was a real divide between them."

"Mama would've had a fit if she knew he was a drinker. Bad enough that he smokes. My parents said alcohol is a tool of the devil. They wouldn't allow a bottle in our house."

"I used to booze it up. Now I don't touch the stuff. It's not been easy and I couldn't have done it without G.K." Elsie chewed her lip. "You're nothing like I thought you'd be."

"What do you mean?"

"Elmer said your family's very religious, and I thought ..."

Looked like religion was a big issue with Elmer. I kept quiet.

"I thought he'd married another fanatic. You're not, though. You're a swell gal, winsome and accepting, I'd say. You're open and real. I can see why Elmer chose you."

"He wasn't attracted to me until I played hard to get. At the beginning, I was only one of the girls on his string."

"You think so?"

"I know so, but when he saw I wasn't coming back from Kansas, he had to have me." Again, that pang. "It was purely accidental. I'm not that clever. I left the crew because I didn't want to share him with other women. When he couldn't have me, then he wanted me."

"All men are alike." Elsie snorted.

"They're alike—and they're different. I still have a lot to figure out. It doesn't get any easier with Reba flaunting herself around Elmer every time she sees him."

"She's a tart. Guess she figures she doesn't have anything to lose. What it comes down to, Claire, is whether your man plans to be faithful. I think Elmer has more character than to chase after any floozy, even Reba." Elsie rotated her wedding band on her finger. "Just keep him happy. Men are so insecure. One time, we had Elmer over for dinner, and he said—he wondered—if he married again, would he be able to meet the expectations of another woman. Said he couldn't please Florence. She always wanted to change him. Especially the religious part. He couldn't fake that. It wasn't in him—at least, how she thought it should be. He had real doubts about pursuing you. Like he was afraid you'd turn out to be another Aimee Semple McPherson and you'd try to convert him."

I frowned at that. "I didn't marry him to convert him. I want him for who he is."

"Fine for you. Make sure you stick to it. If he thinks you're out to change him, you've got a handful. I'd bet there's more to his family history than what you'd imagine."

"Why do you say that?"

Elsie rubbed at a spot on her glass. "It's mostly a feeling, I guess, from things Elmer's said—or really from what he's not said. He hardly ever talks about his family. Changes the subject if it comes up."

⌘ ⌘ ⌘

In the three months we'd been married, I hadn't once asked Elmer to take me to church. He joked around about everybody and everything, but religion and religious people got special attention. According to him, churches were full of hypocrites asking for money and sticking their noses in other people's business. That wasn't new, but surely he'd at least join me on Easter Sunday. Everybody turned out for Christmas and Easter.

On Good Friday, I pulled the nice blue dress he liked out of the closet, pinned on the corsage I'd bought, and held it up for him to see.

"Looks nice. You getting all dolled up for something?"

"Remember, I mentioned last week that I'd like to go to church Easter Sunday? You're going with me, aren't you, big boy?"

He stilled. "Afraid not. I've had enough religion pounded down my throat to last a lifetime."

"Not by me." Playing dumb might make him give the idea another chance. Or at least get me info firsthand. "Who are you talking about? Your mother used to take you to church?"

"Florence." His lips pursed into a hard line.

"Florence?" I looked at him easy-like, but I was all ears.

"Yes. I went to her church, right after we were married. Pen-tea-bab-tist, Apostolic something or other. I went a couple times and didn't care for it. People raising their hands and talking at once. I couldn't understand anything. The second time—the last time—the preacher tried to get me to 'walk the sinner's walk.' I don't like anybody pressuring me so I walked. Walked right out of there. Florence went completely sideways. I told her I'd never go back. If they couldn't treat a man with respect, how was that showing love?"

"Maybe he meant it for your good but didn't go about it the right way."

"They hammered me about 'getting right with God' and followed it with a big show about giving. Asked for money, like they always do."

My throat felt dry. I coughed and laid my lovely dress with the corsage over the back of a chair.

Elmer seemed to have forgotten me as his words continued spewing like a water hose. "Florence figured she'd remake my life. She had her holy-roller preacher stop by the house. I listened to him for about two minutes, but when he started in on me, I told him he was nothing but a hypocrite and to beat it and not come back."

I hadn't seen Elmer this worked up since the time he'd come out of a Missouri farmhouse to find a white goat prancing across the hood of his new car.

He paced the floor, glaring at whatever was in front of him. "She didn't like me running off her old preacher, but I couldn't have cared less. We had one row after another then. You want to know why I left that marriage?" He wagged his finger at me. "I left because she wouldn't let up. She tried to change *everything* about me! After a year of her trying to run my life, I wanted out and would never get myself into a corner like that again. She didn't even want a deck of cards in the house, let alone tobacco or a bottle of beer. Not once did she bring up any of that before we were married, but as soon as she had that marriage certificate, she started in on me."

"I understand that about Florence, and her pastor even, but how can you judge churches and believers by one or two unreasonable people? Could you go with me this time? It's Easter. You'll feel better for it."

"I feel fine the way I am. And I'll feel better if I don't go. Don't *you* start in on me."

We stared at one another for what seemed like two minutes.

Finally I said, "Okay, if you're going to be stubborn about it."

"Call it what you like. I'm not going." He grabbed a newspaper and sat.

⌘ ⌘ ⌘

Under a moody sky on Easter morning, I set out, heels clicking down empty sidewalks to a gray stone church in downtown Moline, Illinois. It was easy to find but I felt lost. I hugged my coat and my unhappiness so tightly around me that I mashed my corsage. I sat alone in that church, thinking how Elmer had flown off the handle— about his ex-wife, no less.

If he'd listened to me, he might have heard how church could help a person.

I wasn't anything like Florence. Surely he could see that.

Chapter Twelve

The summer of 1931 bumped along like a slow freight. Sales had never been so flat. It was little consolation that everyone else complained of the same things. Elmer said whiners hurt morale. Did the man ever feel fear? Or, at least, anxiety?

His unbuttoned shirt flared out like the wings of a bird as he stood before the open hotel window. "More hot sun tomorrow. Might as well be fishing."

I heard a rap on the door and opened it to Elsie.

G.K. stood behind her, swabbing his jowls with a sodden handkerchief.

She waved a little fan in front of her. "We're lost lambs looking for a glass of cold tea and some good news."

"Come in. I can get the tea but Elmer will have to provide the good news."

Elmer re-buttoned his shirt and turned. "You want some good news? Well, Ben finally tied the can to Sweeney."

"Really?" G.K. said. "Because he was always 'sick'?"

"That, and the fact that he lost his sales records three times in two months," Elmer said. "But the real surprise was Harry Doyle. Only him and Spessord had been here longer than me."

G.K. whistled. "Harry? That *is* a surprise. I thought he'd retire from Deluxe."

Elmer snorted. "He'd been here so long, he got careless. Got pinched for bootlegging. He grew up in Jersey City. My guess is he figured the cops would look the other way. Ben had a fit when he discovered Harry was using Deluxe as a cover."

Elsie shook her head. "All for money. The Michelmans were always arguing about money too. It broke up their marriage. Last I heard, she went back to Detroit."

G.K. slid a chair toward the window. "You ask me, money is at the root of most people's problems. Sweeney claimed he drank because he grew up poor."

"That's no excuse," Elsie snapped. "A person has to be responsible. It's part of living." She frowned at Elmer. "What about the company, Elmer? Ben tell you anything?"

"Yeah, but I'm not sure I buy it." He fiddled with a shirt button. "Definitely making changes next week. Intense campaigns with short canvassing times in each town, for starters."

"That's stupid," G.K. said. "We'll have to move before we even get settled."

Elmer nodded. "I don't like it and neither do the other crew bosses. Another thing—Ben is cutting sales bonuses by a fourth."

"That does a lot for team morale." G.K. leaned back in his chair and rubbed his eyes. "He won't have to send people down the road. They'll quit on their own."

"You better have a place to land," Elmer said. "Otherwise, sit tight. I have to remind myself that Ben built this company based on his business sense."

"Meanwhile, we have to survive while he experiments," G.K. said.

I could see this wasn't going anywhere. "Why don't I fix some sandwiches? We'll all feel better about everything with a little food in our stomachs."

⌘ ⌘ ⌘

Elmer and I lay in bed listening to the patter of rain on the window.

I ran a hand along his arm. "I've never seen G.K. so negative. Should we be looking for something else?"

"Always got my eyes open, Sal. Nothing looks any better than what we have here."

His use of my nickname from the song "My Gal Sal" soothed my worry a bit. "You didn't see Pop's letter yesterday. He asked about sales. Wanted to know if we'd seen 'armies of unemployed and starving people in the streets.' We haven't actually seen anybody dead, but panhandlers are everywhere. I don't know how much to tell him."

"Gotta be tough. I've seen down times in the seven years I've been with Deluxe. This one happens to be longer. Might be harder. But you tell your daddy not to worry about us."

I traced my finger from his forehead to the corner of his mouth. "Honey, when are we going to start a family?"

He grinned. "You ask that every night you hear rain outside." He turned serious. "Being on the road is no place for a baby. Pregnant, you couldn't manage door-to-door sales—"

"Marcelle Hogan canvassed up until the eighth month—"

"She was sick three months before she quit too. George almost had to carry her like a sack of meal every place they went. Cut his production. That really stuck in Ben's craw."

"We could work someplace else. A lot of places would love to have a salesman like you."

"Sal, we're lucky to have Deluxe. You ever think about that? Companies—big outfits—are going belly-up all around the country. If we keep sales above expenses, we've got a job."

"But, Elmer, I want to have a family. Mama doesn't think I'll ever—"

"Your mama *doesn't* think. That's her problem. She sees what she wants. But there's a right time for everything."

I rose up on one elbow.

Elmer's profile caught the dim light from the window like a Greek statue. He'd closed his eyes and held his lips in a tight line.

"Honey." I drew his hand to my cheek. "Maybe this is the right time."

His eyes popped open. "No. We've got to keep the money coming. You want us out on the street? We can't take chances, not with sales so hard to get."

The rain stopped.

I dropped to my pillow. "There's more to life than work."

Harold had insisted he didn't want kids. Maybe, deep down, Elmer felt the same way.

⌘ ⌘ ⌘

I looked at what I'd written to Mama and Pop.

> *Sales seem further apart lately. Guess we'll have to work harder. We might have to look at other job possibilities.*

I almost reached for my eraser, but instead I signed the letter and mailed it.

Ten days dropped off the calendar before a response came. I opened the envelope, glad that Elmer was at Ben's Saturday morning meeting with the crew bosses. A quick flip of the two sheets to inspect for Mama's neat cursive showed everything was in Pop's firm hand.

He strung words together like a chicken wire fence tied to prevent the escape of half-formed thoughts. Without introduction, he jumped into his agenda.

> *Henry Minor's filling station is for sale. Aunt in Ohio died. Left a wad of cash that would choke a cow. Talked with him last week. Says that his half-baked son-in-law would run the station into the ground. He and Emma want to travel. Elmer could do very well running that station. It would be wonderful to have you near us.*
>
> *Your mother took a fall Tuesday. Said she must be getting clumsy in her old age, but that's not like her. Better see the doc. Stubborn as she is, I'll probably have to call him here to the house.*

My breath caught in my throat. But not another word about Mama appeared among the complaints about the dry weather and wheat prices, that Myrrl had three new calves …

I flipped to the back sheet.

> *Henry has that station at a good price. I might as well tell you—I've already put money down on it. Talk to Elmer about coming out for a look, will you, dearest daughter?*

If only Elmer would consider it. Lately, we could hardly give anything away, let alone sell it. But Elmer likely wouldn't be thrilled about being in the same county with my family.

Keys rattled at the door.

I stood to greet Elmer. As he came in, I gave him a bright smile and a kiss.

He sat and gave a halfhearted overview of the sales meeting. "I don't like meetings on Saturday." He rolled his neck. "What'd you do this morning?"

I strangled the excitement out of my words. "Pretty quiet, although we did get a letter from Pop."

"You mean, *you* got a letter."

"Elmer, it was addressed to both of us, and it *was* for both of us."

"Yes, I know he has both our names on the envelope, but it's always about your folks. I don't know one in ten people he mentions. What's for dinner?"

I moved to the kitchen. "I've warmed the chicken casserole. But you might be interested in Pop's letter." I snatched it off the counter and thrust the pages at him.

"Okay, what did your folks say to *us*?" He sat on the divan and motioned for me to read, a faint smile playing at the corners of his mouth.

Elmer's expression never changed as I delivered Pop's message. "Pop really believes we could make a go of it. Wouldn't that be something?"

He untied his shoes and shook them off. "You know we can't afford anything like that."

"We don't have to. Pop will carry the note on it until we can start paying it off."

"I won't depend on your folks' charity."

"But it's not charity. We'd pay it back."

"Of course we'd pay it back. That's not the point. You've said more than once that your dad already put a wad into Harold's 'ventures.' I doubt if your brothers and sisters would be pleased if he bought a ready-made business for me."

"Pop gave land or money to every one of them to set up their farms. I admit he helped pay off some of the people that Harold took advantage of. But Harold is gone, forever. You're not like Harold and he knows that."

"I should hope not. I don't want people to think your dad has a full-time job bailing out Claire's husbands."

I grabbed a chair from the kitchen and pulled it in front of the divan so I could face him. "Pop wouldn't be giving us the station—

although he'd be willing to. He only wants to help us. He knows things have been slow."

"Oh? And how does he know that?"

"Because I've told him. Everybody knows things are tight all across the country. That's about all we talked about with G.K. and Elsie. Now George and Myrt have gone back to Texas. There's Thelma. And Leo and Maxine, Alphonse and Dominic. They're all gone."

"Myrt has been after George to go back and herd cows ever since they joined the crew. Leo couldn't sell his way out of a gunnysack. Thelma left to take care of her mother. And—"

"Yes, but what are *we* going to do? You're a super salesman, and I can hold my own. But these are hard times. We've got to make a living. You've always said we'd move if—"

"Settle down, Sal. Let's look at the bigger picture. Ness City is what? A piddling place in the prairie, a long ways from nowhere. And that station? I'd guess old man what's-his-name—Minor—has let that place slide. We'd have a lot to do just to get the business going."

"Elmer, please! Take a look at it." I wanted to shake him. Instead, I took a deep breath. "Pop said the station is in fine condition. And Henry Minor is a reputable man in the community. I know Pop wouldn't put a dollar down on a business until he'd checked the books thoroughly."

Elmer's patience sounded forced. "Maybe so. But what about me? You expect me to trot in there and keep accounts that old bird's had for years? I'm just 'the salesman from Chicago.' Those farm boys don't trade with a man just because his wife grew up next door."

"They judge a book by its cover. They'll find out you're honest when they deal with you. And they trust my father."

"But your father won't be running the gas station."

"People will know he's controlling it—" I could've cut off my tongue as soon as the words passed my lips.

He looked at me, silent.

"Elmer, I said that wrong. It would be ours to make or break. Having Pop's help doesn't mean you have to take it that way. You're the one who'd be managing it. We would own it. It would be ours."

Elmer spoke in that deliberate tone that meant he'd made up his mind. "I don't *want* to run a service station, pumping gasoline till all hours for those hay-shakers. I'd have to run a repair shop too—fixing every busted car and truck on the road. That's what Earl does—he's a mechanic. I'm a fixer. You can't make a go of it just by selling gas."

"Maybe so, but you could learn how to do repairs. I know you could."

He stood and turned to the wall, as if to speak to it. His words came out like dry twigs crushed underfoot. "I keep my own car running, but other people's problems get under my skin. I hardly know another soul in that town. Besides, Gar would have his nose over my shoulder every minute, checking if the city boy really fits his overalls."

Everything had run off the rails. Elmer always got his back up if I pushed too hard. I had let the discussion drift into things he couldn't or didn't want to do. I pulled myself to him. "Pop is making us a wonderful offer." I searched his eyes. "I can't force you to do something you don't want to do. But please, think about it."

He remained silent.

The tears started. "Elmer, what will we do? We can't stay here with Deluxe."

⌘ ⌘ ⌘

In the fall of 1931, Al Capone was jailed for income tax evasion, Governor Huey Long promised the folks of Louisiana a chicken in every pot, and Elmer said to thank Pop but he'd handle his own problems.

I wrote asking about Mama's health, and then I told Pop about Elmer's decision, without apology or further explanation. I tried to be upbeat. Inside, I was shattered.

Ben's experiment with short, intense canvassing efforts in each city was a bust, so he divided crews into two areas at a time so they could stay longer in each location. They also cut costs by staying in rooming houses and apartments instead of hotels. Thus it was that our crew had settled into the Joliet area, although none too successfully.

The fourth Friday after commencing the new procedure, Elmer sat totaling the week's orders. "Not much change from a month ago—except it's down seven percent. Sal, wait on supper. Let's talk."

I refilled his glass of tea and waited.

Elmer stirred in a teaspoon of sugar. "It's time to leave Deluxe."

I wasn't sure if I'd heard correctly. Deluxe Art Studio had been Elmer's life for as long as I'd known him. For several moments, I forgot to breathe.

We could start a family.

"We need a change." Elmer stood and waved his hand. "We can sell on our own, independent of the crew. I can't sit around, waiting for things to get better. I floated the idea to Ben a couple weeks ago so it wouldn't catch him with his pants down. He'll take over what's left of my crew. We'll work on our own and send the orders in here. Then we keep forty percent. I'm thinking of a sizable town—someplace we've not been for a while."

It wasn't all I wanted but more than I expected. We'd be done with traveling on the road. Possibilities whirled in my mind. "Why don't we go where we'll be closer to my family?"

"We'll go west all right. I'll check with Uncle Jim and Smiley in Kansas City first. No place is a hundred percent, but that should be better than back east."

"All I know about Kansas City is that we saw your family there after the wedding." That was a lie. Russell was in KC, working someplace. My face burned and I sneaked a glance at Elmer.

He didn't seem to notice. "Kansas City is bigger than it looks—not as big as Chicago or Philly. All those Pollacks, Jews, and Krauts—"

"Elmer! Mama's parents came from the old country, but Grandpa Stedke forbade the girls to ever speak German in that house. They were Americans, like you and me."

"Yeah, yeah, I know. Anyway, the area around KC is farm country. Real Americans. People we can do business with. People like my family. You met Uncle Jim. Smiley and Henrietta are on their own. Effie says she's helping support the family, but she's a quack, always trying to fix somebody—pills, herbs, whatever. No man will ever put up with that nonsense."

"But Elmer, we'll have our own place. Finally. Do you realize this will be the first time I've ever had my own kitchen?" I pulled a chair beside him and drew his arm onto my lap.

"You never had a kitchen before?"

"Life with Harold was a mess. We got kicked out of nearly every place we moved into."

"No reason we can't stay in Kansas City as long as we like. It's big enough to give us a decent living. Smiley's lived and worked there all his life. Uncle Jim said door-to-door sales would be a cinch, but I take that with a grain of salt. He's never even sold a dozen eggs."

I only half heard Elmer. I was imagining ways to decorate our place—the place we didn't have yet. We could start with an apartment—maybe move into a little cottage next, with a clothesline and garden in back and a fenced yard with roses and a lilac bush.

After supper, I dashed off a letter to Pop and Mama. I wrote that Elmer had worked out a deal with Deluxe for us to work on our own. I tried not to say anything that would alarm Mama, but hoped that Pop could read between the lines and know we were leaving the crew.

⌘ ⌘ ⌘

We began to say our good-byes to the people who'd shared our lives for the past three years—seven for Elmer. G.K. and Elsie had several of us over for supper. For dessert, she brought out apple and custard pies. She said she baked them to remind us how special we'd become to one another.

Fighting back tears, I searched the faces gathered around the table. Even though we promised we'd keep in touch, this was probably good-bye forever. Spessord said he'd stay with Deluxe, but if he got down to Kansas City, we'd all go dancing. Geneva, dear Geneva, wasn't sure what she would do.

Cosmo Grenada came over the next evening and prepared a sumptuous pasta dinner at our place, "just like Mama used to make." He didn't know if he'd stay with Deluxe. Martha and Lowell Dial brought dessert, salad, and Elmer's favorite peach brandy.

Ben was used to hard-boiled business decisions. Having Elmer and me in a satellite relationship suited him fine. Still, he hated to see us go.

⌘ ⌘ ⌘

Kansas City offered so many living choices—duplexes, apartments, garages, basements, and even lean-tos. We found an upstairs apartment next to a cemetery, about a mile north of Uncle Jim's little house. Afterward, we scouted the city for promising areas in which to market our wares.

As the first big city east of the heartland, Kansas City attracted droves of farmers, migrant workers, blacks and sharecroppers from the South, autoworkers and machinists from the east—all looking for a buck. The city had its own Hoovervilles with people living in old car bodies and piano boxes, in chicken houses and tin sheds. Silent men stood on street corners like molting hens, their personalities shed during a prior existence. Some wore shabby suits; others, overalls or rumpled gabardine. Like feathers blown across a hot tar roof, they'd descended on every vacant lot in the city. Now they were stuck—unless something appeared to pluck them from their misery and plant them on a hopeful island. If there was such a place still out there.

Surprisingly, I remembered a Scripture verse Pop had recently shared. *God is sufficient to meet all of your needs.*

Yes, that was what the faithful said, but I didn't count us among that steadfast few.

Chapter Thirteen

An unfriendly tapping sounded on the stairs outside our apartment.

The landlady. She only came if she wanted something.

I whipped open the door before it vibrated from another whack of her cane.

"You have a phone call. Something about your brother."

My stomach knotted as I followed her downstairs.

A pair of gaunt cats eyed me as I entered her living room.

Sure enough, it was Myrrl. His familiar tenor made me smile. But now, his usual calm faltered. Mama had had a stroke. His voice ratcheted up. "Sis, we wanted you to know, in case you can come home to see Mama. Can you hear me?"

"Barely. How bad is she?" I jumped as a kitten brushed my leg.

"We're not sure, but I ... Pop would like you here ... Such a bad connection ... Take the train. Call collect ... let us know when to pick you up." Myrrl's voice faded in a drone of static.

No point calling back. I turned to leave and nearly fell over a bundle of gray that hissed out of the room. Eyes burning from the heavy smell of cat urine, I stumbled to the door.

Elmer met me at the stairs.

I clutched his arm and told him the news.

I caught the first train west, which arrived in Dodge City the following evening as bleak clouds hurried across a thickening sky.

Myrrl and Grace, expressions somber, escorted me to the car for the two-hour drive to Ness City. En route, my brother recited the doctor's explanation—that Mama had probably had a series of small strokes prior to this episode. He had called it a brain attack, caused by a lack of circulation.

My breathing cramped as they told me what happened.

Grace leaned forward from the backseat. "If I hadn't been there, we wouldn't have known any of this. I helped her bake pies for the Shroyer funeral. All at once, she staggered to a chair and slumped down. Said she was dizzy. I helped her out of the kitchen and called your dad. He wanted Doc to come over, but she wouldn't have it. Finally, Pop kept after her until she admitted she'd had other spells too."

Myrrl shook his head. "You know how stubborn she can be. Finally told us that two days before, she couldn't see out of her right eye—as if a shade had been pulled over it."

I clutched my neck. "Mama helped with Floyd Osborn's mother. After Mrs. Osborn's stroke, the entire right side of her face froze in place, like set-up plaster. Had to feed her with a spoon and washrag. She could only open one part of her mouth, and food drooled down from it along her face. Poor woman. I saw her once. I could hardly take it."

Grace eased back into her seat.

Myrrl looked straight ahead. A street lamp caught the bead of a tear on his cheek, glistening like a diamond.

"Myrrl, what is Mama like now? She's going to be all right, isn't she?" I strained to hear over the Studebaker's throaty roar.

He coughed. "That's the way Mama is. She's paralyzed, sis. On the right side." His voice sounded off-key, like a bird's chirp. "Her right arm and leg. And the right side of her face ... it's like Mrs. Osborn." He grasped the hankie that Grace thrust from the backseat.

I closed my eyes as they described the paralysis and inability to speak. I forced myself to think only of Mama's strength, arms open as Myrrl and I trooped in from school. My eyes flooded, obscuring an amber light from a distant farmstead.

⌘ ⌘ ⌘

Home. It seemed barren, as if its life blood had drained away. Only Pop and me alone with Mama after Myrrl and Grace had gone.

I swept into the bedroom to see Mama, to touch her and hold her.

Two lamps lit the room—one atop the maple dresser and the other on the nightstand.

As my face drew close, I thought I saw a flash of recognition. I couldn't be sure. I knelt and leaned my head against her shoulder. "Mama, I'm here. I'm with you. Mama, you know I love you. I'm here for as long as this takes."

Mama was there, but she was not.

I backed out of the room, words a stutter in my throat. When I'd passed her line of sight, I dropped helplessly onto a chair and gave vent to wracking sobs.

Late that night, after Pop and I had talked and prayed for God's mercy, I set up my bed on the couch outside the bedroom door. Uncounted times, I'd awaken to check on Mama.

The next morning and each day afterward, I studied her still form for improvement. I wondered if she would recognize anyone, or if this stroke had taken her into a distant wilderness of the mind. I studied the shape of her face, which was enshrined in the mass of auburn hair. No wonder Pop adored her—she'd been such an elegant woman.

At times, her dark eyes gazed back at me in wonderment, as if we'd just met and she couldn't place who I was.

The doctor examined Mama every day and always departed grim and apologetic.

Myrrl and Ethel came in from their farms each morning.

I looked forward to their visits for my own encouragement. When they were gone, I attacked household chores like a woman possessed.

Once, when I went in to see her, I recited everything I'd done, "It's me, Claire. I cleaned the kitchen stove, washed and ironed the curtains." Then I leaned over and squared my face in front of her line of sight. She had to know all I was doing for her.

Pop came in and put his arm around me. "Claire, it's all right to do these things, but you're acting like it's more important to you than it is to her."

I shook my head, almost frantic. "Pop, don't you see? I need to do these things, so when she's well again, she'll like me and she'll—" I burst into tears.

⌘ ⌘ ⌘

Another time, Pop entered the bedroom and wordlessly bent down and kissed his wife—a kiss so intimate and full of devotion. As if he gave no thought to my presence.

This once vibrant woman now looked like a mummy, shrunken and indifferent to her husband.

I came beside him and bent down into her line of sight. "Mama, it's Pop. Don't you want to say hello to him?"

She didn't respond.

He left the room.

She closed her eyes and her face relaxed.

I pulled the sheet over her bare shoulders. The slackness of her flesh made me shiver, and I backed away and tiptoed to the kitchen. For long moments, I stood in that empty room, hardly breathing.

Mama's kitchen. It was her church, but she no longer worshiped there. Nor spoke to me.

The labored tick of the great clock in the hallway, urgent and impersonal, penetrated my thoughts.

Pop bade me good-night. Was his grief too great to share with me?

I returned to her room. Me and Mama, together. Should I pray? I stared at her still form and tried to recall the good times. We had laughed together on every square yard of our farm. I felt her hand encircling mine as we walked around the pond, mud squishing between my toes. I'd shrieked when a crawdad squirmed under my foot once, and she'd swooped me up, hugged me close, and dried my tears with the flowered apron that always smelled of baking and spices. Now I stood with her left hand within my own, stroking the fingers of the one who'd borne me. "Mama, I so want you to get well. We *all* pray for you every day, every night."

Silence.

I wanted to ask why she hadn't come to the ceremony when I married Elmer. Instead, I spoke with the voice of a six-year-old. "I went to the church Christmas program. I wish you could've been there, you especially. Will you come next time? Can you hear me?"

Nothing.

I dropped to one knee by the bed and kissed her hand. "Mama, I know you'll tell me when you can." I placed my hand along the artery on her neck and watched the second hand of Pop's gold watch, which he'd left on the nightstand.

One hundred fourteen beats per minute.

Two days before Christmas, Mama had another stroke. Her breathing became a furious pant. Although her gaze occasionally darted toward movement outside the room, she was moving further from us, dying.

We five children joined Pop around her bed, murmuring occasionally but mostly silent. There was nothing we could do to deny the beast of death.

That evening, the doctor came in one last time to check her vital signs. He gathered all of us outside the bedroom. "All you can do is pray."

Four hours later, Mama stopped breathing.

⌘ ⌘ ⌘

I'd faced death only once before, when Aunt Priscilla died of typhoid fever. Aunt Priscilla was strange. She didn't visit us, and Pop seldom took us to her home in Ransom. When I was a girl, Mama said Aunt Priscilla claimed she couldn't believe in a God who allowed suffering in the world. I thought how awful for someone to say that about the Heavenly Father. Now, as I gazed into Mama's open casket in the living room, Aunt Priscilla's words seemed prophetic.

Why had God allowed Mama to die so soon? Before I could ask her if she really loved me? If she accepted me, even with the divorce and all the shame to the family?

Elmer phoned that he'd arrive mid-afternoon.

When his car pulled into the driveway, I grabbed my coat and flew out to him. Once inside the car, I fell apart. For what seemed a long time, I wept while Elmer stroked my hair. Finally I could speak. "I'm so glad you're here. I didn't know I'd hurt like this."

"It's okay, Sal." He put his forehead against mine and whispered, "This will take time, but it will be okay." He closed his lips in that unyielding line I knew so well and continued to hold me.

For now, that was enough.

A figure came down the steps, a red bandanna pressed to his face.

"It's Myrrl. I know he wants to see you. He was pleased you could make the time."

Myrrl waited as we got out of the car, then he turned to Elmer. "I'm glad you came. Claire and Ethel are taking it pretty hard. As you can see, I am too." He forced a smile through tear-streaked features.

Elmer averted his eyes, as if offended by the sight of a man crying. Then he stuck out his hand. "Hello, uh, yeah. Claire said you and Grace would be here."

"Not Grace. She's home with the children."

"I see. Well, where is Sam—your dad?"

"He's inside. He's hardly left the place since Mama's stroke. He never lost hope. Trusted her to God, but you're never ready for the end. I know she's in the arms of Jesus." Myrrl's voice caught. His right hand wandered out and grasped Elmer's left arm.

Elmer's eyes widened.

Myrrl drew out the bandanna with his free hand. "Thankfully, God gives us that comfort. I tell you, Elmer, there's nothing better than knowing you're loved by God, that the Lord of the universe cares for you."

I watched, fascinated, paralyzed, as the two men strained against each other.

Myrrl spoke again. "I wish you could've gotten to know Mama better." He abruptly stopped and stared in surprise at his clamp on Elmer's arm. "Oh. Oh my!" He jerked his hand back, as if he'd grabbed a hot poker. "I'm sorry ..."

Released, Elmer moved back a step and smoothed the bunched creases in his jacket sleeve. "Yes, I didn't get to know your mother very well." He became suddenly absorbed in the necessity of knocking ashes from his unlit pipe.

I stepped between them, holding my breath. "Now, Elmer, why don't—"

He suddenly laughed and thrust his chin at Myrrl. "You get a little out of control when you talk religion, don't you?"

"My apologies, Elmer. I'm so sorry. I forgot where I was."

"I came to pay my respects to your mother, Claire's mother. You've both lost ... well, you've lost ... I understand how you'd be emotional. Forget it."

"Yes. Thank you." Myrrl swallowed. "Why don't we go inside, out of the cold?"

⌘ ⌘ ⌘

Platters of food came from the neighbors. Pies and casseroles, scalloped potatoes and baked beans, fried chicken, roast beef and noodles, cinnamon rolls and baked bread, cutlets and puddings, more pies and stewed meats—given as offerings for what the neighbors could not do. They could not bear the grief, replace the loss, comfort the hurting. Instead, they brought quiet words, obligated in their own ways to reach across the gulf that death leaves behind.

The wind had stilled, as if attuned to the arrival of relatives and friends. Ethel and I greeted each one, took their coats, and led them to the living room, fragrant with flowers. Hands folded, Pop sat quietly beside the open casket. I relaxed when Elmer stepped out onto the porch and nodded or spoke to relatives as they went out for a breath of fresh air.

This was the first chance all of the family had to see what kind of man I'd married this time. None of my kin smoked, drank spirits, or had been divorced. Elmer had done all three. Perhaps they'd measure him by what they saw. By his hands and his eyes and, finally, by his words. No calluses on his hands, but inwardly they'd approve of his handsome dignity and firm handshake.

He made no pretense of mourning to be proper, which caused a few whispers. My well-dressed heathen was certainly different from these farmers, although his roots were scarcely 200 miles from Ness County.

But nobody but me knew that.

⌘ ⌘ ⌘

The day after the funeral, Myrrl and Grace returned to town to bid us farewell. When they arrived, I hurried out to join Elmer on the front porch.

Would Elmer still be wary of Myrrl?

Myrrl said, "Elmer, Grace and I want you and Claire to visit us next time you come. Stay overnight if you can."

Elmer nodded, warm and relaxed. "Appreciate that. But I don't expect to get back to western Kansas very soon." He pulled out his tin of Prince Albert tobacco and filled the bowl of his pipe.

Myrrl leaned back, foot against the porch rail. "Where's your family, Elmer? They back east?"

"Yes, if you call Tulsa back east." Elmer grinned. "Mom and Dad are staying with my brother Earl and his wife until Dad can get work."

"Tough for an older man to get hired on. How old is your father?"

"Sixty-six. He said he'd check into working at a garage, but Tulsa's slowed down." Elmer looked into the distance, seeming to find the subject distasteful.

"Pop is sixty-eight but he's blessed to have good health. Losing Mama has hit him hard." Myrrl cleared his throat. "I've never been to

Tulsa, but I'm sure God will provide something for your folks."

Elmer centered the pipe in his mouth and spoke through clenched teeth. "Yes, I'm sure he will." He looked directly at Myrrl, as if daring him to continue that topic.

Myrrl proffered his hand. "I guess we'd better go. We have to pick up our two little ones and get back to the farm. Come and see us when you can."

Elmer smiled, genuinely, it seemed. "We'd like to do that, wouldn't we, Claire?"

⌘ ⌘ ⌘

I went to Pop's study while Elmer loaded our luggage. He was anxious to return to Kansas City, but he'd said we could wait until I felt it was okay to leave Pop. As if there would ever be a good time to leave.

Pop sat waiting, his head silhouetted against the clutter of photographs and books on the shelves beside his desk. He turned as I spoke his name. "Come in, babe. I had Elmer take those ceramics that Mama would have wanted you to have. Sit here with me." He seemed composed, almost as if nothing had happened.

Maybe this wouldn't be so hard. I pulled up a chair and touched his arm as I told him we had to go.

He squeezed my hand as we sat in silence, then turned to look out the window. "When I began courting your mother, her father—I always called him 'Old Stedke'—asked me where my family was. I told him about my mother, not mentioning a father. He wanted to know. So I told him—'I don't have a father.' I was afraid, for a moment, he wasn't going to let me see her anymore. I think if he had, I would've given up the farm and taken her far away. I couldn't think of losing her. Now she's gone ..."

I waited, Pop's grief far exceeding mine.

He began again, softly. "I am alone, but I'm not alone. I have this." He placed his hand on the big King James Bible. "We feel abandoned, but Jesus says otherwise. You know this by heart. John fourteen. 'Let not your heart be troubled: ye believe in God ...'"

As he spoke the passage I'd heard many times, the words now seemed personal and intimate. No wonder Pop believed those promises. They applied to the here and now, not as feel-good

118

encouragement pills. The words swept over me.

"Let not your heart be troubled …"

As if I could control the force of grief.

But maybe that was what it meant. One could be troubled—or not.

"And if I go and prepare a place for you, I will come again …"

If Jesus was in heaven, didn't that mean we had to work things out on our own? I covered the left side of my neck. *I'm not ready for the return of the Messiah. How can I even get ready?* I searched Pop's eyes. "Pop, I know you believe that."

"It's a comfort because it *is* real to me. I don't know how I can live without her. Your mother is the only girl I ever kissed. There was never anybody else. Now, I have to trust the comfort that only God can give." He sighed again and his body sagged. "She's gone, and I hurt terribly. But when my family needs me, I'll be here."

I stood and touched my fingers against the ridge of his cheek, then leaned over and kissed him.

He seemed so composed.

Mama, the only woman he ever loved.

All was silent but for the ticking of the hallway clock.

Could I ever know God like Pop did? I'd not been walking among God's called. The chaos of the past three years interrupted every time I tried to reach out to the God of heaven. Heat flashed across my face. Something had to change.

Tick, tock. Tick, tock.

"Your mother seemed to know her time was short. That's why she seemed unhappy much of the time. She had so many things to do before she could allow life to stop. Aren't we all that way? We fall into bondage to our tasks, all of it this side of heaven. And we've never gotten over being thrown out of the Garden. We were made for Eden, you know. Lilly spoke of heaven but she'd always say, 'for later.'"

His words floated toward me like pieces of truth pried loose from the edge of night.

Night possessed Mama and I was left—separate. My apartness would remain, unless it was healed by the God that I couldn't speak into my existence.

"Claire, you all right?"

I shuddered. "Oh, Pop, I don't know. I don't know."

Pop pulled me against his side and rocked me like a baby.

My hair, matted by tears, bunched against the warmth of his cheek.

Chapter Fourteen

Only three sales to show for a ten-hour day of canvassing. As we approached the apartment, I saw a brown coupe parked in our space.

Elmer squinted. "Remember Earl, my only brother who's figured out how to keep a job? Looks like you're going to meet the folks."

"Oh, Elmer, the place is a mess! Why didn't you tell me they were coming?"

"How would I know? I bet *they* didn't know they were coming. Staying with Earl and Mae is like living in a boxcar, shuttling between towns without a place to stay. Earl probably made an extra ten bucks and decided to bring them up from Tulsa."

I smoothed my blouse. "After nearly a year of marriage, I finally get to meet your parents."

"First, you were mad 'cause they were here. Now you're complaining that they didn't come sooner." He grinned and cut the ignition. "Don't worry what the place looks like, honey."

"Elmer, I wish you'd figure out what matters to a woman." I shook my head. I'd met Earl and Mae. If Earl was the ideal brother, his wife had made me question his judgment.

A dishwater blonde with pouty lips, Mae seemed to think whining made her sound intelligent. She bragged, "Earl was a real sheik." In the next breath, she complained about hussies who flirted with him.

I labeled her *cheap trash* but kept quiet.

As Elmer and I got out of our car, an older man with a walrus mustache and silver thatch emerged from the brown Plymouth. A skinny little woman struggled out, pushing the heel of her hand over her iron-gray hair. The couple looked careworn, like maybe they *had* lived in a boxcar.

Elmer waved them over. "Dad, Mom, this is Claire. My folks, Will and Mary Grace."

Will, tall and spare, returned my smile with a casual handshake and a "Hello, little lady" that had a nice lilt to it.

Mary Grace acted like she'd forgotten something important. She barely shook my hand and quickly turned to retrieve paper sacks from the car.

I looked for Elmer.

He and Earl already had their heads under the hood of our Oakland.

I gathered an armload of samples from the car.

"May I help?" Will took the smallest case and looked down at me, twinkling eyes beneath fierce eyebrows.

Couldn't help but like him. I smiled back. "It's good to finally meet you. Elmer said to call you Dad—is that okay?"

"Call me whatever pleases you, Claire. Dad will be fine."

"You must be hungry. I'll get supper started. I'm sorry, the place is a mess."

"Don't worry about that. Elmer told us what a good cook you are. And I'm ready to eat." Will called over toward the coupe. "Mother, let that be. Claire said she'll fix us a bite."

Earl extracted himself from inspecting our car and gave me a casual nod. He took a drag on his cigarette and exhaled, the smoke hovering under the brim of his soiled felt hat. "Hello, Claire, I wasn't sure we was going to find you home and all. Mom and Dad been after me to carry them up here. I finally had a day off, so here we are."

Who's he kidding? No one these days has to fight for a day off. I wanted to tell him to see a barber. Instead I said, "Hello, Earl, how's Mae?"

"Oh, she's fine, fine. Couldn't come this time, though. She had important things to do." He raised his eyebrows in a knowing way, as if Mae's duties were so complex that he couldn't explain further. Then he made a mini project of dropping his cigarette butt on the drive and grinding it out with first the toe and then the heel of his worn brogan.

Elmer's mother still fussed in the Plymouth.

"Can I help you with something?" I asked.

The old lady barked at Will for assistance. He didn't blink at her waspishness, but strolled over.

Guess I wasn't needed. I went upstairs to unlock the apartment.

Shortly, the men had settled around our small dining table and

Elmer poured coffee.

I mixed up cornbread to go with a pot of navy beans.

His mother appeared in the kitchen, wordless, watching me. Her voice came like the snap of a mousetrap. "Elmer likes his cornbread with more white flour than that. Needs three more spoons of sugar in the mix."

"Oh," I murmured, "yes, I suppose so but I, uh, he seems to like it this way as well."

"Best to measure the lard first. Keeps the eggs from sticking to the cup."

I bit my lip. My temples throbbed and perspiration ran down my face.

"Don't you have bigger plates?" Mary Grace held one of the plates aloft. "Everything will run together on these little things."

"Not in a set. We use what we've got." My face flushed and I turned my back. "Since you've got the dishes, could you set the table? I'll put out the rest of the things and finish supper while you take care of that."

Once the food was ready, I brought it out and saw that my only two large platters were at Elmer and Will's places. Three other mismatched plates completed the assemblage. I glared at Mary Grace.

She wouldn't meet my eyes.

It was a simple meal, but Will complimented my bread pudding.

Supper over, I cleared the table. The others retired to our front room while I began cleanup. A blackened saucer held two Lucky Strike butts. Earl's leavings.

Laughter and voices in the other room transported me home to Mama's kitchen. Images appeared in the soap bubbles dripping from my fingertips. Mama and I had seemed unified then. Leaving home had become more than a separation. I wished I could talk with Pop. Maybe Elmer and I could move back to Ness County. Outside the cloak of these thoughts, the conversation in the other room sparked from comedy to chaos.

"Stopped at a railroad crossing on the way in." Earl's nasal tone. "You wouldn't believe the thievery going on. A big freight had pulled off on a siding. Had at least six cars loaded with corn. I'll be dogged if a buncha blackies didn't come out the ditch by the track. They climbed up and sent that corn flying like pudding hit by an eggbeater. Others run up to grab ears of corn. White folks too. Then somebody musta give the word. Railroad cops come from nowhere. They come charging down on that bunch, swinging their billies. Knocked people left and right. Never seen anything like it."

"Folks is desperate." Will's voice. "There's stealing going on everywhere nowadays. Smiley told me thieves took milk right off his neighbor's porch. Never caught them. I told him it was probably country boys trying to survive. Most of them farmhands are like fish outta water when they come to the big town. But you gotta do what you gotta do. I don't blame them a bit."

"Are you saying it's all okay to steal?" Mary Grace snapped. "You weren't too happy about those Italian boys taking a watermelon from your garden."

"Young pups! Nowadays, youngsters got no respect for their elders."

I resumed rinsing the dishes.

Elmer redirected the conversation. "Anyone hear from Maggie? She and MacLaren still down near the Panhandle? Liberal, isn't it?"

A snort from Earl. "Still there, and still trying to keep a lid on Mac. That's a lost cause. After they had those two kids, Maggie got religion, according to John and Moselle. I'll tell you this—she can go to church every day of the week and twicet on Sundays, but prayin' won't never change a man like Dick MacLaren."

"We figured to visit Maggie, to see those grandkids." Will again. "But she said we better wait till things settle down. She hadn't seen hide nor hair of Mac in a week. Probably off on a toot. I don't see how she manages to feed those kids on what little she makes. Fixes pies for a roadhouse, and the neighbor lady gives her produce now and then."

"John could give her a hand," Earl said. "Adams is less than thirty miles south of there."

"She's not going to call on John." Elmer sounded agitated. "He does well to support the tribe he's got. How many do they have now?"

"Five." Mary Grace's voice, full of alarm. "I'm sure Moselle was expecting again when we left there. When was that, Dad?"

"Let's see, we stayed with them March and April. Mosie wasn't in a family way back then, but John said we ought to go see Maggie. So we called Maggie from the neighbor's. She was really down, said she didn't know where Mac was. Figured he'd come back with a sob story about getting a tropical disease from a train station washroom. So John didn't take us to Liberal. Instead, he brought us back to Tulsa about the first of May—"

"Sixth of May. That's when you arrived at my place." Earl cleared his throat. "John's car broke down. He called me in the middle of the night from Pawnee. I'd be surprised if he got home within a week. Always wanting help for something. The last time his car quit on him, I put eight dollars plus a day's labor into it, and he still hasn't paid me."

Elmer gave a rough chuckle. "You might as well forget your eight dollars."

"I have, but it still makes me sore," Earl said. "John isn't one to honor his debts."

"How you doing in there, Claire?"

At least Will remembered I was alone in the kitchen. "Almost have the dishes done, Dad. How's the coffee out there?"

Mary Grace bustled in to grab the coffeepot and give everyone a refill.

Elmer and his dad sidetracked into a passionate discussion about the Pendergast political machine. It sounded like there were no honest men left in Kansas City.

My feet felt like they'd been pressed in a steam iron, but I put up the dishes and poured a cup of coffee. I could finally join the conversation.

I entered the front room as Earl eased the door open.

He looked at me like I'd caught him riffling through my purse. Full of stutters and explanations, he said he had to get back to Tulsa so he could do a valve job on a banker's Packard.

I opened my mouth.

Elmer, already on his feet, waved me off and went out after Earl.

I followed them and nearly tripped over a pasteboard box and two battered suitcases at the foot of the stairs. Suitcases? And Mary Grace and Will were still in the apartment …

Elmer turned and lugged the suitcases up the steps.

I hurried to catch him, my voice breaking. "Elmer! What's going on? Is he leaving without your folks? What—"

"I guess they'll be staying with us for a while." He threw the words back over his shoulder, as if I should know what was going on.

"But, but, you didn't tell me about them—them staying here!"

"What was I supposed to say?"

"You were—" I gasped for air. "Why didn't you? You were supposed to say *something* ..." My words came out ragged as I fought for breath.

"Yes." He spoke with that forced patience. "I should've said something."

"Well, how ... what can we do? We don't have room." My forehead pounded.

"Claire, Earl's already gone. We'll take care of them."

My choked protest was cut off when Will appeared at the top of the stairs. He stepped back when I followed Elmer in.

Mary Grace came out of the kitchen, mumbling about a missing sack.

I watched her exit and then turned to see Elmer set the two bags in the only bedroom. Our bedroom. "Elmer, why are you—"

"You look like you're a mite upset, Sal." He gave me a quizzical look.

"Yes. I am. What are you doing? Are you giving them the bedroom?"

"They traveled over 250 miles today. I figured we'd get two cots from the landlady and set them up in the front room. It'll be handier for us when we go out canvassing."

Unbelievable. "How long are they staying?"

"Shouldn't be long. Dad couldn't find work in Tulsa, so Earl thought he might have a better shot here in the big city."

A door opened behind me and Mary Grace's voice rasped from the open doorway. "Claire, where can I hang these clothes? And Dad wants another cup of coffee."

I wanted to yell at the stranger in my house. This wasn't Elmer's mother. This was a bossy old lady who'd come in to take over my life. "You can hang them on the nails in the bedroom wall. I'll see

126

about the coffee *later*."

Of the three other people in the apartment, none was going to listen to me. In a few short hours, I'd been disregarded by my husband and moved out of my own bedroom. If I'd had money for a ticket, I'd be on the train for Dodge City.

And to see all those boxes—did they plan to stay a month?

I'd be having a talk with Elmer very soon.

After we got the folks situated, Elmer came over to help me make up the cots.

I couldn't look at him, I was so burned up. Lacking additional bedding, each sheet and blanket had to be spread over both cots, but I made a point of moving my cot away from his anyway.

"Hey, Sal, this reminds me of that weekend we went camping on the Ohio River—except that farmer's cow won't be slobbering all over your face when you're asleep." He chortled. "You sure woke up in a hurry when that old Jersey put her snotty nose against the back of your neck."

I gave him a look. "I remember the other cow. She caught you with your pants down when you were doing your business."

His jaw dropped.

"Didn't know I saw that, did you?"

"You didn't see anything."

I had him. "Oh, yes, I did. A farm boy like you should know better than to get between a cow and her calf. You dived over that fence with your drawers down ..." I laughed so hard I snorted.

He flung a pillow at me, which narrowly missed the kerosene lamp.

"Elmer, you're going to set the place on fire." I retrieved the pillow and changed into my nightclothes.

Elmer began to take off his shoes. When he pulled his stockings off, I whacked him aside the head with the pillow. He dove across my cot and grabbed my leg.

I hopped on my free leg and pummeled his head with the pillow.

The raspy voice again, from the bedroom. "We're trying to sleep in here!"

We froze and then Elmer called out, "Sorry, Mom. Claire fell out of bed and I was trying to help her up."

I picked up my pillow, doused the lamp, and slid into bed. I watched him in the dim light as he undressed. "Next time, you better not start something you can't finish, big boy."

"How's this for a finish?" He pulled me to him.

⌘ ⌘ ⌘

In the following weeks, we drove farther from the city on both sides of the state line to sell enhanced family photographs and frames. Elmer reminded me more than once, "We've got to keep up appearances. If people smell failure, you've had it. Got to make that good first impression."

He practiced what he preached.

The first thing people saw when they peered out their front window was the black Oakland sedan in their driveway. Not as showy as the big roadsters favored by bootleggers, but it gave a look of legitimacy to our enterprise. We dressed as professionals. Elmer always wore a three-piece suit, and I looked classy with the nice wardrobe I'd built up while on the road with Deluxe.

We competed with scores of unemployed to get an audience with the moneyed people. Former shoe salesmen vied with locksmiths and farmhands selling soap and pies, fresh cream and wigs, firewood and bedspreads. Fences, guard dogs, and "No Trespassing" signs appeared in upper-class neighborhoods. Nevertheless, we made sales with two Catholic bishops, an heiress, and a few rich farmers.

⌘ ⌘ ⌘

The day before Thanksgiving, another unfamiliar car appeared in front of the apartment. Since the folks moved in, our place seemed open to any "visitor" who happened by.

Elmer chuckled. "Earl said Bud had a Hudson. That's a Hudson. You're going to meet Esther. A real flapper. She's a beauty, but she never stops running her mouth."

Time for another loaves-and-fishes miracle. I sighed. "Bud's the youngest? You never talk about him."

"Nothing to say. Bud doesn't talk much." Elmer parked the car. "Get ready."

As we entered, I could only think how this place wasn't ours.

It belonged to the in-laws. Mary Grace seemed in charge of the kitchen. My kitchen.

128

Well, maybe supper would be ready.

If I had seen Bud on the street, I would've pegged him as Elmer's brother. He was handsome as Barrymore but quiet as a sphinx.

That suited Esther, who expressed opinions for both. She announced she'd been notified that her Aunt Salome had willed her a pile of money. She could talk of little else. She knew she was beautiful, but now she'd also be rich.

Bud, who routinely worked as a short-order cook, was likewise charmed with the possibilities of sudden wealth. He talked about becoming a chef and fishing in Canada.

When Bud and Esther's 'vacation' ended, even Will admitted the return of quiet to the apartment was a blessing. I had spent two full days in the kitchen. The entire sum Pop had sent for the holidays had been used for the guests who came to hear Esther's stories and eat our food.

Elmer and I sat in the front room, the folks already asleep. I coughed. "Elmer?"

"What is it, my dearest dear?"

Ah, he was onto me. I changed to a diversionary question. "Well, my dear honey, do you believe Esther and Bud are going to be rich?"

"They believe it, so why shouldn't we?" He winked. "No, they won't get rich. I don't know what's going to happen, but something will come up to end the whole business."

"You're a cynical one. Don't you think good things sometimes happen?"

"I'm not sure getting a pile of money would be a good thing for Bud. He's never really applied himself. Maybe because he's the baby of the family."

"They're kind of like Earl and Mae, except Esther's really in charge of that marriage."

"Mae wants to run Earl's life. Bud would probably visit us more if it wasn't for Esther."

Did he think I wanted them around more often? "No. No, I wasn't trying to get them to visit sooner. Uh, Bud will come by often enough. He sure doesn't say much. Esther does all the talking."

"Before her, I'd never met anyone who could speak for five minutes without taking a breath. Bud doesn't have much chance to get a word in edgewise, much less run that team."

"Is that why Bud never takes in your folks?"

"Claire, have you ever been to Bud's house?"

"Of course not. You know that."

"Well, neither have I. None of the family has been to Bud's house."

"You're not serious." I stared at him.

"Very serious. No one knows where Bud lives."

"You can't be serious."

"Sal, you're repeating yourself."

"Oh, *Elmer*." I shoved his shoulder. "He doesn't live in a tree or out alongside the road. He's got to live somewhere." This family I married into was different, but this was bizarre.

Elmer sighed the tired sigh of a man who would play my little game if I insisted, but the ending would never change. He had told me all that mattered.

"Hasn't anybody asked Bud where he lives?"

"Some have. Different times, different ways. He's amazing at not answering questions. I decided if he doesn't want to tell me, it's his business. I don't need anything from Bud."

"It might be nice to have him take his turn with your folks." This was tricky ground, and I wasn't sure if I should tread there.

"Esther comes with the package, don't forget. She and Mom would tangle, for sure."

"So we—and Earl, some of the time—provide for your folks because we 'get along' with them?"

"Yes."

The room held its breath, and it was clear that Elmer would say nothing more to displace its burden of silence.

There'd been few times when I was uncomfortable with my husband, but this was one of them. His family was different. Maybe even strange. I went out on the stair landing. The night breeze riffled my hair, dried leaves rasped against the fence across the alley, and I tried to think of absolutely nothing.

Couldn't do it.

Since Elmer's folks showed up, I seemed to get more confused or angry at Elmer. I'd thought I was marrying him, not the whole lot.

Harold's family had been practically invisible—mostly because they didn't want to be contaminated by Harold. With Elmer and his kin, it was the reverse. Like he was the only one with a future, the only one who knew how to get from here to there. Maybe they came to be near him, to have some of his elegance and smartness rub off on them.

My good cooking probably worked against me too.

Elmer's brothers seemed infected with just enough of skirt-chasing, drinking, and sleeping until noon that they never got well enough to do anything with their lives.

But Elmer's dad? Will was already doing what he wanted to do— sit all day on the front porch.

Pop had quoted something, probably from the Bible, about bad company corrupting good morals. I didn't want to stand in judgment of my in-laws, but what if their habits affected me rather than the other way around?

I hadn't been to church in months and months. In fact, I hadn't thought of going to church for a long time.

That answered my question.

Tired as I was, I couldn't sleep. I went into the kitchen, moved the pile of ironing from the three-legged stool, and sat.

The King James Bible that Mama had given me peered out from under a week-old issue of *The Kansas City Star*.

I opened it and read where my finger dropped. "Let not your heart be troubled ..."

But *my* heart was.

Chapter Fifteen

I sliced the end of the envelope and saw the bills. Pop hadn't sent cash since I'd first written that Elmer's folks were living with us. A quick count—four five-dollar bills. I could practically hear Pop's voice in the letter.

> *Didn't expect to hear in-laws still with you.*
> *Thought it was to be a short visit. Hope you don't let*
> *it become permanent. This gift's for you and Elmer,*
> *not for a man who won't support himself.*

Pop was still smarting over that ghastly afternoon Gar came to his house to rant about Harold's waste of the family treasure.

I stared at the bills. How could I keep the cash from supporting the in-laws?

Impossible. In 1933, hardly anyone had extra cash. Elmer and I both knew to the penny what we had between us.

I took a deep breath. Could I *not* tell him about the money? I'd never kept anything from him. But what good was money if we couldn't spend it on what we needed?

This wasn't going to go away. Myrrl had been blunter in his letter of two days before.

> *Pop said you wrote him that Elmer's folks are*
> *living with you. When Elmer was here, he said his*
> *dad was out of a job. He's younger than Pop, as I*
> *remember. Doesn't seem like the old guy thinks he*
> *needs to work. Kind of like termites, if you ask me.*

I expected sarcasm from Gar but not Myrrl. For sure, they'd been talking. They might even pressure Pop about how to spend his money. Pop would tell them it was none of their business. But what if he didn't?

By the time Elmer returned, the folks were in bed.

I brewed a pot of tea and joined him at the kitchen table as he read the classifieds. "We got a letter from Pop today."

Elmer glanced up. "How's he doing?"

"I think better, but he misses Mama. I do too." My voice caught. Now was not the time to get emotional. I closed my eyes to organize what I wanted to say.

"Hey, that's all right, Sal." Elmer folded the paper and touched my cheek.

I opened my eyes to meet his.

"So, what else did your daddy say? Is he coming to see us?"

I hesitated to break the magic of the moment, but I'd prepped myself and didn't want to put off something this important. "Pop worries about things."

"Like what?" Elmer leaned back, eyes narrowed.

I jumped up to pour tea. *I'd make a terrible poker player. Elmer is so touchy how people talk about his family.* "Pop wonders why we're the only ones taking care of your folks."

"We're not." His voice was flat. "They came from Earl's before he brought them up here."

"Well, yes, but why is it that your folks—" I avoided his eyes "—have to be taken care of? Pop is older than your dad, and he provides for himself. He wonders why your folks can't do the same."

"Why is that any of his business?"

"He wants to help us out, but not by supporting the rest of your family while they … don't put in anything." Had I gone too far? Would he fly off the handle?

"He doesn't have to give us a dime. I never asked him for anything."

"I haven't, either," I said quickly. "But in Pop's letter, he included twenty dollars."

"Send it back," Elmer snapped.

"Pop knows we're hard up. But he doesn't want to support all the rest."

He glared. "Does he expect to control us—what we do—by sending us money?"

"He wants to help us. But he can't help your whole family. There'd be no end to that."

Elmer kept his eyes on the tabletop.

I touched his arm. "Elmer, Pop has provided for all five of us kids. Gave the others houses and land. Then Harold squandered Pop's gift money and didn't pay back loans. Gar got wind of it. Made a big scene, upset everybody. You've heard all this before. Since then, Pop's been real sensitive. I don't want to give Gar a sniff of anything to bellyache about. He's forever been critical of me. If he knows we're putting up your folks, he'll pressure Pop."

"It's no comparison. We're the ones helping Mom and Dad."

"If Pop helps us, it goes to support them, not just us. And the surprise visits from others? They go on and on. Why should we provide for your whole family?"

"You complaining about Bud and Esther stopping by for a couple days?"

"It was four days. And Esther never lifted a hand to help in the kitchen."

"Well, she's pregnant, isn't she?"

"She said she *might* be pregnant. I think she didn't want to get out of bed before noon. She was always into your dad's homemade wine." I didn't like spongers anyway, and Esther's condescending attitude topped it off. Like she was better than anybody else. Better than me.

"Don't forget, Claire, Esther's an heiress." He grinned without humor.

"That doesn't impress me or you, if it's even true. But we can't provide a boarding house every time someone wants a place to flop. There's a limit to everything."

He stood and leaned down on the table. "Why didn't you tell me this bothered you?"

"I'm telling you now." I got up and switched on the bare overhead light.

"No, you're telling me your dad is bothered by it."

"Elmer!" *That man could be so annoying.* Had he paid attention to a word I'd said?

"Look, I hear what you're saying, but what do you want me to do about it? Tell them they can't eat with us? Should I tell them they have to leave so we can have supper?"

"You're just being sarcastic. We can't afford to feed everyone whenever they stop by. And I end up in the kitchen before and after every meal, usually without any help."

"Mom helps you." He fumbled for his pipe.

"She takes over." I watched his face. I'd never spoken against his mother before.

His eyes widened. "What? You want help in the kitchen, but only on your terms. Claire, you can't have it both ways."

"You're not even trying to understand."

"What I want to know is this ..." He waggled his index finger for emphasis. "Is it you, or your father, who has the problem with my folks staying in this house?" Elmer cocked his head at an angle like he always did when he was angry. Then he stomped out to the stair landing.

Fists clenched, I sat there while the door slam echoed through the apartment. *Let him stay out there. He knows what I said is true. Why doesn't he do something about ... all of them?* I watched the door, palms sweaty. Maybe I shouldn't have brought it up. Maybe I should've put up with them. I could go to Elmer and apologize.

But if I talked with him, I would lose any ground I might have gained.

No. I'm not backing off what I said. Not this time.

⌘ ⌘ ⌘

A week later, as we drove home from another fruitless day of canvassing, Elmer waved at a cluster of figures on a street corner. "Look at that—everywhere the same. People down and out. Men, little kids, trying to sell razor straps and shoelaces and pencils and apples. Selling anything. There's bound to be buyers other places. We've got to get out of this town."

I searched his face. "Elmer, do you mean that? I've been ready to leave Kansas City since we unpacked. Why don't we ..." *No. Don't say it.*

"I'm serious. I thought about going to Maggie's, but she's clear across Kansas, dealing with that sot. I won't impose on her." He turned a sharp corner and adjusted his speed. "I told you about my

Uncle Joe, up in Phillipsburg. Lost his leg in a railroad accident, so he's got a pension to get him through this depression. Anyway, he wrote back. Said there were no evicted families out on the sidewalks, no Hoovervilles up there—not in all of northern Kansas. I'd like to give that a try."

Excitement bubbled up at the thought of leaving KC. "When do you want to go?"

"As soon as I can get the folks down to Tulsa. Can you have things ready by Wednesday?"

Words tripped over thoughts as I imagined Phillipsburg. God *had* heard my prayers, infrequent as they'd been. "I'll have it packed, everything, by Tuesday. We don't have so much now since we've sold a few things over the last weeks." Keen as vinegar, I remembered personal property we'd had to sell. A wealthy couple in Liberty had bought my honeymoon dress, three pairs of my shoes, Elmer's tuxedo, and his overcoat. I refused to think more about it. They were just things. Regardless of where we ended up, we'd be closer to having a home.

The best part? Elmer's folks would be out of our hair.

⌘ ⌘ ⌘

We drove out of Kansas City as morning sun brightened the fields with a golden glow. I didn't look back.

Elmer pointed the Oakland west, a bamboo pole lashed atop the car. "Smiley likes fishing the Solomon. Never gets skunked. I'll catch some fish for lunch and save a few bucks too."

We pulled off along the river near Junction City. Elmer took down his pole and cast into a quiet hole before the current narrowed. "Do you realize this is the first time in two and a half years that I've been fishing? Haven't had a chance to relax, always on the go."

"Almost the same with me, except it's been six years."

"Six years?" He gave me a quizzical look. "Six years for what?"

I tied my scarf. "Six years since I felt like I could put my mistakes behind me."

He stared at the bobber resting on the shining water. "I guess you mean the mistake of Harold. Or do you mean me?"

"Things will come to rest when we—you and me—have our own blessed home. When I can be a mother. You can't imagine what that means to me."

"You keep talking like that, you'll scare the fish." He threw me an impish grin.

"I'm serious, Mister Elmer. You've got a few things to learn about women."

"So I've been told." He settled onto a log. "What 'few things' would you like to tell me?"

I slapped a mosquito from my arm and sat beside him. "Men don't understand what it means to be a mother. To start with, you have to put down roots. Can't do that traipsing around the country."

"So we'll get settled. I told you we're going to Uncle Joe's, Phillipsburg or wherever."

"That's what bothers me. 'Wherever,' as if we're simply going to wander around."

"We'll follow the Solomon River. It forks northwest before Salina. I wrote him to expect us. But I can't guarantee how far this car will take us. It's got over forty thousand miles on it."

⌘ ⌘ ⌘

We fried the bullhead catfish Elmer caught, then ate and loaded up the car. The Oakland rolled down the highway, roadside fence posts falling behind us like pencil dominoes. *Thank you, Lord, KC is history.*

But there were no promises ahead, either. No job. No home. We weren't any different from the refugees streaming out west.

Maybe I'd been too dramatic. "Elmer, I hope I wasn't too pushy. I only want to have a purpose, a plan."

He rubbed his forehead. "I want a plan too, Sal. Right now, it's to make Phillipsburg. There are better times ahead. No way will I get beat down like those Detroit factory workers and Tennessee dirt farmers you see at every roadside park. One way or another, we're going to make our own way. Uncle Joe wrote that he's never seen a breadline or soup kitchen. That's reason enough to go there."

"I'm glad we left. Having your relatives underfoot was driving me crazy."

He gave me a sharp look.

I pretended not to notice and gazed at the road ahead.

Two miles beyond Abilene, a pop sounded and the car fishtailed.

Elmer regained control as a row of mailboxes flashed inches from my window. He pulled off the road and found that the left rear tire had picked up a nail. By the time he changed the tire, pinks and oranges tinged the clouds.

The horizon cut the light and a dreary plain spread between us and the dimming sky. A sign showed Niles and Solomon lay just ahead. Unfortunately, Niles was nothing and Solomon was fast asleep.

We couldn't even find a park or a campsite. But speaking of trouble might bring it about, so I kept my thoughts to myself. The drone of the engine made me drowsy.

Elmer said he'd watch for a riverside campsite.

Fog lay across the highway as it curved toward the river. We crested a low hill and a bright beam appeared ahead, ghost-like.

I blinked to comprehend.

The light grew brighter, coming on a collision course with our path.

I jerked my eyes between the phantom and Elmer.

He'd been driving at a good clip along the gravel road, but he seemed silenced by the harsh beam that floated toward us. Now, he slowed the Oakland as an expanding sound grew to fill the air all around.

I screamed, "Elmer! It's coming at us! Oh! God, help!"

The brightness surrounded us, accompanied by a din of clanking, rumbling, hissing, and a deafening howl. I screamed again.

The monster flew past—all blackness, sparks, and smoke—its track turning the locomotive from our path as the road veered in the opposite direction.

I cowered, heart thudding as the train rumbled past, terror easing to comprehension.

Elmer stopped the car in the center of the road.

I watched the retreating dragon as it thrust into the darkness. Trembling, I sat wordless as silence again covered the fields. I looked over at Elmer.

His body shook.

What?

In soundless laughter, he leaned back and wiped his eyes.

I yelled, "You horse's behind! You knew that was a train all along.

Why didn't you tell me?" I whacked him across the leg with my purse. Combs, nail files, a powder puff, and cosmetics spilled onto the floorboard.

He tried to speak, but my pounding only increased his choking laughter.

I grabbed his ear and gave it a good tweak. "You oughta be ashamed." I seized his other ear. He should pay for being so mean.

He dived to grab my leg.

I kicked to keep my shoes on. No luck. He tickled my foot and I shrieked hysterically.

Just then, a horn blared, this time behind us.

We jerked up. We had the road blocked.

Elmer grabbed the gearshift but hit reverse.

More honks and shouts.

He finally got it in low and moved to the side.

The other car pulled around, its passengers all scowls.

Elmer acted as if nothing had happened.

"If you'd behave, you wouldn't get into trouble, big boy."

"That was quite a train, wasn't it?"

⌘ ⌘ ⌘

An hour later, the fog lifted and we found a cove along the Solomon River. By lantern, we laid out blankets and slept under the star-studded summer sky. The next morning, Elmer put out his fishing pole. We shared two crappie broiled over an open fire before proceeding.

The highway ran along dry fields and pastures, collecting stores, houses, and stone-faced civic buildings of scattered towns. There was a sameness to farm towns, but we strove to make each unique, inventing personalities for every hamlet we passed through. Our game ended when the car began to run hot.

Elmer stopped and topped off the radiator with the jug of water he always carried. He backed away from the raised hood. "Water hose is leaking. Wish I'd had Earl replace it when he brought the folks up. With that and the brakes, we better find a place to land 'cause we won't make Phillipsburg without repairs."

"Where are we? We don't know anybody out here." I felt a headache coming on.

Elmer laid his map over the fender. "We're nearly two hundred miles from Kansas City, but only six from Beloit, Mitchell County. Why don't we go to Beloit?"

We limped into the town and found a garage.

The mechanic, a squat fellow who looked like he'd just gotten up, pulled his head from under the hood of a black Buick when we came in. Without speaking, he regarded the Oakland skeptically as he wiped his hands on an old shirt.

Elmer was extra casual. "Nice town. Looks orderly, like a county seat ought to be."

Apparently happy with these words of appreciation, the mechanic spoke. "We're proud of our community. Mostly farmers—wheat, oats, and barley. Good people."

Elmer nodded. "It's a far cry from the cities back east, with their soup kitchens and people lined around the block to get their name on a work list. I like that."

"Ain't no soup kitchens or breadlines here, mister. You folks from the city?" He eyed Elmer's slacks and white shirt and the cane pole lashed to the top of the car.

"Yes and no." Elmer grinned. "My wife grew up in Ness County, and me, Elwood, Nebraska. We left KC. Everybody's on the make. Wanted to look over your town, while you put on a new water hose and check the brakes."

⌘ ⌘ ⌘

After a two-hour stroll, we returned for the Oakland.

The mechanic said he replaced the water hose and adjusted the brakes, but the engine needed a valve job. If we pushed it too hard, who was to say what might happen?

Elmer paid for the work with more of our reserve than I would have liked to have spent. "Appreciate the advice. We'll keep that in mind." He pulled onto the main drag and we headed out of town.

Where would we go? How far could we make it? My stomach churned. I waved him to stop. As the tires crunched off the pavers to the gravel, I flung open the door and vomited.

Elmer strode around the car, eyes wide. "What is it, Claire?"

I wiped my face and sat against the fender. "I want to know where we're going. The car is fixed, but not good enough to travel far. We

140

don't know a soul here and—"

He pulled me to him, his eyes searching mine. "Don't fall apart on me now. It may get worse before it gets better. Have you seen a well-off town anywhere? This car needs work. Two tires are bald ..." He wiped his forehead. "I don't know, Sal. I won't know where we're going until I see it. We'll return and really size up the town. If it looks halfway promising, we'll stay."

Finally something. I didn't expect him to have it all figured out, but I needed to hear a plan. For the first time since we left the Deluxe crew, Elmer seemed real again. "Thank you. When you don't tell me things, it's like you're afraid to trust me, that you fear I'll go to pieces. Tell me what you're thinking. I'm with you, Elmer. You know I love you." I put my arms around him and laid my head against his chest.

He stroked my cheek. "Let's find a decent place for right now. We'll stay long enough to build a reserve so we can fix the car and get to Phillipsburg."

We drove west to Glen Elder and then another ten miles to look over Cawker City. Not a single rooming house there, so we returned to Glen Elder, which featured the three-story Hobart House. Asleep on a corner, it reminded me of an old maid, unloved and taken for granted. A gaunt porch extended down both street sides. The flimsy screen door kept out the insects circling the potted philodendron beside the entrance. The lobby, decorated with brass spittoons at the desk and stairs, was quiet as a church on Saturday night.

Elmer cast about for a sign of management.

Eventually, a short, stout man in his fifties bounced in, an outrageous necktie tucked under his belt. He introduced himself as Felix, the owner, while he eyed me the whole time. For a monthly lease, he'd let us have a furnished apartment with a bath down the hall for sixty-five cents a night.

Elmer got him down to forty-five cents, with the condition that I could set up a manicure table in the lobby.

Glen Elder would have to do for now.

⌘ ⌘ ⌘

Sick again. Just like the day we came into Beloit. I started bleeding, just a little, and Elmer took me to the county hospital. He almost panicked until the doctor attended to me.

Miscarriage. I didn't want to believe it. Eight weeks along, and I'd lost the baby before I'd even known about it.

Before we left, Elmer asked if we could ever have children.

The doctor, a tall, serious man with sad eyes, sat and spoke to me. "You're healthy. No reason you can't get pregnant again."

My doubts of conceiving swept away, I tried to bear the hurt but grew more despondent every week.

At first, Elmer tried to understand. He did nice things for me, like the time he found wild flowers down by a farm pond and picked a colorful bouquet. But when I didn't snap out of it after six weeks, Elmer got frustrated. Really, he never could understand my grief. Eventually, he kind of gave up and went canvassing to the far reaches of the county.

I tried to shake loose from my depression and wrote up several notices about my beauty shop.

Over a three-week period, four women came in for a manicure and one for a cut.

My expectations adjusted to reality, and I made a point to encourage Elmer by greeting him at the door every evening after a day's canvassing. I'd take his felt hat and suit coat and loosen his tie.

He'd tell me about the farmers he met, the dogs that tried to ambush him, and the few sales he made—at places like Cuba, Clifton, and Burr Oak.

Everywhere, decay and defeat lay over the region. Few cars stirred on the dusty roads. Most people walked and some rode horseback. Glen Elder, like all small towns, offered little privacy. Thus, people couldn't—or wouldn't—openly announce their want. Need was as shameful as theft.

A growing weariness seeped into Elmer's eyes. His optimism faded under the toll taken on his body.

I patted him on the back. "I know why there's no breadlines or soup kitchens here—because it's the same as back home. These people are too proud to beg. They won't ask for help."

He looked grim. "I wouldn't have my hand out, either. Nobody wants to be on the dole."

Discouragement swept over me like a wave. If something didn't change, we'd be stuck in Glen Elder. Worse, we had no friends or family here.

Things needed to change, and for the better.

Chapter Sixteen

Clunk.

I peered around my manicure cubicle. I couldn't believe my eyes.

Elmer's dad stood beside those two battered suitcases I knew so well. With a broad grin, he said, "There's that good cook."

That fact settled on me like the dust that daily coated my working area. Three months it'd been just me and Elmer. Now Earl—or somebody—had traveled halfway across Kansas to drop Will and Mary Grace off at our apartment.

I huffed and rolled my eyes.

Will's grin faded when I flung a valise onto the table.

A muffled cry sounded from outside.

Will hustled to the entry and held the screen door with his foot while Elmer's mother struggled in, dragging a pasteboard box tied with binder twine.

He turned back to me. "It's good to see you again, little lady. Earl couldn't stay. Said to tell you he had to get back to Tulsa, but he'll visit next time he comes." He glanced around the lobby. "Looks like a nice, quiet place. I haven't been up in northern Kansas since Hector was a pup. Say, where's Elmer gone to?"

I snapped, "Why, he's down at the lumberyard, hoping to get on. A shipment of cedar posts is coming in, and they'll need men to unload that freight car. You might go down there too, Dad."

Will pitched his felt hat on the counter, where it settled in a spasm of dust. He dropped into a bentwood chair and waved away my suggestion. "He won't have a Chinaman's chance getting on there. Earl passed the lumberyard as we come in. They was several men milling around but no Elmer. You can bet your bottom dollar that the same bunch that unloaded that freight will be there to help. No use for an old buzzard like me to go out there."

I frowned and put away my equipment. Having my in-laws in the middle of our lives again was the last thing we needed.

"And how you making it, Claire?"

I barked back. "How do you think, Dad? These are hard times."

Mary Grace turned from fidgeting with the boxes. "Where's your apartment, Claire? We've traveled a long ways and I want to get settled."

I'd forgotten how much her voice reminded me of a complaining cat. "If you'd let me know you were coming, I could've had something ready."

Will shook his head. "We didn't know we was coming till day before yesterday. Mae's been on the prod. Didn't like Earl going to the dance hall without her. They started going at it so he told us we needed to be somewheres else. She's awful touchy, that gal."

Mary Grace sniffed. "Mae's so whiny the dog even goes outside when she starts up. I'm glad we don't have to put up with that. Why Earl ever married her, I don't know."

I stood tall. "So you're here. Why didn't you go to Jim's? Or John's?"

"We never go to Jim's," she said. "Beatrice won't have anything to do with us. And John and Moselle? That houseful of kids would drive a deacon to drink."

"I'll find Elmer. We barely have room for ourselves. He'll have to decide what to do." I snatched up my sweater as I marched out past the startled pair. Behind me, the screen door hit the frame with a satisfactory smack. I clattered down the wooden steps and almost tripped over the calico cat that cried for a handout every time the door opened.

Kind of like Elmer's folks.

I stalked down the dusty street, not caring if I found Elmer. Losing my self-control didn't concern me as much as losing my privacy.

Pop would say Jesus taught us to love others.

Yeah, well, Jesus had never met Elmer's folks.

I pulled on the sweater and headed for the park on the south side of town. It'd been weeks since Elmer and I went there to roast catfish.

A new bunch of floaters had set up camp. One man had his head under the hood of an old Reo. Two others worked beneath a Model T with Indiana plates, a jumble of greasy parts laid on a piece of cardboard. Two women huddled over a campfire, stirring the contents of a smoke-blackened pot while "Bye, Bye, Blackbird" echoed from a radio. Dirty-faced kids peered from makeshift shelters.

I'd seen that look too many times—hunger, painful and pleading. Poverty's face was as colorless as oatmeal. That joyless group would be there only until they got their flivvers running. Then they'd disappear, like crows flapping off to California or Arizona, leaving only charred wood and oil stains on the ground.

The wind picked up, sharp as a thistle on my face and legs. I headed back to the Hobart House. I'd dreamed of honoring my husband's family, but Elmer's family took and kept taking.

At least Will was likable and Mary Grace was a hard worker.

Too bad God didn't see fit to reverse their personalities.

⌘ ⌘ ⌘

Elmer waved off my plea to send the folks back to Earl's or John's. They'd come to stay and, as usual, we gave up the bedroom. Elmer got another bed from Felix, which he set up in the living room. Elmer stayed up past midnight, talking with his dad about Uncle Jim and Cousin Effie and the rest back in Kansas City.

After breakfast the next morning, I motioned Elmer out to the lobby.

He ambled out as if he knew I was not pleased.

"With your folks here, Felix is sure to charge us extra. If they were back at Earl's, they could stay for free."

"Don't tell me what to do." He clenched his jaw. "I'm not sending them back to Earl's. He's got a marriage in the ditch. We'll make room."

I wanted to kick his shins for not considering my feelings.

We made room all right. It took all morning, but we shoehorned their stuff and ours into two rooms. Boxes of mysterious herbs and potions—Effie's contributions—we stacked on suitcases. Mary Grace's sacks marked every corner. Will's two coats and trousers ended up over the backs of the bentwood chairs and the small settee. Mary Grace insisted that her rug-making enterprise be set up in the front room "where there was more light."

Her rugs buried our sales office.

Flirting with danger, I pushed her boxes out of the corner behind the kitchen table. Our samples, order forms, display valises, and receipt books had to go someplace.

Maybe it didn't matter. We found mostly closed doors and gloomy stares on the sleepy streets and roads of Glen Elder and Beloit.

I had to get away. I grabbed Elmer and told him we were canvassing Cawker City before I flipped my bonnet.

⌘ ⌘ ⌘

Cawker City looked dead, so Elmer headed west, then south, toward the river. Every farmstead along the way had its own peculiar sense of exhaustion or desolation. We topped a low rise.

I waved at Elmer to stop. "Look! Look at that place."

He slowed and idled past a long, tree-lined drive and dry pasture fronted by a whitewashed fence. "A prosperous farmer, by the looks of that house and barn. With the drought, I'm surprised those Guernseys look so good. And no goats."

"Let's give them a visit." I squinted against the morning sun to get the name on the mailbox in black Roman letters. "DeBey."

Elmer turned the Oakland up the narrow lane. "Must be Dutch. Doubt they got this prosperous by entertaining every peddler and salesman who came through the gate. You ready?"

I fluffed my hair and rubbed my lips. "How do I look?"

"Twenty-three skidoo. Go get 'em." He parked in front.

The picket fence encircled a two-story Craftsman house with lace curtains and a sun porch. Everything, even the outbuildings, was white except for the green trim and shutters, and the dark shingle roof.

Elmer remained in the car while I scouted for dogs and pushed through the gate.

A rumpled, old collie lifted his head, tail sweeping the grass.

"Good dog." I kept an eye on him and side-stepped toward the recessed entry, which framed a screen door.

"Hello out there!" A voice boomed from the darkened interior.

I caught my breath and painted on a smile.

A youngish man with twinkling gray eyes, his head forested with a thatch of sandy hair, padded to the door in his stocking feet.

I quickly introduced myself.

A lilting voice chimed out of the gloom. "Bart, be a gentleman and invite the lady in." A fair-faced brunette appeared, wearing cut-off corduroy pants and a man's shirt rolled up at the sleeves. She

147

extended her hand. "Hello, we're the DeBeys, Jen and Bart. Got a couple of kids running around here too. We get so few visitors down this lane, Bart sometimes forgets his manners. Is there someone with you?"

"Yes, my husband, but he'll wait in the car. I won't take much of your time."

Bart headed out to meet Elmer, and Jen motioned me to a Victorian parlor chair in a room set off by Grant Wood and Art Deco framed prints and an oak buffet. She poured coffee. "I've always wanted to have family photographs done but haven't because of the expense."

I smiled and began my spiel. "You'll be surprised when you see what we can do. Deluxe Art Studio produces some of the finest family portrait copying in the country. We'll take any snapshot of a loved one and reproduce it in our studios in Chicago—enlarged true to life and tinted by our talented artists to make a family keepsake that will be cherished for generations." I mentioned the innovations in frame production and design. "Here are some examples of our work. Isn't that nice?"

Jen held the sample up to catch the outside light. "Why, that's so life-like. The colors are so natural. Let me get something." She knelt, pulled out the bottom drawer of the buffet, and held up a fistful of old photographs. "Can you enlarge these, like in your sample?"

"Every bit as good. We have a first-rate selection of frames to complement your order, as well."

"Yes, I'd like to look at your frames."

"My husband, Elmer, will demonstrate the entire selection when he brings back your completed portraits."

Jen DeBey laughed as if filled with joy, then gave me a $217 order.

With Jen beside me, I floated out the door and back to the car.

Bart and Elmer stood leaning against the Oakland.

I caught snippets of talk about Dillinger and Pretty Boy Floyd.

They seemed to have connected, and parted with an enthusiastic handshake.

To celebrate, we stopped at the five-and-dime in Glen Elder where Elmer treated me to a soda and got himself a King Edward cigar, his first since Kansas City.

I gave him a grocery list before he dropped me off at the hotel.

He left to cash the check and go to the grocery.

Will wobbled in from the front porch, rubbing his eyes. "Where you been, Claire? I'm flat out of tobaccy. We thought we was goin' to have to send the law after you."

"Hold your horses, Dad, Elmer's gone for your tobacco. The door, please."

He pulled the screen open and followed me in. "Now ain't you in a fine frame of mind. How did your trip to the country go?"

I wanted Elmer to share the satisfaction of telling, but ... "We had a little luck selling pictures west of Cawker City. I did well with a couple named DeBey. Beautiful farm and nice people. I showed them my portfolio, and it was duck soup after that. Elmer will probably get a good order on the frames when he delivers their portraits."

"Now when would that be?" Will sorted through his collection of pills.

"Generally a month. The order goes to Chicago, where Deluxe processes it and paints the portraits. A week for shipping back to Glen Elder."

"Do they pay you when your order comes in?" Will studied my sample case.

"Forty percent of the total order is ours to keep. But we have to send most to Deluxe with the order. Then they pay us back upon delivery." Would this be too much detail for him to absorb? Or was he interested in trying his hand at the work?

"Sounds like you can make a pot of money."

"Hasn't been the case lately. This was our first sale in three weeks and we're behind on the rent." I shifted my load to my other hand. "Have you checked about a government job? We could use the help."

Will cleared his voice as if to speak but Mary Grace entered, waving cloth remnants. "I can start a new rug. Got this from the dry goods."

Will used the interruption to sidetrack further talk about work. He complained about "Roosterbelt's socialism" while Mary Grace said the government never was fair, what with animal shelters in Chicago giving more food to large dogs than a man on relief received.

A half hour later, Elmer brought in two bags of groceries. "There you are, Mom. I could hear you out in the lobby. Good thing old Felix was out for a walk or he would've thought you'd laid an egg." He grinned and pulled her apron strings.

She swatted at his hand and rummaged in the sacks.

Will came alive and grabbed a red tin of Prince Albert. He waved it triumphantly and retreated to the rocker to fire up his pipe.

Mary Grace put away the groceries, her mood improving as she assessed the spread. "No reason we can't have something special for supper. I'll make a custard pie."

Anything to keep her out of my hair.

After supper, we settled in the front room for our evening cup of coffee and Elmer nodded toward me. "We hit the jackpot today because of this gal. Went right in there and did her stuff. We got a doozy of an order."

I blushed at this unexpected praise. Elmer seldom handed out compliments. "It was easy. They're nice people. I was just being friendly."

He waved me off and leaned back. "Main thing is you did it. I'll bet I get a good frame order. Jen will get what she wants."

⌘ ⌘ ⌘

A month later, Elmer called the DeBeys—their family portraits were ready. When could he deliver them?

Jen suggested the next day and insisted I come along.

Though selling frames was Elmer's show, I looked forward to seeing this delightful couple again.

With classical music in the background, the three of us sat around cups of steaming tea in the DeBey's front room. Elmer began his presentation with ornate designs of gold gilt plaster on wood— Empire, Victorian, Eastlake, and Art Deco. He mentioned the basic frame line, but Jen waved those off and settled on two groupings of floral gesso designs.

An intermittent thumping from the back porch rattled the cups on our saucers.

Jen called back over her shoulder, "Bartel, I've selected twelve lovely frames for the portraits. If you don't get in here, you won't get to choose!" She turned back to us. "Where are you living?"

Elmer squared up the sheaf of order forms. "We've been at the Hobart House for five months. My folks came in a couple months ago from Tulsa."

"Oh, goodness! Bart, they're in the old, uh, in the hotel, the Hobart House."

Bart came in and set down his muddy boots. He greeted us and padded into the kitchen. "The Hobart? How do you put up with the roaches?"

"Bart. Puh-leeze." Jen turned to us. "You have to ignore him sometimes."

"Oh, sorry, folks. I didn't mean to sound critical. My brother, Gert, told me they had cockroaches the size of shoeboxes patrolling the hallway. I used to go there to pick up *The Wichita Eagle*, but not after that. Didn't want to accidentally bring home a monster."

"Bart, Gert always exaggerates. You know that."

"Yes, I guess they were smaller, like flatirons." As if struck with an idea, Bart began a dialogue exclusively with Jen. "The Koster place. Why not?"

We pretended not to listen.

"Yes ..." She dropped her chin and held his gaze.

"Like we talked? That okay?"

"Absolutely fine."

"Yes, now." he replied. He turned to us. "We apologize for talking like you weren't here. I wanted to confirm something with Jen. You see, we have this vacant rental house. It's decent, only two miles down the road. If you'd be interested in moving out of the hotel, we wouldn't charge you a thing."

Frowning, Elmer opened his mouth as if to argue.

Bart held up his hand. "In fact, you'd be doing us a favor. We haven't found anyone to rent it. Nobody to our liking, that is. The bureaucrats will make me put bums in there if they find out it's vacant. Awful what they're doing to private ownership. It'd be a relief to have you living there. Had a break-in last year. So much riffraff in the area. It would get you out of the hotel."

I held my breath.

Elmer leaned back, a grin now on his face. "I heard about that government deal, but for all you know we may be just the sort of riffraff you're trying to avoid. You can't be serious."

"Oh, I'm serious," Bart said. "I'm also a pretty good judge of character. I felt like we hit it off last time you were here."

"We could pay you what we're paying Felix—forty-five cents a night, plus a bit more a week for my folks. It's not much, but I can't take charity."

"Wait a minute, Elmer." I was tired of being shut out of my own bedroom. I turned to Bart. "That's so nice of you. But I'm not sure if we can pay both for ourselves and our parents." I glanced over to catch Elmer's reaction.

He swallowed as if battling his pride.

"Aw, Claire, we like you. You don't have to pay us anything. Jen and I talked about you folks. Ain't something out of the blue." Bart stood. "Let's go take a look at it."

Our apartment in Kansas City had been the only place I decorated and furnished. Three and a half years of marriage and we'd always been on the go, with nothing of our own. The idea of my own sanctuary, be it castle or cottage, was precious beyond words.

Bart and Jen showed us around. The house was a rectangular wood-frame structure with a gable roof overlooking struggling Chinese elms, cottonwoods, and hackberry trees. The south entry porch faced the road. A cellar adjoined the back, and a granary and chicken coop hovered next to the stock tank and fenced pasture. Nothing fancy, but I could dye feed sacks for curtains, and Bart said he had paint. The best part? We'd have our own bedroom.

As we all piled back into the Oakland—Elmer had insisted on driving us to see the house—Bart asked, "What do you think? I'd like for you to look after the place for us. And it'd be nice to have you as neighbors."

"If you don't mind a one-sided deal," Elmer said. "We're getting the best of you—"

"We'll clean up around the place." I pointed toward the corral. "Get those tumbleweeds out of the fences and the stock tank. Elmer's mother can help me clean the house."

"I knew you could use it," Jen said. "Say, do you play cards? We have a time finding anyone around here who does. My folks sometimes come up from Larned, but they're Baptist and won't touch an ace of spades with gloves on. I don't see anything in the Bible against playing cards, do you, Elmer?"

"You'll have to ask Claire about that," he said. "She reads the Good Book."

Jen leaned toward me in the backseat. "Oh, you read the Bible too? Were you raised in a Christian home?" She smiled at both of us.

"Yes. Pop was the first Sunday school superintendent at our country church, south of Ness City. My sister, Ethel, played the organ and Mama led singing. That's something I miss."

"You don't go anymore?"

"Not since I went on the road. It's hard to go when you don't know a soul."

"I can understand that. You must feel the same too, Elmer." Jen nodded. "All that travel, right?"

"Not really," he mumbled.

"I guess I assumed you—" Jen blinked and cleared her throat. "I shouldn't ask so many questions, now should I?"

Bart grabbed the conversational ball that hung awkwardly in the air. "Elmer, I believe Jen asked if you'd like to play cards. We play ten-point pitch. Would that interest you?"

"Oh, we'd love to, wouldn't we, honey?" I looked at Elmer.

"Certainly."

"That's wonderful!" Jen clapped her hands. "How about this Saturday night?"

"Sure, but Claire's still learning to play. I've been trying to teach her the difference between clubs and spades for three years." Elmer snickered and gave me a sideways glance.

Bart rapped the dashboard. "Then it's settled. Why not join us for supper, say about six? We'll have a good time, and I promise Jen won't pressure you to join the Lutheran church."

Jen lifted a hand to her crimson cheek. "Elmer, I'm sorry. My mouth got to running, and I didn't know how to stop."

Turning his head over his shoulder, Elmer raised his eyebrows in mock dismay. "Think nothing of it. Bart and I will take on you and Claire. Loser slops the hogs."

"Claire, I hope your husband knows how many pigs Bart has." Jen grinned.

Back at the DeBey's house, Bart stuck his hand out. "Shake. This is a good deal for both of us. And remember, you take care of the place and you won't owe us anything. You can move in anytime you want. Lemme get you a key."

We drove back to Glen Elder in silence. Every now and then, I couldn't help but giggle.

"Yeah," Elmer said. "That Jen is a corker."

"It's too bad that house doesn't have two kitchens."

Chapter Seventeen

"Where you been? We've been waiting all day!" Mary Grace's voice cracked the quiet like dentures dropped on a plate.

I ignored her and continued into our apartment. Her bellyaching because we didn't meet their time schedule couldn't kill my good mood.

"I thought you was just going out to get your order. Cawker City is only ten miles, or did you have to go over into the next county? We don't have nothing but a little lard here and nothing to cook with it. What are we supposed to do?"

Whoa, Nellie. I opened my mouth to give her a piece of my mind.

Just then Elmer entered with a box. "Hold on, Mom. We had a good day. A great day, really. Look at these groceries. Something else I want to tell you and Dad. We're leaving the hotel." A barely suppressed smile crossed his face as he waited for their responses.

"But you can't do that," Mary Grace cried. "We don't have no place to go."

Elmer had told me about his mother's fear of practically everything—tornadoes, drought, floods, holdup men posing as women, getting kicked by a horse, snakes, and so on.

I shook my head. They wouldn't be in a continual fix if Will found a job. Always yipping he was too old. If he'd worked and planned like Pop, they could support themselves. Instead, they end up wherever they're dropped off.

Mary Grace waved an indignant finger at the men. "You sit there and nod like you agree with every word. But it goes in one ear and out the other."

I'd heard her get cranked up before so I went out on the porch.

An epiphany hit—that likeable old coot was the problem, not the victim or a bystander. If he'd take charge of his household … But he'd be in for a fight at this stage of the game. Maggie and the five sons were their inheritance. Kids took care of their parents. That's what he had figured on.

I couldn't fathom having to house and feed them the rest of their lives. Through the open door, I heard Elmer announce the DeBeys' offer of the Koster place.

Silence.

Then Mary Grace's voice chastised him for scaring her.

Will rumbled that it'd be nice if he could plant a garden for a change.

Maybe the move would stop their complaining. Me, I was happy to have my own bedroom.

The only downside to the new place was that it would take a pry bar to get them out of there.

⌘ ⌘ ⌘

Bart dropped off paint and brushes two days after we moved into the Koster house. I started painting the interior right away. I guess Will helped. He found a pile of feed sacks in Bart's granary. Mary Grace began braiding a rug for the living room, using the sacks and rags from her perpetual collection. With leftover blue RIT, I dyed extra sacks to cover the orange-crate furniture.

Bart came by later that week, admired Mary Grace's rug, and said he didn't know feed sacks had so many uses. She repeated Bart's words of praise when Elmer returned that evening.

I got irritated at the third telling, but then I realized how starved she must be for appreciation.

Sure enough, she started work on a rug for Bart and Jen.

⌘ ⌘ ⌘

I'd finished washing Elmer's work clothes when I heard the familiar sound of the mail car's muffler. Eleven o'clock on the dot. Will said one could set a watch by that noise. I dropped the shirts and khakis in the rinse and stepped out into the bright sun.

Will barely stirred in the old rocker.

I looked at the Oakland, parked under the hackberry trees. Another aggravation. With no sales in the three months since Bart and Jen's order, Elmer said we better save the car for essentials. The money from the DeBeys had just about dried up. If we went anyplace, we walked.

At the mailbox, I pulled out two letters—one from G.K. and Elsie

Swank and one from Pop. *Glad somebody from Deluxe still remembers us.* I tucked the Swanks' letter in my apron and opened Pop's letter.

Three five-dollar bills!

I glanced toward the porch.

Will and the rocker remained motionless.

I leaned against the mailbox, savoring my private moment. One of Pop's first questions—had I found a church? I could have gone with the DeBeys, but I wouldn't know what to do in a Lutheran church, robes and sacrament and all.

Pop suggested, for the second time, that we visit him for several months. He said the house felt so empty and Elmer could surely get work around Ness City. He'd keep his eyes open anyway. Something would turn up.

> *I won't support that old man and woman, especially since he doesn't seem interested in working.*

A blunt closing from Pop, not that I blamed him. I tucked the money inside my apron pocket before going inside. I handed Elmer the letter from G.K. and Elsie, then showed him the greenbacks.

"We can go into town first thing tomorrow morning to get groceries," he said. "You and Mom make up a list."

"I'll make the list right now." I grabbed a pencil stub and scrap of paper. I didn't need Mary Grace giving advice on how to spend Pop's money.

⌘ ⌘ ⌘

The $15 lasted twenty-seven days, with most going for groceries, $1.40 to Felix for unpaid rent at the Hobart House, ten gallons of reserve gasoline, and half a load of coal for the cook stove.

Except for the seventy-five cents Elmer kept, I had all our money left—two dollars—to buy groceries. I got everything on the list and waited for my change, scarcely breathing. What would I have to put back on the store shelves?

Nothing, and twenty cents change besides. Enough to get a used pair of shoes at the Salvation Army store in Beloit.

I pulled off my scuffed lace-ups and held them to the morning light. The cardboard liners were shot.

Elmer's shoes were just as bad, but not a peep of complaint from him. Not about the limited variety or amount of food, not when a tire blew, and not when he went weeks at a time without a single order.

Politicians and weather were another story.

I sighed. I could put a new liner in my shoes. At least cardboard was cheap.

⌘ ⌘ ⌘

Another cloudless morning. I hurried, hoping to be the first in the kitchen.

Mary Grace already had the coffeepot on the cook stove, re-using coffee grounds for a fourth day.

"Good morning, Mother. It feels chilly. We might have an early fall."

"Yes, it was a cloudy sunset, but nothing but clear sky this morning. Did you get flour, Claire? And did anybody gather eggs last night?"

"The hens have stopped laying. And flour—only if we had a way to grind the wheat."

"My stars! What do we have to eat around here?"

I gave her a blank look. "We've got Bart's cow and she's fresh, so we've got milk."

Her eyes widened. "You mean that's all we have to eat?"

Surprisingly, I remained calm. "We ate the last of the beans last night. Everything else is gone." At last, the folks would have to face facts.

Mary Grace worked the side of her cheek. "So we don't have nothing." She paced the kitchen. "You say there's wheat?"

I pointed out back of the house. "Wheat in the granary. Belongs to Bart and Jen."

"Well, surely they wouldn't mind if we used some of it. How much is out there?"

"Elmer said there must be five hundred bushels."

Mary Grace said nothing but stalked out to the granary.

I followed her and watched as she filled a gallon can full of wheat. She soaked it for an hour in a galvanized bucket half-filled with water. For breakfast, she cooked six cups of the wheat, gingerly pouring milk over it like a wizard concocting a brew. The old gal knew a thing or two.

Will came into the kitchen, his gaze moving from the simmering kettle to us women. Finally he spoke, "I swan to goodness—"

The men sat down to the steaming pot of gruel on the table. Will glanced around, apparently to see if other choices were available on the stove, the wash stand, maybe even on the floor.

Mary Grace spooned a glob into his bowl with a dull splat. "You want milk on it, Dad?" She shoved the pitcher at him.

I told them where the meal came from.

"I expected it might come to something like this." Elmer helped himself and chewed methodically without further comment.

Two cups of the weak coffee followed. Everyone took a portion of the wheat, and we all ate quietly.

Will stirred his serving a full minute before consuming it, then another helping. He wiped the remnants from his mustache and finished with a glass of milk.

My stomach felt full, yet I still possessed a desire for pastry, meat, fruit, anything different.

Afterward, I asked Elmer what his plans were for the day.

He rubbed four days' stubble on his face. "Car won't start. Battery's dead. I didn't want to fiddle with the tires now, so yesterday I blocked the car up. We can get along without it. It's three miles into Cawker, but yeah, I'll walk in again."

"Did you eat enough?" I didn't say that cold wheat mash was all we had for lunch.

Defeat lined his face.

It brought tears to my eyes. I glided to his chair and pulled him to me.

He touched my face, lingering the slightest, then stood and went outside. For a long while, he stood on the porch and simply gazed at the eloquent but empty sky.

⌘ ⌘ ⌘

We repeated the milk and wheat menu three times the next day, and the next. The lack of variety was somewhat offset by the quantity. I expected Elmer to resist against us taking Bart's wheat. When he didn't, I asked, "Shouldn't we ask Bart if it's all right to use his wheat?"

"If we say anything, they'll know we're out of food. Then we'll be a charity case. The very thought disgusts me."

"I guess you're right. They're such decent people. I don't think of them as landlords but as friends. It's just that, well, we're taking what belongs to them. Do you think they'd mind, if they knew?"

"No. It's hardly anything, and it's not like we're robbing them. Remember, Bart wanted to pay *us* to watch the place." His tone softened. "I don't like to take without asking. But we can't bring it up. Not now anyway. What little we use won't be missed. If Bart knew we didn't have two nickels to rub together, he'd be over here with a side of beef. We can't have that."

"I suppose so. I guess we can figure out how to make do."

"We'll take care of ourselves. I'll shave and clean up—go into Cawker tomorrow and nose around to see if I can flush out something. We won't have to do this long."

The next morning after breakfast, Elmer prepared to hike into Cawker City.

I tied a pint of the cooked wheat in a double muslin bag. "At least it's something," I said.

He only nodded.

ELMER

Claire's hug still warmed my arms. I slipped the bag of wheat into my pocket and hastened my pace. Not that I was expecting much by going into Cawker, but I had to do it. If Claire had tried to talk about anything after kissing me good-bye, I'd have gone haywire.

Wise people say that doing without is supposed to build character. I could do with a little less character, myself.

Once in town, I roamed the streets like a lost hound, eyes open for anyone needing hired muscles. Hardly anybody was out and about, and those I saw kept their heads down. They seemed to signal their own lack of goods or money, as if saying, "Don't ask. Let me be. I've got nothing you need." Those who looked prosperous—a well-fed look, decent clothes, a sack of goods in the crook of their arm—they avoided eye contact or conversation. I knew better than to talk with another man; likely as not he'd hit me up for change, a smoke, maybe a place to stay.

I rounded a corner and nearly bowled over a scruffy figure propped against an unpainted door.

The man grunted as I jerked back. His gaunt stare hit me, a hot poker laid against my cheek. He looked pale, maybe Irish. Grimy pants and bits of grass still on his shirt. The raggedy coat bunched around his shoulders looked like it'd been cut from a canvas tarp.

I closed my eyes and headed out of there.

Right away, I hated myself.

I stopped, swallowed hard, and turned toward the now-expectant face. "Hey. I wish I had something for you."

"Aye, I wish ye did too, mate." His voice sounded barren, even separate from the body, as if its fifty or so years had used up all energy to get to that moment in time.

My teeth worked at my lower lip. Something compelled me to reach for the man's arm, to connect. Maybe to let him know I accepted him as another member of the human species. As soon as I touched his coat, I almost threw up.

His arm was fleshless, little more than a stick of bone in a sleeve. Yet this was a man, struggling to get through that day in hopes that the next would be better. A man the same as me.

Somehow, I knew this old derelict was alone.

The man's eyes, now alive with blue and wide in surprise, stared at me.

My left hand felt the bulge in my pocket—the packet of wheat. I didn't dwell on my needs. I pulled out the muslin sack and thrust it at him.

His long fingers, nails rimmed with dirt, reached out like a hawk's claws to get at the bag.

I backed away, overcome by a sense of unworthiness. Shame washed over me. How could I watch another human honor what I'd taken for granted? I dropped my eyes, aware only of a cry like that of a small animal. I turned and stumbled back the way I'd come. I got as far as the nearest corner, and then I pushed my face into the crook of my arm, bawling like a baby. I couldn't stop blubbering against that cold brick wall.

Everything, the way we were, the folks ... no matter. I was better off than this man.

I didn't care if anyone saw me. I swiped a sleeve across my face and started back home. The wind had quit. All I could hear was the scuff of my shoes. Louder still, my mind registered the scuffling of his fingers to open and devour the contents of that muslin bag.

CLAIRE

Elmer waved me off when he first got home, but the story of the Irishman soon spilled out. At supper, he silently joined the rest of us for the wheat porridge. Afterward, I went out on the front porch with him. Together we watched the sun paint the thin clouds that stood high above the dry earth.

For two more weeks, wheat and milk was the only choice in our house. Mealtime became a ritual. Elmer sometimes joked about it, which irritated his mother. Usually, we ate as if in a race to get it over with, then spent a half hour to nurse our cups of dishwater coffee. Our hardship brought a surprising closeness among us. Even as I resented it, it seemed very precious.

One quiet evening, Will spotted a cottontail rabbit near the windmill. He rushed into the house for Elmer's .22 caliber rifle. Two shots cracked out, and that evening we had a break from the gruel. For several evenings thereafter, Will patrolled nearby roadsides. He found a skunk, but we weren't that desperate. The coyotes and drought had cleaned out everything else.

Over the next three weeks, Elmer walked into Cawker City several times to look for work. Once, he got two dollars and a sparse lunch for re-building fifty yards of picket fence. Every time he returned from his trip into town, he sought my face and told me how important it was to see me waiting for him at the door. He couldn't get the Irishman out of his mind. The derelict probably had no one to care whether he lived or died.

A month of the wheat and milk diet. I told Elmer we ought to keep an eye on his folks. Who could know, this strange diet might drive them to some wasting disease? Aside from a common grumpiness, they appeared as alert as ever. Five weeks of the wheat and milk fare stretched to six. The infrequent stop by Remus, the mailman, was our only contact with the outside world.

Bart and Jen hadn't stopped by in over a month. Perhaps they'd found others to play cards with.

One evening after Mary Grace and I had cleared the table, Will stood up. He'd been fidgeting all evening. "Anybody wonder where I was all day?" He paused a beat. "Well, I guess I wasn't missed. But I'll tell you anyway. I noticed a Diamond T truck headed for town so I told Mom I'd catch a ride."

"You hitched a ride, Dad?" Was he getting addled from the food?

"I did, and the fellow took me near into Glen Elder. Young man from Iowa drivin' truck to haul pigs for that big farmer outside of town. This farmer heard Roosterbelt is gonna raise hog prices by makin' farmers kill their pigs. Can you believe that? That's what this boy told me. Anyways, he said I could hitch a ride on his way home too, and that's what I done."

Elmer grinned. "I'm impressed, Dad. You heading to California with the rest of them?"

Will snorted. "You ain't heard all my story. I went to city hall and asked Irma, the old-maid recorder, if I could use their telephone to place a collect call."

Mary Grace looked impatient. "Ain't nobody taking a collect call from you."

"Earl would." He met her gaze and held it.

"You're lying. Earl don't have a telephone and we all know it," she said.

"Well, for your information, I called the shop where Earl gets work, and *they've* got a telephone."

It pleased me to see Will stand up to his wife for a change.

"So you called." Elmer leaned back, hands behind his head. "You talk to Earl?"

"And why call him?" I asked.

"Listen, and I'll tell you how I done it. No, Earl wasn't there. Mom, you didn't know this but, back in Tulsa, me and Winfield, the foreman, we was like this." He raised his crossed fingers. "He agreed to get ahold of Earl. I left the city hall number for Earl to call back. I waited around, talking with Irma—she's got kin back in Kentucky. Earl called back and ... Let me say first—" He turned to me. "I don't want you to think poorly of me, Claire, but I asked Earl to come get us 'cause, I've got to admit, we've been eating this wheat mash for a long time."

I couldn't help but smile. "I understand. It has been a long time."

He seemed to lose some of his fire. "Yeah, Claire. It ain't that we don't appreciate you putting us up. I been ... I been having troubles with my elimination lately."

Mary Grace snorted. "You believe everything Effie told you she learnt from that quack in Kansas City. Every time you pass gas, you think it's an ulcer or a stroke."

"Ain't so," he retorted. "You know you've had enough of that wheat mash yourself."

Elmer laughed. "Dad, I'll put a bag of mash in your suitcase so you won't miss it."

"So when's Earl coming to get you?" I said.

"Day after tomorrow." He glanced at Elmer. "If you got any gas for his car, that'd help."

"Might be some out of our reserve." Elmer stood. "So you're leaving us? Well, tonight you and Mom sort out your things. Earl won't wait around. We'll start packing after breakfast."

Morning ignited a hunt for boxes, twine, and misplaced keepsakes. Progress hit a snag when Will hefted the latest braided rug. "No way this'll fit in Earl's Plymouth. We'll have to leave it here for the next time we come to see you, Claire."

"No. You'll need to take everything you want to keep," I said. "We don't know how long we'll be here. If we move, we can't take that big thing."

Mary Grace screeched in from their bedroom. "We're not leaving my rug. Will, don't just stand there—help." She dropped to her knees and began to roll the rug, puffing and pushing.

"Ain't gonna fit, Mother," Will said. "Look how big a wad that makes. Can't put it inside or it'll hang out the window like a bull's tail. Best to tie it on top of the car."

"Not my rug." She stood, arms akimbo. "For the time I spent on it, it's going inside."

Elmer waved his hands as if parting the Red Sea. "Whoa, it'll be safe on top. Earl will make sure." He sent me a cautionary look and raised his voice. "Mom, get all your things from the bedroom. What about your kitchen stuff? Anything in the attic?"

The search for stray belongings defused the anguish over the rug. By day's end, all the boxes had been filled, tied, untied, emptied, re-packed, and re-tied per Mary Grace's instructions.

Earl arrived mid-morning the next day and we had his car full by noon. Elmer asked him to check the Oakland. Earl gave it a tune-up and, after a jump to his battery, he got it started. He prioritized repairs on a box top and shook his head as he handed it to Elmer. "Get those brakes done before you run into somebody. Valves and the rest as soon as you can. Hope you're not stuck here."

Elmer and I watched the Plymouth chug out of the driveway, the folks wedged amongst their worldly goods, the rug tied on top. They'd surely be back, escaping some future affliction. Earl usually found enough car repair work to pay bills. He could afford to put them up for a while. Assuming he got Mae settled down.

We sat on the porch and talked out our options. There weren't many. California? Not a chance. Elmer said I could go stay with family and he'd do something, but what? He'd lost all faith in Uncle Joe's rosy assessment of northern Kansas. With the Oakland doubtful, talk of relocating elsewhere seemed like a joke.

"No matter what, we won't starve like that Irishman." Elmer didn't speak with much conviction.

Chapter Eighteen

I had entered the granary to restock our supply of wheat when I heard a bump. Maybe the wind. I hoisted the gallon bucket, half full of grain, and turned to go.

A figure stood silhouetted in the rectangle of light.

My breath caught in my throat. I squinted to make out who it was.

A familiar voice called out, "Claire. You're here. I thought—"

I exhaled. "Jen! You scared me half to death. I didn't know who was …"

Jen DeBey moved inside as she pulled the scarf from her head. "I'm sorry. Didn't mean to startle you. I hadn't seen you for a spell. Decided to take a break and come visit. How are you and Elmer and the folks? Whatcha doing here—"

I stammered and set the bucket down, hands waving as if they might help me to manufacture an explanation. "I'm … Oh, Jen, I'm taking your wheat." My voice slid into a bog of shame.

"Wheat? Claire, you can have all the wheat you need for those old hens. We don't mind."

I lifted my head. "Forgive me. I have to tell you. We took the wheat for ourselves—to eat. Jen, we took it without asking." I chirped a weak laugh.

"You've been eating wheat?" Jen stared at me. "Why've you …? Oh, Claire, Claire! *I'm* the one who should be ashamed for not checking on *you*."

"We didn't want to ask. We knew you'd give us something, so we ended up taking—"

"And we would have given you—"

"No. We can't have you treat us like charity."

"Claire. You're *people*. Oh, I feel awful. You needed it. You *should've* taken it." She laid her hand on my arm. "Let's do this. Let's have you come help me. I'll tell Bart and that's what you can tell Elmer. Then, I'll see that you get a few things."

The next day, I had just posted a letter to Pop when a column of dust rose in the distance.

Bart's pickup.

I waited beside the rusted mailbox.

Bart's big grin shone through the windshield as he rolled to a stop and cut the engine. "Hi, Claire! How you folks doing?"

"We're fine. Elmer's folks went back to Tulsa early in the week. Kind of quiet now. How about some coffee?" Hated to offer our brew. It tasted like cow-track water.

"They're gone? Sorry I didn't get to say good-bye to Will, and Mary Grace too. What with maize harvest and Jen's family visiting, we plumb forgot our friends. I did notice you been staying closer to the place. Not trying to be nosy, but thought I'd check on you."

Jen hadn't told him anything, then. I tried to sound upbeat. "You don't miss a thing, Bart. Sales, well, nobody's buying, so we're doing some … other things. Glad you stopped by."

He started the pickup. "Sorry about that. Can't take time for coffee. I'm going into town. We're butchering a shoat tomorrow. Jen said I better get to the bank before Roosevelt shuts it down. Another reason I came over was to ask if you had time to give her a hand with rendering lard and putting up the meat."

"Oh, I'd be glad to." *Don't sound too eager.* "What time?"

"Jen said about seven thirty. Frosted last night, so heat shouldn't be a problem. We can get him cut up in a good day's work. Is that okay for you?"

"I'll be there. I can help all day, if she'd like."

"Expect we'll need that. I better go. Tell Elmer we need to get together again for pitch. We'll beat you girls next time." A wave and he was off.

Oh, God, thank you. I'd get two meals out of the deal.

Jen dropped a silver dollar in my apron pocket once when I had helped her before.

Elmer had snagged a one-day job at the creamery, so he'd walk to Cawker City about the same time I went to the DeBeys. Hopefully, he'd finish in time to eat supper with us.

⌘ ⌘ ⌘

A meadowlark trilled as I set out. Fencepost shadows striped the road ahead and diamonds of frost sparkled in the sun. I sang "Red Wing," "Swanee River," and "America the Beautiful." So long since I'd sung anything. I got through "Amazing Grace" twice before I walked through Bart and Jen's front gate.

The old collie barked and waddled out to greet me.

Bart and his school-age boy, Johnny, worked beneath a crossbeam secured between two cottonwoods. The pig carcass hung from the beam, glistening entrails flowing into a cut-off oil drum.

Jen came from the house, set down two steaming buckets of water, and hurried toward me with a big smile. "Oh, Claire, you walked all that way? Elmer too busy? We could've picked you up."

"Yes, he's working today at the creamery. It's such a beautiful morning. I didn't mind walking. Besides, we don't drive the car much."

"I understand." Jen glanced toward the cottonwoods. "Let me get this hot water to Bart. There're cinnamon rolls on the kitchen table. Help yourself. We'll be busy, but we'll have fun."

Cinnamon rolls. The thought made my mouth water. I wiped my lips and hurried toward the house. I burst into the familiar kitchen and groped for the table in the dim interior.

Sugar and cinnamon glazed the mounds of dough, which glistened in the dreamy light like jewels.

I swooped a spatula into the soft dough and lifted it to my mouth. I tried to savor each bite but was overcome by desire. Too much. I coughed and caught my breath. It tasted so good I almost wept. I wiped my face as Jen came in.

She gave me two buckets to fill from the boiler. We must have carried twenty buckets of hot water out to a rectangular wooden vat.

Bart lowered the carcass into the trough and began scraping off the hide.

Jen had pots, pans, a meat grinder, bone saw, and knives set out. We began our work of dividing the meat. Hams, chops, and bacon went into a scrubbed wheelbarrow, which I pushed to the meat house—for curing with Bart's "old family recipe." Extra fat went back to the kitchen to re-heat on the stove. As soon as it went jelly soft, we poured off the lard and set it aside. Thankfully, an occasional breeze through the windows cooled my face and the nape of my neck.

168

As we worked, Jen entertained me with tales about her in-laws, and I shared stories of our days on the road with Deluxe.

Suddenly weak, I sat. Effects of the wheat and milk diet, I supposed. I thought of Elmer, working alone, with only the wheat mash to eat.

Jen put me to work at the big six-burner Wedgewood gas stove. The fat sizzled and popped, stung my arms. It'd been months since I'd had tasty meat in front of me. I pictured it on our table. To awaken any morning and choose pork chops, gravy, bacon, biscuits, eggs … I closed my mind to the savory smell. Otherwise, I'd have stuffed a wad of it in my mouth, then and there.

Bart came in for a water jug. "You gals gonna have this meat put up by evening?"

Jen looked at him with mock amazement. "Surely you don't doubt us. If you get the rest of that pig in here so we can make sausage, we'll be drinking tea on the porch before you're done."

"Glad to hear it." He smiled at me. "What's Elmer up to?"

"He's working at the creamery in Cawker. But he'll stop by to walk me home."

"He's not driving the car?"

"No. We need to save expenses, so we're not using it much."

"I guess lots of folks have stopped driving." He squinted. "You in that kind of pinch too?"

"Well, we decided that since sales are slow, we, uh, better not drive more than we need to."

He and Jen glanced at one another. Then he went back outside.

Jen and I spent the next two hours grinding sausage. I formed patties and put them in Mason jars. I topped off the sausage with lard and then sealed each jar.

Jen heated another pot of grease, and together we began a donut-making operation, just like Mama and I did when Pop butchered. Pop had said he used everything but the squeal.

It was nearly dark when Bart and Johnny came in to eat. I could only think of how weak Elmer must be. Trembling seized me. I was sure Jen would put the food away any moment. I debated asking her to make a plate for Elmer.

No, that would never do. Maybe, if I dawdled a little, we'd still be at the table when Elmer arrived. I jumped up to serve coffee. A glance out the window lent no sight of my man. Back to the table to finish eating. I washed the dishes and scrubbed the cutting board as Jen and Bart checked on the meat.

Jen swept in from the meat house. "Oh, I was going to do the dishes." She peered outside. "Is that Elmer coming up the road? He looks like the wind is going to blow him away."

Heedless of my dripping hands, I rushed to the door. "Oh, he's coming! He's here!"

Bart poked his head into the kitchen. "Wow. I wish Jen would be that excited when I return from a day's work."

I froze, embarrassed. "Well, he's coming. We didn't get to, uh, talk this morning."

Jen reached up and clasped Bart's lower lip between her finger and thumb, puckering it ridiculously. "Bart, will you be nice? And I am excited to see you ... when you behave."

Elmer, hat cupped against the wind, carried a large sack over his shoulder. He reached the lee of the house and looked up. His face was streaked with dirt where his eyes had teared from the lash of the wind.

Jen followed me out the front door. "Elmer, you poor thing! Come in and wash up. I saved you biscuits and pork chops. I'll bet you'd like a piece of pie too." She waved him inside.

He plopped the gunnysack inside the door and hugged me to him. "Sounds good, Jen. Smells great in here!" He gestured toward the sack. "Sal, I got a silver dollar and forty pounds of spuds for washing about two hundred cream cans."

I got him a towel and watched as he cleaned up.

God hadn't forgotten us.

Swallowing hard, I squeezed his shoulder. "I'll be back in a bit. Jen said to eat all you want." I cleaned every inch of the kitchen while Elmer ate the first decent meal he'd had in months.

Afterward, Bart drove us back to the Koster place. Before he left, he pulled a large sack from the trunk. Jen had given us "a few extra things from supper."

I laid the assortment on the table and wiped away tears, then I giggled.

Elmer slumped into a chair. "For Bible-thumpers, Bart and Jen are mighty decent people."

⌘ ⌘ ⌘

Gravel crunched.

I peered outside.

A blue Plymouth? My brother!

"Elmer, it's Myrrl! There's others with him!" I hurried out the front door. "Pop!" I buried my face against his shoulder, my tears staining his neatly pressed shirt.

"There, there, babe, it's all right. Your last letter kind of got to me, so … And there's Elmer." One arm around me, he extended his other arm to shake Elmer's hand.

My father's face never seemed more precious. Myrrl and Grace joined us and caught Elmer in our five-person hug.

He squirmed to get away.

Too bad. He'd just have to endure it.

Myrrl waved us to the back of the pickup. "We got something for you. Remember that red steer I said kept getting out? Well, there's a quarter of him."

"Elmer, you've got a place to keep this meat cool, don't you?" Pop said. "Some you should eat pretty soon but we've cured most of it."

Elmer hesitated. "Yes, we have a cellar."

"I'll go open it up." I grabbed a lantern off the porch and hurried around the house before anyone could follow and see the cellar's emptiness.

Grace's voice came behind me.

Too late.

I opened the inclined door, lit the lantern, and descended into the gloom. I hadn't entered the cellar since Bart showed us the place but knew it would be orderly. I'd grabbed a stick on my way in to swipe at the mass of spider webs which draped the passageway.

Grace stepped down behind me. "You don't use your cellar much, do you?"

"Well, there's plenty of room … and it's secure, if that's what you mean."

"No, Claire, I'm sure it's a good cellar. But you don't use it much, do you?"

"Yes, that's right, we don't use it much." I looked up at my sister-

171

in-law.

She moved down two steps and put her arm around me.

Both of us began to cry, like two mourning doves.

I blew my nose. "Thanks for coming, for all you brought. But we have to get this wiped down before the men bring the meat."

Pop made a point of checking the cellar afterward. He never missed a thing. He saw the only food in it was the meat we'd just stored.

As Grace and I prepared dinner, I breathed thanks that Jen had included lard, eggs, bacon, and seasonings with her sack of "a few extra things." Our neediness wasn't so obvious. With the potatoes, and some canned goods Grace brought, we had a delightful meal.

We walked our visitors around the place. Will's garden was reduced to a latticework of sticks and twine choked with tumbleweeds. Aside from stark trees, the windblown yard was little more than a few patches of dried buffalo grass. The windmill clanked as the wind shifted and two bobwhites' wings tattooed into the air. They'd come to drink where the wind had whipped the water out of the stock tank. Seven red hens and a solitary rooster clucked about the visitors, and Bart's Guernsey stared at us through the barbed wire fence.

"Are your hens laying?" Pop asked.

"Bart's hens, but the eggs are ours. Lately, we haven't been getting any eggs."

Myrrl said he'd bring a few of his pullets next trip.

We looped around the house to sit on the porch in the fall sunlight. The Oakland, parked by the hackberry trees, marked the right side of the front yard. Dead elms, limbs cut off for firewood, stood opposite like ghosts. Ridges of dust lay on the leeward running board of the car and window moldings, and the right rear wheel was blocked up.

Pop glanced at the Oakland.

I knew what he was thinking.

Finally he spoke, with a few polite questions about the DeBeys, which I'd already covered in my letters. Elmer explained how we'd met Bart and Jen. I chimed in that we'd helped them on butchering day. My excuse that "we'd just run out of coffee, and I'd neglected to get it at the store" prompted Grace to disappear into the kitchen. She said she had a box of tea leaves.

The three men offered their observations about the weather, near-Sahara conditions for nearly three years.

Pop asked, "Elmer, how long do you figure to stay here in Mitchell County?"

Elmer tensed up. He knew as well as I did where this was going. "Hard to say. I'd go back to Kansas City if we could make a living, but my cousin Smiley said the town is one big unemployment line."

"Anything holding you here?"

Elmer rediscovered his pipe and inspected it as if it were a laboratory instrument. Finally he gestured at the Oakland. "I need to spend some time on the car before we go anyplace." He spoke as if time was the only issue. "Another thing, we can't pick up and leave without giving reasonable notice. They don't charge rent, but they depend on us to look after the place."

"So they're not paying you, except for free rent."

Myrrl stood. "I'll help Grace with the tea." He hurried into the house.

Elmer watched Myrrl leave. "That's right. No money to us. Cash is scarce. Most people barter for what they need." His voice signaled frustration.

"It's been awfully quiet at my place." Pop's voice grew husky. "I don't think I'll ever get used to living without Lilly."

Elmer remained silent.

Pop cocked his head, thumbs hooked behind his blue suspenders. "I'd welcome having you and Claire visit. Whenever it suits you. And for as long as you'd like, several months or more. What with winter coming on, you could use it as a base till you get your feet on the ground. I know what it's like to work yourself to a nub and get nothing for your sweat. I was fifteen when I was kicked out—completely on my own. No one gave me a nickel. You're working hard, doing your best. But these are hard times. Very hard times."

The two men had been talking as if I wasn't there, but it didn't offend me. They both understood Elmer's pride. This had to be his decision.

Myrrl and Grace reappeared, bearing a pasteboard box with cups, condiments, and a pot of tea.

As Grace poured, Pop leaned toward Elmer. "Remember. Whenever, as long as you like." He took a sip and grinned. "My compliments to the tea makers. Nice tray too."

I tried to seem nonchalant about Pop's offer.

Elmer knew Pop had the situation pegged. Jen had said she might need me one or two more times to help with canning. No way would that keep us afloat. We needed something a lot bigger to happen.

My family stayed the night and prepared to return to Ness the next morning. After breakfast, Pop slipped me two bills—*forty dollars*. Before they loaded into the pickup, another round of hugs caught Elmer off guard again.

As they left, the wind came up and a dull cloud of blowing dust drove us inside. Elmer talked about everything but Pop's offer.

I couldn't stand it any longer. "What do you think about what Pop said?"

"He's making himself open to criticism from your brothers if we were to stay several months. I won't let it go that long. I can't stand the thought of depending on another man's charity. Even from your father. He's an okay guy. Can't say that about Gar."

⌘ ⌘ ⌘

Three weeks later, we invited Bart and Jen over for supper, courtesy of the red steer. We played pitch until well past two in the morning.

The DeBeys came again two days later. By then, the Oakland was packed and Elmer had repaired the brakes, put on a new tire, and replaced the battery. Both Jen and I had our hankies out.

As Elmer got in the car, Bart touched his elbow. They locked hands and eyes.

Jen hugged us both. "We're going to miss you so much."

I could see Jen, still waving her hankie until the Oakland dropped over the first hill west of the Koster place. We spent that night in Phillipsburg with Uncle Joe, and then drove south the following morning toward Ness City.

I almost couldn't stop smiling. Back home was the only place to keep Elmer's folks from being part of our baggage. Such a relief, and maybe, just maybe, it would last. If we were in Ness City even a month, Elmer would see my family in a different light. They'd respect his beliefs. They weren't religious fanatics like his first wife.

Elmer had made it clear he didn't want a big commotion when we arrived at Pop's. Said it was bad enough we had to come in like beggars. "Your brothers will be watching to see if I'm out to fleece the family."

"Not Myrrl," I said. "He's not that kind of man. Remember, he's the one who brought that quarter of beef for us."

"Maybe so, but there'll be others watching to see if we plan to stay forever."

"Pop said we could stay as long as we wanted. Why do you have to be so suspicious?"

"Because of the way you've acted about my folks living with us." Elmer gave me a sharp look. "I'd feel a lot better if I could carry my own water. You sit too long at another man's table, you soon forget you have to work for yourself."

⌘ ⌘ ⌘

The smell of pancakes and sausages greeted us as we came downstairs the third morning after our arrival. Like every day since we'd arrived at Pop's house, he practically fell over himself to make us feel welcome. It was heavenly not to worry where our next meal was coming from, but Elmer was concerned about appearances. Like Mama.

I'd never before thought of the similarity.

"Help yourself to more toast and potatoes, Elmer. There's plenty." Pop rose to refill our cups with steaming coffee.

Morning light burnished the oak table, laden with enough food for a week.

Pop looked at Elmer. "You have plans for today?"

"Thought I'd look for work but no one's hiring." Elmer tossed the Hutchinson newspaper aside. "I need to work on the car. Any particular place you'd like me to park it?"

"There's room in the garage, and feel free to use my tools. I'll see Brian Fitzgerald today. He'll know if anyone is looking for a hand." Pop sipped his coffee and without looking at either of us, said, "You're welcome to join me for church tomorrow. I could come back for you after Sunday school. That way, you might avoid Matilda." He grinned.

Elmer said, "The garage would be best as I need to block it up several days."

I smoothed Elmer's hair as I stood behind him. "I'll go with you tomorrow, Pop. I'll be ready and waiting at ten forty-five." As I cleared the table, I mentally counted how long it'd been since I'd been in any church.

⌘ ⌘ ⌘

I would've preferred a back pew, but Pop, as Sunday school superintendent, had to give his report, and that meant sitting up front. I cringed at the customary welcoming of visitors. My departure from Ness nearly four years before had been little short of a disaster, and I expected sly remarks from the less charitable attendees, within earshot of others, of course.

A heavyset dowager with a fixed smile clenched my hand as we entered the narthex. "Well, if it isn't your youngest, Samuel." She rambled into a story about her cousin and a frazzled redhead with three urchins needing assistance.

I pried my hand loose and waved at Pop to go ahead—I'd escape to the ladies' room. Most females needed at least five minutes to take care of business. I took fifteen, then paused before entering the sanctuary.

Pastor Lewis introduced the call to worship.

As the congregation stood, I hurried down a side aisle and slid in beside Pop. The hymns swept over me in a blissful wash of memories.

Pastor Lewis typically scanned his notes during the singing and therefore didn't see me until halfway through his sermon. He stopped in mid-sentence, coughed, and announced that Claire, Sam and Lillian's youngest, was a visitor that fine morning.

So much for an unnoticed entrance.

No one mentioned the chaos of my hasty marriage and the abrupt closure of the beauty shop. Matilda, of course, made a beeline for me after the benediction, and I spent the next fifteen minutes trying to gloss over our extended captivity in Mitchell County. She'd get her story for the grapevine eventually, unless I avoided church altogether.

⌘ ⌘ ⌘

Elmer spent that first week repairing the Oakland. Pop talked with

176

Brian Fitzgerald several times, but there were no jobs anywhere. After that, when Myrrl invited him out to the farm, Elmer jumped at this opportunity to pay Myrrl back for that quarter of beef with some labor.

I divided time with Pop and catching up with Helen Schweitzer.

Elmer stayed overnight at the farm. To save gas and time, he said. Maybe he felt Myrrl was less of a threat to his comfort level than Pop and his Bible.

Pop and I spent several afternoons together studying God's Word. My frustration at not understanding it increased until Pop took me into the book of John.

Jesus the man, the person, became real, even caring. Not simply as a spectacular healer and preacher—which I always took with a grain of salt—but as someone I wanted to know.

Still, how had Mary, one of Lazarus's sisters, always sat around listening to Jesus?

As Pop read their story, I interrupted. "I guess I'm more like the other sister, like Martha. She kept the place going, preparing the meals and cleaning house."

"Both did important things," Pop said. "We do what's most important at the time. Mary let the housework go so she could talk with Jesus while he was there. Remember that other verse we read? 'That ye love one another, as I have loved you.' It's better to show love and be with your friend than to scrub floors, don't you think?"

"But the house needs to be clean. Can't we do both?"

"Perhaps. If we have the choice. However, we can always clean the house later, but we better spend time with Jesus while he's available. He puts love and listening ahead of doing the chores." Pop sat back. "What relationship means the most to you, my daughter?"

"Well, being with Elmer. But it seems like ... like *his parents* are more important to him. I don't think that's right."

"That's probably because he doesn't understand what God's Word has to say about marriage. Let's see ..." Pop turned to the front of his Bible. "In Genesis, chapter two, it says, 'A man shall leave his father and his mother, and shall cleave unto his wife.'"

I shook my head. " What does 'cleave' mean?"

"'Be one flesh.' See there." He pointed. "The two persons are to become one body. First, they must *leave* their parents. That allows them to cleave. Can't cleave if you don't leave."

"Leave? How far?"

Pop laughed. "It's not a matter of distance. It means to leave the security of belonging to your parents and commit yourself to the love and well-being of your husband."

"Isn't he supposed to do the same for me?"

"Yes, but since Elmer doesn't look to God for guidance, this idea will be strange to him. That's probably why you're having problems."

"Oh, Pop, he won't read the Bible."

"Then ask God to help you." Pop smiled, a faraway look in his eyes. "Start by making sure *your* heart is right, so you can do the right thing, God's thing, at the right time. It's called listening to God's Spirit. Listen, and he'll tell you. Through circumstances, a word, a sense of rightness—confirmed perhaps by other sources—he'll let you know. I've found that to be true."

⌘ ⌘ ⌘

We'd been with Pop less than a month when I realized it wouldn't last. Elmer was cordial to my kin, but I saw something in his heart.

Shame.

Moving in with Pop meant Elmer couldn't handle life on his own. I read it in his eyes, in the clipped conversations with family, and sometimes with me. My complaints about his folks probably echoed in his mind, adding fuel to the fire.

I tried to dismiss the thought. Pride should take a backseat to reality. Lots of people were in the same boat.

But Elmer wasn't "lots of people." He was proud that he'd always made it on his own. His self-sufficiency had impressed me from the beginning. Top sales manager with Deluxe, then going on our own in KC when slow sales forced us from the Deluxe crew.

Mitchell County simply relocated the setting for failure. Those hellish months of denial peeled away Elmer's belief in himself, layer by layer. To him, one truth probably remained—he couldn't provide for his wife. Maybe he was no better than his father, the career freeloader.

I couldn't talk about what I now understood.

Elmer was too fragile, too vulnerable. He hadn't fallen into a

raging fit or jumped off a high building like others did back in '29.
But I wondered how close he might be to that very thing.

Chapter Nineteen

I looked up from the ironing board as Pop came in.

He waved an envelope. "Somebody knows you're here. Letter for Elmer, postmarked Liberal."

I set down the iron and scanned the inscription. "From his sister. He said he wrote her. I'll give it to him when he comes in from the farm."

Pop gazed out the window. "Saw Brian Fitzgerald at the post office. No work possibilities yet, but he'll try his uncle over at Bazine."

"Nothing in town?"

"These things don't happen overnight. I hope Elmer will give it time. I'm glad I can have you around. And not only because you iron my shirts and bake biscuits like your mother." He grinned and patted my arm.

⌘ ⌘ ⌘

I handed Elmer the letter.

He dropped into a wicker chair on the front porch and sliced the envelope with his pocket knife. "Let's see if Maggie has anything."

I sat, waiting for him to read aloud. Only the rustle of paper and the rattle of cottonwood leaves next door reached my ear. I couldn't stand it. "Elmer!"

He glanced at me and tucked the sheets in his breast pocket. "Let's go over to the park."

We settled on a bench next to a broken teeter-totter.

He flourished the letter, and I peered over his shoulder. He laughed and jerked the pages away. "What are you doing, Sal? She's got some personal stuff in here. You sit still, and I'll read it to you."

I jabbed him in the ribs. "All right, get to reading."

He scanned down the first page and began. "'I want you and Claire to visit me in Liberal. I'm dying to meet her. Here you been married over four years, and I've never met your wife! She must be a

180

saint, to put up with you.'"

I snickered.

He frowned in mock anger. "'Liberal isn't much, compared to the places you've been, but it's the biggest town in this windblown part of the world. In case you haven't heard—Mac is gone for good, so I'm raising the kids by myself. It's no cakewalk, but I bake pies for a local café, and we're making it. I've got more money now that it doesn't go for booze. The kids need a dad, though.'"

Poor kids.

"'You can have the bedroom. I'll sleep on the couch. It's probably not as fancy as your father-in-law's place, but this'll be our first chance to talk in years. Haven't heard from Mom in two months. Guess her and Dad are with Earl. Last time the folks went to stay with John and Moselle, John brought them up here the very next day, but Mac was rip-roaring drunk and ran them off. Wouldn't let them out of the car. Maybe the best thing he ever did for me.'" Elmer paused, as if maybe he was recalling events that he'd never mentioned to me. "'About your last request—my neighbor has something you'll surely be interested in. Make sure you bring that wife with you.'" He folded the letter and tucked it away. "Maggie always did a sorry job in picking men, and Dick MacLaren was surely the sorriest."

"She was married before?"

"No, but she was no match for any sweet-talking cowboy with a hard-luck story."

"What's this about 'your last request'? What did you ask her?" I searched his eyes.

"I told her to let me know if there might be a farm for rent down there."

"You think that's what she meant? Does she know we don't have any money?"

"Sal, you should know by now that you don't always have to have money to make a deal. That's why I want to see what she's got." His voice took an unmistakable cadence.

"You mean to go there? Why not write her again? Find out before we go."

He cored the bowl of his pipe and rapped it on the bench. "Maggie's got possibilities. We've got nothing here."

"We've got plenty to eat and a wonderful place to live. We practically starved for months until we came here. Pop loves having us, and no one is pushing us to leave."

"Can't make a living in this town. Your dad has nosed down every rabbit trail, and he hasn't come up with a sniff. At least Maggie's onto something."

"Elmer! We can't drop in on a single woman with little kids. I don't want to go through more of what we——"

"We're done with that. Put it in the past, where it belongs."

"Remember, we couldn't afford to put gas in the car, much less food on the table."

"We've talked about this before. I haven't changed my mind. We need to make it on our own." He spanked each word, as if that would cancel any argument I might have.

Just like always, and I don't get a say in it. "Elmer, you don't care what I want. It's always got to be your way." I took a deep breath. If I threatened that he should go without me, he might. I wasn't ready to let that happen. "Okay, do it your way."

Elmer gentled his voice. "Look, I appreciate what your dad has done, but we're the ones who have to make it."

"He's going to miss us so much."

"Do you want to tell him, or do you want me to?"

"Aw, honey, you know Pop'll be hurt. He really went out of his way to help us."

"I know that. But I didn't expect him to start a rescue mission explicitly for us."

"He cares for us! We're family. He's not trying to set us up on welfare." I glared at him. "Can't we give more time here? Don't you trust anybody? Why are you so dead set against getting any help from *my* family—really, from Pop? And besides, I don't want to leave."

"Hold your horses! You're way off base." He stood and leaned toward me, his foot on the bench. "It's not a matter of trust. I'm not against your family, for crying out loud. It's about us getting back on our feet." He pursed his lips, as if weighing whether to say more.

Back on our feet. Making it on our own. Coming under Pop's roof, Elmer's pride had suffered.

My husband started sharing that same feeling, slowly at first, then gathering speed and intensity as he warmed to his subject. He felt like a whipped dog, not being able to provide for his own.

Had he meant the two of us? Were we "his own," or did that include his folks who showed up any time they wanted? I would have asked, but he displayed his emotions so seldom, I wasn't about to interrupt.

"Claire, a woman doesn't know what it's like for the family's welfare to depend on chasing the right job, finding the right person to talk to, knowing when to take a risk."

I had a few things to say about that too but held my tongue.

He leaned back and started again, like a fire hose flowing full force. About how things wouldn't get better unless we made them better. And if Maggie had a lead on something good, we'd better chase it. He said I'd like Maggie too. And it would be good to be close to his favorite cousin, Ray, who lived with his wife, Edith, and their two little girls "next door in Harper County, across the line in Oklahoma."

Elmer never talked in such complimentary terms about his brothers, which I could understand.

"Ray knows livestock like nobody's business. We can buy some cows as soon as we get the money."

I had to interrupt on that. "Wait a minute. You never said anything about farming or raising livestock before now."

He grinned. "Well, why not? I told you working with Myrrl on his farm was like tonic. I can do that again."

I stared at the floor. "Elmer, I've made my case to stay here awhile longer, to be sure before we go off. Again. You've said things about yourself I never heard before. Not only that, but it seems every time we find a place, your folks move in."

Elmer gazed at the thunderheads towering in the northeast. "Before Kansas City, it'd been ten years since I'd had time with family. You lived with your folks before we married."

Time to make a stand. "All right. But if we get a house, it's *our* house. Not a boarding house for whoever drops in."

"And what if they do? I was taught to be hospitable."

"And I am hospitable. I'll put out a meal for guests." I shook my head. "You know what I mean. I like your dad ... and mom. I just don't want them staying for months on end."

"I don't plan on that. But if they need help, I can't turn my back on them."

"They always need help," I murmured. I stood and trudged back to the house. I didn't turn to see if Elmer followed. I didn't care.

⌘ ⌘ ⌘

We stopped in Dodge City long enough to check the water and air up the tires. I handed Elmer the twenty dollars Pop had given me before we left Ness. He took it without comment. I knew that was within the limits of help he'd accept this time.

By noon, we'd almost finished the 130-mile trip to Liberal. The outline of the town rose above the plain like a child's drawing—low scattered blocks setting on a horizon as flat as a board.

I drew my hand to my neck. It was nothing like I'd hoped for.

After the comments about MacLaren, I expected to find Maggie living in a dump. Instead, the address took us to a tidy, white bungalow with lap siding and green shutters. As we got out of the car, a willowy brunette in her late thirties launched herself from the front porch.

She carried a little girl, and a young boy shuffled behind, his face hidden in the folds of her print dress. Maggie flew to Elmer and pulled his head down to kiss his cheek. She released him and put her arm around my waist. "Now, who's this lovely lady, my dear brother? Ain't you someone to behold!" She stepped back and regarded me with eyes as blue as a china plate, a puckish grin across her face. "I'm glad Elmer got you. He doesn't say much about his feelings—you know that—but he wrote very nice things. Now I see why."

"Hello, Maggie. So good to meet you." Face burning, I glanced at Elmer.

He cleared his throat. "Well, are you going to make us stand out in the street all morning? What's for dinner?"

Maggie ignored him and introduced the children, caressing each as she spoke their names, Gracie and Billy. Maggie reminded me of Ethel—an island of calm in a sea of activity. Something in those sparkling eyes and high energy spoke of a fragility caused by hurts and loneliness.

I eyed the simple dresser, the chest of drawers, and side chair. The knickknack shelves and a framed print of Jesus looking down on a sleeping town seemed fit for a home. *Can't have such when you're living like refugees.*

After feeding us all toasted cheese sandwiches, Maggie put the children down for naps. She tiptoed out of the bedroom and led us outside, throwing words over her shoulder. "I want you to meet Jenny Washburn. I told her that you worked for a big company back east. She's a special gal to me. If it hadn't been for her and the Lord Jesus, I couldn't have put up with Mac's carousing. She's held my hand and listened to my sorrows many a night."

Would I ever be as open as Maggie? She spoke about knowing Jesus. I glanced at Elmer for a reaction, but he didn't blink.

Next door, a leprechaun-like figure in a faded sunbonnet and coveralls knelt by the front stoop, fingering packets of seeds. At our approach, she popped up like an ant on a hot stove. "Hel-lo, Maggie. Is this that brother and his wife we've been waitin' to meet? My, I didn't know she was in the cinema." A smile at me. "Honey, you're the spittin' image of Mary Pickford, and so shapely. Welcome to the High Plains!" She stuck out a hand and then pulled it back to beat it against her thigh, knocking crumbs of moist earth from her fingers.

I blushed. "It's easy to keep trim because we haven't been eating a lot over the last year." I caught my breath. Had I embarrassed Elmer?

Jenny's brow wrinkled. "Oh, look at you, honey. It's hard out there for everybody, ain't it? Well, you're just fine. Come on in, and let's sit for a spell. You too, Elmer. It is *Elmer*, ain't it?" She hurried up the steps, waving us to follow without waiting for his answer. Over coffee and cookies, Jenny asked where we'd been and what we'd been doing. Her dark eyes bore in on Elmer, then at me. "I got a need for someone to farm my home place. Maggie said you was both brought up on farms. So you know what farming is all about. It's hard work, but it's a good life for them that sticks with it."

"Farming's not easy, that's for sure." Elmer rubbed his hands together. "We struggled to make it when I was a kid up in Nebraska. But times have changed in the southern plains. Wheat prices over two dollars a bushel. With that new Turkey Red, farmers have raised wheat to beat the band."

"Yeah, but everything dropped into the outhouse about the time

Harding got elected." Jenny seemed thoughtful. "Everybody made money during the twenties—except the farmers. Then the drought. Hardly a sprinkle since the spring of '31. Dirt storms come up without warning. Turns daylight as black as pitch. Might go on for half a week. But it's bound to rain eventually. If you put your mind to it, you can do about anything, including running a farm." She looked at Elmer, eyes challenging. "Think you could make a go of it?"

Elmer cleared his throat. "Yes, I did it twenty years ago, and I can do it now." He locked eyes with Jenny and gave a smile that looked forced.

Jenny's tone turned deferential. "Maggie said something about you staying in Ness City and running a service station for your daddy-in-law. I wasn't sure what your plans were."

"I'm not pumping gas." Elmer stood. "Let's go out and look at your place." That flat, measured tone again.

"You bet!" Jenny grinned. "I'll drink to that. And how about another cookie?" She jumped up to snatch a fistful of gingersnaps from the blue hen cookie jar on her maple buffet.

Maggie leaned over to me. "I told you she was something, didn't I?"

I nodded but couldn't escape the feeling that things were moving too fast.

⌘ ⌘ ⌘

The house on Jenny Washburn's place was an L-shaped half dugout, cut into the north side of a bleak prairie hill. If the outside wood had ever seen paint, none remained to identify the color. Its front shell stood weathered and sad, like a starving cow hunkering against the wind. Light entered through small windows in the east entry door and the north kitchen wall. The front room lay to the west, and the small bedroom backed into the hill.

Elmer remarked that it looked solid, even though its flank deflected from the heaped earth.

It reminded me of pictures I'd once seen of military bunkers in France. Pretty it was not, but shelter counted for more than beauty. The thought of having my own place brought a lump to my throat.

Elmer and I walked back and forth outside from one edge of the house to the other, like children discussing what we'd do with toys in a Christmas store window. A trellis here; plant a row of elms there. Curtains over the windows. Get some scraps of lumber and build a henhouse next to the barn. Best of all, we could grow crops on sixty acres of farm ground.

My temple throbbed. If we dropped anchor, we might be here forever and never return to Ness County.

After staying in Pop's house, the dugout seemed tiny. Certainly too small to put up squatters—like Elmer's family. Confusion and delight debated in my mind. Ever since we left Deluxe, I'd had the idea that, somehow, having land to grow things would set us free.

But was this place an opportunity or a snare?

The quiet prairie awakened a dormant part of me. The smell of the earth, even the prairie wind, brought stabbing memories of when I was a little girl, of Mama, and of sitting high on the buggy behind Pop's black team. From before Pop bought his first car, before I had left to work for Deluxe, to marry Harold. Before Mama and Pop bought a place in town. Life had moved on, and me with it. Staying home wouldn't have, couldn't have, preserved those blissful, carefree days.

I sighed and looked above to the great bowl of blue, pure and uncomplicated, the way life should be. Elmer, strong and protective, yet so fragile that he couldn't share decision-making with me.

He wanted Jenny Washburn's place. Maybe I did too.

But I knew I wanted to be asked.

My preoccupied husband acted as if I didn't need to be consulted. Maybe I should simply be nice. That's what the Bible said. Being Christian meant being nice to others, pleasing them before I pleased myself.

Then I remembered the Golden Rule, which Mama had helped me memorize a long time ago—Jesus said, "And as ye would that men should do to you, do ye also to them likewise." But somehow it wasn't as simple as being nice.

Maybe that was why it was the right thing to do.

⌘ ⌘ ⌘

We returned to Liberal for more coffee and gingersnaps. Elmer let Jenny carry the conversation. When she wound down, he said, "Jenny, you've got a fine little place there. We might be interested."

She perked up. "I'd be tickled pink if you take it. You was talking about how you'd fix it up. Too much for a woman by herself but duck soup for a couple. You can do right smart out there. Crookneck maize thrives in the sandy soil. 'Course, it has to be harvested by hand. Leonard grew some of the biggest watermelons."

"Who's that?" I asked.

"Leonard Washburn, my husband's brother's second boy. Him and Emma lived there until he got a chance to rent the Eagan place. It's a 400-acre farm, so him and Emma moved over there. Hated to see them go, but you can't deny your own kin a chance to better theirselves. By the way, you can have it for a third of the net. That's the goin' rate."

Would Elmer consult me?

He stuck out his hand. "Sounds good to me. Where do we sign?"

She shook it. "Nothing to sign. Just take care of the place and send me some money if you make a little on the crops. Grows good corn too. You've got yourself a whopper of a deal, you know." She grinned at us and turned to Maggie. "Boy howdy! Thanks for the referral."

I hoped she was right. By taking this tumble-down farm, we were stuck right in the center of the Dust Bowl.

Chapter Twenty

Home. The dugout smelled of cool earth, as though I'd walked into a cave. I set down the chair I'd carried in and walked through the rooms. In the semi-darkness of the bedroom, my fingers tripped across the row of twelve-penny nails Elmer had spiked into the east wall to hang our clothes on. Back in the light, I traced a line in the condensation on the galvanized water bucket.

It sat on a rickety wash stand next to a chipped enamel basin, gifts from Maggie.

And dear Pop. As soon as he heard we'd rented the farm, he drove down from Ness to bring a used bed, ten bushels of seed for milo and corn, and a young Berkshire sow. He also brought some of the precious things from Mama—the delicate ceramic peacock figurines, a moose head cream pitcher, and a crystal jam server. He told me he could help us get a team of horses but said not a word about our abrupt departure. Before he left, he slipped me thirty-five dollars "for expenses."

I rested for a minute as Elmer brought in another load of boxes. "This house must have been real special to Jenny."

He set the boxes down and wiped his face. "Maggie said she lived here six months after her husband died. Jenny's family had a tizzy about her wanting to run the farm on her own. Good for us she finally gave in."

"We could've farmed with Bart and Jen DeBey."

"I doubt they even thought of that. We were still trying to sell when they met us, remember? About time we got us a farm. It's what we've needed all along, crop ground. The well is good enough to pasture several cows and keep a garden. I better find a team of horses so we can plant when it rains. If it rains. Melons do well in sandy soil. God knows we've got plenty of sand."

"I want to get the house put together. We still need a few things—shelves, mostly."

He ran his fingers through his hair. "All right. The house first.

Jenny said she'd always had luck scavenging in Forgan. It's about ten miles away. I'll check the lumberyard and see what I can find. You fix us a bite to eat, then I'll go into town."

⌘ ⌘ ⌘

Elmer returned that afternoon, roped bundles of random length boards sticking out the back windows. The backseat and passenger side overflowed with orange crates and feed sacks.

I circled the car as he pulled to a stop. "How'd you get all this?"

He opened the trunk and motioned inside. "Man at the hardware store, Coldwater by name, sold me the crates and sacks for practically nothing. The rest came from the lumberyard bone pile."

I began removing the conglomeration from the car. "You are some salesman, Elmer. These crates will do for shelves, and there might be enough for a nightstand and cupboard too."

He laughed. "I guess they don't see many people moving into this country, so folks are happy to help out newcomers."

"Meet anybody else besides this Coldwater?"

"A man named Wiley where I got a dollar's worth of gas. From the miscellany in the car, he knew I wasn't merely passing through. Several people gave me the eye, but not in an unfriendly way. Just curious."

The wind kicked up, and we hurried to get everything inside the house.

⌘ ⌘ ⌘

A loud rap sounded on the door. Through the window I spied a rawboned man wearing a high-crowned felt hat and a pinched expression, a Chevrolet truck behind him.

A pert little redhead with him held her purse like a Tommy gun. She turned first one direction, then another, as they waited on the stoop.

The couple wheeled when I opened the door, as if attached to the handle.

"You the new people? We're neighbors—names are Lew and Kate Buffalow," he said and gave Elmer an emphatic handshake. "Coldwater told us that some folks from back east moved into the dugout, so we thought we'd better make sure you knew how to survive out here on the plains."

190

Elmer grinned. "Yeah, we're from Chicago and Kansas City and then some. My wife, Claire. She's got the coffeepot going. Have a seat."

The woman turned to her husband. "Why don't you go ahead and get those things out of the car?"

He nodded and disappeared out the door. Within minutes, he returned with a pasteboard box and a shiny tin can. He placed the box on the table with a flourish.

She lifted the lid to reveal a layer cake, a sack of produce, and yet another box, which held a platter of fried chicken.

For a moment or two, Elmer and I stood there, unable to speak.

Kate broke the ice. "I guess we'd better explain. Lew got a fairly positive report about you from Coldwater, which is rather remarkable in and of itself. Anyway, we decided to welcome you to the neighborhood."

I laughed. "Well, we're pleased you came. You're our very first visitors."

"We figured that," Lew boomed.

"But we still hadn't met you," Kate murmured. "So we didn't want to—"

"—to waste a good cake on some Arkies, regardless what Howard said. So we left the food in the car until we could meet you first."

"You got anything to eat with? We didn't think to bring silver." Kate's elfin face crinkled into a sun-freckled smile.

"Just washed the dishes." I pulled crockery off the shelves.

"What's the tin can for? You taking up a collection?" Elmer grinned.

Lew turned solemn. "If it's acceptable in your house, Claire." He held up the bright can and a brick of chewing tobacco for inspection. Lew's voice sounded like a bass harp down a deep well.

"Of course. Go ahead."

The afternoon visit by this lively couple extended into evening. The Buffalows played pitch, which brought back pleasant memories of Bart and Jen. Elmer found a political comrade-in-arms in Lew, a deathless Republican. Together, they griped about the New Deal and speculated how Alf Landon could beat Roosevelt. When Elmer said he needed to find a team of horses at a good price, Lew said he'd

191

check around.

⌘ ⌘ ⌘

Kate had said she'd seen abandoned furniture two miles north on Bluebell Road. The next morning, we pulled a wooden table and two chairs out of a plum thicket near the Lauderback place. We put the chairs in the Oakland and tied the table to the roof. After we cleaned it up, I propped it against the living room wall as one of the legs was split to pieces.

The Buffalows returned two days later, Lew eager to announce that John McCarter had a team of horses. "You could probably get them for less than thirty dollars, with harness."

While they discussed the deal, Kate motioned toward an open-top pasteboard box she'd set by the front door. "Dozen little chicks for you, newly hatched. Do you have a hutch for these babies?"

"Elmer can make one if he gets more lumber from Coldwater."

"Keep 'em in that box, right in the house, Claire," Lew rumbled. "We lost eight chicks one night to a skunk, so I'd never leave them outside until you get that henhouse built. Won't nothing get them in your house, unless you got rats."

"No, we don't have rats!" How dare he think such a thing?

Elmer grinned. "Settle down, Sal. You might tell Kate about the 'pets' you found in our bedroom the other night."

I shuddered. "It was awful. I carried the lamp into the bedroom and saw something shiny move on the wall. Centipedes! I must have screamed 'cause Elmer came out of bed like a shot."

Elmer shook his head. "Never seen centipedes that big. They're not as poisonous as a rattler, but I've heard they can make you awful sick. I beat them to pieces with my belt."

I shuddered. "After that, I took the lamp and searched every inch of the walls, the floor, and the ceiling. We found a crack down by the floor where they must've come in. I plugged it with oakum. They'll never get in there again, but mornings, I still shake every piece of clothes before I get dressed. I'm not taking any chances."

⌘ ⌘ ⌘

I stared out the kitchen window, again thinking of the centipedes. We'd seen rattlesnakes on three different occasions that summer. I sighed. Maybe I wasn't cut out to be a farmer's wife in this raw land.

God, please send a sign, a positive sign, that you'll take care of us.

I prepared ham hocks and black-eyed peas for supper. While Elmer washed up, I glanced outside for my ritual check of the weather.

A few ragged clouds rimmed the otherwise empty sky. A tawny form loped out by the barn.

"Elmer, get the gun! A coyote! It'll get the calf!"

He lurched toward the window, skittering a fork off the table. "That's no coyote." He expelled his breath. "Looks like a dog. Yeah, he's part collie. See the white blaze on his chest? Muzzle's too broad for a coyote."

We stared at the animal. It stood some thirty yards away, eyes on the stoop.

Elmer quietly unlatched the screen door and stood in the opening.

"Don't scare him, Elmer," I whispered. "Isn't he pretty? Here's a piece of bread. See if he'll take it."

Reaching back, Elmer took the morsel and stepped down from the stoop.

The dog didn't move.

Elmer walked toward the animal, the bread held in front of him, speaking in a low, continuous murmur.

The dog remained motionless, only the brush of his tail flicking.

Elmer moved closer.

The animal's ears went erect, not once flattening against his head. His teeth lay sheathed out of sight, except on the right side. The dark muzzle twisted upward in a curious grin, evidence of an earlier savage encounter.

Elmer squatted and held out the bread.

The dog downed it in a single gulp.

I murmured and the sound of my voice brought the dog's tail to a full wag. I sidled up by Elmer and extended my hand.

"Careful, don't be reckless."

The brown-white muzzle stretched forward to sniff my fingers.

"Look, Elmer, he smells bacon grease on my hands. He's hungry, not dangerous." I reached out to pet the animal.

Its nose followed my hand.

"Oh, Elmer, he's so pretty. But he has cockleburs in the ring around his neck and all over his body. I'll brush those out. What shall we call him?"

"Call him? What do you mean? He's not ours."

"Why not? He came to us. He's been abandoned, Elmer. Every farm needs a dog. There's no reason we can't take care of him, is there?"

"He'd have to get by on table scraps." He chewed his lip. "Better give him a name."

"I had a dog before named 'Old Blue,' but that doesn't fit. Maybe 'Shep.' Look at that white ring around his neck. It's like a collar."

"Uncle Joe had a dog that he called 'Ring.' How about that?"

"Ring. I like that." I crouched again. "Come here, Ring. Oh, Elmer, I'll bet he hasn't had water in days." I dashed to the house, grabbed a gallon can of water, dashed back out, and set it before him. As we watched the dog drink, I murmured, "Elmer, this is a sign. I asked God for a sign. Ring is our sign."

He glanced at me. Then he scratched the dog's head. "Looks like a good dog."

⌘ ⌘ ⌘

Pop wrote, saying he'd bring down another brood sow. Elmer was fine with that as long as Pop would accept two pigs from the first litter, and then two more from the second litter to go to Myrrl for his contribution months before. Another month without rain, but Jenny had put in a good well, so we always had plenty of water for the livestock.

I fed and watered the chickens. Then I crossed the yard toward the house.

The skinny elm whipped toward the southeast. Unusual. On a hunch, I turned back and closed the door to the hen house. The cow and calf should be inside the barn if a storm came up. The tree stilled.

Behind me, Elmer's voice crackled. "Sal, something's going on. Wind's been out of the northwest. Now it's quit altogether." He faced the direction of the Cimarron Canyon. "Look at that!"

A wall of darkness glided toward us. Soundless and menacing, it extended upward and to the east and west without visible limits. We stood wide-eyed as it enclosed us, blotting out the sun.

Elmer cursed and grabbed my arm. "Come on! Get inside!"

We lurched toward the dugout, the dog beside me. The wind pulled the blanket of darkness over us. Within seconds, it became a howling beast, ripping at our clothes and sucking the breath from my lungs. Where was the dugout? Sand lashed my face and arms, stinging with hellish fury. I stumbled as Elmer pulled me forward.

He stopped, forearm over his brow, and then whirled back, thankfully, toward the faint line of the house. Crab-like, we edged along the wall to the door. He pulled it open and thrust me inside.

We stood, gasping. The wind shrieked with such force, I expected the walls to collapse. A piece of roof flashing chattered above the wind.

Elmer groped in the darkness for the kerosene lamp. He found a match, then lit the wick, the flame flickering before he slipped the globe over the base.

I glanced around. "Ring! Where's Ring?" I started toward the door.

"Don't open that door!" Elmer bawled. He stepped past me and eased the door open. A gust caused the lamplight to tremble like a dying moth. Before he could push the door closed, Ring's nose appeared in the narrow slit. Elmer pulled the door back a few inches, and the dog slithered through the narrow space.

"Oh, he's in! He's in!" I shrilled as the lamp flickered out.

Ring pressed against my knees, a mass of comfort, as Elmer re-lit the lamp. Light again blossomed throughout the kitchen and we stood, arms about one another, as our pet sat regarding us.

"How long—"

Elmer held up his hand. "Listen."

"What is it?"

"Can't you hear that? It's the barn door!"

I cocked my head and held my breath. Sure enough, a distant banging could be heard above the unleashed wind.

"If that cow doesn't keep her calf in the barn, we'll lose them for sure." He grabbed his coat and hat and strode toward the door.

"No. Wait, Elmer!"

He slipped sideways out the door and rasped, "Stay inside. I'll be right back."

Before he could close the door, the dog glided outside as the wind again snuffed out the lamp.

Frantic to recapture light, I fumbled for the box of matches. I found the lamp globe but jerked my hand away from its hot touch. My palsied fingers located a towel, and I removed the globe to re-light the wick.

Bizarre shadows danced on the wall beside me.

I swept to the window and stopped.

Darkness, only darkness, loomed beyond its smooth face. Nothing moved but the grit that sifted inside.

Again and again, I circled the room. Never had I felt so cut off and abandoned.

Over the next three hours, I raised the lamp to the window many times, staring out at the pit of blackness, as if by concentration I could find Elmer and bring him into the house. Every passing minute lessened the chance of his return. I looked a last time and saw only my tear-stained face in the cold glass. I turned away and set the lamp down. Great choking sobs shook my body as I swayed against the dust-covered table.

I finally collapsed in a wretched heap on a chair and cried out to a God who seemed unable to hear above the wind he had sent. Exhausted beyond measure, I fell into a deep sleep.

⌘ ⌘ ⌘

The chill of inactivity finally brought me awake. I looked about with the confusion of one awakened from a dream. Dust coated every exposed part of my skin, hair, and clothes. The lamp burned faintly, and I jerked up to look around. Pain flashed from my stiff neck. My right arm had gone to sleep. Shivering, I struggled upright, possessed by shame that I hadn't stayed up to watch for Elmer's return.

The wind—the endless wind! Jenny had said dust storms could last for days. In the dim light, whorls of dust sifted in around the window jambs.

I twisted up the wick, brightening the room.

Perhaps …

I ran to the darkened bedroom and held my breath, waiting to hear the sound of breathing. "Elmer?" My voice caught and I released a deep sigh. I whirled to the kitchen window and clawed the curtains aside.

Only a reflection met my gaze.

"Get ahold of yourself, woman," I whispered. "You can't fall to pieces now." I held my breath and listened for any sound above the cruel, cutting wind.

Wolfish in its attack on the earth, it would overwhelm me if I left the cover of the dugout.

Where might Elmer be?

Yet, I could not despair. I wanted to fling open the door and scream his name. Then I listened again and heard it—the faint banging of the barn door. Elmer had gotten to the barn too late to keep the cow and calf inside. He must have left the door open in case they came back. What then? Then he went to look.

Or maybe he never reached the barn. *Lord, help him find his way back.* That banging door would've led him to the barn … if he was close enough to hear it. But he was out there. And it wasn't like Elmer to be reckless. Fighting the impulse to break down again, I knew I had to focus, keep my mind clear.

My nerves seemed to crackle inside my head. As abruptly as fear had enveloped me, I grasped the idea that I should speak to God.

Listening for the unreachable beyond a seemingly endless storm, I prayed to the invisible God, saying words from the Psalms that I'd not repeated for years. "I will say of the Lord, he is my refuge and my fortress: my God, in him will I trust." I asked for protection for Elmer. For myself, that I might overcome fear and unbelief.

My Bible lay on the nail keg.

I picked it up and gazed at its clean outline in the dust that coated the percale covering. I cocked my head for the sound of a voice or a dog's bark, and then flipped the pages.

Isaiah.

"Who … walketh in darkness, and hath no light? Let him trust in the name of the Lord, and stay upon his God."

Back to the Psalms.

A cry of anguish caught my eye. "My God, my God, why hast thou forsaken me? Why art thou so far from helping me … O my God, I cry in the daytime … and in the night." My heart stopped pounding, and I settled in. I'd never read this book in quite the same way.

Throughout the Psalms were cries for mercy, assurance of God's presence in times of distress. He was a rock and a fortress, strength and light and salvation. His eyes were upon the righteous. He heard the cry of those who were lost, afraid, alone, those who had failed. It seemed written for people in trouble. Like me.

I always accepted God as mighty, as a ruler who pardoned sin and brought justice to a wayward, confused world. But maybe God was closer than I'd imagined.

I arose and pulled the curtains back from the window. The wind seemed less violent, though it still swirled in the thin light. To the east lay the outline of distant hills. With a new day, hope seemed sane. A strange peace seemed everywhere. Had I only been mesmerized by the events of past hours?

No, something had changed. Something inside, deep and forceful.

Maybe I could see out the front door. Hardly any kerosene remained in the lamp anyway. I'd need to refill it from the five-gallon can. As I pulled the front door inward, a stream of sand poured onto the floor from the drift that covered the stoop. Opening the door farther only let in more sand. And meant I couldn't close the door.

There was nothing in the Psalms about mountains of sand. Those middling aggravations were probably for people to work out on their own.

I covered myself against the still-blowing sand and inched outside to find the shovel and kerosene can.

The long-handled shovel still hung from the dugout wall, but the fuel can was nowhere in sight—undoubtedly blown into the next county. My back to the wind, I set about clearing the sand so I could close the door.

I looked to the southwest, which was dark and forbidding, imagining where Elmer might be. He wasn't one to give up easily, but he could be as far away as the kerosene can—lying at the bottom of a canyon in a pile of thistles. Anger rose like bile in my throat. *He left me—alone—just to get two dumb animals ... But if he's lost or hurt, how can I be mad at him?*

Chapter Twenty-One

A whine cut through the unleashed wind.

I whirled, the shovel raised over my head, and then gasped and stared.

There stood Ring.

"Ring! Oh, Ring!" I dropped to my knees and hugged the furry ruff to me. "Where's Elmer? Where'd you come from?"

The dog pulled away and dashed down the lane through the curtain of dust, then stopped and looked back.

I squinted past him toward the county road, scarcely breathing.

Tumbleweeds appeared out of the gloom and bounced past. At the end of the driveway, the tamarack whipped as if the gale would wrench it from the earth.

A form separated from the tree. Then another figure, then two more.

"Hello! Who's there?"

No answer. Then a wave and a muffled call. "Claire!"

I stumbled down the lane. "Elmer!"

The dog romped beside me.

I fell into my husband's arms as tears streamed down my cheeks.

"It's all right, Sal. I'm okay. What about you?" He nuzzled my cheek and held me. Then he gestured toward the dog. "Ring, he rescued me—really, all of us. Never saw the like before."

I buried my face against his shirt. "I thought I'd lost you. The wind was a monster, and you were gone. Oh, darling, I couldn't ... I wouldn't let myself think of you alone out there. God brought you back. He saved you."

"Hey, what's for breakfast?" Another voice, familiar, sounded behind Elmer.

There stood Will, with Elmer's brother Earl beside him. Mary Grace brought up the rear, her face framed by a dark shawl.

My in-laws? Had the storm blown them in? I struggled to sort it out.

They had found our new home. Like cowbirds that laid eggs in the nests of others, again they'd pushed my dreams and possessions aside to hatch their own.

I finally mumbled, "Hello, Dad, Earl. Hello, Mother."

Elmer waved them toward the dugout. "It's a long story, Sal. I'll tell you, but let's get everybody inside first." He trudged to the house and halted. Only a third of the structure protruded from a great dune of sand.

I shouted above the wind. "The sand flowed in when I opened the front door. And the kerosene, I don't know——"

"It's taken care of. I got the fuel can. Put it in the barn." He picked up the shovel I'd dropped and thrust it at Earl. "Move that sand back so we can close the door." Earl sent the sand flying, and then we crowded inside.

I made a quick swipe of the washstand and table before putting the coffeepot on the still-hot stove. We circled its warmth, emotionally drained. In that moment, a deepened kinship with my husband's family rose up inside of me.

Elmer set a lamp on the table.

We broke out laughing, all of us pointing at each other's raccoon-eyed appearance, painted by dust against tear-streaked faces.

I washed my face and hands, and stirred up pancake batter.

"Elmer, what in the name of heaven was you doin' wandering outside in the middle of a cyclone?" Mary Grace asked with a motherly voice.

"I was after that fool cow. If she'd stayed in the barn ... But I got there too late." He pulled off a shoe and sand streamed onto the floor.

"A fool mistake, son." Will pulled on his pipe. "I thought I learned you better than that."

"Yeah, it was dumb. I knew they'd go with the wind, so I tied a handkerchief over my nose and mouth and headed southeast. It was so bad I couldn't see my hand in front of my face. Ring stayed right with me. He nudged my leg. Guess he tried to circle me back to the house. Got almost to Garrett's when I took a header. Landed in the bottom of a ten-foot draw."

I turned from the stove to rub his shoulder. "You could still be lying out there." My voice cracked. "I'm glad I didn't know. I fell apart as it was. I don't know how many times I held the lamp up to the window, hoping you'd see it."

"Well, that fall took the starch out of me, but I guess I came out all right."

"Lucky you didn't break your neck, stumbling around in that storm," Will said. "We was stalled, right in the road, and then you come along. How in blue blazes did you find us?"

"Ring found you. When I crawled out of that ravine, I was totally discombobulated. Sand blowing hard enough to take off my hide. Ring led me to the road. I looked for a tree or a shed nearby where I could wait it out."

"You could've laid there till springtime," Earl said. "We'd *all* be out there, if your dog hadn't brung you along. Big dust storms build up enough static electricity to kill a car engine. No big deal to fix, but I sure wasn't gonna do it in the dark with a duster blowing around my ears."

I spooned more batter into the skillet. Earl must have been mighty desperate to get rid of the folks for him to come hundreds of miles from Tulsa and head into that storm.

"Ring led me right to your car."

Will laughed. "I believe you was as surprised as us when you opened that car door and poked your head in."

"Everybody was glad to see that dog," Mary Grace said. "I got a chill in the backseat. He laid down on the floorboard and warmed my feet."

I flipped the pancakes and turned back from the stove. "Did you know where you were?"

Elmer stirred his coffee. "No, but the wind eased off, and I figured Ring would lead us home at daylight. Then I saw that tamarack by the drive."

⌘ ⌘ ⌘

After breakfast, Elmer and Earl went back to start the car. Their return brought in the familiar suitcases and paper sacks. I pulled Elmer aside. "Why bring their stuff in? You know there's no extra room in this house. And there's definitely not space in the kitchen for *two* women."

"Don't get excited. They're only here for a while."

"Only for *a while*? Like the months they stayed with us in Mitchell County—"

"Elmer!" The front door burst open and banged against the wall, followed by a wide-eyed Mary Grace holding a lantern. "You've got a visitor in your privy!"

"What is it, Mom?"

"Bullsnake, that's what it is!" Her voice ratcheted up half an octave. "There's a snake down in that outhouse, and I'm not gonna use it until you get it out of there."

"Mom, he can't hurt you from way down in the bottom."

"I won't use the outhouse until that thing is out of there!" Her voice bordered on a screech. "That's it! I will not—I'll say it again—I will not go out there until that snake's gone." She clattered through the kitchen and into the living room where, head down, she commenced sorting her paper bags. After a minute, she stopped and glared at Elmer. "Well, when are you going to do what I asked you? I can't wait forever."

He stood and clomped toward the door, grabbing the still-lit lantern on the way out.

I wrestled into my blue sweater. "Wait, I'll help."

Elmer waved me back.

I ignored his irritation and crowded behind as he went around the corner of the dugout and into the outhouse.

He thrust the two-by-four he'd grabbed from the porch down the platform hole.

I was going to say my piece. No way would I let him brush me off. "Leave it, Elmer. We barely have room for two—"

"Take this light so I can see."

I tilted the lantern out at arm's length. "Why are we doing this? She could use the slop jar, and then we could send them back to Tulsa. Elmer, listen to me!" Once I started shouting, I couldn't stop. "Last night, I couldn't sleep a wink with them on my mind. Wasn't sure if I'd have to run this farm without you, but I decided some things. First of all, I'm through being a doormat, for you or anybody else. I'm a person. I have my opinions. I expect to be treated with as much respect as anyone else."

Elmer whirled to face me. His shadow hovered on the wall and underside of the roof. He squinted, like he couldn't believe what I was saying.

My arm ached from holding the light, but I wasn't about to twitch. He needed to see I wasn't simply making noise.

Although the door stood open and the wind moaned in the darkness, the walls seemed about to close in.

He grunted. "You think I don't hear you? It's not about respect. Look. The folks are here. Not the first time. I didn't ask them to come but they're here. Earl needs ... Mae's on a tear. Wouldn't surprise me if they separate. Mae won't talk—not with the folks there. You're not the only one that locks horns with Mom." He peered down the hole. "Hold that light again. There's that sucker. Unhh!" He shoved the two-by-four down again. "Got him. Now, tear out some sheets from that catalogue. We'll cover him up. Mom won't know the difference. Let's get out of here."

I grabbed his arm. "Listen to yourself. What Mae said about it being hard to talk with the folks there—why is our house any different from Earl's? We can't talk over things, not with your folks sitting in the same room."

He shook loose, frowning. "That's no problem."

"It will be if they move in. Even in Beloit, we didn't—couldn't— talk things out. Them sitting there listening to every word. Maybe they don't mean to take away our privacy, but they do. You've got three other brothers besides Earl. Let them take a turn."

"It's hard times, Claire. Families have to help one another. Your dad helped us. Why are you so dead-set against sharing the space we've got?"

"Because we don't *have* space to share! Ever since we had that apartment in Kansas City, we've put up with your family. And don't ignore what I said about your other brothers."

"Oh? You want me to drive the folks all over creation just so they're gone from here?"

"Hardly. Jim lives at Buffalo, and John moved to the McCarter place. That's only four miles from here. Take your pick. Besides that, we don't have room."

"We don't have kids, either. That makes a big difference."

"Elmer, what makes a difference is that the other wives don't allow your folks to park in their house. I haven't liked it, and you know it—"

"You're being unreasonable. They're here and I'm not showing them the door."

"Call it what you want. This is my house too."

Eyes flashing, Elmer grabbed the lantern and wheeled out the door. Circles of light bounced ahead as he marched back to the house.

I wanted to jump on his back and throw him to the ground. Instead I yelled at his back, "Just you wait, Elmer!"

He didn't turn around, but I'd blown his arguments to pieces. If he wouldn't stand up to his mother, I would. Beginning with putting their blankets on the floor.

I wasn't giving up my bed at night anymore.

⌘⌘⌘

Once the storm lost its punch, Earl returned to Tulsa. Elmer drove away shortly afterward. I had an idea what he was up to. Sure enough, he returned before dark with a bedstead, springs, and mattress lashed to the top of the Oakland. I watched from inside the house, but when Will went outside, I followed.

He waved at Elmer. "Found your cow and calf, Elmer. Man named McCarter stopped by. He'll take care of them till you get over there."

I waited for Elmer to look my direction. "I see you got what you wanted."

He turned back to Will. "That all McCarter had to say?"

Will glanced between us. "McCarter got a visit from the Federal Land Bank man last week. They're peddling farms they picked up. Said they're talking to everyone around here."

I waved toward Elmer's cargo. "We need to talk about this."

Will made as if he was going into the house but remained on the stoop.

I struggled to speak. "It looks like my feelings don't matter."

Elmer flexed his jaw muscles. "Yeah. They matter. But I'm not sending the folks anyplace." A shadow, perhaps pain, drifted across his face.

Let him squirm. "Doesn't it matter what this does to us? *We're* a family."

He spat crosswise to the wind, now reduced from a howl to a moan. "You're overreacting."

"If what I feel matters, why do you ignore me?" I stormed back into the house without closing the door. I snatched my coat off a chair and flung it over my shoulders.

A sleeve caught a pie tin and skittered it to the floor.

Mary Grace looked up from her sewing, eyes wide and mouth open as if ready to straighten me out.

I glared, daring her to say a word.

Our eyes locked, her face questioning, mine surely looking fierce, until she dropped her gaze.

Jaw set, I cocooned myself in scarf, gloves, and coat. A check to make sure the lantern had fuel, then I lit it and marched through the still-open door. I nearly collided with Will.

He staggered backward.

I whistled Ring to my side and half ran into the gathering darkness, toward the road. I dropped a hand to the dog's neck. "Good boy."

Will's voice rang out behind me. "Elmer, forget that bed! See about Claire!"

The darkness enclosed me like a net. Not since Myrrl and I walked home the time Pop's car ran out of gas had I taken off into the night. My breath came in choppy gusts despite the wind, which had turned to the southwest. The sand would be in my face once I turned west at the road.

Behind me came a clatter and Elmer's voice. Within moments, footsteps thudded behind me.

Calmed by the distance I'd gone, I stopped when Elmer swept up and around me.

He started to grab my arm but stopped, panting. He seemed hesitant to touch me. "Claire, what do you …? Stop this. Where the dickens you going?"

I turned away. So many times he'd ignored what I said.

He could make me feel secure, even precious, and then discount me a millisecond later. Harold had made me feel discounted almost all the time.

Now Elmer seemed befuddled. Had he run after me to pressure me again? To get me to cast off the only thing I truly owned, my claim to being me? I glanced up, wishing I could have seen his expression when he ran after me. Had he been frantic? Maybe even desperate? Had he chased me out of anger or because Will told him to?

I raised my voice above the hiss of the wind. "I'm going to see Kate. Kate will make room for me. She'll listen."

Elmer took my hand.

I felt numb, unable to respond.

Ring leaned against my legs, whining.

Elmer spoke, his first words almost erased by the wind. "I'll listen to you, Sal. Look, you can't go out in the dark by yourself. I … I don't want something—anything—to happen to you."

"I've got Ring."

"Yes, you've got Ring."

"And I've got the lantern."

"Yes, Claire, and you've got me." He leaned down as if on a hinge, maybe afraid I'd pull away. He drew me gently to him. "And I've got you, 'cause I'm not letting you go."

I allowed the embrace but kept my arms at my side. "You know I meant what I said?"

"Yes, I believe you." He sighed, a quick in-and-out breath. "You're quite a woman. And I'll say it again—you've got me. This, this whole thing, is … yeah, about us. Not only the folks. You see things different than I do, probably different than I ever will, but I need to see your face, to look at you. Let me have the lantern." He tugged until I released it.

His fingers brushed across my hand, and I shivered.

His forehead came against mine, then his mouth next to my ear. "I can't have anything happen to you. I don't know how to say … to tell you that I don't know what I'd do without you. You can't leave, Claire. This is crazy. You know I'm for you, honey. I admit that I've been so set on taking care of Mom and Dad that I didn't see … see you." Elmer took another deep breath and leaned back. He removed his hat and swept his hand across his forehead.

As his fingers trailed through his beautiful hair, I almost threw myself into his arms.

He drew the lantern up again. "You *are* important to me. The most important thing in my life. I know I'm not perfect, but if you want me to really listen, I will. We have to work this out, the two of us. But I need time. Mom and Dad are always in a jam. Nothing comes easy. Dad's not up to snuff, and Mom—well, she just knows how to bark at him—but I'll tell them what needs to be said. Can I have that time?"

"How much time? If it's going to take six months, I might as well keep walking."

"Two days? Three? Okay?"

I gave a slight nod.

"Okay. Now, let's go back to the house. Together."

I let him take my arm. It would have been a long three miles to Kate's house. I hoped I'd never have to walk it all the way.

Chapter Twenty-Two

At first light, I slipped out of bed and into the living room. The sound of deep breathing stopped me. I peered into the gloom toward the corner.

Elmer had put the bed up after he escorted me back to the house, 'cause he couldn't leave the folks sleeping on the floor.

Anger, demanding and righteous, heated my face as I backed away from my sleeping in-laws. I tiptoed back to the bedroom and gathered a shawl about me. Then I quietly went outside and sat on the stoop.

The morning sun bloomed before me like a new flower. Wrapped in the shawl and my thoughts, I shut out the visitors inside the house.

I replayed in my mind Pop's Bible quote about marriage, about leaving and cleaving, especially the cleaving to one another. Not only did it make sense, it would have prevented meddling in-laws. Elmer had left his folks but *they* always returned to him. And that kept him from cleaving to me, if cleaving meant putting me first, which I thought it did.

Cleaving and commitment—same thing.

Mid-morning, Elmer put on his coat and hat. "I'll take Ring and get my cattle from McCarter."

I watched him a moment as he and the dog headed down the lane.

Fine, I needed time to think.

I refilled the water for the chickens and then struck out toward the canyon rim. The cut in the prairie always amazed me, as the flat terrain parted to reveal an unreal world of cliffs and ravines stepping down to the Cimarron River. It seemed forbidding yet exciting, and I felt like a kid again. I shaded my eyes.

The drought had dried the current, leaving only scattered pools glinting in the hard sunlight. Cottonwoods, bright with the leaves of summer, fringed the channel. Other than yucca plants sprinkled across the hills, that was the only green in sight.

A voice called behind me. Will.

Probably wanted to complain about his "artheritis" or "Roosterbelt."

A mass of white hair spilled out as he lifted the crumpled hat to wipe his brow. "Man gets to be my age, he has to keep fit. Can't work like I used to, but I enjoy a good walk." He caught his breath and spat in the dry cow path. "I ever tell you about the time I unloaded railroad ties off a flatcar down by Joplin? Me and one other man. Actually a wet-nosed kid. We pulled off that entire stack of ties. It was high as a buckskin pony in tall clover."

I waited, silent.

He tamped the tobacco in his pipe and drew a match from his overalls. After lighting his pipe, he shook the match in the still air and knelt to thrust the blackened head into the sand. Grunting as he stood, he said, "Yessir, it musta been about a hunnerd degrees, and it took us seven hard days to unload those ties. You ever try to lift a railroad tie, Claire?" Without waiting for my response, he rumbled on. "Each one weighs one, two hunnerd pounds, I'd say, so you can imagine how many tons of wood we horsed around."

"When was that, Dad?" I walked ahead on a path that followed the canyon rim.

"Right before the World War. You was probably a kid. When was you born?"

I answered over my shoulder. "Aught-six."

"So you were born when Teddy Roosevelt was president. Best president we ever had. Doubt you remember him. Too bad he ain't runnin' the country now. This cousin of his is a socialist. You mark my words, we'll see changes the likes of which you ain't never seen."

"So, Elmer was a young man during Roosevelt?"

"Yes, he was in his early twenties. Him and ... him and, uh—"

"Florence. Elmer told me about her." I turned around.

He squatted and watched two glistening tumblebugs work on a cow pie.

"Where was Elmer—and Florence—when you worked in Joplin?"

He looked up. "As I recall, he had a job with a farmer outside of Elkhart. Maybe that's where her family come from. But we still had Jim and Maggie and Earl, yeah, and John at home. Bud came later. I tell you, it's tough feeding a houseful of hungry kids."

"I understand. I was the last of five children, but my father always provided."

"He a farmer?"

"He homesteaded in Ness County. You know where that is?"

"I surely do. Passed through there once. Homesteaded, did he?" Will seemed impressed.

We continued along the canyon in silence.

He seemed buried in the past, then found his voice. "I gave some thought to joining the Cherokee Strip Land Run back in '93. We could've had our own quarter-section of prime Oklahoma land."

"So why didn't you do it, Dad?"

He ducked his head.

I stopped and looked at him. "A lot of people got in on that free land. It was only a matter of getting there and staking a claim. Why didn't you make the run?"

Will stared across the canyon, chewing his upper lip. "'Cause I decided not to. I'm getting a mite chilly. Let's keep moving."

My jaw dropped, and I shook my head as I headed down the cow path.

His voice sounded behind me. "When Elmer gets back, I'll talk to him about taking us over to John's. Maybe Jim and Beatrice's. Although Beatrice ... I don't know. But we'll clear out till you get settled."

⌘ ⌘ ⌘

The folks cleared out, all right, but it wasn't long before they were back. Elmer had taken them to John's. That lasted five days. I didn't get the full story, just the tidbit Will offered: "No way I could sleep, what with seven kids raising Cain all night."

So John took them to Jim's.

Mary Grace gave a snappish report about their reception at their second son's house. "Beatrice prackly met us at the door. Said we could have supper, but she weren't going to have us stay. I told her we wouldn't eat if she had to act like that. Jim stood there like he had mush in his mouth. So John loaded us up, and here we are."

I wasn't sure if I should faint or swear. Silently, I plopped into the rocker on the front porch and watched as Will and Mary Grace moved back into our house. *My* house. Which now seemed to be *their* house.

Would a screaming fit do any good?

⌘ ⌘ ⌘

The first frost sent Elmer and his dad into Forgan for a load of coal. I went out to cut more of the crookneck maize. The sun worsened the white spots on my arm and face, so I wore Elmer's long-sleeve shirt and my big slat bonnet for protection.

I walked each row, topping the maize with a large wooden-handled knife. The cut heads went into a gunny sack tied to my waist. Once a sack was filled, I simply dropped the heads on the ground. It was a sure way for a backache hours after I quit, but what could I do? As the sun rose, sweat matted the shirt to my back and the collar chafed my neck. Even the dog flopped into the shade.

Mary Grace's cry broke the quiet. She stood beside the scrubby elm, waving her arms like a railroad flagman.

That performance always irritated me. An exaggeration intended to get my goat.

Sunlight glinted off a maroon sedan in the driveway.

What was this all about? I hurried across the rows toward the house, blinking from the sweat that ran down my face.

Mary Grace gave another impatient wave.

I slowed just to spite her and squinted through the shimmering heat.

Ring barked as a chunky man in a suit got out of the sedan. He emerged from the shade to the edge of the sunbaked field.

I studied him, my head buried in the recesses of the bonnet.

The man lifted his hat to wave, revealing hair slicked straight back like Fred Astaire. That was the only resemblance, with his below-average height and above-average weight. Probably laughing up his sleeve.

Elmer's pants, gloves, and shirt fit me like a saddle on a sow. To cap it off, I'd had to tie Elmer's brogans on with binder twine looped around my calves. I felt like a clown as I shuffled up to this finely dressed dandy. At least his patent leather shoes were coated with dust.

"Hello, there." His voice had a surprising alto pitch. He stepped toward me, hand extended. "Name's U.J. Ingraham, regional manager of the Federal Land Bank in Dodge City."

I allowed my fingers to touch his hand in the briefest of

211

handshakes and mumbled a hello. I backed away as far as I decently could, hoping he couldn't smell me. I could hardly stand myself. *State your business quick and get out of here.*

"Is, uh, your husband … might your husband be around?"

I caught anxiety in his voice, which charged my confidence. "No, and he won't return until evening. Can I give him a message? You say your name is Ingraham?"

"Yes, U.J. Ingraham, from the Federal Land Bank in Dodge City. My business card."

The big shot McCarter mentioned. I made as if to turn back to the field, hopefully indicating my interest in limiting the discussion.

Ingraham commented on the heat. *Swell, now he expects me to feel sorry for him.*

He leaned forward again and raised his voice against the tunneled opening of my bonnet. "The Federal Land Bank has acquired several properties in the High Plains over the past several years. Frankly, we're not interested in being in the farming business. That's the work of you good folks. When your husband returns, please tell him that I'd like to talk to you about financing ownership of one of the farms in our portfolio. The bank is making a comprehensive effort to contact farmers currently engaged in the community, like yourselves, to advise you about our attractive lending terms." A hint of a smile crossed his face. "We want farmers like yourselves to be aware of this new option for farm ownership." He paused as if wondering if I'd heard him.

He could squint all he wanted, but I wasn't taking that bonnet off. "Uh, yes, farmers need to be aware." Farmers like ourselves, indeed. We hadn't seen a dollar bill in months. The whole business smelled fishy. He probably had to meet some kind of quota.

"Wonderful. I assume you'd be interested in a farm in this community?"

"Perhaps." I thought of telling him I'd be interested in flying with Amelia Earhart. And maybe a vacation in Spain. Instead I said, "We already have friends in the neighborhood. My husband and I will have to discuss this."

"But of course. I'll return in a month or two so I can talk with you both. Good day." Mr. Ingraham touched his hat to Mary Grace, who stood near enough to listen but back far enough to signal she didn't want any part of the exchange.

⌘ ⌘ ⌘

Elmer and I went over to Lew and Kate's the following Friday evening to play pitch.

Lew shook his index finger. "A dollar to a donut that Ingraham fellow hit every house in the area. Got both Mintons before he caught me and Kate right after dinner. I watched him head north to Corzines when he left. By the time he finished his tour, I doubt he remembered what *anybody* told him."

Kate said, "I 'spect he wrote things down, don't you, Claire? I know I sure would." She stared at her cards. "I bid six, by the way." She arose and opened a window.

Lew lifted his spit can and ducked his head before saying, "He's catching us little farmers when he oughta be talking to the Barbys and MacFarlanes and Mrs. Maple, even that Miles bunch, if he wants to get rid of his land. They's the ones with the money. And you can bet Wilgus has his nose in there. Seven—we can do seven, can't we, Elmer?"

I quickly bid eight.

Lew said, "Eight! I knew I shoulda bid higher. Elmer, can't you stop these women? They get one more hand, and then they're out."

"I'd bid if Claire would deal some face cards," Elmer growled. "We'll have to set these smart ladies. I'd guess the Land Bank has already sold several properties to the big farmers, but if one of *them* goes under, that'd make a splash. So they need to spread their exposure ... Lew, we can't let these gals clean our clocks again."

"It's a free country." I grinned. "You boys can bid it up if you think you've figured out how to play cards. Elmer's been trying to get his cousin in Harper County to move over here for six months. Why don't you tell Ray that the Land Bank's looking for people to farm their land?"

Kate laid a card down.

"Oh, goodie! I was hoping you'd have that queen, Kate. Game."

"We can't beat that kind of luck." Elmer tossed his cards on the table. "Yeah, Ray said Edith wants out of Harper County. I think they'll move our way."

213

"The Meisenheimer place is still available, from what I hear." Lew spat into the shiny can and slipped it under his chair.

Elmer perked up. "Hear that? Coyotes."

We cocked our heads to the high-pitched laughter-bark in the darkness.

I shivered. "They run a chill up my back when they yip like that. I can imagine them getting my chickens."

Lew laughed. "They come around here, and I'll blast them."

Elmer crowed. "I'd like to have somebody clean out that nest of coyotes over by us. They get one of my watermelons nearly every night. I've never seen the like—and the best ones too. Always seem to know when they're ripe."

Lew spat again. "You might try sleeping in your watermelon patch for a night or two. Pull your wagon out there and spread a blanket on the bed. You hear those varmints, and you raise up and let 'em have it. Might keep the Corzine boys out of there too. When Leonard farmed that place, he slept in his melon patch more than once. Nailed a couple big coyotes. Kept them away for a while."

Kate giggled. "That you did, Mr. Coyote-Hunter. Lew, didn't you say Leonard applied for a job with Seward County? If he hires on, he'll have to live in Kansas. The Eagan place will be available."

"That so? Well, I saw Leonard the other day in Forgan. He commenced telling me about this county job. Figures he's got a little pull with one of the commissioners. 'Course, it may be months before he gets on."

Elmer looked at Lew with keen interest. "Leonard moved to the Eagan place right before we rented Jenny's farm. I wouldn't mind farming that place."

Kate stood. "Anybody for a piece of chocolate cream pie?"

"Better check into it, Elmer," Lew said. "You never know who else might be laying in the weeds to pick up a nice little farm like that."

"Maybe I will. Sal, tomorrow let's write that yahoo from the Land Bank. Chocolate pie, you say, Kate?"

I twined a strand of hair around my fingers and stared at Elmer. So what if we rented the Eagan place? We could never buy it. I could see us meeting with the Land Bank man: *Yeah, we'll offer you thirty-five white hens and a red rooster, twenty-seven pigs, eight cows and five calves, and Diamond and the team as collateral for your money.*

My husband had always been the optimist, but this didn't make any sense at all.

Chapter Twenty-Three

The windless morning hinted at a delightful fall day. I hugged one of Elmer's khaki shirts over my blue print dress and stepped out of the dugout. With the dog at my side, I headed toward the canyon rim as early light scrubbed Venus from the sky. High clouds, shot through with gold, blushed crimson. In minutes, the sun would glint where the Cimarron River lay like a trail of syrup at the bottom of the valley.

I had asked Elmer to join me. We needed to talk about getting the folks on their own. Anywhere but with us.

He must have suspected what I was up to, because he said he had to go see a cow. Stucks Potter had a four-year-old Hereford for sale.

A cow.

I shook my head. Now that the Land Bank man said we could rent the Eagan place, Elmer said we needed to buy more cows. I had suggested the same thing two months ago, after Pop sent us thirty dollars. But no, Elmer only listened to Ray when it came to cows. As if I knew nothing about livestock.

Ring pranced ahead, eager for adventure.

The screen door slapped closed. "Hey! Where you goin'?" Elmer's dad again. He mopped his hair in place with one hand before mussing it with a flop of the gray felt hat. "Wait up. I'm gonna scout for cottontails."

"It's barely light, Dad, and I won't be out long. I'm only going over to the bluff." I stroked the dog's head as he shuffled over. *Will, pick up your feet, for heaven's sake.*

Will admonished the dog to watch for rabbits and listen to that meadowlark and don't be gallivanting too far ahead. He pushed up his hat brim, exposing his pale forehead. He huffed and waved his arm across the canyon. "This was fine country, Claire, before the big plows busted up the prairie twenty years ago. Buffalo grass everywhere and antelope, wild turkey, bobwhite quail. You ever hear of Coronado? He was a Spaniard. A con-keest-a-dor. Them was the

216

explorers that followed Columbus four hundred years ago. He and his men come down those canyons and crossed the Cimarron."

How did he know all that?

Will pointed toward the river. "Ain't nothin' to cross the Cimarron—it's never been more than three inches deep and a quarter-mile wide at flood stage. Them Spaniards heard about cities of gold. Supposed to be right out in this country. Seven Cities of Cibola was what they was called. As the story goes, they traipsed all up and down this prairie."

I couldn't help but wonder at that. "Did they find gold?"

Will pulled the felt hat down over his brow. "Nah. They ain't no golden cities out here. Never has been. Anyways, what would you do with all that gold? Buy land? They's plenty of land hereabouts, and I like it the way it is. If it'd only rain once in a while. By the way, did you and Elmer ever hear from that Land Bank fellow about rentin' the Eagan place?"

"Didn't Elmer tell you? We got it. The Washburns are moving next month. Then we can move in. Do you want to help?" I waited for the usual excuses.

"I don't know, Claire, my artheritis ain't gettin' no better. Maybe we oughta have Earl come and get us while you take your stuff over there. We'd be out of your way. Earl's in Enid now, which is a right nice town."

"Elmer said he's in Woodward."

"Yeah, Woodward, that's it. Anyways, that's a lot closer than Tulsa, so it'll be no trouble for him to fetch us."

Just then, two quail, then three more in quick succession, burst from the fencerow and whirred toward a brushy draw.

We jumped at the flurry of wings and watched as the birds disappeared.

"Look at that, Claire! Five of 'em. Knew I shoulda brought the gun."

I suppressed a smile. His impulsiveness and childlike love of nature seemed to be what bound him to everlasting irresponsibility. I couldn't help but like the old coot.

Elmer had returned by the time we got back to the house. He sharpened his corn knife with a hand file and listened with a knowing smile while Will detailed his plan to bag the quail. "That sounds good, but you've got to be a better shot than me to hit a quail on the fly with a rifle. I guess you haven't lost your eagle eye." Elmer grinned and gave me a wink. "Tell you what, Dad, why don't you help me get a load of feed? Get the rifle. Shells are on top of the dresser. Once we load that hayrack, you'll be able to ride on top and see anything that moves. Just don't shoot any of my cows. Or me!"

"Pshaw. I been huntin' long before you was dry behind the ears, Elmer."

⌘⌘⌘

Out of the north, a sharp wind picked up. Elmer and Will, bundled against the cold, had been gone about an hour. Mary Grace rolled out dough for sugar cookies, while I got the boiler and canning jars ready to put up peaches from Kate's trees. A muffled racket from the main road brought me to the kitchen window.

A battered pickup slowed, backfired, and then turned into our lane. Ray, Elmer's cousin. Maybe he'd made a deal with the Land Bank people too. Someone was with him ... but who? Too big for Edith.

Hastily drying my hands, I hurried to the front door at the same time as Mary Grace, who had lurched up from the breadboard. "Look who's here, Mother. It's Ray."

"Yes, I can see that, but who's that strapping young man?"

Ray approached the house, followed by his passenger.

I stared past Ray at the square-jawed face framed by a shock of black curly hair.

Nobody I'd seen before.

I stepped outside and greeted them. "Hello, surprised to see you, Ray. Get in out of the wind." I gave the visitor a smile.

Ray struggled out of his mackinaw and waved his companion in. "Hello, Claire. Yes, it's nippy. Might have an early winter. Aunt Mary Grace, didn't know you was here too. How you doin'?"

I discreetly observed the young visitor as the two men rubbed their hands above the potbellied stove. Ray's companion was a solid six feet and appeared to be in his late teens. The high cheekbones made me think of Indian blood and maybe something else.

Mary Grace stared boldly at the stranger for several seconds before muttering, "Oh, just fine, just fine, Ray, uh, where's your wife?"

He barked out a curious little cough. "Edith wants me to find a house over here before she makes that sixty-mile trip from Buffalo again."

"Why don't you look at the Meisenheimer place while you're here? It's five miles west."

"I might do that. Where's the menfolk?"

I clattered cups on the table and motioned them to sit. "They took the team and hayrack out to get a load of feed. Dry as it's been the last four months, we've got no pasture." In my haste, I slopped coffee on my wrist. I winced, then smiled at the stranger.

Ray seemed to have forgotten his manners. Weren't introductions in order?

The ill-fitting clothes and the hair over the young man's ears marked him as affected by hard times, maybe more than us. Even so, he was a guest—someone I could serve.

Not so long ago I'd been enjoying a three-year ride at Deluxe with fancy jewelry, marcelled hair, and expensive clothes. Now here I was, queen of a half cave/half house.

As Ray and Mary Grace discussed family, the visitor looked around the room. His gaze touched on the printed feed sack valances over the windows and my favorite glass figurines. He fingered Mama's doilies on the end table and chair arms, which most men hardly noticed. I'd never seen a man so observant. He seemed about to bend down and touch the rug Elmer's mother had braided.

He'd stood all this time but now moved to the folks' bed. As he scooted to make himself comfortable, the bedspread bunched against the wall.

Mary Grace frowned.

I wanted to chortle.

Elmer's mother again stared at the visitor. Then her eyes widened in comprehension. It seemed I was the only one in my house who didn't know this man.

Ray coughed again. With a wave of his hand, he announced, "Claire, this is Durward, Elmer's boy."

The words hit me like a blow to the stomach. I blinked to clear my eyes from the fog that seemed to fill the room.

No one said a word.

Ray and Mary Grace each shifted their gaze between me and Durward. *Elmer's boy.*

Elmer had once fathered a child. "A boy." That's how Elmer had put it when he told me a full year after our marriage. "I've got a boy. He's with Florence." Nothing more, as if discussion were too painful to bear. Our childlessness was because of me—my barrenness. I'd pushed the knowledge into the recesses of my mind.

Doubly flawed. A failed first marriage and, except for the miscarriage, unable to conceive a child in seven years with Elmer.

Too bad Elmer had disappeared from his child's life. This young man who stood in my house was Florence's son too.

I swiped my hand across my eyes.

It'd been a long time since anyone had spoken. All eyes waited for my response.

Of course. I'd just been introduced to my husband's son. A hoarse sound rasped out my lips. "Yes, you are finally here."

Was that how one greeted a lost son?

My face burned—such a loutish response.

But you're not a visitor. You're the offspring of my husband, the child I've not been able to have. Surely, you've always been part of our family. You've simply waited for us to notice you. I lifted my eyes to this boy-man, Durward.

My mother-in-law stared, her lips curling into a smirk.

He looked back at me.

Ray erupted in a coughing fit.

Focused on Durward, I caught only snatches of Ray's words. His voice hovered in the background, reciting to no one in particular the circumstances that had brought about the moment at hand. I felt inept, trivial as dry leaves rattling across the ground by the wind. A rush of questions inundated me.

This boy was flesh of my husband, but not of me. Did he see me as the wife of his father? As a substitute for his own mother? Or did he reject me as both? Why had Elmer not brought him into our lives earlier? I'd do as I should. Treat Durward as an honored guest.

Elmer had once sent a suit to Durward. Florence wrote back only to say it fit him.

Ray's voice wound tighter. He babbled, mixing phrases with a nervous cough. "I tell you, Claire, I debated whether I should even bring him over from Buffalo. Didn't know what Florence would say. You know how she is."

I shook my head.

"Well, I guess you don't. I thought, uh, I thought Elmer should see how his son had growed up, and here he is. Now, ain't it good the both of them can get together?" Another cough. It seemed he'd been talking for hours.

Mary Grace got up and pulled the tray of cookies from the oven.

I leaned toward Durward, wanting connection.

He regarded me with sad eyes.

I laughed nervously.

He laughed in return.

We laughed together, and I beckoned him over. "Wouldn't you like to sit at the table with us? And can I get you more coffee?"

"I could do with another drop." He moved to the table with an easy grace.

Conversation resumed.

Mary Grace suddenly acted as if she'd anointed a new prince in the family and gave him the royal treatment.

Durward brightened when she asked if he'd found work. "You bet. Put in a mile of fence for a rancher north of Buffalo. Worked cattle for two weeks on the XI. Them calves can kick!"

This provoked a round of stories about getting stepped on, kicked, run over, or knocked down by livestock.

Mary Grace pushed the plate of sugar cookies toward Durward.

"Can you stay over? I think we can make room." What was I saying? Only last week, I'd complained to Elmer about his folks crowding the place.

Durward's eyes widened. "You asking me to stay?"

"Why, of course. You're family." I paused. "As far as I'm concerned, you're welcome to spend the night. You too, Ray."

Durward seemed about to tear up. "That's real thoughtful, Claire, but I can't stay. I ain't got around to telling you, but I'm married. Wed two years and—"

"But you're not—" I stopped myself before I said too much.

"Yes, I surely am. I'm nineteen, and May's eighteen. We've got a baby girl, Sandra Lee. She'll be a year old Christmas day. I'll bring them over to show them off. You can see my baby too, Grandma." He smiled at her.

His baritone voice had a resonance that reminded me of the revival preacher who spoke at our church when I was ten. Pop had said he was a man of conviction. "How long since you saw El—your father?"

"Dad came to Buffalo a couple times, but I guess he missed us. Mom and I'd gone to Elkhart. I figured he'd come again. I was only eight the last time he saw me." He flicked a glance my way. Anyone could read the hurt in his eyes.

Eleven years! How could Elmer have done that? He was a man of feelings—did he not care for his own blood? I whispered the question that troubled me. "Do you think he'll know who you are?"

"Hard to say. He might not. I've growed up. Makes me wonder what will happen, what he'll say."

Such innocence. I paused and then said something which wasn't exactly true. "We've talked about you. More than once. Lotsa times, I guess. He'll be proud to see you." I had no idea if Elmer would be mad or glad, but Durward needed to be built up.

Ray coughed. "Like I said, your dad mentioned you last time he was in Buffalo. Wondered if you was growed up okay. I told him he'd be right surprised. That pleased him. He's had a lot on his mind, trying to make a go of it and all. It ain't easy to make a living in this country. Besides that, it takes a dollar's worth of gas to get to Buffalo and back."

Durward seemed to be avoiding eye contact. "Well, I guess you're right." He splayed his fingers before him as if he wanted to number his options. "I'm a mite shaky, thinking about when Dad sees me. When I meet him. Ray told me about you and, to tell the truth, I wasn't sure how *you'd* cotton to me, Claire. Or if I'd even like you. But you're nice, and I'm real glad of that." He lowered his voice again. "Claire, could … could you be with me when Dad meets me?" He gave a sheepish grin.

I caught my breath. "Well, yes. You want me there, I'll be there."

"Good." His voice almost broke and he swallowed.

I reached across the table and touched his arm. "Durward, you're not afraid of him, are you? He'll want to see you."

"No. I'm not afraid of him. No reason to be. But it's been a long time. Him and Mom had their differences. Maybe he *won't* want to see me. But you're sure you don't mind being right there, Claire, when he finds out who I am?"

I gazed at him, again seeing the little boy in his earnest eyes. "You can count on me. I won't let you down."

⌘⌘⌘

By late morning, I began getting dinner ready. Around noon, we heard the team and hayrack outside.

Ray stood. "Come on, son. Let's see if they need help."

After bundling up, the two men ambled outside.

I watched through the kitchen window. Durward had his collar up and hat pulled low. Would Elmer ask who he was? I wanted to be out with them, but that would be too obvious. Mary Grace was running the kitchen but, for once, I didn't care.

Ray and Durward had pitched in to help unload the hayrack. Nobody standing around talking. Even Will doing his part.

I went to the stove and started the gravy. Another look outside.

The men drifted toward the house, puffs of conversation in the chill air, but Durward strode ahead. Was he still an unknown?

I went to the door and waved them in.

Elmer and Will came in last, their faces ruddy from the cold. As they washed up, I whispered to Ray, already in the living room. "Does Elmer know?"

Ray shook his head.

Elmer and Will shared a towel and then went right to the stove. Elmer faced it, talking about the early frost while he massaged his hands over the heat. Durward stood on the opposite side, eyes averted. Will ignited a spark of static electricity when he placed his hand on Mary Grace's shoulder, and she barked in irritation. The room seemed to vibrate with tension.

I took a deep breath. "Elmer, do you know who this is?"

He ceased rubbing his hands together, and looked directly at the visitor.

The little clock on the table ticked desperately.

Elmer seemed a bit embarrassed and shook his head slightly.

I wanted to cry out for him to see the similarity with his own high cheekbones, his hazel eyes. Even though I'd missed it.

Durward simply looked into the face of his father, a stranger waiting to be known.

My lips moved but no words came. My tongue stuck to the roof of my mouth, which felt dry as sagebrush. I tried again, and, as if from afar, heard the strange sound of my own voice. "This is your son."

The two men stood, neither moving.

Had Elmer heard me? I spoke again. "Elmer, this is Durward, your son."

Bright dust particles danced in the sunlight reflected into the room, suspending time and thought over the hot stove. Something clunked inside it.

Elmer suddenly lurched around the heated thing, as if dodging through hell itself. He'd never learned how to be vulnerable. Now, he allowed himself only the luxury of grabbing Durward by the right hand and shoulder, seemingly unsure of the danger of an embrace.

The son reciprocated the gesture of his father, and so, the two men stood close, unable at that moment to come any closer. And unable to stanch the unbidden tears that coursed down the faces of both.

Chapter Twenty-Four

When we moved to the Eagan place in the spring of '38, I should have expected trouble. Sure enough, a week after we unpacked, Earl showed up with Will and Mary Grace.

My forehead throbbed like it'd been hit by a skillet.

Elmer met them outside.

He promised he'd put a stop to this. I better go see which way the wind is blowing. I caught Earl's end of the conversation as I opened the door.

"Bigger place, more room for them to get situated. Dad can have a garden here."

That's what they always said. *What a deal—giving us the chance to watch Dad grow peas.* "Oh, hello, Claire. How are you?"

As Earl carried in the two suitcases, I whispered to Elmer, "Don't forget our agreement. They can stay for a few days, but this is *not* to be a permanent arrangement."

"Nobody said it was. Now isn't the time to talk about it."

"Nothing will be done until you talk it out with Earl. Once he leaves, things happen. Tell him we're not putting them up for weeks on end, just because we've got 'more space.'"

"And just what do you propose we do?" he muttered.

"It's not for me to decide. You and your brothers need to work it out. You said you needed time, yet here they are again."

"All right, all right." He sauntered over to Earl's car and, with a bear-with-me-a-minute attitude, said, "Earl, how long did you plan to leave—have—the folks stay here?"

Earl squinted, as if he hadn't heard right. "I didn't know there was a time limit." He gave a fleeting look toward me and frowned. "I guess it'll be about as long as it, uh, suits you."

My frustration frothed into a sigh. "Elmer, it's not how long. What needs to be done is something permanent."

Both men looked sideways at me.

225

I glanced back to make sure Will or Mary Grace wasn't coming out to give their two cents' worth. "Elmer, can't you settle this so your folks don't drop in here at unexpected—"

"What she wants, Earl, is for the folks to have a place. A place where they can settle."

Earl looked at me incredulously. "Claire, you gotta realize Mom and Dad hardly have a nickel to their name. They can't go out and buy a place."

"So does this mean they'll forever live with us, or you, until they die? Surely—"

"Claire? Elmer?" It was Will, on the front step. "Which bedroom we got?"

"Look, Elmer, I got to get back to Woodward. Can't this wait?" Earl opened his car door.

Elmer waved his hand. "Go ahead. We'll settle this later."

Earl didn't look up as he started the old Chevy.

I was fit to be tied.

⌘ ⌘ ⌘

For the second day in a row, the southwest wind chased tumbleweeds past the house. Where did they all come from?

Elmer joined me in the kitchen. Backed against the wash stand, he laced up his shoes. He pointed. "Sal, that wind wasn't all bad. Look there. We might get some rain this week."

Sure enough, a moody murk of clouds had piled up in the northeast.

Will padded up behind us. "Nah, it ain't gonna rain. Wrong kind of clouds." He glanced at Elmer. "Your herd all there?"

"Depends on how that pasture fence held up. I'm fixing to take a look." Elmer put on his hat and went outside. He skirted the barn and headed toward the pasture.

Will rubbed his back. "My artheritis is acting up something fierce."

Mary Grace barked at him to get fuel for the stove. He ignored her and stirred a third teaspoon of sugar in his cup of coffee. "Quite a blow. Sand's drifted some, but ain't no reason to believe it tore the fence down."

I glanced at him. "It's not what you believe, Dad. It's what *is*."

He crushed his hat across his eyebrows. "I'm going out to my chair."

I shook my head.

Twenty minutes later, Elmer came from the barn, head down, like when he was upset. "We got work ahead of us," he said as he came in. "Sand drifted off the field west of the barn. Must be a hundred yards of pasture fence buried. Good thing I got the cows penned in the corral. Can't leave them there long or we'll run out of winter feed. Let them in the pasture and they'll be all over the county. I need more posts to fix that fence."

"We have a little money Pop sent last month," I said. "I planned to save that for baby chicks. We'll need wheat and maize seed, and—"

"I *know* what we need. I'll build over the buried fence where I can. If we run out of posts, we'll dig the rest out. Dad can help, and Ray's coming Sunday." He ran his fingers through his hair. "I'll get an idea how many more posts we'll need. You say your dad sent some money?"

I went into the bedroom and emerged with an envelope. "I can help dig postholes if I have to, but pulling posts and wire out of the sand is too much for me."

He tapped the envelope, and four ten-dollar bills slipped out. "Your dad's a good man. But I don't want you working out there. Dad can help until Ray gets here. The three of us will handle it. Biscuits ready?"

"Yes, biscuits and gravy."

After we ate, Elmer went out to the cottonwood and pointed toward the pasture.

Will gestured toward his back.

I could guess what he had to say. His arthritis again—or gallstones.

⌘ ⌘ ⌘

We delayed putting Sunday dinner on the table for over an hour, Elmer insisting we wait for Ray to show.

Apparently Mary Grace could take it no longer. "My stars, Elmer, the mashed potatoes will be hard as rocks and the gravy like cement. Let's go ahead and eat."

Magically, it seemed, Will was at the table.

Elmer sighed and joined him. "Ray's pickup probably quit on him. We'll get started on that fence without him."

Will swept two pork chops onto his plate. "He'll be here Tuesday. No reason to work out there in that wind before Ray gets here."

I started reheating the potatoes and gravy and glanced at Elmer.

"Dad, you and I'll get started tomorrow. That fence can't wait."

"I don't know, Elmer, my back. Like I said, it's artheritis. Can't we wait another day or two for Ray to make it over here?"

Elmer appeared not to hear him. "This afternoon I'll round up every post and piece of wire we've got on the place. The wind might stop tomorrow."

By mid-morning the next day, Elmer and Will had made real headway on digging out the buried fence. When they came in for the midday meal, Will announced, "I told Elmer I couldn't do no heavy work like I used to. Man my age shouldn't have to be doing this. What's to eat?"

I motioned him toward the table.

He filled his plate and carried it outside to the wicker chair.

I turned to Elmer. "I think you've lost your helper."

Elmer turned to me. "Get your work clothes on. He'll recover if he sees you helping me."

The wind drove Will inside. He pretended not to notice when I went out to help Elmer. However, within fifteen minutes, he'd joined us. He gestured at the wire stretchers I'd flung over my shoulder. "Gimme that, little lady. Can't have you out in this wind. This is man's work."

I shrugged the stretchers off my shoulder and onto his forearms. Without a look back, I trudged toward the house.

It was no surprise when Earl arrived a day later to take the folks back with him to Woodward. I figured Will had posted a distress letter when the fence project reared its head.

Elmer was philosophical when the folks left. "We made a good start on that fence, and Ray should get here tomorrow to help finish it up."

John McCarter and Durward showed up the following afternoon. Durward explained he and Ray had gotten as far as Gate before the pickup quit on them. He'd hitched a ride to Forgan, where McCarter had picked him up. Ray was looking for parts to get his pickup running.

⌘ ⌘ ⌘

The men worked dawn to dusk. The second evening, Elmer went to bed early, but I could tell Durward wanted to talk. He again brought up the fact that his dad stopped coming to see him when he was eight.

"How did that make you feel?"

A shrug. "I knew he worked someplace. Mama never mentioned you. But I started thinking Dad didn't feel I was important enough to come see me. That hurt a little."

"More than a little. Maybe he didn't think. Did you feel he was an awful person?"

"Well, I don't hate him. But if him and Mama hadn't argued so much, I would've seen more of him. He could've helped me understand things. Things a mother doesn't even think about. Mamas teach kids the indoors things, how to count and read and get along. I wanted him to show me how to be a man, to know when to be tough, when to follow and when to lead, and when to listen. A boy who never leaves home never grows up. Boys don't look to their mamas to show them how to get things done."

"Are you saying a woman doesn't know how to run things?" I didn't try to temper the sharpness in my voice.

"Now, don't get your dander up." He grinned. "Mamas listen and hold you on their laps and doctor your hurts. We need them most when we're babies, little boys. But, when I needed to prove myself, I'd watch how other men did things. Every little boy wants to grow up to be a man. Sometimes, I don't know how to act around other men, when to say my piece and when to listen." He sighed. "A few years ago, I realized I had to untangle myself from Mama's skirts so I could find out who I was."

I blurted, "Oh, you too?"

He smiled. "Maybe that's what everyone's looking for. Who they really are."

I dropped my eyes. "Hard times bring out what we're made of."

He leaned forward. "I love Mama, but I don't want to be anything like her. I want to be *me*, and my own dad would've

229

taught me how to do that, how to see myself." He said he hoped the future between him and his father would make up for what he missed as a boy.

"I'll do everything I can to help that along."

A smile creased his face. "I know you will, Claire. You take me at face value. Dad and Mama ain't never going to get along. She believes what she believes. One time when I was a kid, I drank six beers with my friend Eddie, and we took his twenty-two and shot up a bunch of mailboxes. Of course, she found out about it. I knew I was in trouble, but I was ready to face the music. Then she called me a drunk and wouldn't let up. Six beers and I was a drunk. I figured if she was going to call me a drunk, I'd be one. I went on one toot after another—just to show her."

"Now you can show her something else."

⌘ ⌘ ⌘

By the end of the week, the men finished the fence as a steady rain began to soak the parched pastures and fields. The life-giving moisture almost moved me to tears.

Ray's old pickup putted into the front yard Saturday morning to take Durward back to Buffalo. Before they left, I pulled Elmer aside. "Elmer, we've still got twelve dollars left from what Pop sent. Don't you think you should give five of it to your son for the help he's given us?"

He jerked his head up. "I like that, but don't forget you almost had a fit when I suggested we spend a few dollars on the folks."

My face burned. "It's not the same. Durward came to help, and he has a family to feed. Your folks expect us to take care of them. You saw how hard it was to get your dad out to help build that fence."

"Sal, you want to help Durward, 'cause you cotton to him. If you want to be consistent, put yourself out to help the folks." He gave me a so-there look.

I glared at him, stuck for a response.

"I agree about paying Durward. He's my son and I want to help him. Mom and Dad are family too. You're being a mite hypocritical in how you're deciding who gets our donations."

I wanted to smack him. Instead, I turned and stomped back into the house.

Chapter Twenty-Five

A letter from Pop made me want to cry. Myrrl and Grace were expecting another child.

> *I know you'll be pleased at this news. Myrrl said to tell you that if it's a girl, they'll name her after you.*

They already had three children. Wasn't that enough? When would I get a turn? I told God I was still waiting. The days fell off the calendar like pebbles dropped into a dark pool. After a while, even the ripples disappeared. I gazed out the north window, seeing nothing.

Back to the letter. It was three ... four ... five pages. Pop probably took half a morning to write it. I looked at the sheaf of papers, ashamed at feeling sorry for myself.

> *Another grandbaby. Someday you'll give me one too. All in God's time. Read Hannah's story in 1 Samuel. God answered her prayer and he'll answer yours. One of my favorite passages. Did you know that my name—and his—Samuel, means "ask of God"?*

I shook my head. God wasn't going to answer my prayer. He hadn't before.

Except during the sand storm.

Okay. I pulled my Bible off the sewing machine cabinet. Finally I located 1 Samuel.

Right from the first verse, I got bogged down—Elkanah, Tohu, and Zuph—and skipped down. Elkanah was mentioned again.

"He had two wives; the name of the one was Hannah, and the name of the other Peninnah: and Peninnah had children, but Hannah had no children ... And she was in bitterness of soul, and prayed unto the Lord ..."

I skipped Eli, the priest, to continue with Hannah.

"'I am a woman oppressed in spirit but I have poured out my soul.' And the Lord remembered her. She gave birth to a son; and she named him Samuel. But Hannah said ... 'I will not go up until the child is weaned; then I will bring him that he may stay there forever ... for this boy I prayed, and the Lord has given me my petition. As long as he lives he is dedicated to the Lord.'"

The dog barked.

I closed the thick book. What did it mean? *Stay there forever.* Why was God so demanding? I pulled on a sweater and went outside to help Elmer carry the sacks of coal from the car trunk and stack them in the west end of the milk house.

He told me Durward and May had just had another little girl.

I began to cry.

Elmer didn't ask why, but he put his arms around me and rocked me until I quieted.

After supper, I explained it all.

He listened to the very end and told me he loved me.

⌘ ⌘ ⌘

Elmer's brother John, his wife, Moselle, and their eight kids had come and gone, staying for dinner and supper, as they did most Sundays. I rinsed the last of the dishes while Elmer sat nursing his pipe. I picked up a dishtowel. "Did John say anything about how they were doing?"

"He says he's going up to Colby or Dodge. Some place to find work."

"He'd better consider his wife. I don't see how she takes care of that houseful of kids. John never lifts a hand. Louise and Bonnie are old enough to work, but I never see them helping their mother. I'm worried about Mosie. She's not well, and he doesn't notice."

"Aren't you a tad critical? John didn't say anything about her being poorly."

"That's because he's oblivious. That seems to run in the family."

Elmer leveled a look my way. "Oh, yeah? And *your* family is a sterling example of moral sensitivity? Didn't sound like they treated you so nice after you left Harold."

I had no chance to win that argument. "Did John tell you they were going to have another child?"

"Another kid? No, he didn't say anything."

"Well, Mosie did. She said, 'Claire, I'm expecting. Worries me to death. I can't bear another child.' She sounded desperate, said how run-down and tired she feels all the time. After Phyllis was born, Doc McCreight told John straight-up that she wasn't to have another child or it would kill her. That poor woman can't go on having kids forever. She won't make it."

⌘ ⌘ ⌘

Heavy snows in the winter of 1939 appeared to end the drought and the suffocating dust storms. Spring brought news of another storm— Hitler had invaded Czechoslovakia. But we still hadn't gotten through the depression, though the President said it had already ended.

Elmer snorted at this. "More of the same from Roosevelt. I haven't seen any change in our finances. When we can make a decent living, I'll believe it's over."

John still brought his family over for dinner every Sunday that spring. Mosie was such a sweet woman, but I could hardly tolerate John. He whined about his pasture fence blowing over and that he couldn't afford to fix it.

Elmer slipped him a five-dollar bill.

I tore into Elmer after they left. "I don't think the money Pop gave us should be used to cure John's stupidity. Let him fix his own fence."

Elmer frowned. "How do you square that with the religion your family talks about? Besides, that's the exact amount you suggested I give Durward."

"One act of charity to your kin and it gets thrown back in my face." I glared at him. "Religion doesn't mean we pay for John's problems. He's a grown man. Besides, when Earl showed up last week with his 'friend,' you had a different take on it, remember? I asked where Mae was, but you said you didn't know and didn't care, 'cause your brothers' personal lives weren't your business."

"That fat dame won't last long. I'll bet Earl goes back to Mae."

"I've seen her kind. This Gertie—Gertrude—is reeling him in.

233

Makes no difference that he's married. She hung on to his arm like he'd float over the barn if she didn't hold him down. To think he can bring that hussy into our house while Mae sits at home …"

"Mae's whiny. Never has trusted Earl."

"Doesn't this Gertrude woman prove her point? And Gertie hardly stepped inside our front door before she had her mouth running. The only time she closed it was to light up a cigarette. How she got all those stories about John's family is beyond me."

"Well, she's a gossip. Earl's probably taken by how she fills out a dress."

I snorted. "She reminds me of those fat woman paintings we saw back in Cincinnati."

Elmer's eyes twinkled. "You saying she looks like a cow?"

"Oh, Elmer, enough about Earl's women. We were talking about John. Please don't give him any more money."

⌘ ⌘ ⌘

Ray came over to tell us that Durward had called to say his baby girl had died in her crib. Not even one year old. I was heartsick for Durward and told Elmer I'd join him at the services, but the morning of the funeral, I couldn't stop vomiting. I told Elmer to go without me.

He said he'd probably see Jim and Beatrice but didn't expect to spend much time with Durward and May if Florence was there.

I was still sick when Elmer returned and hardly heard his report about the trip to Buffalo.

The next morning he took me to Liberal to see Dr. McCreight.

The doctor examined me and called Elmer in before he gave his diagnosis. "Claire, you're going to have a baby."

Elmer's Cheshire cat smile disappeared.

I could only gasp. "Would you say that again?"

He repeated himself and smiled.

"Since my miscarriage …" I burst into tears. "Do you realize I've waited to hear that for almost six years?"

⌘ ⌘ ⌘

After waiting another month just to be sure, I sent a letter to Pop. Then we drove over to tell Ray and Edith and completed the circuit to share the news with Lew and Kate. For the time being, we wouldn't tell anyone else.

Gertie would be the last to hear.

Earl stopped by in early August—with Gertie.

Elmer pulled him over to look at the carburetor on the car.

From the kitchen window, I peered out to see if Gertie was coming in.

She stood behind Earl, her slip showing, primping in a mirror she fished out of her purse.

I double-checked. It was an automobile rear-view mirror she held. Earl had probably picked it up from a junk yard.

She turned toward the house and headed my way.

I braced myself. *Might as well be decent.* I poured her a cup of coffee and asked about her family.

Instead of answering the question, she gave a blow-by-blow account, which I'd heard before, of how she met Earl at a honky-tonk outside Catoosa. "I came in with my cousin Mildred, and Earl spotted me right away. He stood there, his devil eyes looking across that dance floor, an arm around a girl on each side. Really gave me the once-over. I stared right back at him, and he came straight toward me and introduced hisself, leaving them two hussies fuming. By the way, Claire, you got any more of that chocolate cake you had last time? I ain't had dinner yet."

I set a piece of custard pie in front of her and turned to finish the dishes.

Between bites, she said, "Now why don't you set down and have a piece with me?"

Before I thought better of it, I said, "Better not. My stomach's been unsettled lately."

"Now don't go telling me you're pregnant too." She stared at me like a cat with a mouse.

My jaw dropped. I couldn't find words to send her off that track fast enough.

"You are!" She raised her fork and licked the back of the tines. "I'll be. You really are. I'll have to spread the word. Moselle pregnant and so are you!"

Chapter Twenty-Six

ELMER

Gertie was bending Claire's ear when Earl and I came in from the barn. Talked like she was a founding member of the clan. She turned to tell me what she thought about John.

We all knew he was worthless, but nobody liked to hear it from an outsider.

She talked like she had inside dope. "I'll tell you, Elmer, I don't see how Mosie takes care of them eight kids. She's as big as a house, and *she's miserable*. John only took her to see Doc McCreight ten days ago. Can you believe it? McCreight hit the ceiling. Said he couldn't take care of her if John didn't get her in there until the baby was due. That woman is in bad—"

Earl interrupted as if he meant to shut Gertie up. "The doc said Moselle's got poison in her system. Told John in no uncertain terms to bring Mosie to the hospital. John—you know how he is—he said they didn't need no hospital for the other kids. He's not gonna do anything if it costs him, mostly 'cause he ain't got a red cent."

Gertie fumbled in her purse. "You know what he'll do, Earl. He'll make her have that kid right at home in her own bed. He won't spend a dime for proper care of his own kin."

Earl brought a lit match to her cigarette.

She squinted through the smoke swirling around her moon face. "That ain't all. Bill and Kenny, the oldest boys, was smoking behind McCarter's shed when we drove up. It wouldn't surprise me none if Tommy isn't into his dad's tobacco too, and how old would you say he is, Earl—maybe eight?" Without waiting for an answer, she rolled on. "I know Bonnie ain't even eighteen, and she's seeing a guy who's pushing thirty. Alfred somebody. Last time we stopped by, Louise took off with a young smart aleck in an old flivver. Nearly ran us off the road, laughing like they didn't have no sense."

Earl rubbed her arm. "Now, honey, you don't know nothin' about him. Moselle said Louise's boyfriend was a Headrick. Comes from a decent family, she said."

"Maybe so, but I wouldn't let *my* LaVonne go out with a man nearly twice her age, I'll tell you that. Seems like this whole family is out of control." She tapped ashes from her Chesterfield into the saucer.

I stared at this woman. Wasn't Earl going to shut her up? *You don't talk trash about someone else's family. Especially if you're trash yourself. Well, this floozy isn't running things in my family.* I threw the door open. "Earl, step out here a minute."

Earl jerked his head up, eyes wide. "Yeah. Sure, what's up?" He pushed his chair back.

Gertie immediately stood to join him.

I stepped right in front of that old heifer and slammed the door in her face. I started in on Earl before we got off the steps.

⌘⌘⌘

Earl and Gertie showed up a month later, her in the lead, which Claire would be sure to bring up. Mosie had gone into labor and John rushed over to a neighbor's to call Edith. Edith told him to get the doctor out there. Ray had gone to Forgan, and Edith had no transportation.

Dr. McCreight barely got there in time to deliver a baby boy. He told John to call him if Mosie's condition changed. Edith went over later that evening. She found Mosie half-conscious, her bed soaked in blood.

By the time McCreight returned the fifteen miles from Liberal, Mosie was dead. Gertie said John went crazy, screaming like a madman and blaming the doctor and Edith.

Claire almost fainted.

I helped her into a chair.

Her lips moved, but it took a minute before she could talk. "Remember what Mosie said? 'I'm wore out, so exhausted I can hardly stand.' Mosie was afraid no one would be there when she needed them. That's what happened."

I knelt and cradled Claire's head against my shoulder.

Her whole body shook and her tears wet my shirt. "Moselle never had a life of her own, nothing for herself."

That was true.

The door clunked.

I glanced up.

Earl had taken his woman and gone.

Claire rose up and gazed past me. "Now Gertie will be telling how I got delirious, how unstable I am, or some such thing, but I don't care. Moselle is dead. Honey, she's dead."

I whispered to her, imagining Mosie's struggle for life while the family blundered outside that closed bedroom door.

Claire would be giving birth to our baby in less than a month.

I'd never given it much thought. It would be simple, I assumed, like when Durward was born. That had been during another life, which I'd put behind me when Florence and I split. Claire was my wife now, and I figured I'd only have to get her to the hospital.

Strange, all sorts of what-ifs seeped into my mind. Hamstrung as I was, all I could do was be there when Claire's time came.

⌘ ⌘ ⌘

Two days after they buried Mosie, John drove down. Said he needed to talk.

Claire was busy with breakfast dishes, so I motioned him outside.

John didn't beat around the bush. "Elmer, I been through a lot here. Big responsibility. I was wondering if the two youngest girls could stay with you until things work out."

I hoisted a leg over the front fender of his sedan. "What needs to work out?"

"Well, now, it's a lot of responsibility, taking care of eight kids."

"Eight? Did you forget about the last one?" I squinted at him under the brim of my hat.

"Oh. Well, yeah. Maggie, she has the baby."

"And the others? Anybody got them?"

"Uh, Mosie's folks—Weldon and Hassie. I thought you met them at the funeral. They'll help out, I expect." John cursed softly. "It's hard, Elmer, all by myself."

I looked away. Not a situation I'd want.

"So, what do you say? If you could help me out, take the girls ..."

I glanced toward the kitchen window. "Why don't I get back to you?"

"Oh, I see. You have to check with the boss."

I glared at him. "I'll let you know. Tomorrow."

John cranked the Hudson and revved the engine a few times before he tore out of the yard.

So he was mad. I didn't care. It was an easy call—him or Claire on the prod.

I hung my hat on a nail and scooped a cup of water from the galvanized bucket.

Claire hovered by me, waiting to hear the news. John never came by unless he wanted something, and she knew it.

"John wants us to take the two little girls."

She got this stricken look in her eyes. "Us? What did you tell him?"

"I almost said we'd take them. Then he mouthed off. So I told him I'd get back to him tomorrow." I shook my head. "He won't take care of those kids by himself."

"Elmer, we're having our own baby next month! I can't look after that bunch. Those kids are John's responsibility. It's about time he started acting like it."

She was right. No use even talking about it. I told her to forget it.

She leaned over her belly and dropped her head against my chest. I realized how vulnerable she was. How much she needed me. I'd better be ready. John hadn't been there for Mosie. It'd be easy for me to make the same mistake. I shook my head at how I'd bulled along, doing things my way.

Actually, I'd been that way for most of our marriage.

⌘ ⌘ ⌘

Claire milked the cows Christmas Eve. She'd had to remind me the day before was our ninth anniversary. I wasn't much good at remembering dates. I'd never learned to milk a cow, either. Didn't know how I'd manage after she went to the hospital.

The wind started to howl.

I broke the ice in the stock tank, fed all the cattle, and checked my new pigs.

That sow had mashed half her previous litter.

At the back of the barn, movement caught my attention.

Claire waved from the dark rectangle of the open barn door. Two full milk buckets.

I waved back and peeked into the hog shed. A quick count of the pink bodies nursing—all present. I carried the pails across the road to the milk house, Claire and the dog beside me.

Suddenly, she lurched and grabbed my arm.

Made me almost spill the milk. "What's wrong? You all right?" I set the buckets down and bent to her.

"It's only a cramp." She leaned against me, biting her lower lip. "It's hard … worst yet."

I touched her forehead. In the chilled air, her perspiring skin felt cold under my hand. Wisps of snow swept the yard. "Let's get you inside."

I helped her to the house, brought the milk in, and put bean soup on the stove.

She shook her head when I offered her a taste. Shortly after eight o'clock, Claire called from the bedroom, "Elmer, my water broke."

I got in there quick. "Do we go now?"

"No, not yet. I helped Mama when my sisters gave birth. Several times. Could you get some towels?"

I hurried in with the towels.

Back to the north window. Bits of snow appeared out of the inky blackness and pecked at the glass. Frost edged the window.

I grabbed a lamp. As I opened the front door, the wind snuffed the flame.

Dummy.

I pulled on my mackinaw and went back outside. The wind nearly took my breath away. Snow smacked my face—a blizzard in the making. If we didn't beat the storm, it would destroy us. But if we went out and got stuck in that storm, we'd be goners.

Under these conditions, I wouldn't be able to see the edge of the road. Eighteen miles to Liberal. Might as well be to the moon. How long did it take a woman to have a baby? Claire had to hang on. What could I do to help? I went back inside and paced in the kitchen, cursing, more a cry of anguish than anger.

I heard Claire praying and shut my mouth.

Feeling sorry for myself wouldn't help. *Wish Edith was here. Somebody. Anybody but just me. Why did this storm have to come up now?*

The moaning wind subsided to an impatient sigh. Snow fell at an angle.

I let Ring onto the porch and went back into the bedroom.

Claire gripped my arm. The strength in her hand seemed to power right into me. "I think I'll be able to hold things together for a while. Contractions have stopped, but I'm wet. Can you get more towels? And read to me from the Psalms?" She caught her breath. "Honey, my Bible ... on the sewing machine cabinet."

I brought the towels.

She dried herself off, her voice steadying me.

She was the rock; I was nothing but a pile of sand. But I couldn't let her know how shaken I was. "The wind's backed off, but we can't let ourselves get caught in a blizzard. With daylight, it'll be a cinch to drive into Liberal. Think you can you hang on until morning?"

"I think so ... I hope so." She was quiet.

I studied her face in the glow of the lamp. She was really a beautiful woman.

"But I ... we may have to go before dawn."

I wanted to call for help, but there was nothing outside but the snow and wind. "If it's storming too much, I'll ride Diamond across the section to get Edith. I'll—"

"No, Elmer! Don't leave me."

I held up both hands. "Sorry, Sal, that was dumb. I'm staying right here." *So stupid. I can't go off and leave her. What if the baby comes while I'm gone?* I picked up her Bible. "What was it you wanted me to read? Psalms? Where's that?"

She closed her eyes. "It's right in the middle. Just read anything from it."

I stared at the words I opened to. They seemed to fit, so I leaned toward the lamp. "I will love thee, O Lord, my strength. The Lord is my rock, and my fortress, and my deliverer; my God, my strength, in whom I will trust; my buckler, and the horn of my salvation, and my high tower. I will call upon the Lord, who is worthy to be praised; so shall I be saved from mine enemies."

Every so often, I glanced over to see how she was. I was glad I was some help, even in this little way.

Before first light on Christmas Day, the storm let up again. Claire said the contractions were coming more frequently and getting stronger.

When she said we'd better go, I hopped to it. Grabbed the extra blankets, her clothes, and the other things we'd set out. After I warmed up the car, I got her settled in the back, and we headed north.

Blue Bell Road headed us right into the teeth of the wind. That wasn't all bad, as it scoured snow off the roadbed. After the turn west at Lauderback's, the snow had drifted sharp ridges across our path. At times, the earth seemed to blend with the sky. The road seemed tilted, like we might slide off the edge of the world.

I let out a curse.

Claire's voice sounded behind me.

Thank God—yes, *God*—she was talking to him. I couldn't hear all the words but knew she was praying. Like she'd done back at the house.

We needed all the help we could get. It seemed dangerous to acknowledge him—whoever he was. But the fear lifted, and I didn't cuss after that.

Two long hours later, we crossed Highway 54 and punched through the drifted snow toward Epworth Hospital. Nothing could stop me now. I breathed easier. The streets seemed as empty and worn down as my dear wife must've felt. Not a soul to watch us arrive. Everyone was hunkered down to wait out the blizzard.

The two-story red brick structure loomed ghost-like out of the flying snow. We'd already been through so much—would the place be shut down? A soft glow through southeast windows said otherwise.

I pulled the car close to the lower entrance. Snow had piled in front of the door of the hospital, like they weren't expecting anyone to come through the blizzard. I managed to get part of the snow cleared when a frowning nurse appeared from somewhere inside.

At the words "my wife," she retreated to the interior and returned with two helpers. They got Claire covered up real quick and on a wheeled bed before rolling her inside. The hallway surprised me with its warmth. I caught a whiff of rubbing alcohol, and a radiator banged somewhere.

Claire clutched my hand as I walked beside the bed, but before I knew what happened they'd eased me off to the side, like I was in the way.

Chapter Twenty-Seven

CLAIRE

"Where's Elmer? Honey!" I tried to see where he'd gone, but another spasm hammered my back.

The nurse beside me motioned. "Probably to the waiting room. You don't need him for what you have to do anyway." The squeak of her shoes on the linoleum floor sounded official.

"But I *want* him with me. He brought me here, through that blizzard. Don't you ..."

Neither nurse was listening. The bed on wheels swept through double doors into a space off the hallway.

The older nurse, Bertha, announced we'd entered the delivery room. All organization and purpose, they got me onto the real bed, chatting back and forth as if they were putting laundry out to dry. After they got me undressed, I began to relax, glad to be under the care of women. Nothing against Elmer, but I needed people who knew what they were doing. I was about to be a mother, the event I'd been waiting for all my life.

They gave me a quick scrub and whisked a hospital gown over me. I looked for Dr. McCreight and asked what time it was.

Bertha, a wisp of a thing whose pasty coloring belied her warm smile, said, "Time don't mean anything, honey, until you take care of business."

Another cramp brought a gasp. I squeaked, "I wanted to check. My sister, Ethel, said her babies always came in four—or was it fourteen hours? I can't remember."

They chuckled. The young sprite, Norma Jean, took my temperature and said I'd have plenty of time to work out my personal theories on birthing.

An evergreen Christmas wreath on the far wall took me far away, and I thought of Pop. He'd be praying for me. For me and this baby, and Elmer too. I asked for Dr. McCreight twice more before I got an answer.

"He'll be in here when you're ready for him."

I must have fallen asleep for seconds ... or several minutes. I drifted in and out of wakefulness. My baby was full term, and I was ready. At least I thought I was.

The alternating back massages and warm compresses eased the pain, but I couldn't stand for them to touch me during contractions. I must've changed positions fifty times.

Hours later, I caught a grim look on Bertha's face. My baby was in trouble, no two ways about it.

Dr. McCreight still hadn't come to see me. Why?

The head nurse was in and out.

Bertha said she'd only had two mothers exceed thirty hours of labor, but if I didn't get busy, I'd break their record.

I wasn't interested in records; I wanted to have my baby. Ridiculously, they still wouldn't let Elmer in.

ELMER

"You Claire's husband?"

I turned, a smile coming.

No dice. It was the chunky, blonde nurse waving at me from the end of the hallway. Said she'd like to do the paperwork before she went off shift.

I almost gave her a smart answer, but Claire had told me to be nice.

The nurse motioned me toward a desk in a corner of the lobby. What with the popping of her chewing gum and clacking of that typewriter, I had to ask her to repeat the questions several times. She went at it like she intended to pound the thing through the desk top.

"Are you through with your questions? Because I have one of my own."

Ten seconds later, she met my eyes.

"We've been here quite some time, and I haven't seen anything of a doctor. Isn't McCreight supposed to be here?"

She stopped chewing and glanced around, frantic-like. Too bad the head nurse wasn't there to help her out. The blonde pushed a stack of papers from one side of her desk to the other and then moved it back.

"So?"

"Doctor McCreight isn't here. He left yesterday afternoon to deliver a baby at Adams. With the storm and all, we haven't heard from him. But you can be sure your wife will be well taken care of until he gets back."

I gave her a look that brought her wad of gum to a standstill. "You mean to say that, after us coming eighteen miles through a blizzard, you don't have a doctor available? Woman, this is an emergency! What about my wife and baby?"

She shook her head and ducked.

I backed off. She hadn't ordered up that snowstorm any more than I had. But it irritated me that the self-important people running these hospitals couldn't be straight-up. The blonde had already made sure I was prepared to pay the standard forty-dollar charge for hospital births.

I left her sitting there and went to the waiting room.

Adams was thirty miles south. McCreight should have delivered that kid and already returned to Liberal. Unless something had happened.

Not long afterward, the head nurse came out of her office, tapping a lead pencil against her notepad as she approached. Her message was short and sweet. McCreight hadn't been heard from since he'd left Adams at four that morning. That meant he was lost someplace between there and Liberal. She'd already called the sheriff to organize a search party.

I knew Ed Bartlett. He'd find that doctor if he had to go on foot.

She asked me if I wanted coffee.

Coffee? Woman, are you crazy? This is no time for a tea party. Let's take care of my wife first. I shook my head.

I'd beat the blizzard to get Claire in there, but it looked like the storm might have the last say.

Claire needed to know I was still there. I headed toward where I thought she'd be. The same nurse who'd wheeled her in blocked the door and pointed me back to the waiting room.

I paced and fretted. Finally I grabbed my coat and went out into the fading light to walk the two blocks to Maggie's house.

She insisted we pray.

I half listened while she called upon the Almighty to help my wife and baby.

Still no word about McCreight when I returned an hour later. Told the front desk I was going home. I still had my coat on, so I was out the door before the nurse could respond. Had to feed my livestock, and those fool cows would be due for milking. Wished I'd thought to have Ray and Edith come over and do our chores. I returned five hours later.

The head nurse was waiting for me. Her hand whipped like a flag in the wind and pointed me toward an adjoining room. "Sit down. I have some things to say to you."

I wasn't used to such talk, especially from a woman, but I saw the weariness in her face. I waited for the completion of a one-sided conversation.

Her voice started ragged and quickly ascended loud enough to be heard in the hallway. "Whatever possessed you to take off like that—while your wife was struggling with every ounce of her strength to give birth? What if we'd needed to contact you?"

I started to tell her I had to break the ice in the stock tank, that I had livestock to feed, that I was so worried I couldn't think straight—but she waved me off.

"Never mind. I don't want to hear it," she snapped. "You better listen to me. Your wife has been in labor for over *twenty-four hours.* She's a remarkably strong woman but she can't keep this up if the doctor doesn't get here soon. We'll do what we can, but at her age—thirty-three, I believe—and this being her first childbirth, her pelvic structure is quite rigid." Her tone softened. "The worst is this, Mr. Hall. The infant had a bowel movement, which may have poisoned the uterus. From all my years of experience in obstetrics, I'll ... I'll tell you straight. There's no hope for the baby, and there's very little for the mother." She dropped her eyes to allow me the privacy of my own response.

Her words came like ice clattering off a roof. So that's why she was so worked up—Claire was in bad trouble.

I imagined Moselle lying on a blood-soaked mattress while Edith tried to revive her and John screamed blasphemies at the heavens.

The room swam around me in a murk of shadows and violent light. I forgot how to inhale. Backed against the wall, I remained sitting up. After what seemed like several long minutes, I sucked in a breath.

The head nurse still sat across from me, a frown on her face. She shouted, "Get the smelling salts!"

"No. I'm all right. And my wife will be all right. Claire will get through this. And our baby will make it. My wife prays, you hear!" I stood, weaving.

"Maybe you should pray too."

Yeah, if I knew how.

Several times that evening and night, I almost bolted out to Maggie's house but didn't want to face the head nurse's wrath again. This part of the battle, I'd do by myself. Late that night, I heard someone say the search party had found McCreight stalled in a snowdrift.

And Claire? Nothing I could do. Nothing except "be available to her."

CLAIRE

I called several times for Elmer.

A turnip-colored face crossed my line of sight. "Your husband's right outside, Claire, waiting on us to finish our job. It depends on you."

I felt like my insides had been twisted, pulled, and squeezed. I'd resisted the pain at first, but couldn't for long. Fighting it only made me feel worse. I cried to God for strength. Like our old mare, I took the bit in my teeth and bore down.

Someone said it was past midnight. Pain came in waves. I tried not to wonder if I could last.

A man's voice echoed beside me, and I looked up, expecting to see Elmer.

A cloth wiped perspiration from my face.

I blinked. "Doctor McCreight!"

He squeezed my hand and did a quick exam. "The head is too

high. Let's get to work."

In the blurred minutes that followed, I knew I was on track to deliver this child. Hannah and Samuel—*Ask of God.* God had responded to her request. I hoped he'd answer mine. I had asked God. If he answered my prayer, I'd name my baby the same as Hannah's baby boy. The same name as my dad. I never stopped to think that it might be a girl.

ELMER

"Hey, Elmer, wake up."

I jerked awake and tried to figure out where I was.

Somebody stood over me. Bartlett, the sheriff.

"Ed! You're back. McCreight? Where's the doc?"

The big man clapped me on the shoulder and slumped into a nearby chair, his face ruddy. He nodded at the admitting nurse as she handed him a cup of hot coffee. "Much obliged." He perched his Stetson on his lap. "Be glad you didn't have to go out there again, Elmer. Tough sledding, let me tell you. Almost didn't find McCreight. He missed the jog at the section line south of Highway 64—ran smack into the ditch. Snow would've covered him up if we hadn't seen the top of his Buick poking up. I hope he's thawed out by now. Boy, he was glad to see us."

While he rattled off the rest of the story, I realized the doctor had already gone in with Claire even though the man probably hadn't slept in two days.

Bartlett retrieved his hat, clapped me on the shoulder again, and trudged out of the waiting room.

Once more, it was just me in the quiet. After an hour of pacing, I finally sprawled back on my nest on the big couch.

About three in the morning, the day after Christmas, somebody shook me again.

One of the nurses. "You better scrub up. You're the father of a seven-pound, six-ounce baby boy. Everybody's doing just fine. You can come see your wife and son now."

I bawled like a little kid.

Chapter Twenty-Eight

CLAIRE

The land bank man's maroon Packard thudded up the washboard road and pulled into our grassless yard.

I hurried from the bedroom, where I'd put the baby down for a nap.

Elmer smirked as he stood. "Your boyfriend's here."

I swatted his backside with a dish towel. "Shut your mouth, smarty-pants. You better not say a word to him about what I looked like last time he came to see us, you hear?" I pushed him out the door.

That first time, the bank man never did see my face hidden by that big bonnet and my body lost in Elmer's clothes.

But that was then and this was now.

I'd scrubbed and polished the linoleum floor, even where it'd worn down to the planking. I could serve that big-shot U.J. Ingraham fresh coffee in my shiny kitchen. I smiled at Elmer's complaint about my starch job on his blue cotton shirt, that he knew what a knight felt like getting into a suit of armor. I made a last check on Sammy and caught my reflection in the bedroom mirror.

The simple print dress hugged my small waist. Not bad for having a baby ten months ago.

Elmer looked confident as he stepped outside to greet the man.

I dabbed on a bit of lipstick.

That banker was going to forget about the clown in clodhoppers and men's overalls.

I waited at the door, wishing I could hear the first words between these two men who'd never met before.

Ingraham had a paunch, but he knew how to dress. His brown pinstriped suit looked tailor-made. The gold watch chain draped across his vest glittered *money*.

Most farmers practically bowed in the presence of the money

lenders. This banker was going to get a surprise if he thought he could pull anything on my husband. And Elmer was at least half a head taller.

Ingraham, big valise in hand, stumbled in like a confused barn owl, eyes blinking as they adjusted from the outside light.

I gave him a twenty-carat smile and held out my hand. "How wonderful to see you again, Mr. Ingraham."

He stood stock-still.

I figured I'd better help him. "I met you when you stopped by the farm we rented from Jenny Washburn. Elmer was—"

"Yes, yes! Of course, I remember. The last time was so, uh, hurried. I almost didn't recognize you. A pleasure to see you again."

I gestured toward a chair. "Please, have a seat. Would you like some coffee?"

Elmer settled himself at the table and shot me a quick grin.

"Certainly, and call me U.J., please." He sat and fumbled in his black leather valise. All business now, he arranged a sheaf of papers on the table. "I wanted to meet with you folks, as your letter said you'd be interested if this property came up for sale. We've now placed it on the market. This is called, in local parlance, the Eagan place, and it consists of four hundred acres, including one hundred seventy-five acres of pastureland, the house, barn, a producing water well, and various outbuildings."

Elmer seemed bored. He stared out the window and laid his pipe carelessly in the ashtray, as if he had better things to do. "Not sure we're interested. I'll tell you straight—your outfit better not abuse farm people like the banks did over the past eight years."

"Oh. Yes, absolutely." Ingraham sat back like a scolded child, his chin tucked in.

"Farmers were treated like the dirt they planted their corn in. Land and machinery was repossessed if a note was *a day late*. They'd take a man's horses and plow, condemn his family to starvation. That how your people do things?"

Ingraham blinked, his hand rubbing the mole on his chin. "No, sir. We are not a private operation. We are the *Federal* Land Bank. My letter stated you have first right of refusal to acquire this property, by virtue of renting and operating this farm. The Federal Land Bank is willing to liquidate the entire parcel and improvements for the sum of three thousand dollars." He paused and looked at Elmer as if to emphasize what a great offer that was.

At less than ten dollars an acre for the farm plus the house, it *was* a great offer. The place was easily worth four times that amount. But we had only $6.38 left from the $24 Elmer had gotten for the trailer he'd sold in Forgan. We'd get more Saturday from our eggs and cream but, even if Elmer sold all the pigs, this meeting seemed like a charade.

My husband had fooled me before, pulling money out of the unlikeliest places when we were in traveling sales, but those resources had all been used up.

Elmer remained silent.

Ingraham seemed to panic. He rattled off terms as if afraid Elmer would disappear before his very eyes. "We, that is, the Federal Land Bank will need a deposit of one dollar per acre—four hundred dollars—on the account, delivered to Lawson Title in Beaver. Do you folks want to pursue this?" A bead of sweat slid down his face and onto the collar of his fancy silk shirt.

Cool as custard, Elmer said, "We like the place, and we'll get you the deposit. I don't suppose you'd have time for a piece of banana pie, would you?"

Ingraham's eyes widened. "Oh, yes, I do like homemade pie. If it's no trouble."

After one bite, he'd be putty in my hands. "Surely. Would you like more coffee too?"

"Good coffee. Yes, please."

I swept a freshly baked pie onto the table. The banker seemed to forget his paperwork, almost drooling as I cut a large piece and set it before him.

Elmer pushed the legal papers aside and took a small wedge for himself.

I almost laughed.

Elmer said, "I suppose you're disposing of other properties in the community?"

U.J. Ingraham looked up from the plate before him, trying to swallow before he replied, "Yeff, um, yes. I've talked with the

McCarters, Roy Leaming, Jess and Nellie Ingland—never saw such a mess of kids. Claude Wriston, Wilgus, both Mintons, Stucks Potter, Lew and Kate Buffalow—she makes good pie too! Orphie Hall and— oh, is Orphie a relative?"

"No relation. So, any takers?"

"Oh, yes, there's considerable interest. A great deal of interest, for sure."

"But no takers yet?" Elmer was gently insistent.

"Well, I'm not at liberty, you see, to comment on negotiations in process."

"I understand. What are the standard terms you typically offer on your loans?"

U.J. wiped his face with a napkin I'd laid out. "Of course. The Federal Land Bank, as you may know, is part of the Farm Credit System, established in 1917." He went on an extended monologue about the land bank, until he suddenly remembered his pie, which he again attacked with relish.

Elmer watched Ingraham and then, in a flat tone, said, "So, I'm assuming we could get a thirty-year term on our loan."

Alarm replaced a contented expression as the moneylender swallowed his last bite of pie, "Nuff … thith … ack, yes. No. No, I think not. For such a modest loan amount, ten years at three percent would be appropriate."

"Anything short of a twenty-year term would be considered outright usury." Elmer spoke as if this was fact.

Ingraham ran his tongue over his teeth, licked his lips, and vented a deep sigh. "We could write it up with a twenty-year term, yes."

Elmer swiveled toward me. "Good. We could handle a twenty-year loan. It hasn't been easy out here. You don't know from one day to the next what to expect."

"Indeed, no one knows the future but God himself." Ingraham slid the last page toward Elmer. "Sign there. Both of your signatures, if you please." While we signed, he scraped up the last crumbs and licked his fork. "Claire, that was some of the best pie I've ever tasted."

"Thank you. I'm glad you enjoyed it." I couldn't believe how well things were going.

Ingraham gathered his papers and whisked a few crumbs from his vest. "This would be a nice little farm for you to raise a family on. I'm sorry to be in such a rush, but my appointment in Turpin put me behind schedule. Before I go, are there any more questions?"

Elmer tilted his chair back. "We'll get our financing together and send you that deposit in a couple months."

The financier stopped, expression frozen. An uneasy smile swept his face. "No, you have to ... I thought you understood. Here—" He scrambled for the copy of the offer he'd thrust at us and half stood as his finger raced across each line of the document. "Yes, here, it's called out on the second page. The twenty-first. Two weeks from Monday. That's when your check has to be at Lawson Title in Beaver City."

Elmer frowned. "A reasonable price, but less than six weeks to get the deposit is absurd."

"I'm sure I mentioned that." Ingraham's eyes watered. He pulled at his collar.

"You didn't say when the deposit was due. We'll get it to you in two months, when we've made arrangements. I can't write you a $400 check at the drop of a hat." Elmer hadn't raised his voice, yet it had an unmistakable edge.

Ingraham's discomfort was as obvious as a frog on a dinner plate. "I apologize for the misunderstanding, but I'm afraid the date can't be modified."

"Why not? This agreement is between us and the land bank. We initial the date change and it's done. It's unjust to require a deposit in two and a half weeks. Takes time to get money together. It's been over two weeks since you set up this meeting."

Mr. U.J. Ingraham evidently decided it was time to come clean. "There's another party, ah, name of Wilgus, who lives in the community—"

Elmer's voice came like the lash of a whip. "What's he got to do with it?"

Ingraham took a deep breath and spoke very fast. "Mr. Wilgus delivered a check for $400 to Lawson Title, as the deposit on this property, in case you, uh, chose not to exercise your first position to purchase the property. That accelerated the liquidation to this time line."

I couldn't believe that. "Wilgus? No. Anybody but him."

U.J's eyes widened. "I gather you know something about Mr. Wilgus."

Elmer snapped, "Never dealt with him. But practically everybody in the neighborhood knows something, either from what they've heard or because they were undercut by him. Doesn't make any difference if they're neighbors or not. He'd step on his grandmother's neck if it'd give him a leg up. Obviously you've had dealings with him."

"Yes, the Federal Land Bank has done business with him. He's acquired a few properties in this community when the former owner or other interested party, like yourselves, had difficulty raising the necessary capital. He's quite focused, and he's been able to position himself to pull it off."

"I'll bet," Elmer said.

"But you still have first right of refusal."

Disbelief and then despair sucked the air from my lungs. I struggled to breathe and dropped into a chair, vaguely aware of Elmer getting into Ingraham's face. After all our hopes ... I was afraid something like this would happen. We'd be perpetual tenants, never able to establish ourselves, independent and free. The Eagan place was right for us, and there was little chance we could ever find another place like it, small enough that we could afford it yet large enough to support us. With both pasture and cropland, we wouldn't have to depend on a single source of income. It was just right, and now this land hog was going to steal it.

My head started to clear. No way could we let Wilgus horn in.

The agreement lay on the table, right in front of me. I placed my index finger on the front page and flipped it over to the second page. "What's this about termination of intent?"

My voice hadn't been heard in a while, so I repeated my question, only louder.

Ingraham coughed. "Well, at this time, there is not yet a contract, *per se*. So, when Mr. Wilgus submitted the deposit check to Herb Lawson, that established a time limit for other parties, like yourselves, for example, to redeem their option to—"

"But that 'time limit,' as you call it, was not—should not have been—set by Wilgus." Elmer's words grated like ground glass on rock. "Is that shyster running your land bank?"

Another cough. "I apologize, again, for the misunderstanding, but we must honor that date."

Elmer came as close to losing his composure in a business deal as I'd seen. He drew a wash of air through his nose, then stood and seized the coffeepot like he meant to bludgeon the banker.

I imagined Ingraham lying faceup on my clean kitchen floor, eyes closed as if dreaming of cream pie.

Thankfully, Elmer simply banged the percolator on the table. "First right of refusal means squat if we don't have time to raise the money. No reason for you to even come out here. That date has got to be pushed back. It's the only right thing, the fair thing, to do."

"Yes, I see." Ingraham licked his lips. "The problem is Wilgus. The receipt for his deposit stipulates he acquires first option to buy after the twenty-first."

Elmer drummed his fingers on the table and appeared not to hear him.

Ingraham's eyebrows went up hopefully. "Plenty of time for you to talk to your banker."

Elmer shuffled the change in his pocket. "We don't *have* a banker. We've had no reason to talk to one of those—to a bank."

"I see, uh, yes." He seemed unable to process this information.

"Do you have any names of lenders?" I needed to settle Elmer down.

Ingraham jumped at the chance to offer helpful information. "George Cafky at Bank of Beaver City, Bissell at Meade State Bank, Harlow Brisendine at Citizens Bank in Liberal—"

"You understand our problem, don't you?" My womanly perspective might keep Ingraham from feeling alienated. "We've had high hopes of getting this place."

"Indeed. Oh, yes, indeed. I hope—I'm sure—there's a way to protect your interests." Ingraham stood and jerked his arm out to shake our hands. "And now, I really must go. I wish you folks the very best. I know that you'll honor your commitment."

The maroon Packard was nearly out of sight, headed north to the state line, before Elmer spoke. "Ingraham didn't know I was aiming for a twenty-year note. Other than that, he didn't do us any favors. We'll see about this. Somebody ought to tie a knot in Wilgus's tail."

"What will we do, Elmer? Shall I ask Pop?"

"No. We'll handle this ourselves."

I stared at him. Just like I thought—nothing but our butter and egg money left. I wouldn't suggest anything else to my hard-headed husband. He'd have to figure it out for himself if he wouldn't listen to me. There was no way on earth we could raise that kind of money by the twenty-first.

Chapter Twenty-Nine

Maggie frowned from her front door, a squirming child in her arms. "Claire! You and Elmer were supposed to tell me what the land bank man said."

"Sorry. Only me and the baby this time. Elmer's working cattle with Ray. They ran short of blackleg vaccine, and I came in to get it. The vet's expecting a batch this afternoon, so here I am."

Maggie put the child down. "Gary, you throw those toys again and I'll swat your behind." She waved me to a chair. "Kid's as headstrong as John. Now, did you get the money?"

"Things went well as long as Ingraham was eating my cream pie." I told her the whole story. "I wanted to ask Pop to loan us the money. Elmer wouldn't hear of it."

"Elmer would sooner pour lye down his throat than ask for help. All the while, my brothers and the folks expect you to provide them bed and board without a stutter. They got *no pride* and he has *too much*."

"They get what they want and we do without. Really, with Elmer, he never wants to be seen as needy."

"Well, that's pride, isn't it? Always appearing to be in control, not worried, never having to ask for help—Elmer's always been proud to a fault."

"Knowing what's wrong with Elmer doesn't get us the money," I said.

"You ain't got no choice but to talk to a banker, if not for this farm then for another. Else you'll be like our folks, not established anywhere."

"Don't say that, Maggie. We *won't* be like them." The very thought made me ill. The way Will accepted failure so easily, like he didn't have any pride, probably bothered Maggie too. "You should be telling this to Elmer. He's the one prejudiced against banks. Besides, we never needed a bank until now."

258

Maggie gave a wry smile. "Gotta keep up with the times. You can't stuff it under your mattress forever. I'd talk to Citizens Bank. Brisendine is the big wheel there."

"Again, tell this to Elmer."

"You're saying Elmer's too proud to ask your dad for money, yet he won't deal with the banks 'cause they starved out the little farmers? I don't know, sis. Life goes on." Maggie pulled me beside her to the couch. "We better pray about this."

⌘ ⌘ ⌘

Evening shadows rippled across the furrowed fields. One less day to come up with Ingraham's down payment. I carried the baby outside so we could be with Elmer.

He sat on an upside-down bucket on the knoll beyond the windmill, whittling a stopper for the water barrel. We always went to that spot to survey the farm, our property.

Or what we called ours.

I spread a blanket next to Elmer, sat, and visually traced the horizon from the green hills of the northwest pasture to the bounds of the eighty-acre field that surrounded the house on the north, east, and south. We had every right to claim that land. It brought a lump in my throat. "This is like heaven, Elmer. It's our home. We should stay here forever."

He closed his pocketknife and slipped it into his bib overalls. "We can do it if we find a moneylender to give us four hundred dollars for a smile and a handshake. Seems they only loan money if you don't need it. Makes no sense."

"Have you decided where we should go to get that deposit money? I can hardly sleep, thinking about this."

"Liberal. Lew heard the banker in Meade has run crosswise with Ingraham, or vice versa. Maybe the Beaver City bank—if Wilgus doesn't already have him sewed up. Not sure I want to chance that."

"So you will see a banker? It's due in less than two weeks."

"Don't remind me. I'll set something up when we go to town on Thursday." He whittled for another moment. "I got another letter from Broyles from Deluxe. He says things are looking up."

A rush of heat came across my face. "Elmer, you already know my thoughts on that."

Maggie took Sammy from my arms, cooing to him like he was her own.

Elmer set a sack of diapers on the table. "Don't wait on me for dinner, sis. This may take all afternoon."

Maggie's eyebrows went up. "You got your deposit money yet?"

Elmer removed his fedora and smoothed the feather in the band. "No, but I will."

"Maggie's got some ideas. Why don't you ask your sister?" I gave him a sideways look.

"He's never been very eloquent when he's upset." Maggie chuckled. "What do you have up your sleeve, my dear brother?"

"Looks like I'll have to deal with some bloodsucking banker."

"Nice way of putting it. At least you have a plan, don't you?"

"Somewhat. What do you know about the high and mighty bankers in town?"

"Get off it, Elmer. You know I don't run in those circles, but I've heard good things about Brisendine at Citizens Bank."

"They must be lies if they're 'good things.' I always try to wash my hands right after I meet with one of the moneylenders."

Maggie heaved a sigh that could've been heard outside. "You better change that attitude. You don't, and they'll boot you right out onto the street."

He gave her a tolerant smile and headed toward the door. Over his shoulder, he said, "I'll stuff my attitude in my hip pocket. Anything else you know about this banker?"

"Why don't you see Jenny?" Maggie said. "That lady knows everything about everybody. I think she's home right now."

As Elmer went outside, Maggie and I eased over to the window to see what he would do.

He headed over to Jenny's, all right, but he didn't look very happy.

I shook my head. "I'm glad you mentioned Jenny. He wouldn't listen to me."

Maggie shooed the children outside and hefted a basket of clothes. "Always been that way. Bring your baby and let's talk while I hang up the laundry."

I followed her into the bright sunshine and put a blanket over Sammy. I passed the damp clothes to her. "Elmer's stubborn, but he's head and shoulders above his brothers. John thinks we ought to provide him dinner and supper every Sunday."

Maggie said, "It doesn't surprise me. When I was a girl, my brothers treated me like their personal servant. All but Elmer. Frankly, that's why I left home and married Mac."

"You had to cater to them?"

"It seemed that way. I never understood why neither Elmer nor Dad stood up for me."

"You hold a grudge about that?"

Maggie sighed. "Oh, you have to forgive—whether they ask for it or not. They probably don't realize how hurt I was."

I should have hugged her or something after she said that, but I let the moment pass. "Seems like men get special privileges in your family. John's still angling for us to take his two little girls. Irks me that Elmer considered taking them after Mosie died."

"Really? I thought you got Elmer's attention that night you took off in the dark."

"I thought so too. Nevertheless, every time some of the family drives in, he thinks they'll starve if we don't put them up. And the extra work involved—it doesn't seem to matter."

Maggie gave a mirthless laugh. "They do it so often I've come to expect it. Sometimes, all that keeps me from despising them is the fact that they *are* family. When Bud left home, Dad decided he'd raised us kids, and now it was our turn." She had a faraway look in her eyes. "Mom can really be hard to live with. I never knew her folks, but she claimed her mother was full-blood Cherokee. She never talks about her childhood. You notice she hardly ever laughs. But she takes care of Dad, and she gets things done. The brothers— they are what they are. Might as well accept that."

I gave her a look. "I don't accept it, and I won't. I'd like a little respect from that crew. I'll not be treated as their servant."

"They'd have tried the same with me if I hadn't been married to a drunk. For the life of me, I don't know how you teach grownups good manners." Maggie picked up one of her children and waved the other inside. She sounded melancholy. "I learned to stand up for myself or get run over. That's what you'll have to do. Can't take it personal. You can't change other people anyway, just yourself. That's where you run into trouble, Claire, when you try to change them."

"If they're selfish, they ought to change."

"Yes, but that's God's responsibility, not yours."

"If I mention God, Elmer says I'm preaching at him."

"So don't preach. Ask God to love him, to give him what's in his best interest. It makes life a *whole* lot easier. God gave us the truth about all this. It's in the Book."

I frowned. "I haven't had much luck with *the Book*."

She shook her head. "God's given us his truth. *His* truth! Don't you get it yet?"

Her self-righteousness could be so annoying. "That bunch doesn't care what's in your black book. So don't you preach to me too. They'll only throw it back in my face."

"Claire, simmer down." She squinted and leaned over, almost in my lap. "I'm not saying to shove it down their throats. Their burdens are *their* burdens, not yours. Dad's laziness isn't your problem. It's his, which he's passed on to his sons. If they won't change, pray for them."

"Well, it doesn't mean you give what's yours to people who refuse to work. What about the story of Ruth? That proves God expects people to take care of their own."

"Exactly. So you provide for Sammy and let John take care of his kids."

"But he doesn't. You know that."

"Forget John. You said people have to provide for their own. That's your first responsibility as a mother and wife. If someone gets in the way of you taking care of Elmer and your baby, you bypass them. The way you're handling it now, sitting in judgment of them, doesn't work. You get riled when John or the folks show up."

"I am not judging them. I haven't said they're bad people." I glared at her. *Whose side is she on anyway?*

Maggie smiled back despite my indignant tone. "Not in those exact words, but a minute ago you said they're disrespectful. You get upset when they expect you to fix a meal, or—"

"You would too, if you had a crowd of spongers show up at your door." What was wrong with Maggie? *She's acting like this is all my fault.* "And Elmer lets them get away with it."

She took a deep breath. "He's not taking your side, because he can put you off. You don't stand up for yourself, so what do you expect? There are better ways of handling this than complaining. No man likes a nag."

"I am *not* a nag!"

"Sis, listen to me." Maggie gave me a big-sister look. "Something has to change, but you're not going to change them. You change yourself and the way you do things. That's all you got control of."

I stared at my sister-in-law. *Is this entire family nuts?* "What are you saying?"

She took a deep breath. "In Matthew, I believe, Jesus told his followers he was sending them 'out like sheep among wolves. Therefore be as shrewd as snakes and as innocent as doves.' You remember that passage?"

I did, but the snakes and doves part never made sense. Confusing passages like that frustrated me and kept me from trusting the Bible.

Maggie explained why Jesus said we're like sheep. "We get in trouble without even trying. Sheep aren't very smart. If they aren't in a pen, they have to be constantly watched or they'll get lost or attacked by wolves."

That sounded too much like me.

"The same as sheep need a shepherd, we need Jesus. You can trust him to change the attitudes and actions of your in-laws, but first you have to stop trying to do it yourself. Let go of control and do it without complaining, trying to get even, or saying things that aren't exactly true."

I nodded along, even if I didn't understand it totally.

"Okay, lesson's over." She gave me a big grin.

I didn't have it in me to say anything.

"Do you want to try it Jesus's way? Or do you want to keep doing things your way?"

I tried to bluff an answer. "I'm not sure about that, Maggie. I thought I was already doing things the way I was supposed to."

"Well, good." She wasn't going to argue with me, but she wasn't buying it. "Claire, most of the time I think I'm behaving like one of God's little angels too. But if I ask Jesus to kindly open my eyes to my wrongdoings, I don't like what I see."

I'd about had enough. Maggie tried to be nice to me, but I didn't like being preached at. "I do nice things for your folks. I can't count the number of times I've gotten up at all hours of the night to fix a meal for one of your brothers. Without complaining, I might add."

She stood, quick-like. Then she whirled and faced me. "Claire, you need to get off that. I know you've done those things, but Jesus is more interested in your attitude than in what you do. You resent it while you're doing it. You are, if I may be so bold, a people pleaser." She leaned toward me.

If I slapped her smiling cheeks, would she stop preaching at me?

"And when they don't appreciate your sacrifices, you get riled."

"A people pleaser? I'm only trying to do right."

"Do you ever say no when my brothers or the folks crowd into your life?"

"Yes, I do. I say—"

"Name one time, *one time*, you told them you weren't running a boarding house when they expected you to fix a midnight meal." Maggie looked calm as a cow while I was boiling inside. "You don't stand up for yourself. You're afraid to say no."

I lurched up. I wanted to put her in her place, but no words came. *I'm trying to be decent to that bunch. Nobody cares.*

Maggie laid her hand on my arm. "I think I better say something else, dear sister, while I have the courage. I've been where you are. You're afraid, afraid they won't like you if you don't please them. But if they respected you, they wouldn't run over you."

"Maggie, I'm not scared of them." One of the kids whimpered in the bedroom, so I lowered my voice. "I was taught to be polite. They don't have the decency to appreciate it." I shook her loose and stomped into the bathroom, slamming the door behind me. I faced the mirror, tears streaming down my face. *Is she right? I try and try, but nobody appreciates what I do. And Maggie, of all people, calls me a nag?* I wanted to hit something—or someone.

She didn't even knock on the door.

After a bit, I simmered down and went back into the living room.

Maggie beckoned me to sit by her on the couch.

I sat and let her put an arm around my shoulder. We must've sat there for five minutes, neither of us saying a word.

Finally I said, "They take me for granted. I wish they'd leave us alone."

"Claire, wishing for my brothers and my folks to get out of your lives won't ever make it come true. They're your family, too, because you married Elmer. He doesn't wish them away. They're his flesh and blood."

"Why can't I have my own home?"

"This may not make sense, since your people were so different from ours, but Elmer, as the oldest, took over responsibility for the family. When I was fourteen and Elmer about seventeen, things changed. We all knew Dad wasn't up to ... to leading the family. We lost our farm right about then." Maggie sighed again, heavily. "Elmer still looks out for everyone. My brothers are all grown men, but in many ways, they never learned to really grow up. Elmer has always cut them slack, like they're cripples."

A silence fell over the room, so strong it seemed to stick to every surface, like cooked gelatin flung at the walls.

Head bowed, I tried to form words. None came.

"I'm sorry, Claire. I stopped at the sheep and the wolves and never got to the birds and the snakes, did I?"

"Yes, 'wise as serpents and innocent as doves.' How ...?"

"Reverend Fultz said it means to not be taken in. Use your head. Know what and who you are. When Jesus said to be innocent, he meant don't be two-faced. That's the hardest for me—trusting God with my life instead of running it my way. I promise you though, when I give Jesus my troubles, he does better than I ever would."

"What you're saying, I—I don't know if I can do it."

"*You* don't have to do it, Claire. Jesus changes people. Trust him to change you so you can do what you need to do. You care about justice, but when you fret and stew over people, *they* become your problem. Except you can't do anything about them. You can only pray for them. When they're ready to listen, then you talk. If they're not, they'll undercut you at every turn."

Maybe she was right. Life didn't seem so black and white

anymore. I threw my arms around my sister-in-law and bawled.

Maggie pressed her cheek against my face and patted my back. "That's all right, sis. It's okay to cry. We all have to cry sometimes."

Chapter Thirty

A few hours later, and still not a word on Elmer's contacts with local bankers. I nursed Sammy while Maggie finished ironing. "Downside of getting the farm is that it gives the folks more excuse to move in with us. Of course, your brothers will show up at all hours ..."

"You're casting your worry net far and wide, aren't you?" Maggie gave me a sad look. "Bud and John treat your home like their personal hotel because it's like coming home to Mama, who takes them in because that's what a mother does. With them, it's a game. My brothers and the folks pretend it's really Mom and Dad's place."

I searched her face. *Nobody thinks like that—nobody but this family.* Maggie's words percolated like leftover coffee on a hot stove. "How can I stop that craziness?"

"Start by saying no. Respect yourself first, remember? You're starting your family. Don't let the folks move in."

I chewed my lip. "But if Elmer tells them it's okay, what do I do?"

"Remind him of your agreement. He may want to ignore it, but appeal to his sense of honor."

A car door slammed.

Maggie went out on the porch and hailed Elmer. "Get in here, brother. I'm giving Claire a class in family history."

He entered, a puzzled look on his face. Instead of asking Maggie what she was talking about, he shared news of his own. Brisendine was out of town, but Elmer had finagled an appointment with the banker in precisely one week.

⌘ ⌘ ⌘

We sat on the front step, watching the sunset. Elmer was preoccupied with coring out the bowl of his pipe. He still hadn't said what he'd do if the banker turned us down for a loan.

I swatted at the cloud of gnats that niggled at my face. "I can't stand the thought of us having to pack up and move if that banker doesn't come through."

"You worry too much. Granted, bankers are cold-hearted, probably by training." He stood and flung a stone at the trunk of the big pear tree. "But I'll make him see that a loan to us is the right thing to do, and it's good business sense, as well."

"How do you expect to do that?"

"Get him to understand how much blood and sweat we've put into this place. Put a face on his calculations. Show him this is a chance to help hard-working people with a new baby, not just a gamble of his precious money." Elmer threw another rock.

It smacked the tree.

"I'll size up his office, how he greets us—to see if we're going to get a hearing. Gotta head off Wilgus, in any case." Elmer cursed. "He never seems to have enough. Always ready to put his foot on the neck of the little man, as if it's his sovereign right to own the whole county."

"You're letting this get your goat. I'll pray for God to give us that money."

"The brass of Wilgus is unbelievable. A decent neighbor would give us the chance to come up with the dough first, but not him. No matter. I know sales, and Wiseacre Wilgus will get a surprise. You and me and the baby, we'll be that banker's collateral."

"Maybe this banker likes banana cream pie too?"

Elmer snickered. "Who knows? That might be just the ticket. It'll come down to what kind of man he is. He's heard lots of people come in and promise the moon. Then they couldn't pull it off, so the bank foreclosed. Yet they'll give a skunk like Wilgus second and third chances merely because he plays the big shot. We'll see if fairness means anything to Brisendine."

"It will, Elmer. A hundred times, I've seen you get a sale when everybody else would have given up."

Stars found their places in the silent sky. Venus stood like a searchlight above the mulberry trees to the southeast. Pop would say it meant God watched over us. Soon the Seven Sisters appeared in the northeast and the Milky Way spread across the heavens like a glistening robe.

A sharp high-pitched bark sounded from the east.

I shivered and Ring sprang to his feet.

A series of yips answered from the north.

"Elmer! Those coyotes are close. Gives me the creeps."

"They sound like they're in the next room, don't they, Ring?" He stroked the dog, who stared into the darkness with a rumble in his throat. "Their song carries because it's a quiet night. I think it's a promising night. We'll see old Brisendine and give him what-for."

⌘ ⌘ ⌘

The seventeenth of September was typical of fall on the High Plains—hot and windy. I looked in my Bible for words of assurance, then said a quick prayer. *All I've ever wanted ... it all depends on this meeting.*

I wore my simple blue dress and the jacket with the rhinestone pin Elmer had gotten me in Pittsburgh. I'd laid out Elmer's suit, but he wore his starched khaki shirt and pants. Said he didn't want to appear overanxious.

As we entered the paneled lobby of Citizens Bank, the baby squealed.

Uh-oh, I was pinching his leg. My nerves. We sat, watching people scurrying about in the solemn institution.

A scowling matron disappeared down a long hallway. She reappeared and ushered us into the office of a youngish-looking man who reminded me of a Sunday school teacher.

Coatless and with his shirt sleeves rolled, he shook our hands and motioned toward two straight back chairs.

While the men sized each other up, I did a quick inventory of Brisendine's office. A wire basket and brass table lamp anchored one end of the polished oak desk. On the opposite corner, a framed photograph of a pretty blonde and two tow-headed children smiled back at the banker. An ornate clock dominated the entry wall. Behind him, an open bookshelf separated photographs, certificates, and a glass-covered board with news clippings.

Elmer presented our loan request with the finesse and organization I'd seen in company boardrooms. He emphasized that we'd both grown up on the farm and knew the hard work required to succeed. Through it all, he presented himself as an equal.

Brisendine nodded when Elmer listed the improvements we'd made to Jenny's place.

I talked about running my own business.

Elmer wrapped it up with highlights of his management career with Deluxe. Then he laid his hand over mine. "What you're looking at, Mr. Brisendine, is my collateral—my wife and our baby. I expect that boy to grow up on this farm."

Brisendine flicked a glance at me and Sammy and then to the picture on his desk. "I see. I'd like to help you folks, but it's not been our practice to make substantial unsecured loans."

"Four hundred dollars is hardly substantial for a substantial bank." Elmer gave a tight smile and leaned forward. "Wouldn't you agree?"

The banker acted surprised. "No. That is, yes, we are a sub—"

"Good. So we agree on both counts." Elmer's words volleyed out, controlled as a fireman's hose. "That being the case, why—"

"Not true. We're talking about two different things." Brisendine gripped the edge of his desk, knuckles gleaming.

Isn't he going to ask about Ingraham and the land bank?

"Our bank didn't achieve its considerable standing by undisciplined lending."

"What is it about our request that's 'undisciplined'?" Elmer should have ignored the question, but he was enjoying this. Too much, I was afraid.

I blurted, "Have you contacted U.J. Ingraham at the Federal Land Bank?"

The men looked startled, as if they'd forgotten I was in the room.

I gave him a sweet smile. "Mr. Brisendine, don't you think Ingraham considers us good credit risks? That he trusts we'll be as good as our word? He's counting on us to repay *thousands*, not just a few hundred dollars. Otherwise, why would the land bank bother to talk with us?"

Harlow Brisendine rocked forward and backward in his chair. Even if he wanted to agree, he was supposed to be in charge. Also,

I was only a woman. He swallowed and looked at the clock. "I've another appointment waiting. How about I let you folks know tomorrow if my bank can be of service?" He jumped up, quickly shook our hands, and just like that, we were out of his office.

Elmer stopped in the hallway and glared at the closed door. "I've got a notion to go back in there and tell him off. You don't treat someone like that." He whirled and nearly collided with a small man pushing a document cart. He grabbed my arm and pulled me into the lobby, toward the exit. We passed the sour-looking matron as she beckoned to a man slouched in a chair on the far side of the lobby.

I caught the man's profile before we left. "Elmer, that was Wilgus. I'll bet he's going in to see Brisendine. Did you see him?"

"Are you sure it was him?" Elmer stopped, his hand pressed against the door.

I nodded.

He didn't speak, but his jaw muscles twitched all the way back to Maggie's house.

⌘ ⌘ ⌘

Maggie listened to our story. "Jenny dropped by earlier. She knows Brisendine well, even calls him by his first name. Maybe he had you confused with someone else. You'd best follow it up."

"Elmer, remember how Brisendine acted when I asked if he'd called U.J.?"

"He looked embarrassed. He should've already done that." Elmer stood. "You made him sit up in that big chair. I better catch him before we go home."

After Elmer left, I turned to Maggie. "Will you pray with me?"

We clasped hands across a corner of the dining table.

What if Elmer can't meet with Brisendine? What if Wilgus already has it sewed up? Felt like morning sickness all over again.

Maggie flopped her Bible on the table and flipped the pages. She read a verse in Jeremiah, something about being like a tree planted by the water, which meant I needed to relax.

Well, I was anxious. I'd never prayed out loud in front of people before, but I started talking anyway, like God was right there. "It's me, Claire. You already know what I'm going to say.

Help us get this farm. Maybe we don't deserve it. You know how I am, awful selfish sometimes. Maybe a lot of the time. And Elmer swears when he's upset. I don't think he means it, but I promise you we'll make this little farm a grand place to raise our kids and have friends over. I'm asking, God, that this banker lend us that down payment so the Federal Land Bank will sell us the place."

Maggie said, "Yes, Jesus," and squeezed my hand.

"Thanks for Maggie. She's such a good woman and knows so much. Help me make Pop proud of me, and please be with Elmer now so we can get that loan from Mr. Brisendine. Amen. Oh, and help Pop too. I worry about him, all by himself. Yes. Amen."

Maggie gave me a big hug. "That was a wonderful prayer, Claire. Don't forget, you're a gift from God, and he listens to your requests."

Less than an hour later, Elmer returned, all smiles. "Harlow wants Claire to come back with me so we can sign a loan agreement for $500. I got him to sweeten the deal for operating expenses. Leave the baby here, Sal. We'll be right back, sis."

⌘ ⌘ ⌘

Harlow Brisendine told us he thought he was a good judge of character and felt we'd honor our obligations. He thanked me for suggesting he call Ingraham. That had cleared up what he called a "confusion of identities." He slid the loan agreement across his desk. "Both of you need to sign right down there."

So, I'm part of this operation too. I wanted to cry and laugh at the same time. I felt important, independent.

When we got outside, I hugged Elmer until he pulled back in embarrassment.

"All right. Let's go celebrate with Maggie. She'll be plenty tickled," he said.

"My baby boy finally has a home! His mama and daddy have a home—for the first time since they got married!" I practically danced to the car.

Maggie was waiting for us, Sammy on her hip. She had us tell all about the meeting and signing the loan agreement. "I wish I'd been there when Brisendine told Wilgus that he wouldn't be getting your farm." She set to fixing us sandwiches. "You barely missed Earl. He was on his way back to Woodward from working at Garden City. Not to take the bloom off your excitement, but he already plans to bring the folks with him next time so they can move in with you. He said everyone thought it was a good idea since you had a big place now."

I was floored. "We've only got a two-bedroom house. They can't crowd in like that."

Elmer said, "Earl was only thinking of the folks. With him working off at Garden City for weeks at a time, he doesn't want to leave the folks alone at his place."

I snorted. "More likely, he knows John's crowd will clean out his kitchen."

Elmer acted like he hadn't heard me. "Anyway, Mom and Dad need a place to stay."

"I guess they'll have to find someplace else then."

He drew back like I'd hit him. "You ought to make allowances."

I didn't back down.

He got huffy, but I didn't much care.

We went on like that all the way home from Liberal.

There we were, just made the biggest deal of our lives and then plopped ourselves right into an argument over who could live in the house we'd just bought. What was wrong with us?

Chapter Thirty-One

The guttural bark of Lancaster's pickup drew me to the west window. Maybe my baby chicks had arrived in the mail. One arm raised against the wind, I hurried outside and headed across the road.

The mail carrier lurched away without a glance my way, which meant no chicks.

I retrieved the solitary letter. It was addressed to Elmer.

What could be inside?

Nothing good, I was sure. The postmark tracked above our address like an ant dipped in ink, but I recognized the jagged script.

Broyles.

I dangled the envelope between my fingers.

The wind would carry it to the state line if I let go.

But that would never do. He'd only write again, and I might not intercept the next one. Once inside, I flung it on the kitchen table as if it were about to burst into flame.

Elmer came in from the field and asked if Ray had stopped by with word about the two cows Otis Minton was looking to sell.

I shook my head. "You planning to get some things in Liberal?"

He plucked the letter off the table and opened it without taking time to wash up.

I finished preparing the pork chops and gravy. What did the letter say? Probably more of the same—Deluxe pressuring Elmer to make money for them. A tightness across my shoulders increased the longer I thought about it. How did those meddlers dare to keep hounding us? We'd left the crew ten years ago and it wasn't only because of the depression. We left that gypsy life to start a family. Now that tinhorn Broyles had tracked us down just to help Deluxe fatten its coffers. Ben Dial probably offered him a bounty if he could reel Elmer in.

Elmer folded the single page and thrust it back in the envelope. He avoided my gaze and turned as if he'd simply read the sorghum futures from the Chicago Board of Trade.

I spoke, voice shrill. "Well, aren't you going to tell me what that letter is all about?"

"What? You mean this?" He waved his hand over the envelope.

"Yes. That."

"Yeah, Broyles. He's says he's going to be canvassing the Liberal area. Wants to know when I could meet him. He'll be here in a month or so. I'd like to hear what's on his mind."

"I can tell you what's on his mind." I put my hands on my hips. "He wants to get you back at Deluxe! Why would you even give that a second thought? We've started a family now."

"Sounds like Deluxe has more prospects than they can keep up with. There's a lot of money to be made out there."

"Well, that's fine for him. But there's no way we're going back on the road. We've already talked about this. You might as well tell him to save his stamps."

He puckered his lips. "Now, Sal, you don't want to—"

"Now, nothing! You know that would be chasing after the wind. And after we've soaked our sweat and tears into getting what a lot of people will never have a chance at having. Right here, we have our own home, a place we can come back to every night. Not someplace down the road, when you never know where you're going to be a month from now." My emotions could barely be controlled. Elmer responded better to logic.

He shrugged and moved to the washbasin.

I sat, suddenly engulfed in memories of the shame and betrayal caused by Harold's infidelity. I hadn't thought of that life for a long time. Hadn't allowed it, actually. A deep breath, again and again. The memories seeped into my mind, an infection that hadn't yet healed.

Elmer washed at the basin and massaged his face and hands, water splashing, dripping, cleansing.

Like a baptism, Jesus could wash away all the hurts and fears from when I'd been with Harold. I'd never trusted Jesus to handle all that stuff. I'd never allowed the cleansing, purging of his pure life to wash me clean.

Not till now.

And Maggie'd been trying to tell me that since I'd met her.

I stood and turned to the dish pan, poured warm water off the cook stove into it, and methodically washed my face, arms, and hands.

Harold's duplicities and lies, even Mama's critical words—*especially* her judgmental attitudes—I rinsed them all off. I accepted the Lord's offer of forgiveness. Jesus accepted me. I accepted me.

Elmer spoke, a muffled voice through the towel. "You ought to see how dry those fields are. Plowing that ground is like trying to cut concrete. This drought isn't over. I'd lay odds that we're headed for more of the Dirty Thirties." He hung the towel on the nail spiked into the wall and looked across the room at me. "Well, what are you so smiley about? That's a nice change, but let's eat."

The tone of my voice now soft, I said, "Yes, let's eat. Maybe the drought isn't really over. But remember, we had a good rain last month. Sure it's dry now, but this is dry country. We knew that when we moved here. We have to take the bad with the good."

He sat as I pulled a pan of biscuits from the oven and joined him at the table. "That's just it, Claire, it *is* dry, and there's no sign of more rain. That means I can't plant fall milo or corn or feed for the cattle. Our friend Brisendine will be watching every crop and cow operation in the Panhandle. He's got loans with a quarter of the farmers between Greenough and Forgan." He sliced his pork chops in the methodical fashion he approached anything when he knew exactly where he was going. "These bankers—we miss our payment at the end of the year, they could foreclose. The wheat we already got in the ground won't make a crop, and we'll be lucky to get seed for next year. Sales possibilities at Deluxe are practically a sure thing for a good income. Farming right now is one of the easiest ways to go broke."

So, he felt his own pack of wolves nipping at his calm demeanor. He hadn't yet forgiven bankers for what they did to the farmers during the last decade. "That's not so. If you believed that, you'd have taken Pop's offer to run that service station in Ness. We both believed we could make it here." I poured the iced tea. "Before we bought this place, we agreed we'd make the Panhandle our home."

"I'm not saying we should leave. But without rain, we won't have a choice. There's no reason to live a hand-to-mouth existence when an opportunity like this falls into our lap."

I studied his face. "Elmer, it isn't like you to be so negative. We don't know the future. With a good rain, we could plant the fall crops, and the pasture would green up for the cattle. If it doesn't rain, we can always ask Brisendine if he'd extend our note. I know the land bank would. They don't want to take our property back."

The baby whimpered.

I got up and fetched him.

Elmer extended his arms to receive his son when I returned to the table. With Sammy tucked against his shoulder, he resumed his rundown of farms in trouble. "The bank in Beaver City pulled the plug on several farmers over by Laverne. They didn't get a second chance. If a banker gets scared, he's not going to let you get behind."

"Elmer, you surely don't plan to go on the road and leave me and Sammy here alone."

"Oh, I'd get back as often as I could. May not be gone but a week—ten days at the most. Besides, you can run things. You were rock solid when we went through that blizzard to get to the hospital."

He almost never complimented me for anything. I wanted to revel in his praise. Maybe do a nice pirouette, like those fancy French ladies we saw when the crew worked three weeks in New Orleans back in the day. But I didn't want to be in charge. I wanted my husband. "Elmer, I'm glad you see me as more than a cook and bottle washer. But I'm a wife, and I want to keep that role. I can't do that if you're gone for days or weeks at a time." A lump in my throat, I searched his face for understanding. I didn't want to have to spell out the risk of us being apart.

"Don't jump to conclusions. I'm only asking that you keep an open mind." He stood as if the conversation was over, but then turned. "I think it'd do you good to sleep on it." He took the baby with him back to the front room.

"Sleeping won't change my mind, Elmer. We need to stay together."

⌘ ⌘ ⌘

It didn't rain all that week, nor the next. As if to prove Elmer's dire weather predictions, we got no rain for the next two months, clear into early June. To add to our distress, the wind blew nearly every day. It went hard for a week at a time, sending vast clouds that darkened the sun. I hated to see it as it would push Elmer further away from keeping the farm.

Sure enough, he got another letter from Broyles.

A headache began a drumbeat over my left eye.

Elmer had invited Lew and Kate Buffalow to come over to play pitch that evening. We needed to have fun for a change.

They'd barely come in the house before Lew bet Elmer he could name more people in the Greenough community who had decided to quit farming if we didn't get a rain by the Fourth of July.

Elmer colored a bit but quickly insisted that if we got one good shower by the end of the month, he'd bet on a milo crop.

Sure, Elmer, but you don't think we'll get that rain.

Kate set one of her famous coconut cream pies on the counter.

I'd found Mama's family recipe for deviled eggs, so with that and ice tea, we had special treats that evening. Kate bragged up Elmer's sweet corn, and then she and I won four straight games of ten-point pitch before the boys won a single game.

Elmer shuffled the deck at least three times before he'd let Lew deal. "Lew, you been talking about the neighbors leaving. What will you and Kate do if this dry spell hangs on?"

Lew didn't speak. Instead, he dropped his hand down to the shiny tin can at his feet.

So Elmer wasn't the only one considering other options.

Kate casually cut the deck. "We've talked about that, more than once. We'd hate to leave the community, but if we had to, we'd go back to Pond Creek and raise honey bees."

Lew shot a stream into his spit can and wordlessly nodded.

They looked at us expectantly.

I jumped in before Elmer could answer. "My family is too important to even think of moving somewhere else. Elmer and I plan to stay in the Panhandle."

Elmer's face contorted ever so slightly. "Well, what she says is true. That's the plan, but if we have to adjust, we'll adjust. There's no point hanging on to one end of the rope if you're upside-down and a wild steer is on the other end, dragging you face first through a patch of cockleburs. Me, I'm going to let go of the rope."

Leave it to Elmer. We all broke up laughing. Lew slapped his leg and then the table. Kate got the giggles, which sent the rest of us into hysteria. I finally got up to serve everyone a piece of Kate's pie. We forgot our troubles, and with it being nearly midnight when Lew and Kate went home, Elmer and I forgot Broyles's letter.

⌘ ⌘ ⌘

Neither Elmer nor I wanted conflict but we both wanted our own way. Breakfast done, I cleared the table and started washing the dishes.

Elmer's fingers drummed the table top. "Broyles will be in Liberal until Wednesday. I aim to see the man, hear what he has to say, and then make a decision."

My best efforts to stay calm failed. My breath caught. Without turning from the washstand, I said, "Have you already made a decision? If he makes you an offer on the spot, I mean?"

"No, I said I'd—"

"But you're going ahead with it, even though I'm opposed? Why not put a stop to it?" My lower lip quivered.

He arose and I felt his nearness. He moved beside me, and put his arm around my shoulders. I dropped my head against his chest.

His heart pounded, like mine.

For what seemed a long time, we stood without speaking. I wanted to bring us together, but without finding a field of compromise, I knew it was impossible and suspected he felt the same way.

The dog barked as Cousin Ray's beat-up Ford pickup drove into the yard.

Elmer stepped out the front door.

I peered at the figure getting out of the old pickup. Not Ray; it was Durward. Nice. We hadn't seen him for a while.

Elmer waved at him, and they came in together. It struck me how much Elmer had changed, softened maybe, since that day Durward came back into his life. Elmer wasn't one to bare his soul, but I sensed a shame in his heart that he hadn't done more to reach out to his son. I put the coffeepot back on the stove and turned in time to get a hug from Durward. Besides Pop, Myrrl, and Elmer, he was the only other man I let put his arm around me.

Durward told us he'd borrowed Ray's pickup to chase a job in Elkhart, seventy-five miles west. He'd hired on with a trucker, so he and May would be moving away from his mother. He seemed as pleased about that as getting the job. He said the job should last several months, but even if it didn't, there was big money in the oil fields down near Borger. Like Elmer, he was optimistic and can-do. "How are Grandma and Granddad? You heard from them lately?"

I glanced at Elmer but kept mum.

Durward looked at his dad.

Elmer leaned back and ran a hand through his hair. "Since we last saw you, we've become part of the landed gentry. Federal Land Bank man came through. Wasn't easy, but we're financing it through them." Casual-like, he added that his folks might be moving in with us.

I opened my mouth to set facts straight.

Durward spoke up. "Permanent, huh? I didn't know if that might be wearing thin. May can't stand to be in the same kitchen with Mama."

"It's worn thin, all right." I said, "Elmer's mother acts like she *owns* my kitchen." Durward understood far better than my own husband.

"Grandma treats me like royalty." He sat up straight. "Say, why not have them stay with us for a while? Grandparents are different than parents."

Elmer shifted in his chair. "No, son, they're not your problem. We'll take care of it."

"That's right, Elmer," I said. "They aren't his problem. Shouldn't be *ours*, either."

My dear husband snorted loud enough to make old Ring bark outside. "They're family."

"There are a lot of people in this family. My brothers, John and his kids—"

"Don't be foolish, Claire. They can take care of themselves and their own."

"Not to hear John tell it. He almost had you agreeing to take his girls."

Durward frowned. "I didn't mean to interfere. It just seemed like maybe I could lend a hand. I'm proud to belong to the clan."

Elmer refreshed his coffee. "You're family, by blood. Nothing required for you to lay claim to that. We wouldn't be talking about this if Claire hadn't brought it up."

I swabbed the table where he'd slopped coffee. "I brought it up, 'cause nobody else will."

Elmer scowled.

Durward rose from his chair and peered out the front window. "Looks like you got more company. Who drives a Plymouth?"

"Why do they always show up at exactly the wrong time?" I bit my lower lip to keep from saying more.

Elmer moved to the window beside Durward. "It's Earl, with Mom and Dad."

The wind had kicked up again, and in they came, Mary Grace with three paper sacks and her sweater buttoned up. Will lugged a familiar suitcase with his right hand while he mashed the crown of his wide brim fedora with his left, holding it against the wind. Earl carried a new pasteboard box that was filled to overflowing with cloth remnants, while he clutched the handle of a second suitcase underneath.

I jumped up and hurried to the bedroom to assure myself that Sammy was snug on his little bed. I briefly entertained the image of chaining him to the floor, to remove any doubt as to whose bedroom it was.

Durward played the host, greeting his grandparents and shaking Earl's hand.

Mary Grace made as if to carry her sacks into the baby's bedroom.

I stepped in front of her. "The baby's asleep."

Without changing her expression, she said, "Where do you want me to put these, Elmer?"

A tilted silence came over the house.

All eyes turned to me, as if they were waiting for me to back off so they could proceed with their intentions.

Durward took the bags from her hands and set them along the wall. "Grandma, Granddad, sure good to see you. You too, Uncle Earl. In fact, we were asking where you might be. Have a sit." He motioned to our four kitchen chairs, and then turned to me. "Claire, okay if I serve another round of coffee?"

I nodded, hoping our baby would stay asleep.

No one had said why Earl had brought the folks, but their baggage dominated our front room. Evidently they planned to move into the house for as long as they cared to stay. Just as they had for the previous eight years of our marriage, after we left Deluxe.

My inclination was to invite unexpected guests to stay for a meal, but it being only two in the afternoon, I wasn't about to do any such thing.

Durward carried most of the conversation, asking for updates on the family. Earl fidgeted, surely wanting to finalize arrangements for the folks so he could go. Mary Grace kept darting hard glances at him. Elmer seemed perplexed, probably expecting me to bow to the pressure of the moment.

Not this time.

Finally he asked Earl to check the clutch on the Oakland. They both jumped up, as if relieved for an excuse to go outside.

Will settled onto the couch, lit his pipe, and asked Durward if there was a good water source near the garden area behind their new apartment at Elkhart.

Without either of her sons in the house to contend with, Mary Grace acted like she'd been abandoned, going to the window several times to see where they were and then returning to paw through her many sacks.

I waited, simply waited, enjoying the boundaries I'd established. Boundaries that belonged to me, but that I'd never before claimed.

Chapter Thirty-Two

Durward, full of eagerness, pivoted a chair toward Will, putting him at the kitchen table opposite me, with Will and Mary Grace on my left. "Say, I guess you and Grandma are looking for a place to stay for a while, isn't that right?"

"Sure was. Figured Elmer and Claire would have room for us like they always done before, now that they already boughten this farm. We—"

"Land sakes," Mary Grace shook a fluff of cloth remnants onto the table. "We 'spected to have a room to sleep in like always. Elmer said Dad could easily put in a big garden area, so when Earl said we'd oughter go to stay with them, well, that's why we came here."

I took a deep breath. "I've got something to say. Something I should've said a long time ago." I swung my gaze from Mary Grace and over to Will and then back again, as perspiration laced down my spine. "This, *this*, is my home, our home. The first place Elmer and I had ever owned in more than ten years of marriage. It's a dream come true. But of all the places we rented, not one time did anyone ever ask me if you could stay with us. You just showed up, unannounced, no forewarning. I made a place for you. Every time. We shared our food with you, no matter how often you or any of the other family came to eat and … to …" I gasped. My breath deserted me, turning my mouth to cotton. I cast about for something to drink, anything to avoid cutting short the speech I'd rehearsed thirty, forty, maybe seventy times.

Durward caught my eye. He was nodding, a look of approval on his face.

I could have kissed him. He reached over to the washstand and swiped a half-full cup of coffee—maybe Earl's. He shoved it across the table toward me.

I thrust it to my dry lips and guzzled it so hastily that an unladylike belch popped out.

Will and Mary Grace both jerked back as if I were about to vomit.

Durward's face contorted with silent laughter, and tears slid past his nose until he whipped out a bandanna to conceal his amusement.

My embarrassment gone, I plunged ahead. "I was always willing to open our home to my husband's family. People showed up, and I was expected to provide, which I always did. But can you understand how hurtful it was to have it expected of me?" My businesslike approach crumbling, I soldiered on.

Durward was nodding again, encouraging.

"The worst was to *never—not once*—be given the courtesy of someone asking, or at least giving an advance warning that—"

The front door opened as Elmer and Earl barged back in.

By the looks on their faces, I figured they were united in purpose. Never mind. They might as well hear it too. I flashed Elmer a determined look to let him know this was my picture show. I picked up my speech where I'd left off. "What I was telling you, was that … that when you would show up out of the blue, unexpected and never asking me if it would be all right, I felt disrespected. Like a doormat. Everyone else was happy to have me cook and clean, but no one checked if I was happy." A look around the room revealed that at that moment, they weren't exactly happy either.

Except Durward. A faint smile on his face, he gazed at an invisible point above the table, as if rehearsing an old memory.

"Claire, what's going on here?" Elmer appeared caught between the impulse to bark or to try to be polite.

I locked eyes with him. "Your dad said they were expecting to move in with us, like they always did before. I explained that always is different now."

Earl, one leg cocked over a corner of the washstand, rolled his eyes.

Will and Mary Grace whispered to one another.

Elmer shook his head, as if to be sure he'd heard right. "What do you mean 'always is different now'?"

Durward rose and nudged his chair against Elmer's leg. "Have a seat, Dad. Here, take my chair." As tall and every bit as brawny, he fixed on a sunny smile.

Elmer seemed to consider blustering on but finally sat.

I started to get up, prompted by my habitual impulse toward assuming the server's role.

With a slight shake of his head, Durward leaned across the table and pushed me gently down in my chair. Still standing, he said, "Hear me out on this. Before you all came"—he nodded to Earl and the folks—"I was telling Dad and Claire that May and I can put up Grandma and Granddad at our place in Elkhart for a couple weeks or so. I got us a nice apartment over the hardware store, back of Sixth Street. That'll give you time to, uh, work this out. You can manage stairs, can't you, Grandma?"

Mary Grace made as if to get up. "Do I look helpless? Yes, I can climb stairs."

Elmer bent toward his mother. "No, I don't want you climbing any stairs. Can't have you getting crippled up." He looked up at Durward. "Son, I think you're going off half-cocked, offering your place without checking with May. The folks aren't your—"

"Elmer, let him speak for himself," I said. A curtain opened, revealing my husband's approach to people he differed with. "Listen to yourself. You're making everybody else's decisions for them! 'Durward, check with your wife.' Then you told your mother she shouldn't be climbing stairs. How's she going to go upstairs in Woolworth's to look for remnants? And while you're telling your son to ask *his* wife, you never once asked *me* whether your folks could move in."

Wide eyes all around.

Will cleared his throat. "Elmer, Claire's got it pegged. You're right-on most of the time. But everyone needs to decide things for theirselves. If'n they don't, they'll soon depend on you to do their thinkin' for them." He sent a puff of smoke toward the ceiling, as if that settled it.

Elmer's face crinkled into a weak grin. "Dad, you think so?" That was as close as Elmer would come to admitting his fault, particularly in the presence of all the others.

Will struggled to his feet. "Isn't anybody going to ask *us* what Mother and I want to do? Where *we* want to go?" He looked around the room.

Another uncomfortable silence.

He took out his pipe and smacked it onto his left palm. "I didn't think so. Now, while I'm at it ..." He sucked on the mouthpiece to clear it. "Claire, you're missing something here. You never *ever* told us you didn't want us to stay with you and Elmer."

Face burning, I finally manufactured the words. "Elmer, I told you. I asked you, 'what's going on?' and I'm sure I asked you why your folks showed up, unannounced, without warning, and we had to shoehorn them in. No room to even throw down a mattress at some of the places we stayed at."

Mary Grace said, "But Claire, *you* never told *us* we shouldn't—"

"Elmer knew." I shot him a glance. "From the first time Earl left you at our apartment in Kansas City. But you stayed, and we made room. And it kept happening."

Will leaned back in his chair, hands behind his head. "Well, that may be. But no one told us we weren't welcome. I knew you was kinda edgy sometimes, but—"

"I wanted you to feel welcome, Will, but I wanted to be asked. Not just be told you were moving in. We were newlyweds. Still, we've really never had a place to ourselves." I gave Elmer another look. "Is this true, Elmer, that after I asked, you didn't tell them? You ignored what I asked you to do?" That was too much to handle. I slumped back into my chair, tears flooding my eyes.

Durward hurried to change the subject. "Dad, it's not like May is in the dark about all this. We've talked. She's already packing. We'll have our belongings ready to go in three days at the most. Frankly, she'd like some help, maybe advice, from Grandma or Claire about running a household. But not from Mama." He glanced at Earl. "You can bring the folks over next weekend, or whenever you like."

Earl shrugged, and looked at his brother. "Elmer, you care which direction this goes? I can take Mom and Dad back to Woodward for a few days."

I held my breath. *If he dared to try to keep them here ...*

He said, "Yes, sounds like that would be best for all concerned."

⌘ ⌘ ⌘

The folks went back to Woodward with Earl. Then it would be to Elkhart with Durward and May. For a week or two? Who could know? I wondered how May would put up with Elmer's mother. I told Elmer that he and his brothers had to figure out something for the folks, but that I wasn't going to sacrifice our second bedroom—our son's bedroom—for a temporary solution.

Durward was taking a risk, but he didn't see it that way. It was more important to him that he help the family.

At the moment, we had bigger fish to fry. Early June and still no rain. Elmer planned to meet Broyles in Liberal on Wednesday. I decided I'd go to Liberal too. Since I hadn't been feeling so well, I'd see Dr. McCreight while Elmer had his big meeting. Afterward, I'd walk over to Maggie's and wait for him.

Elmer wasn't happy about me tagging along, but I reminded him he'd have to make a special trip back to Liberal if I didn't go that day. Neither of us said much as we drove to town. I expected him to ask about my health but he seemed preoccupied about seeing Broyles.

Once we turned west on the Blue Bell Road, I pointed. "Clouds to the northwest. The most encouraging sky we've seen in weeks."

"Yep. But those morning clouds always wilt before they get to us." He hummed Hoagy Carmichael's "Stardust."

"You know, Elmer, there's no substitute to having a father around to help raise his boy."

"Hey, I'll be around for my boy." He flung his arm over the backseat to touch Sammy.

"Not if you're gone for weeks at a time. I know how Ben Dial operates. After we left Deluxe, people wrote that the five-day overnight trips for contract employees strung out for ten or twelve days. Our son needs his father, and I need you too. With twenty-seven head of cattle and all those pigs, how could I take care of everything while you're gone?"

"Look, I'm not gone yet. And I sure wouldn't leave you with a herd of animals to take care of. I'd sell the pigs and most of the cattle; that would leave us with a few milk cows and your chickens."

He made it sound so easy.

But I'd have to run the farm by myself or give it up.

⌘ ⌘ ⌘

Sensible people didn't travel the Blue Bell Road when it rained. Wet, the caliche roadbed became slick as glass. But, post-meeting and on our way home, we weren't acting too sensibly anyway. Elmer and I began arguing again about him rejoining Deluxe and didn't noticed a storm moving in behind us until a barrage of rain pummeled the car. In minutes, the heavens opened, hiding the edge of the road.

My heart in my throat, I looked back to check on Sammy, but he greeted each swerve of the car with a piercing giggle. The drumbeat of the rain isolated Elmer and me within our individual cones of anxiety. I remembered to give thanks for the moisture even though the car fishtailed all over the road. Elmer swore and I prayed and, somehow, he kept us out of the ditch.

The storm settled to a steady soaker by the time we passed Skinny White's place. Right at the state line, we caught up with Ray Hunter's familiar old pickup. We followed him all the way to our farm, but again it was Durward who piled out as Elmer parked next to the front door.

I covered Sammy up and made a dash inside. Elmer and Durward brought in our groceries and got the cookstove going. I dried off real quick before laying the baby down for a nap. I put together a casserole and got it in the oven. Another check of my baby, and then I began setting the table, half aware of Elmer's discussion with Durward. All about working with Deluxe again.

For the next hour, Elmer talked specifics—things like salary, bonuses, schedules, and sales territories.

I spun from the stove. "Elmer, you didn't *agree* to anything with Broyles, did you?"

He looked down at the new Deluxe brochure Broyles had given him. "I certainly did. Had to, to get my choice of new territories. That way, I can be home more often with less travel. That's one of the things you were worried about, wasn't it? You sa—"

"I said nothing about signing any papers, Elmer!" I thumped the casserole dish on the table, burning my fingers in the process.

Durward ducked his chin and edged his chair back.

"Sit still, son. You're okay here." Elmer looked up at me and spoke in a tone that sounded patronizing. "Claire, why don't you finish getting everything on the table, and then we can all sit down and discuss this calmly?"

I glared at him, but by the time I'd put the rest of the food on the table, I'd calmed down. I had also devised my own little plan to share my information.

Durward relaxed a bit, probably 'cause he figured I wasn't going to dump the coffeepot on Elmer during supper.

Elmer made the long range plans of Deluxe Art Studio sound like gospel as he explained them to Durward. After turning and grabbing several sheets of paper and a pen off the buffet, and pushing the green beans aside, Elmer jotted down dollar amounts, dates, circles representing sales teams, and market areas.

I listened without interest and said nothing the whole mealtime.

Durward glanced at me each time Elmer paused.

As we finished eating, Durward said, "A couple from Mama's church saw we were short of furniture. They gave us a bed and dresser, all sorts of plates and dishes from his mother's estate. I took a load over to Elkhart this morning."

My insides were in turmoil, as I'd never had the courage to openly state my feelings about my family. I wanted to begin living, speaking, and acting according to what I thought God wanted. But how? "My mother gave me judgment when I really needed encouragement after I divorced Harold. I'd like to help May however I can. That's what God would want me to do."

His eyes widened. "You're not gonna preach at her, are you?"

I slowly shook my head. "She's been preached at enough, if I were to guess. But no, just because I trust God's Word doesn't mean she has to do the same. It's because it's part of me."

At that, Elmer arose and leaned against the wash stand, seeming to peer out the window into the rainy afternoon.

Chapter Thirty-Three

Rain. Blessed rain. We hadn't seen that much rain at one time in all the years of our marriage. It showed no sign of stopping and was certainly enough to trump Elmer's concern about another drought. He could forget about going back to traveling sales with Deluxe. But I had a better reason for him to stay at home.

I set a piece of pie—I'd get Durward some after he came back in from checking on the animals—and a cup of coffee in front of Elmer and slid into the seat nearest him. "Honey, can we put our disagreements aside so I can tell you something? Something wonderful?"

His fork stopped mid-way to the pie. "You serious? What's your news?"

"Remember I saw Doc McCreight? I'm pregnant again, due in November, maybe Thanksgiving."

He gave me that cheesy grin and extended his arms.

I fell into his embrace and laid my head on his chest as we listened to the rain patter the window.

He pulled back. "During your labor with Sammy, that nurse told me we'd lost our boy for sure, and maybe you too. I can't go through that again."

"Doc McCreight said the first childbirth is always harder, especially because of my age. He didn't promise this one would be easier, though. After all, I'm almost thirty-five, but I've already had one child. We'll pray for God's care, like last time."

He gazed at me with his beautiful hazel eyes. "You're my gal, Sal. Think we're having a boy or girl?"

"I say girl. I'd like a girl to share secrets with. We can name her Valerie Claire."

"Sorry, Sal, I've already put my order in for another boy. No secrets for you." That mischievous smile creased his face from the sides of his mouth up to the corners of his eyes. He pulled me into Sammy's bedroom, looked at his son, and bent to kiss me.

The front door opened and closed.

"I fed old Ring." Durward's voice.

Elmer called, "In the bedroom. Claire's telling me secrets."

I swatted his fanny. "Are you going to make the announcement, or should I?"

"I'll take care of it." He turned, a smirk on his face. "And I'll take care of you … later." He went out and told Durward that we were going to have another little farmer.

I dropped onto the bed, suddenly remembering that we hadn't settled the unhappy discussion of Deluxe. With a new baby due, Elmer couldn't consider leaving me to run the farm.

But … he'd been known to be oblivious. Maybe he could.

⌘ ⌘ ⌘

So tired from everything, I had lain down beside the baby and fallen asleep. I jerked awake and hurried toward the living room. Had Durward left?

His voice came from the kitchen. "May won't expect me as long as this rain keeps up. The roads will be a mess past Knowles."

I moved to the door.

Durward sat down across from Elmer, who'd been playing solitaire. "So, when do you expect to start selling again?"

Elmer shuffled the cards and put the two jokers on top before sliding the deck back into its box. "He wants me there next week. I told him July first."

Just like that, Durward had again pulled our conflict out from under the rug where we'd stuffed it.

I slipped into the room and sat between the two. "Listen to the good sound of that rain. Elmer, you only considered Deluxe because you thought we were facing another drought. Seems to me that three inches of moisture should end that worry."

Elmer rubbed the back of his neck. "I've got the rest of the month to get the maize and corn planted. I'll get Bill Kizer to cut the wheat. Then I'll make sure I can be back here when the maize and corn need harrowing and cultivation. Ray is coming over next week, and we'll figure out which cows and calves to sell."

Durward glanced at me. "Sounds like some pretty tight maneuvering, Dad."

Elmer ignored my point about the drought being over.

"Problems happen on their own schedule." I shook my head, overwhelmed at the thought of managing it all. "Animals get sick, things break, cows get out. That brindle heifer heads right for Flanagan's garden every time she jumps the fence. Can't you see me and old Ring out there getting her back in? Afterward, I'd have to reset the posts she'd knocked over, mend the broken wire, and then get the wire stretchers out and stretch it without cutting my hands to pieces on the barbed wire."

"That brindle heifer is going to be on the first load out of here." Elmer's voice was a little louder than was needed, being that I sat right next to him. "Besides, you make it sound like Armageddon if I work with Deluxe."

Durward scooted his chair back from the table.

"Elmer, it's that you won't be here, with me and Sammy. After the baby comes, with a newborn and toddler in the house, I can't give you backup. *I'll* need backup. But that's only the tip of the iceberg. Nothing has really been settled regarding your folks. If they show up, I won't be able—"

"That's the idea, Claire. With what I'll make with Deluxe, I'll be able to get them their own place. That's part of why I'm doing this. They won't be in your hair."

"Well, that's really for them, not me." If not for the patter of rain and the rush of wind against the house, I probably could've heard my heart beat. "I don't think you've given much thought to the danger to our marriage. Think what it was like on the crew. Infidelity seemed to come so easy. Harold was only one of many. And with the wife left at home, even for a few months, a salesman has lots of time on his hands after hours."

Elmer clouded up like the weather outside. "You think I'm that kind of man? Look, I could've been a rounder, gone drinking every night. I haven't done—"

"Honey, I know that. But being apart, living in two different worlds? It strains the marriage. Instead of building our relationship stronger, we'd end up trying to pull the scattered parts back together. It's too easy to imagine things, bad things. Being apart, we would begin to doubt because we don't have the daily closeness to remind us what we have." I looked at this man—my man—willing him to understand. "You need to hear me, dear husband of mine. Listen to my concerns, my fears. I'm afraid for our marriage."

He shook his head. "Sal, our marriage will be fine. You'll be fine. I'll be here well before that baby comes."

"No, you're not hearing me, Elmer. You ... you see our marriage differently than I do. I think you take it for granted. I see our marriage as the center of my life, after Jesus. I see it as something precious and special, to be cherished, guarded and cared for, like a garden with high walls around it." My breath came in choppy fragments.

Durward stood and eased away from us.

I needed to say much more, hating all the while that I had to say it. Of all the things that could jeopardize our marriage, I feared separation the most. Tears streaming down my face, I wanted to fling myself into his arms. But I could do only what I knew I must do. "Elmer, I love you. I never want to lose you. But if you go on the road again, leaving me here, I *will* lose you. I can't live with that uncertainty. If you go, when you return, don't ... don't expect me to be here when you walk through that door. I *won't* be here." The words tumbled out and my tears brightened the oil cloth on the table.

Durward, who was starting to put his coat on, turned, a look of panic on his face.

Elmer's eyes widened. Without a word, he lurched up, chair banging the wall behind him. He grabbed his coat and threw it on.

One sleeve flew across the buffet and caught the little hummingbird figurine Mama had given me when I turned thirteen.

It shattered in a faint tinkle of porcelain and glass.

"Elmer!" I cried. I scanned the floor, as if to resurrect bird and marriage. Had both evaporated in those fluttering heartbeats? Who would've thought? Was my ultimatum so reckless?

Sammy yowled.

Elmer crammed his hat on his head and stomped out into the downpour.

I hurried into the bedroom to calm the baby and returned, anxious about Durward's reaction.

There he was, on his hands and knees, searching for pieces of the shattered figurine.

Whole body trembling, I wiped condensation off the window so I could see where Elmer had thundered off to. Probably the barn. "I knew he'd react, but I would've never guessed anything like this would happen."

Durward stood, poking at the porcelain pieces in his palm. "Well, I saw Dad act like that one time before. With Mom. As hot as he is, he won't have a drop of water on him when he comes back in."

While Durward laid the hummingbird pieces on the table, I told him how the folks had followed us with every change of address— KC to Beloit and Cawker City, then to Jenny's farm.

Sammy whimpered again.

I beckoned Durward to follow me into the bedroom.

He plopped on the floor and leaned against the wall while I changed Sammy.

"I'm sorry you had to see us at our worst."

"Hey, I'm part of the family. I *want* to be part of this family. Unless you or Dad objects, that's the way I'll play it. That means I get to share the bad with the good."

I searched his face. "Of course you're part of our family. You're Elmer's son. He's proud of you. I'm pleased, really thankful, that you accept me ... as his wife, as someone you can trust." I bit my lip. "Please don't ever refer to me as 'stepmother.' I don't like the sound of that."

"Not a chance of that, Claire." He gave me a quick smile.

"As bad as that fight was, I won't let him go on the road, away from us for weeks at a time. He knows he shouldn't leave us here, no matter how much money he can make. Six months will stretch into a year. You can imagine what that could do to a marriage." I sighed. "Not to mention how hard it would be for me to run the farm while he's gone."

Durward traced his finger around the doily on the nightstand. "I understand why Dad left Mama. Constant criticism. When he came back to see me—the last time he came ..." He drew his hand over his eyes. "I was eight years old. Mama griped about him not coming often enough. She complained about his pipe, his nice clothes, even him being a salesman. Got on him about not going to church. He put up with it for a time. Then he told her that what he did with his private life was private, and he didn't have to answer to her for anything. Like you saw him here, he tore outta there like he wasn't coming back. And he never did."

For minutes, neither of us said anything.

A clunk sounded from the doorway of the bedroom, followed by a stern voice. "Does it take two people to change that baby?"

I jumped. "Elmer! When did you come in?"

He shook off his wet coat and barked at Durward, "You plan to stay the night?"

Durward struggled to his feet. "I aimed to if it's ... if I won't be in the way."

"You'll be all right." Elmer took a deep breath. "Sal, where are my dry socks?"

"You can find your own socks. I'll get supper ready." I followed Durward into the living room with Sammy on my hip.

Durward grabbed his coat and made as if to go outside.

I shook my head and pointed to a chair.

Elmer came out of the bedroom, socks in hand, as I set the table. He put on a grim smile. "So, you want to tell me all the good things you had to say about me while I was outside working off my snit?"

I stopped and faced him. "Well, you *were* mad, Elmer. Your coat knocked my little hummingbird to the floor—broke it to pieces. And you stomped out in a huff."

Elmer caught his breath and looked at the floor. "Flying off the handle like that was ... not good." He met my eyes. "You threw me, with what you said."

I pointed to the broken bits on the table. "That was my humming—"

"Sal, I'll get you another one." He looked away, working his jaw.

"Elmer, I didn't want to make you mad, but I had to say what I did."

Durward suddenly stood. "Wait a minute. Gotta get something." He headed outside and soon returned, holding a damp paper bag. "Claire, see what I brought you." He set the bag on the table and removed a potted geranium in bloom. His face glowed with delight.

I couldn't speak for a moment. "Oh, Durward, that's beautiful. You're so thoughtful. I haven't had flowers in a long time. Why for me?"

He ducked his head. "Got them in Elkhart for May and Mama. Thought you'd like some too. Mama said a woman always likes flowers."

"Remember the red roses you sent me, Elmer, before you came to Ness to propose? They came at the right time, just like these did, from my handsome son." I smiled at each in turn.

Elmer nodded. "That's my point, Claire. You say you don't think you're important to me. Out there, I was fuming. I thought of all I've done to provide for you. I've always given my best, but I know I'm missing something."

"Yes, you provide for me—food, clothes, a roof over my head. But I need to know that you cherish me. If you leave this farm, that says the opposite."

Durward stared at his hands. "Maybe I should leave."

"Sit down, son. You wanted to umpire this ball game. You'll stay for the last inning." Elmer faced me.

He had come back, not like what Durward had seen, because I *was* precious to him and he didn't want to lose me. "I need to know that you believe in me and accept me, even when we disagree. I need to be free to express my feelings."

Elmer waved for me and Durward to sit at the table, one on each side. He nodded at me.

My mouth felt like cotton, but I plunged ahead. "You haven't tried to see my side. If you'd really listen to what I have to say, I'd feel respected."

"Well, you just want your own way."

I huffed. "Can't I express my opinions? If you don't listen, I might as well not be here. I don't size things up as quick as you, Elmer, but sometimes you're so impatient. When I make a mistake, I still need you with me."

Elmer leaned forward.

My voice dropped to a whisper. "You know my father was born out of wedlock. His mother told him that didn't matter, that he was a gift from God. She kept telling him he was God's gift. Finally he believed what the Bible says, that God loved him *just as he was.* Knowing how God felt about him gave him strength. He accepted who he was, what he was."

Elmer didn't react to the God talk the way he usually did.

I pushed on. "This isn't about being religious, Elmer. It's about how I look at myself. Pop said I'm God's gift too. I'm special. I've been saying those words to myself lately. I can't change my education or how smart I am or what people think about me, but my father and your sister helped me believe that I'm accepted by God." A deep breath. "It would mean so much if you'd believe in me too."

It appeared that Elmer was afraid—yes, afraid—of giving away too much of himself. Giving me equal standing fell into that category. Maybe Durward and I wanted more of him than he felt he could give. Maybe he was petrified at the idea of revealing his real self, of not always having the answers.

If I'd learned anything about men, it was that, deep inside, they were scared—scared of coming up short. Maybe we were all scared, apart from the protective arms of God.

Silence.

Maggie's words came to me. *You can't make people do right, feel right, be right. So you commit them to God.*

Sitting there, in that thin minute, that's what I did. I closed my eyes. Out loud, I said, "Jesus, help us trust you and be willing to change, so we can trust one another." I kept my eyes closed. Though others could hear, this was between me and God and there was more I needed to tell him. "Father, keep us from hurting each other. Show Elmer and me how to love and believe in one another. Thank you, Jesus, for listening."

Elmer and Durward listened too. The room seemed wrapped in a blanket of heavy quiet. I thought of the frosty night I saw a comet streak over the Cimarron canyon. Peace seemed as close as Jesus. Like it marked the beginning of something great and precious.

I wanted to laugh and cry at the same time. I reached up to Elmer and pulled him to me.

He let my cheek touch his, but I could tell he was holding back.

"Isn't it wonderful what this son of yours has done, Elmer? He gave these flowers from the heart. So thoughtful. I'm blessed to have such men."

Durward turned his chair toward his father. "As a boy, I felt like

297

Claire's pop. I didn't feel like I had a father, either. Not until that day Ray took me over to meet you. You accepted me. Both of you did."

I swallowed. The rain had stopped.

Elmer cleared his throat. "Yeah, well. I better say some things." His index finger ran up to his eyebrow and slid down across his cheekbone a couple times. "Words mean a lot." He began a drum beat on the table with two fingers of one hand. "Words come easy for me as a salesman, but right now I feel tongue-tied."

"Take your time, Elmer." Opening up what had been shut away for so long wouldn't be easy.

"What you're saying, son, is that you've been hurt by ... by what I didn't do. After your mother and I split, I stayed away because I didn't want to deal with her. That kept me from you too. Wasn't fair to you, and I let you down all those years." Elmer stopped, wordless. He seemed unsure if he should go down the path he'd started.

Then, I knew. Percolating inside Elmer was what had tormented me—the fear of being genuine, which really was doubt that he was acceptable. He knew he'd done wrong, but here he was trying to make it right.

He tried again, looking at me, voice husky. "I've been so leery about someone else changing me that I got hard as flint. Claire, in no way did you ever try to change my beliefs. That never hit me until I was out in the barn a few minutes ago. In the ten years of us being married, you never asked or demanded that I be different than I am.

"You said you want to be part of the team. Respect, you call it. I reckon I haven't been doing my best." A big sigh. "So, we do our decisions together. I've got some ideas about the folks, but I can't change everything overnight."

I touched his arm. "That's wonderful, honey. I only want for you to hear me, whether you agree or not."

Gently, he pulled me to him, like we were the only ones there. "Out in the barn with no place to go, I thought it through. You thought I wasn't being fair. I couldn't see that before. Probably didn't want to. But a man's got to be fair. Sorry. Sal, you're still my gal."

I forgave him, told him I had some changes to make.

He put his head against mine. "I wish I could do some things over."

I drew my hand to his face. "Elmer, we *are* starting over. Right now. Counting our baby boy, I've got my three men by my side. I don't wish for anything else."

⌘ ⌘ ⌘

Neither Elmer nor I believed we were really good enough the way we were. We each did our own style of pretending. I wept sometimes when I thought about how close we were to losing it all. Had it not been for Pop and Maggie's prayers and pep talks, for the love of Jesus, I wouldn't have been brave enough to drop my pleaser-of-people mask, either. And Elmer probably wouldn't have listened to me. Thankfully, he stayed with his family, where he belonged.

It was a new freedom, and kind of scary, not knowing what people would think. But as Maggie said, if I wasn't going to please everybody, why not just be myself?

My brother Myrrl came down occasionally. Elmer was still unsure about "this religion thing" but he listened to Myrrl. Elmer said change came hard for anyone, but he joked that if it could happen to me, it could happen to anybody. We both laughed at that.

Maggie was thrilled to pieces when I told her about all that God had done.

I didn't have to give Pop all the details. He said he knew his prayers were being answered with every sunrise that brushed the light of God's love upon our family … and that was good enough for him.

The End

Bio

Samuel Hall grew up in the American Heartland.
He lives with his wife near Salem, Oregon. Their three adult children continue to teach him about family relationships and authenticity, core subjects of this novel.

Visit his website at
www. samhallwriter.com.

Sign up for the newsletter at www.ashberrylane.com to hear the latest about Sam's book.

Acknowledgments

This book is dedicated to my parents, Claire and Elmer. Their story embodies the sacrifices, grit, courage, and innocent faith of those whose hardships of the Great Depression were compounded by the Dust Bowl of the 1930s. That calamity distilled them to the core of their being and provided the soil for the flowering of "The Greatest Generation."

This story is also dedicated to my children, Allison, Loren, and Ethan, as they carry forward that heritage.

My sincere thanks go to my family for their belief that, of course, I could and should tell Claire and Elmer's story. In particular, my brothers, Dick and Jerry, collaborated and pointed me to others in the family and around the Oklahoma Panhandle who knew many of the characters named herein or who shared their experiences from the Great Depression.

D.J. Young, ultimate encourager, gave me the opportunity to give and receive as part of the Oregon Christian Writers' leadership team. Before that, Marion Duckworth launched me on the road to learning the craft of writing, a journey I feel I've merely begun. Fellow writers in OCW, John Avery and Lindy Swanson flavored their demand for excellence with encouragement and Biblical application to the lives of my characters. I owe a considerable debt to my critique partners in Willamette Writers, in particular Heather Cuthbertson and Naseem Rakha.

I can't say enough about my editors and designers at Ashberry Lane Publishing, Christina Tarabochia, Sherrie Ashcraft, Nicole Miller, Kristen. Johnson, Andrea Cox, Tami Engle, Amy Smith, and Rachel Lulich; their unflagging enthusiasm for the story and professionalism, particularly relating to cover design and editing, have been invaluable. Many thanks to J.D. Bilbro, PhD, author of *The Dust Bowl Kid*, and to V. Pauline Hodges, PhD, Harold Kachel, and Joe Lansden, whose *Images of America/Beaver County* provided helpful background material.

My deepest gratitude goes to my wife, Gloria, for giving me the support, space, and time to write this story. She was always in my corner. Besides reading drafts, she increased my understanding of the so-called "weaker sex" and opened my mind to the wonders of the female psyche.

Like
THERE'S NO
Tomorrow

Scottish widower Ian MacLean is plagued by a mischievous grannie, bitter regrets, and an ache for something he'll never have again. His only hope for freedom is to bring his grannie's sister home from America. But first, he'll have to convince her young companion, Emily Chapman, to let the woman go.

Emily devotes herself to foster youth and her beloved Aunt Grace. Caring for others quiets a secret fear she keeps close to her heart. But when Ian appears, wanting to whisk Grace off to Scotland, everything Emily holds dear is at risk.

CAMILLE EIDE

ASHBERRY LANE

ASHBERRYLANE.COM

Like a Love Song

CAMILLE EIDE

When she finally surrenders her heart, will it be too late?

Susan Quinn, a social worker turned surrogate mom to foster teens, fights to save the group home she's worked hard to build. But now, she faces a dwindling staff, foreclosure, and old heartaches that won't stay buried. Her only hope lies with the last person she'd ever turn to—a brawny handyman with a guitar, a questionable past, and a God he keeps calling Father.

ASHBERRY LANE

ASHBERRYLANE.COM

The Journey of Eleven Moons

Bonnie Leon

A successful walrus hunt means Anna and her beloved Kinauquak will soon be joined in marriage. But before they can seal their promise to one another, a tsunami wipes their village from the rugged shore … everyone except Anna and her little sister, Iya, who are left alone to face the Alaskan wilderness.

A stranger, a Civil War veteran with golden hair and blue eyes, wanders the untamed Aleutian Islands. He offers help, but can Anna trust him or his God? And if she doesn't, how will she and Iya survive?

ASHBERRY
LANE
ASHBERRYLANE.COM

On the Threshold

Sherrie Ashcraft &
Christina Berry Tarabochia

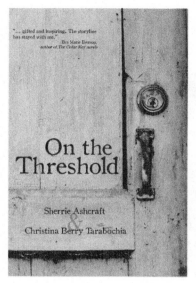

Suzanne ~
a mother with a
long-held secret

Tony ~
a police officer with
something to prove

Beth ~
a daughter with a
storybook future

When all they love
is lost, what's worth
living for?

ASHBERRY
LANE
ASHBERRYLANE.COM

BROKEN Wings

THE Thistle SERIES
BOOK ONE

DIANNE PRICE

He lives to fly—until a piece of flak changes his life forever.

A tragic childhood has turned American Air Forces Colonel Rob Savage into an outwardly indifferent loner who is afraid to give his heart to anyone. RAF nurse Maggie McGrath has always dreamed of falling in love and settling down in a thatched cottage to raise a croftful of bairns, but the war has taken her far from Innisbraw, her tiny Scots island home.

Hitler's bloody quest to conquer Europe seems far away when Rob and Maggie are sent to an infirmary on Innisbraw to begin his rehabilitation from disabling injuries. Yet they find themselves caught in a battle between Rob's past, God's plan, and the evil some islanders harbor in their souls.

Which will triumph?

ASHBERRY
LANE
ASHBERRYLANE.COM

CPSIA information can be obtained at www.ICGtesting.com
Printed in the USA
BVOW08s0303061215

428845BV00012B/45/P